Friedrich Schleiermacher, Frederica Maclean Rowan

The Life of Schleiermacher

As Unfolded in His Autobiography and Letters

Friedrich Schleiermacher, Frederica Maclean Rowan

The Life of Schleiermacher
As Unfolded in His Autobiography and Letters

ISBN/EAN: 9783744687416

Printed in Europe, USA, Canada, Australia, Japan

Cover: Foto ©Raphael Reischuk / pixelio.de

More available books at **www.hansebooks.com**

THE LIFE

OF

SCHLEIERMACHER,

AS UNFOLDED IN

HIS AUTOBIOGRAPHY AND LETTERS.

TRANSLATED FROM THE GERMAN

BY FREDERICA ROWAN.

IN TWO VOLUMES.

WITH A PORTRAIT.

VOL. II.

LONDON:

SMITH, ELDER AND CO., 65, CORNHILL.

———

M.DCCC.LX.

LIFE

OF

FRIEDRICH ERNST SCHLEIERMACHER

AS

UNFOLDED IN HIS LETTERS.

PART III.

FROM SCHLEIERMACHER'S APPOINTMENT IN HALLE (OCTOBER, 1804) UNTIL HIS MARRIAGE IN MAY, 1809.

In Halle, whither Schleiermacher went in October, 1804, he formed a warm friendship for Steffens, which continued for many years, although their direct co-operation in life ceased already in the year 1806, in consequence of the stormy times which led to the dissolution of the University. While at Halle, he took his half-sister Nanni to live with him, and she remained in his house, even after his marriage, until the year 1817, when she became the wife of E. M. Arndt. In February, 1807, Schleiermacher's friend Willich died, at the age of thirty, in Stralsund, of a nervous fever that raged there during the siege, leaving his widow, then only eighteen years old, with a little daughter, and a son, who was born shortly after the father's death.

Subsequently, Henriette von Willich lived with her children in the island of Rügen, in close proximity to her relatives; and her correspondence with Schleiermacher continued and gradually assumed a more and more intimate character, until in the summer of 1808, during a visit to Rügen, he engaged himself to her. In May, 1809, they were married, and Schleiermacher took his bride to Berlin, where he soon obtained a regular appointment, and a new sphere of activity, at the re-constituted University. Schleiermacher was then forty-one years of age, and his wife only twenty-one; but though at first very reserved, and, as it were, overruled by the superior and far more mature mind of her husband, her peculiar nature, nourished by him, gradually developed itself more decidedly and more independently, as was indeed quite in accordance with his wishes; and the influence which she on her side exercised over him is repeatedly expressed in his subsequent letters.

[The subjoined passages, borrowed from the *Memoirs of H. Steffens*, afford some interesting characteristics of Schleiermacher at the period of his first appearance at Halle. Speaking of his own appointment as professor of natural philosophy at that university, Steffens says: " I was there to meet a man whose acquaintance was destined to form an epoch in my life. This was Schleiermacher, who was at the same time as myself, or a few weeks later, called to Halle as *professor extraordinarius*. Schleiermacher, as is well known, was small of stature and slightly deformed, but so slightly as hardly to be disfigured by it. His movements were quick and animated, his features highly expressive. A certain sharpness in his eye acted, perhaps, repulsively at times. He seemed, indeed, to look through every one. He was a few years older than myself. His face was long, his features sharply defined, his lips firmly and severely closed, his chin prominent, his eyes lively and full of fire, his look always earnest, collected, and self-possessed. I saw him under various circumstances in life—deeply meditative and sportive, mild and fired with anger, moved by joy and sorrow—but ever an unalterable composure, greater, mightier than every passing emotion, seemed to dominate his being. A slight expression of irony played round his features; the sincerest sympathy ever animated his heart; and an almost childlike goodness shone through the outward calm. His constant presence of mind had sharpened his senses in a most remarkable degree. Even while engaged in the most animated conversation, nothing escaped him. He saw everything that was passing around him, and heard everything, even the most low-toned conversation. . . . We attached ourselves at once and unconditionally to each other. . . . We lived on the most intimate terms, we shared each other's views, thoughts, and even likes and dislikes. With the family Reichardt,* Schleiermacher lived as I did: we walked together, made excursions together, went into society together, and our best auditors, those who were in full earnest, we had in common. His lectures on ethics, and mine on natural philosophy, seemed to our hearers to be intimately connected, and to supplement each other. We mutually communicated to each other what we knew; and if Schleiermacher profited by my lectures

* The family into which Steffens had married.

on physics, he, in return, opened up to me Greek philosophy, and through him I became acquainted with Plato. . . . The more deeply, the more earnestly, the more religiously Schleiermacher regarded life and science, the more decidedly he discarded, in life as in science, everything that seemed to him hollow and useless. Nay, he seemed, indeed, sometimes to delight in setting outward forms at defiance, and many exaggerated and even false reports about him circulated in the town, and probably spread even further. People used, among other things, to tell each other of how the Professor of Theology went about botanizing in a green jacket and light-coloured trousers, with a tin case slung across his back." *

This picture is confirmed and completed in a passage in the work *Die deutschen Universitäten*, by Karl von Raumer, who, having lived in Halle from 1806 to 1808, describes Schleiermacher as follows:—" A small, quiet, ever self-possessed man. In society, he never fell into speechifying. He followed attentively what others said ; formed a clear perception of it, and expressed his agreement or his disagreement with his well-known dialectical acuteness and skill. He was never seen in a state of passionate excitement ; even when anything roused his indignation, though he expressed his displeasure energetically, he never lost his self-possession, and never overstepped the bounds of moderation. His command over himself was further shown in his power of concentrating his attention even on subjects into the depths of which it was not given to him to enter. In this

* **Heinrich Steffens.** *Was ich erlebte.*

way he made himself at home in such matters also as were in fact foreign to his nature. The almost tyrannical mastery which he exercised over himself was likewise shown in small matters, and perhaps more in these than in others. On one occasion, for instance, when a dispute had arisen as to whether the Low-German pronunciation of *sp, st,* &c., or the South-German pronunciation of these letters as *schp, scht,* &c., were most euphonious and most correct, Schleiermacher gave his vote in favour of the Low-German. 'Why then,' asked some one present, ' do you not adhere to this pronunciation in the pulpit?' Instead of excusing himself with early habit, he replied, 'From next Sunday I will begin to do so.' I have been assured that he carried out his determination without once forgetting himself."]*

Schleiermacher to E. and H. von Willich.

[ccxxvi.]   *Halle,* 17*th October,* 1804.

You cannot but know, dear friends, that my heart has communed with you, though my pen has not, and therefore I need not tell it you. Yes, you must be aware that through your felicity you bestow upon me a happiness such as I have never before known, and such as I can never again know, except through you. For although I cannot possibly wish or predict for you a more beautiful wedded life than Wedcke's, I did not witness and share in his from its first holy commencement, as in your case. Spare me, then, the expression of what I felt on reading the first accounts of your new and full life. They were to me also a wedding feast, a bridal embrace of my most beautiful and most cherished ideal. I was with you, and around you ; and indeed I am so still, and it is impossible to imagine a stronger contrast than between

* The passages between brackets have been added by the translator.

my constant living with you in thought, and my total abstinence from writing. Do not punish me for what has already caused me so much pain, but satisfy my longings very soon. Anything new you cannot indeed have to tell me ; the same spirit, the same life must prevail throughout, yet the separate events of that life are as important to me as they are to you, and I long to go through them with you. Did I not prophesy about you both in the *Monologues?* Do you not repeat my feelings in new and living truth, Ehrenfried, when you say that your wife is to you daughter and beloved maiden, and mother ? Believe me, dear souls, I become quite romantic and fantastic when I think of you ! I seem to love your marriage, independently of yourselves, as if it were a distinct being. I love it passionately, and yet tenderly and reverently ; and thus it ought to be, for it is indeed a true, a beautiful, and a holy union. I am already counting by half-years, when I shall be able to go to you, and behold your heaven with my own eyes, for it is only in reference to this that I now keep any account with time. I wonder when the moment comes whether I shall take my own heaven with me, and thus introduce if not a clouded heaven into a heaven of joy, yet a pale German sky into a bright sunshiny Italian atmosphere ?*

Henrietta Herz has probably already written to you about the wretchedly disjointed life I led in Berlin. As to enjoyment, I had but very little of that. I lost much by the unexpected death of the excellent old Mrs. Spalding, whose society I had looked forward to with great pleasure, and who had a similar feeling with regard to my coming. Intellectually, the meeting with Johannes Müller, the Swiss, was very pleasing to me, though it made me feel my insignificance in point of learning, more than I have ever felt it, in comparison with any of the scholars whom I have as yet met in this place. For very different reasons I was pleased to become better acquainted with Delbrück, the tutor of the princes. He sought me out, and spoke long with me about the religious

* At this period Eleanore had renewed her relations with him.—
TRANS.

education of the Crown Prince; he seemed to listen to me with pleasure, and in a great measure to agree with my ideas. I preached once, during my stay in Berlin, and seemingly produced a desirable effect on many of the persons present. But although a place in the cathedral became vacant immediately after my arrival, the ministers would not allow me to remain, but preferred sending me hither. Many persons were surprised at this, but to me it seemed very natural, as steps had been taken in regard to my appointment here, which no government would like to have made in vain. My reception here, on all sides, was very satisfactory. The principal point, it is true, still remains to be proved, namely, how the students will like me, and how I shall succeed in the lecturing line. On Monday next I commence, and shall give three lectures on that day, in order to force myself into it at once. Instead of beginning with Christian ethics, I have been induced, by various circumstances, to commence with philosophical ethics, and perhaps it is as well that I should lay the foundation in this way; the worst of it is that I have not quite completed the arrangement of the whole, and fear that I may forget a great many points the first day. As yet I have not distinctly worked out anything, and during the three days that remain I have still to make a general sketch of the three courses. With respect to my preaching to the academy, the prospects seem still very distant, as the choice of a building, and other external matters, have not yet been settled.

And now, dear friends, God be with you. God bless you, children! Do you often realize to yourselves how we are all ever with you? My resolution, to take my sister to live with me after Easter, remains unchanged.

Schleiermacher to Henrietta Herz.

[ccxxvii.] *Halle, 22nd October, 1804.*

I have been inducted into my office, and have already commenced three courses of lectures. I am tolerably satisfied with myself, better than I expected; whether the students be so likewise, I do not know; but a great concourse there certainly has not been. Only very few have put down their names, but there were more present to-day than have done so ; many of these must consequently be supposed to have come merely from curiosity, and will probably speedily disappear. You know that I rather feared than desired applause at first, and I am therefore pretty well pleased with the present aspect of things. . . . .

Schleiermacher to E. and H. von Willich.

[ccxxviii.]   *Halle, 30th October*, 1804.

Yes, certainly I did know it, my dear, dear daughter, when I comforted you; certainly I did see in spirit the glorious period which has now dawned upon you both. And when you feel yourselves very happy, then remember that this happiness is not shut up within your walls ; but that it reaches me and makes me happy too. When you can find leisure, dear Jette, you must describe to me your whole mode of life : how you divide your time, how you feel as mistress of a family, and how you get on as such, and also what kind of intercourse you keep up with other people. For you must not begin with isolating yourselves. Though you may suffice for each other, that is not enough. Every family, and more especially such a family as you constitute, must from the beginning adopt the missionary spirit, and be on the look-out for some soul that it may draw towards itself and save from the desolate waste of life.

I always think of a family as a pretty snug little room in the great palace of God, as a sweet, contemplative resting-place in His garden, whence the whole may be overlooked; but also as a snuggery in which one may bury oneself deeply, and feel around one its narrow, cozy limits. In such, the doors must not be closed, but every one must be admitted who possesses the magic key, or who knows how to find his way in by bending aside the branches that conceal the entrance. Is there nobody in your neighbourhood, who might be inclined to knock at your door and to participate a little

in your life? You can hardly conceive how impatient I am
to see everything connected with you develop itself; and I
should, therefore, like to know that you are already letting
your light shine before others. It always seems to me one
of the great privileges of a clergyman, that being entitled by
his office to lead a retired life, he may keep aloof from burdensome conventional connections, while, on the other hand,
his calling points out to him the true nurslings and friends
of his household, whom he ought to lead by his example to
undeviating morality, and to a simple, rational enjoyment of
life. How heartily have I not rejoiced with you, my Ehrenfried, that your office is of this blessed kind! Surely a great
deal may be done in this way, in individual cases; and I
become daily more convinced, that even as regards the world,
this is the only way of proceeding, as, indeed, the true, must
ever be the only, way. If the idea in its purity could but
be brought home to the hearts of those who are led astray by
foolish disputes about the dead letter, and by the dialectical
effrontery of empty reasoning, it would be strange, indeed,
were they not to become friends of Christianity.

As yet I cannot say anything similar about myself and my
new vocation; but in faithfulness and perseverance I shall
not be found wanting; and when I have acquired a degree of
self-confidence and freedom from restraint, proportionate to
the extent of order which I have now introduced into my
new office, I trust that my teaching will not remain without
fruits. I have been lecturing since the 22nd. Quite satisfied
I cannot possibly feel with my beginning, yet I have gained
the assurance that I shall not come to a standstill. You
will readily imagine that I only note down the leading
thoughts, and that otherwise I speak extemporarily, and I
shall persevere in this plan; for although I do, indeed, sometimes omit certain things that I ought to have said, or I find
when I return from the lecture, that I might have placed the
whole matter in a clearer light, I feel, at the same time, that
I shall improve in regard to these points. My *Philosophical
Ethics* give promise of shaping themselves into a very good

whole, and, indeed, this is more likely to take place under the present circumstances, than under any others, because of the constant elaboration of the subject. The same holds good of my *Introduction to the Study of Theology*. My *Lectures on the Fundamental Doctrines* suffer, indeed, somewhat in consequence of the others, and assume a fragmentary character; but their chief object, to teach men to seek for the idea underlying the conception, I trust they will attain. My functions as preacher have not yet commenced, and, in fact, I am glad of the little delay; for I should otherwise have felt myself too much overwhelmed just at the beginning. As it is, I can now and then give a little time to the third volume of *Plato*. Adieu, dear friend. God bless you now and for ever.

Schleiermacher to Henrietta Herz.

[CCXXIX.] *Halle*, 15th *November*, 1804.

. . . . . I cannot beg you too urgently and too often, my dear Jette, not to look so much into the future. With such energy as you possess, you could not fail to feel conscious of your power to bear and to control each event as it occurs, were you not so much depressed by your anticipation of coming events. Your sufferings consequently arise from your habit of condensing all your difficulties. It is easy to see through *one* pane of glass, but through ten placed one upon another we cannot see. Does this prove that each one is not transparent? or are we ever called upon to look through more than one at a time? Double panes we only have recourse to for warmth; and just so it is with life! We have but to live *one* moment at a time. Keep each one isolated and you will easily see your way through them; but if you will arbitrarily double them, then let it be only to warm yourself with sunny prospects towards Rügen. . . . . .

All my friends desire a little advice from time to time; and when I can thus be of comfort to them, I am glad that they apply for it. If I do not ask for any in return, it is because, merely by the fact of being my friends, you afford me guidance.

Schleiermacher to E. and H. von Willich.

[CCXXX.]   *Halle, 21st November, 1804.*

How I wish I could to-day say a word to all those whom I love! To each one the same, viz., that I feel how their thoughts are with me to-day more especially, and that their love is my highest good, without which neither the world nor anything in it would have any value in my eyes. To you both, more especially, you beloved ones, I say it. You know how my heart cleaves to you, how I behold in you the realization of the most beautiful union that I know, introduced in a peculiar manner into the circle in which I live ; and how, while all that regards myself is uncertain and incomplete, I always look to you and feel satisfied. Not in the year that commences to-day, but in the ensuing one, I hope to see you. The beautiful summer time I spent with you has given life new value in my eyes. I have experienced with regard to you all how far more fresh and enlivening is the effect produced by communion face to face, than by even the most intimate interchange of thought from a distance ; and my new sphere of activity, which is one of no little importance, has also created new ties for me. With you, in you, and for you, and all our other dear ones, then I live, and the world must be content with what I can do for it in the way of my vocation.

Henriette von Willich to Schleiermacher.

[CCXXXI.]   *25th November, Sunday morning.*

It is only to-day that I am writing to you in reality, but in the long interval my spirit has often been with you, and answered your dear letters ; and it so happens that I am able to write to you on my much-loved Sunday morning. From my earliest youth Sunday morning was always very precious to me. While I was at school in Greifswald, this was the only morning I had to myself, and on which I could prosecute my favourite occupations. I always kept it very quietly and unobtrusively. I was generally alone in the schoolroom, where I could hear the tones of the organ and of the human voices from the church close by. Among the many books around me, I had selected a few in which I read on these occasions—mostly old devotional works. I cannot describe to you what my feelings were; how inexpressibly happy, and yet how sad, and how much those hours of quiet devotion elevated my being, and inspired me with an earnestness that followed me through the bustle of the whole ensuing week. Now I feel what those hours were to me; they appear to have been the preparation for my present life. At present, I often go to church with Ehrenfried on the Sunday, and afterwards we talk over the sermon, and I tell him what touched me most, and he tells me in his turn with which parts he was satisfied, and with which not—and this is like a second service to us. . . . .

We are never happier than when we are quite alone together, and yet there are few days that we find it possible to be so; but then we have so much to chat about, and to read and to write, that it always seems to us that the day has taken wings to itself, and we long for an hour to devote to our absent friends. It seems so strange that time should slip away thus—for, after all, what have I to do?

I will describe to you our life as well as I can. It is our intention to rise at five in the morning, but as yet it has very rarely been carried out. When we have got lights, and have dressed, we go into the parlour, where we find the fire burning in the stove, and the breakfast table ready laid. Ehrenfried then reads aloud a chapter in the Bible, or some other serious book—at present we are reading Plato. Your *Discourses on Religion* we have finished, and also a delightful book, "*Die Herzensergiessungen eines kunstliebenden Klosterbruders*," by Tieck and Wackenroder. You may imagine how I value these hours, and how my mind communes with yours during the reading. You will also, I am sure, feel gratified at the thought that we have chosen your writings for our edification and refreshment, and that they do us so much good. The early morning is ·in itself so delightful, everything without so dark and tranquil, but the mind of man so revived and wide awake. When it is daylight I begin my little household business. You ask me how I feel as head of a family, and how I get on in my vocation? The feeling of being the *housewife*, who takes care of the whole household, and who may arrange everything according to her own will and pleasure, is, I think, always precious to a woman, and I also value it very much, and am proud of the dignity. But the special household occupations do not afford me particular pleasure, though they are by no means irksome to me.

[CCXXXII.]   *26th November.*

    . . . How I value your letter, how I feel and prize your love; were I only not so often troubled with the thought that I ought to have made more progress since all the happiness and good fortune that has fallen to my lot, and that you must believe that I am growing faster in good than is really the case. How often I long for your presence, that you might participate· in our quiet life, and witness my great and unmerited happiness! Oh, dear Schleier, great as it is, how shall I ever become deserving of it! Thank God, and love Him with my whole heart and my whole soul,—that I can and will.

Schleiermacher to E. and H. von Willich.

[CCXXXIII.]   *6th January,* 1805.

    It is kind of you, dear daughter, to have introduced me, by your letter, to your home life, for some time may still elapse before I am able to become an eye-witness of it. That time passes quicker than we calculate, that in general we do not carry out as much as we intend, is a common experience, and must therefore also be that of housewives, and more especially of young ones. Very seldom, and in special cases only, have I ever succeeded in carrying out my intentions to the full, or in exceeding them, and since I have been in Halle, I believe it has not once happened to me.

Plato is not good morning reading. Very few parts are in their entirety comprehensible or agreeable to women. Ehrenfried ought first to peruse the volume alone, and then to read aloud to you, with the necessary explanations, such passages as he thinks would be likely to please you. On your side, dear Ehrenfried, I wish you would in reading mark such passages as seem to you difficult to understand or incorrect, or in any other way defective. Your remarks would be very welcome to me, as I contemplate bringing out, in a couple of years, an improved edition of this, my literary firstling.

Farewell, dear friends; continue to love me.

[CCXXXIV.] *No date.*

. . . I am quite surprised that I should have let so long a time pass without indulging in a little chat with you. It is true, that a new friend, and one who can only remain a short time with you, is a very time-consuming luxury, and of such you will find an account in my letter to our Lotte. It is another acquisition, for which I am chiefly indebted to the *Monologues*. How often already have I not had reason to thank the happy instinct which induced me to write that exposition, and the blessing goes on increasing! However, I am also beginning to taste some of its bitters, but I will bear them patiently. The little book has, I do not know how, got into the hands of the students here, and this causes me great annoyance; for I know they will connect it with that empty word—philosophy, and vapid mysticism, which begins to be the fashion with the cleverest heads among them, and which I am endeavouring to counteract, but with little success.

I was half and half hoping to get letters from you to-day, but the hope has failed, and also that of receiving a few lines full of the renewed maternal joy of our excellent Lotte. Do not let me wait long. You must not keep a debtor and creditor account with me; but, taking into consideration what a laborious and outwardly unsettled life I lead, you must write to me as often as your hearts prompt you to do so. I am very often with you in spirit, as you cannot but know, you dear ones, who have been the first to make life of value to me again.

Farewell, and let me have a happy hour soon, and write me much joyful news after all these storms.

Schleiermacher to Henriette von Willich.

[ccxxxv.] *Halle*, 1*st March*, 1805.

. . . How willingly would I not be with you to witness your glorious life! Kind, dear soul! No father can think oftener, and with warmer, and more heartfelt affection of his dearest daughter, than I think of you; nor in greater measure draw renewed youth from participation in her sweetest happiness.

Well, by the time the ensuing year is as far advanced as the present, I hope to be able to determine when I can pay you my visit. Oh, God grant that it may not be *alone*, but with the excellent Eleanore! What exquisite joy you and our admirable Charlotte have caused me by bestowing upon this beloved woman the deep and tender affection, which has suddenly been kindled in your hearts, and by the bewitching tones of sisterly friendship in which you address her! How rich am I not through you all, you dear people, and how I delight in the thought of bestowing all these riches on Eleanore, and of introducing her into this sunshiny heaven of friendship and love! I alone might have been too little for her; but with this help I may hope to heal all her wounds, and to crown her life with unfading flowers.

[ccxxxvi.] 12*th.*

Within the last few days I have once more had an opportunity of preaching. I quite long for the time to come when I shall be able again to give utterance to the most sacred

truths from my own pulpit, and I think, when I shall have
Eleanore here, a new and beautiful spirit will pervade my
sermons, and they will all be what, hitherto, only the best
have been. I wonder if Ehrenfried does not feel the same
when he is working at your side? It cannot be otherwise,
for everything grows brighter in the presence of love.

I bid you adieu, sweet daughter, with a look of sincere
satisfaction into your dear, clear eyes. You and Ehrenfried
know that my spirit dwells with you.

Schleiermacher to E. von Willich.

[CCXXXVII.]   *No date.*

About a week ago, I preached here for the first time,
but only for another, not from my own pulpit, the prospects
of doing which are still far distant. However, on this occasion a great pleasure came to me through Steffens, who had
accidentally been informed of my preaching, and came to
church to hear me; and afterwards, with the most lively
enthusiasm, wished me joy of my noble vocation, which he
maintained was the only one in which a man might place
himself at once in the centre of his subject, and give full
utterance to his thought; wherefore the religious aspect of
things is a necessary correlative of the scientific aspect, which
is never more than half completed—just as I have expressed
the relation in my ethics. Steffens' profound and inexhaustible mind, joined to his childlike and amiable nature,
so susceptible of every generous emotion, gives me new pleasure every time I spend a few hours with him ; and the more
so, as wherever the extreme points of nature and science touch
each other, our views always coincide.

Lecturing becomes day by day more easy to me; and
though I take less time for preparation, I feel that my mode
of arrangement and of expression has become more lucid; and
the ethics, as well as my treatment of doctrinal theology, will,
I hope, produce good effects. Nevertheless, I dread every
new course. This summer I am to begin hermeneutics; to
fetch up the interpretations from the depths of the subject, is

no slight undertaking, and one in which I have no practice, and yet in less than two months I shall be obliged to commence. But then this will be the only new course of lectures which I shall deliver this summer, for Plato will press very hard upon me. I am glad that you are reading this author in such a sensible way with Jette, and I often think of this while at work. In the third volume, also, she will find many deep and noble views, and many thoughtful and subtile meditations.

Schleiermacher to Henrietta Herz.

[CCXXXVIII.] *Halle, 27th March, 1805.*

A few days ago, I should have liked so much to have written to you and all my dear ones, while still under the influence of the enthusiasm awakened in me by an excursion to the Petersberg with Steffens and two of his most intimate friends. On my part it was, in fact, a mad freak to undertake it; for we only started on the Saturday, and did not return until the Sunday morning, just an hour and a half before I was to enter the pulpit, to deliver a discourse in honour of the memory of the Queen, at which, I had reason to suppose, the greater part of the Academy would be present. But I am grateful to my instincts, which often impel me to commit such mad pranks; for it is long since I enjoyed so much pleasure. I believe I have not for some time spoken to you about Steffens; and as I have in the interval learnt to know him more intimately, I can now speak of him very differently. You know, dear friend, that if I am not modest, neither am I presumptuous; but never have I with such sincerity of heart placed another man as high above myself in every respect as I do this one, whom, were it seemly between man and man, I could almost adore. First of all, his marriage is a true marriage in the highest sense. Outwardly this is not so apparent, but inwardly it is a beautiful truth. With what enthusiasm he speaks of their connection! with what childlike simplicity he cites to his more intimate friends traits illustrative of her depth of feeling, of her religiosity, of her originality! and always with tears in his eyes! And then the man is altogether so indescribably attractive—as deep, as spontaneous, and as witty as Friedrich Schlegel at his best. But though he philosophizes with still greater animation than the latter, and even in our, to him, foreign tongue* expresses himself with burning eloquence, he is not only always just and entirely free from party spirit, but through and through sanctified and gentle in the sense in which I honour and love the quality. Picture to yourself the greatest natural philosopher of the times turning away, with tears in his eyes, from the sunset, which we witnessed from the mountain! But he is also a true priest of nature. It was the first time since his marriage, that is to say, for about two years, that he had been separated from his wife for four-and-twenty hours. You may imagine how full of her he was; and then our encampment under the old rocks, and the glorious prospect from above, and the delicious freshness of the air, and the freedom from all restraint! The holiest earnestness and the most extravagant mirth alternated so wonderfully, and were blended into a whole so beautiful, as is rarely experienced in life. And in this state we were the whole of Sunday, at dinner at Steffens', in the evening in Giebichstein.† There

* Steffens was a Norwegian.

† The reader may find it interesting to compare with this, Steffens' account of the same incident.—Trans.

"At the same time (as he was appointed professor) Schleiermacher had been nominated preacher to the University. An old church was arranged as university church; and when the Queen Dowager died, Schleiermacher was called upon to deliver an oration in honour of her memory. It was in the month of March. A lovely spring day lured us to the Petersberg, the day before the one appointed for the oration. We spent the night at the inn, in the village of Ostrow. This night will be to me ever memorable. Never did we draw nearer to each other, or look so deeply into each other's hearts. Never did Schleiermacher seem to me intellectually greater, morally purer. Even to this day that night appears to me one of the most remarkable of my life, as if sanctified. In the background lay the delightful day we had enjoyed, the wide-spreading, fertile landscape with its villages, is also between Steffens and myself a wonderful harmony, which is a great source of pleasure to me, and is, as it were, a new guarantee to me of the soundness of my views. When,

animated by the first breath of spring. Nature in its infinitude embraced us like a holy temple vault, bore up, penetrated, lent wings to every thought, and germinating spring fecundated our spirits, as it did nature around us. I have a testimony of the impression this night made upon him, in a letter to his dear friend, Mrs. Herz. [The one in the text.] It was the reflection of his own purity that made me appear to him in a glorified light during these truly holy hours. Never did the deep religiosity of his morality strike me more forcibly. The Saviour was with us, as He had promised to be 'when two or three are gathered together in His name.' . . . . It was past midnight ; and the following forenoon, between nine and ten o'clock, Schleiermacher was to appear in the pulpit. The subject of the oration required to be treated with the utmost delicacy. We awoke after a few hours' sleep, and had still a walk of a mile and a half before us. There had been frost in the night. The preceding warm days had melted the snow, and had made the road almost impassable. Schleiermacher, who was an excellent pedestrian, walked briskly in advance along the rough road and cloddy fields. We could hardly keep up with him. We perceived that, in spite of his swift pace, he was sunk in deep meditation, and we did not disturb him. Arrived at home, I had but just time to change my dress before church. When I appeared there among my colleagues, a general commotion took place. 'Ah!' they exclaimed, 'as you have come, we may also, we presume, expect to see Mr. Schleiermacher!' His pedestrian tour, immediately previous to his delivering the oration, was known through the town, and the fact of our having spent the night at a tavern had not escaped comment. Early in the morning a message had been sent to his house, and as it was little more than an hour before service was to begin, and the bells had already commenced ringing, and he had not returned home, people seemed to expect, and some even to hope, that he would not return at all. I remained silent, and let the gentlemen talk. Schleiermacher went up into the pulpit. Every one who has heard him knows how imposing his composure and earnestness were in the pulpit. His discourse gave evidence of the careful artistic arrangement of all the parts, which was his distinguishing characteristic as a preacher. The thoughts were lucid, the subject worthily treated. In spite of the outward calmness, nay, even apparent coldness, of his delivery, he, nevertheless, produced a deep impression, and every one present must have left the church with the conviction of the

in our conversation, he gives expression to moral ideas, they
are always mine, and as much as I understand of nature and
give utterance to on the subject, always coincides with his
system.   Even those who listen to us are struck by the way
in which we work into each other's hands, and in which our
views meet in the centre, though we start from opposite sides
—a proof that it is entirely and purely the existing inward
harmony that leads to the result.   .   .   .   .

Schleiermacher to Henriette von Willich.

[ccxxxix.]   *Halle, 6th April,* 1805.

     .   .   .   .   And now let me turn to you, dear, sweet
daughter, and dwell upon your perfected happiness, which
still, when I think of it, brings tears of joy to my eyes.   The
highest consummation, the crowning dignity, of your life has
come to you, beloved child of my heart !   How shall I express to you my paternal joy !   Every thought of you is a
prayer and a blessing in the name of love and holy nature.
I forget myself in gazing at your image with the new happiness beaming from your eyes, exultingly, proudly, and yet
meekly !   And how pure, how holy, and how naturally the
first maternal feelings must spring up in your noble heart !
Ah ! how I thank you for being willing to be my daughter;
you have thus conferred a happiness upon my life which I
can compare with no other; it is a peculiar, singularly beautiful, and lovely blossom added to the glorious wreath which
happy destiny has twined for me.   And there is nothing
artificial in this bond between us, but I am as really and
truly your father, as your natural parent could possibly have
been !

nothingness of all earthly rank, even the highest, in comparison with
the divine destiny of man.   My colleagues could not but express
approbation, nay, even admiration, of the discourse.   The idea that he
who had delivered extemporaneously, and with perfect self-confidence,
so well-digested, artistically arranged, and lucid a discourse, could
have spent the preceding hours in frivolous and dissipated frolic,
must have appeared to all as perfectly absurd, and I believe that the
rumour produced no lasting effect."

Yes, you will be a happy mother in every respect. I prophesy it and stake my prophetic spirit on the issue. . . . . In a true marriage like yours, with minds ingenuous and free from care, and hearts pure and loving, education is an easy matter. It starts with the confiding trust that good must beget good ; it aims at nothing more than a gentle stimulation of the noble germ, which can hardly fail to be present, and desires not unnecessarily to interfere and to constrain in every particular. Oh, dear Jette, we will frequently talk of this during the present happy time, and I feel certain that we shall always agree, and that our imaginings on this noble subject will also meet and embrace each other like parent and child.

And now,' for a bit of news. On Wednesday next I contemplate going to Barby, to visit the Herrnhut school, where I spent three of the best years of my youth, during which my love of knowledge and my religious feelings first developed themselves. At that time the school was located in a different place, which I also intend to visit on my return from Silesia, and Barby was then the seat of the Herrnhut University, to which I subsequently resorted, and at which my inner life and thoughts grew, until they burst asunder the fetters of the dead letter, and eventually drove me out of the congregation into the world. At that place I shall spend the holidays; and, if possible, I will partake of the holy communion with the congregation on Maundy Thursday, and remain there long enough to share in the glorious religious services of the brotherhood on Good Friday and Easter Sunday. You may imagine what feelings and memories will throng in upon me on those occasions. They will be delightful days to me, I hope ! . . . . .

Schleiermacher to Charlotte von Kathen.

[CCXL.]   *Halle, 5th May,* 1805.

Poor friend, how long you are made to drink of the bitter cup of sorrow, and how often you have been forced to put it anew to your lips, after you thought it already drained!* In such cases, alas! your absent friend can afford no help and little consolation. He can do no more than share in your anxieties and suffer with you, and when it comes to the worst, feel the bitterest sorrow of all, at a time when he may hope that you have already got over the first shock. May the hope which, after such long anxiety has come at length to cheer your birthday, prove lasting and increasing! and may I soon be apprised of it! After so many relapses, I cannot help feeling very anxious. It often seems to me, that I ought to remind you how you had at one time yielded up the little angel into the hands of his heavenly Father, and how, even after his first recovery, you used to feel as if he were only come back for a time to comfort you, and would soon be called away again. Hard, indeed, it would be were you not to keep him after so much suffering—very hard! But I confidently hope that my Charlotte's self-control and pious resignation will not fail, should Heaven determine otherwise in regard to the sweet child. I am only anxious that you should not feed yourself too much upon hope, so that should the dreaded blow come, its unexpectedness may not prove too overwhelming. And are you sure that you do not neglect the necessary care of yourself? A suffering child is, at the time, an all-absorbing object to a mother, and I fear, therefore, that you may not often enough recall to mind that you are the mother of the other children also, and that as such you must spare yourself and take care of yourself.

I did not know, dear friend, that your birthday fell on Easter Monday, yet I thought much of you that day during my solitary journey; for the Easter festival, I must tell you, I spent with the Herrnhuters in Barby. Delightful, sanctified days they were to me, full of wonderful memories and many enjoyments of the present. Formerly the seminary or university of this congregation was in Barby, and hence I went forth from the community to follow my own path, and came here to Halle, it may now be about eighteen years ago. At

* One of her children was again dangerously ill.

present the brotherhood's educational institution for boys, which was formerly in Lusatia, is located in Barby; to this my father entrusted me four-and-twenty years ago, and while there I became a member of the congregation, impelled by a true inward desire. The locality, therefore, recalled vividly to my mind the opening and the close of my career within the congregation. Even the rector of the institute, from whom I first learnt Greek and Hebrew, and who loved me like a father as long as I was under his care, was still alive; and, though an old man of seventy-seven, was still active and cheerful, and heartily rejoiced to see me again. Then there was the beautiful service on Good Friday, based altogether on the great idea of the Atonement, and consisting of the reading of the whole history of the Passion, without any sermon, and only interrupted at intervals by appropriate sacred music and a few verses of a hymn, and concluded at the hour of Christ's death with an impressive prayer.

On the Saturday was the love-feast at the grave of Christ, and on Easter morning the celebration of the Resurrection at sunrise in the churchyard. Verily, dear Charlotte, there is not throughout Christendom, in our day, a form of public worship which expresses more worthily, and awakens more thoroughly the spirit of true Christian piety, than does that of the Herrnhut brotherhood! And while absorbed in heavenly faith and love, I could not but feel deeply how far behind them we are in our church, where the poor sermon is everything, and even this is hampered by meaningless restrictions, while, on the other hand, it is subject to every change in the times, and is rarely animated by a true and living spirit.

It will soon be my duty to institute divine service here, which is to present a pattern, and to act as a stimulus, to new and far-spread generations of religious teachers; but how wretchedly cramped am I not as to means, and how much I deplore that I cannot transplant hither the best and most attractive elements of what I witnessed at Barby! I might have had one other gratification while there, had I ventured to ask for it. They would not have refused me permission to partake of the Lord's Supper with the congregation, but I would not ask for what I knew to be contrary to rule. Nowhere is the form of communion so edifying as there.

On Easter Monday already I accomplished the half of my homeward journey, my old rector having accompanied me a good bit beyond the town.   The next morning, while moving rapidly onwards in enjoyment of the most delicious weather, and leaving the bearer of my portmanteau panting and groaning far behind me, delightful memories of the days just past blended with affectionate longing for you all, my excellent friends.   While dwelling on my loneliness in the world, and on my separation from those whom I believe form the truest Christian community which exists in the outward world, I consoled myself with the thought of the secret and scattered Church to which we all belong, and of the common spirit that animates us, and of our piety and our love for one another. Do you not feel, Charlotte, how I then thought of you more especially; you, the purest and most holy among us all.

Henriette von Willich to Schleiermacher.

[CCXLI.]   *16th May.*
How shall I thank you for all the gladness that you pour into my heart ? As you feel it, none of my friends have felt or participated in my happiness.   Ah, how I love you for it, even more tenderly than before !   When I feel blessed and content, I see your eyes fixed on me with fatherly affection. Ah! dearest, what a happy creature I am !   What a treasure your letter is to me !   It is so unutterably grand and beautiful to feel oneself a mother, to be a mother.   God be praised and thanked that I feel it, and that it has so deeply moved me ! It gives me such pleasure to think that you know and understand so well the state of my mind, for I can only imperfectly express it.   Good father, my heart clings to you ; you are intimately bound up with my whole happiness, with my every

feeling. You will also be a second father to my child; you must love it very much. I shall not stop my entreaties until you promise that you will adopt my child among your children, and that you will place it very near your heart, and I promise in return, that I will not force or over-educate the young soul, but honour the individual nature of the child. What a blissful time the little creature's first period of utter helplessness will be to me! I will throw off every other care, and be exclusively its nurse and handmaid.

Schleiermacher to Henriette von Willich.

[CCXLII.]   *Halle, 13th June, 1805.*

How were it possible, dear Jette, that, with the exception of our Ehrenfried, any one should feel and participate in your happiness as I do? It is not only in name that I am your father, you dear, dear daughter, but in the very depths of my heart; how, then, could anything have made a stronger and more solemn impression on me than even this? Is it not a matter of course that I should love the little creature with a parent's love? I do so already, and feel pleasure at the thought that I may possibly be able to do something for it directly, during those years when it is supposed to be a great art to know how to treat young minds, but when, according to my opinion, the whole 'secret is truth and love. He who is not saved from evil by these, or reclaimed by them, even should a germ of corruption already have developed itself, for him there is no remedy. You see, dear Jette, how I enter into your maternal life, from its first beginning till the period of its last sorrow, and of its sweetest harvest-time of joy. The prospect of meeting you once more, is the brightest spot on which my eyes at present dwell. Should destiny favour us all, as in so many respects it favours you two, the young mother will soon have an opportunity of presenting her dear babe to me, and she will rejoice at the tenderness with which I shall take it for my own, and at the confidence with which, with prophetic sight, I shall then already greet it as a new temple and organ of the higher spirit. Surely, dear friends, if all marriages were like yours, all children would be a joy to their parents, and the good spirit that would breathe around them in early infancy, would continue to live in them. When I reflect upon the matter, it always seems to me that the usual over-straining in regard to education arises solely from a bad conscience, *i. e.*, from the consciousness that the example shown to the children is not such as it ought to be; wherefore else should there be so much restless activity? I think, dear little Jette, that there is no need of your taking the resolution not to over-educate your child. You cannot be otherwise than good, because your goodness has found its anchorage ground in the noblest love, and the richer and more blessed your life becomes, the brighter will your worth shine forth ; and our Ehrenfried is a man of firm character, long and deeply rooted in everything that is just and holy; and your union will be to the end as lovely as from the commencement it has seemed to us all. The more distinctly you feel this, the more the beautiful harmony of your lives is revealed to you in calm happiness, the less you will ever think of over-educating your child, or ever experience the necessity of guarding against this ; and all sentimental exaggeration of the natural feelings, every tendency to devote yourself exclusively to the life and duties of a mother, will remain as foreign to you as all other affectation. Farewell, dear daughter, I must have a little chat with your Ehrenfried, and unfortunately my time is very limited.

Schleiermacher to E. von Willich.

[CCXLIII.]

Yes, dear brother, a blessed life lies before you, and will in time unfold itself more beautifully still, and reveal riches which are as yet hidden in the future, and each of its joys, and each of its beauties, I will make my own, as long as I remain among you. Everything else in regard to myself is still shrouded in darkness, but my joy in you, and in all our friends, is a bliss such as perhaps few persons are able to understand.

I want to write you a long letter about my various undertakings, but more especially about my lectures, and the interest which I myself, as well as my auditors, take in them. I am teaching hermeneutics, and am endeavouring to raise that which has hitherto been nothing more than a series of disconnected and unsatisfactory observations into the dignity of a science, which shall embrace the whole language as an object of intellectual discernment, and penetrate from without into its innermost depths. As a matter of course, my first attempt has not been successful, as I have had no previous works to serve me as guides, and I am more especially in want of a number of examples and vouchers, for I have never taken notes with a view to this object, and cannot indeed make any such collection with a salutary result, until I shall have before me the whole system, which is only gradually developing itself as my lectures progress. In future, however, the collecting of such notes shall always be a secondary object with me when reading, and as I contemplate delivering a course of exegetical lectures next winter, and shall continue these during a year and a half, I hope that by the time I am to repeat the present course, I shall have been able to collect sufficient materials. You see I am working myself deeper and deeper into my vocation, and with real zest. But for this very reason, I shall most likely do nothing else, except continue Plato; and when, as is often the case, the conviction forces itself upon me, that I shall hardly survive the completion of this work, I feel quite grieved that so many things that I have been planning will have to be left undone.

I wish that it would suit your plan of reading, soon to begin my sermons; the new edition, which is required, will give me an opportunity of introducing emendations, and I would be much pleased if you would mark such passages as may seem to you obscure, or ill-arranged, or otherwise unsatisfactory. And when reading them to Jette, I wish you would make her speak to you about them as she does about your own, and let me hear what she says also.

[CCXLIV.]   *Halle, 15th July,* 1805.

. . . . . A recent occurrence which has taken place here has kept me painfully occupied for some time. A young man from Berlin, of whom I was very fond, came hither with his children and his wife, who had been educated here, and whom he had learnt to know and to love here, to pay a visit to her adoptive parents and to the friends of her girlhood, and while here she died. In him I saw grief in a beautiful and holy form; and I knew nothing more consolatory to say to him, than that in seeing him in his sorrow, I could not but wish that I were in a position to lose what he thus felt the loss of. It must be a far heavier trial for a man to lose the wife of his heart, than for a mother to lose a child. A child is, after all, but an offshoot from the living plant; but a wife is the crown, the innermost heart, whence buds forth into life everything that blooms, and ripens, and shelters. With her everything is gone; and all that follows can only be remembrance, a shadow of life. And yet I wish daily, with a heavy heart, that our friend may be spared the deep sorrow that has so long been impending over her. How much she must have suffered again, poor dear, since her letter in which she expressed her hope that the lovely child was improving— a hope which I do not even now venture to entertain! To yield up a child to the grave and to heaven, to bury all the hopes of the most holy love, must, indeed, cause deep and bitter anguish.

Yesterday I was at Weissenfels, where I made the acquaintance of two brothers of Novalis. The younger seems to have a thoughtful and serene mind, and is certainly the most like the deceased, whom we both value so highly. The elder has already written a good deal in imitation of his brother. I do not know what he may be in reality, but he offends me by a self-sufficient and repellent manner, which can hardly be favourable to a calm observation of men and nature, and of the workings of the latter within the human mind and without it.

I am glad that you like Novalis so much, and more especially the *Fragments*. A great deal of what he has written is, indeed, of so strictly scientific a character, that its immediate significance may not be fully comprehended by you, and much of what he has said was, perhaps, not sufficiently mature for publication; but the spirit that pervades the whole, the childlike simplicity combined with deep insight, is no doubt that which attracts you. So also it is probably those passages in my *Discourses* that bear upon prevalent opinions and vices which, happily, are unknown to you, that are the least comprehensible to you. Quite recently I have derived a new and very great pleasure from these *Discourses*, in consequence of my sister Lotte having read them for the first time. I had endeavoured to prevent her doing so, and wished her to wait and read them with me, lest she might otherwise misunderstand and misinterpret many passages. But her pious heart has been so simply and beautifully touched by the devout spirit in the book, that I may say that few things have for a long while afforded me so much satisfaction as the manner in which she has expressed herself in reference to it, and the hope that this gives me that she will in future be able to understand all my works. When you are reading this, dear friend, I shall probably be on the way to my sister. Although I shall be back in five weeks, I feel as if I ought to take regular leave of all my dear ones. I have still much upon my heart to say to you especially, but I must reserve it for another time. Think of me sometimes, and fancy me rejoicing in the sublime majesty of my native mountains, and with foolhardy boldness shunning no danger that promises the enjoyment of a beautiful prospect; and then, again, picture to yourself the happy, quiet days with my Lotte in Gnadenfrei. In the meanwhile, farewell, dear friend, and if you can, prepare for me the pleasure of finding a few affectionate words from you on my return.

Schleiermacher to Henrietta Herz.

[ccxlv.]   *Halle, 27th July,* 1805.

. . . . For what I did during my journey you must not upbraid me, dear Jette. It was not possible for me to do otherwise. It came over me so strong in the mountains that I could not resist, but felt impelled to proceed upwards ; and I am sure I was better able to bear the fatigue while in a state of great physical excitement, than if I had proceeded leisurely downwards, had left Konopak in the lurch, and had abandoned my plan, thereby causing my sister and brother mortal anxiety, and rushing into more certain destruction, by getting iced through in a lumbering vehicle, while giving myself up to deadly passivity. Besides, dear Jette, anything that we undertake after mature deliberation—and the doctor himself advised the journey, though aware of my state of health—ought to be considered an obligation incurred ; and in this case I could do nothing less than carry out mine calmly, bearing you all in my thoughts the while. And I conscientiously took every precaution in regard to my health that circumstances would admit of. All the pictures which you present to my imagination passed a thousand times before my mind, and, nevertheless, I acted as you have been informed. Must I, then, not have a good conscience ? . . . But it will come to this at last, if not immediately, and though I may not know how. All of you, whom I love best, and even my dear Lotte, whom I feared to lose so soon, will survive me, and I feel with you the deprivation and the grief you will experience. But, dear Jette, let us in the meanwhile cling to each other, and live together healthily and joyfully. Sometimes, when I look upon myself as the centre of the loveable circle that surrounds me, I feel what you must all feel in like manner, that it is not my personality that forms this centre, but the spirit that dwells alike in us all. Let us rejoice in this, and ever become more clearly conscious of it ; to you my loss will then be no more than the loss of an organ is to the body ; it is always missed, because the same life that animates the whole animated it ; but the loss does not destroy life itself. You know how sacred I hold the beautiful aggregate, and therefore, also, myself as part of it ; and you may rest assured that I shall not render myself guilty of wilfully destroying it.

Schleiermacher to Henriette von Willich.

[ccxlvi.]   *Halle, August 4th,* 1805.

Had you satisfied your longing to commune with your father, dear child, and sent forth your sweet loving words, I should have had the great pleasure of finding them here to greet me on my return; as it happened, I was back in Halle several days before your letters were even written, and I was just on the point of knocking at your door and asking for your welcome back, when it came without being asked for; and you cannot but know, dear daughter, what heartfelt joy it has occasioned me. Yes, verily, the affection we bear to each other is a great treasure, to me as well as to you. Through you I have learnt to know in rich measure that sweet tie which I had long accustomed myself to think would never in the course of nature bind me to another being, and your loveable childlikeness will never vanish, as it does in the case of so many women ; but you will ever remain the child of my heart ; and the joy and the blessing of this relationship will ever remain to us.

. . . . About my journey, I shall by degrees bring out one thing and another ; in the meanwhile, I can only give you a brief sketch of the whole ; and in so doing, I must, in order to touch upon the best, begin with the worst, and tell you that during our pedestrian tour through the mountains, we were by no means favoured by the weather, and were most shabbily treated just when we were upon the highest summits. In addition to this, our longest and most interesting day's journey I went through under intense suffering from cramps in the stomach ; yet I did not give in, or allow the state of my health to cause us one hour's delay, nor did the diffi- culties and sufferings in any way impair my enjoyment; and now they seem as nothing compared with the glorious and lasting impression which the sight of nature in its sublimity has made upon me. After this came other pleasures: making acquaintance with my brother's humble home, but pleasing and happy domestic life, with a kind, loving, cheerful wife, full of mental energy; my introduction to her and to my half-sister, who is now here with me; the improved health not only of the latter, but also of my dear Lotte, whom I found together with her in Schmiedeberg, and who was far better and more cheerful than I ventured to expect; and the ease with which my unknown relatives accustomed themselves to me, and learnt to love me; then my stay with Lotte in Gnadenfrei, which was, however, very short; and, lastly, my having now in my younger sister a friendly heart always near me, and my being thus relieved from total solitude; all this has made me very, very happy, and whenever I have felt most so, I have wished that all my dear ones could be with me, and you, dear friends, in particular, have been in my thoughts.

Henriette von Willich to Schleiermacher.

[CCXLVII.]   *4th August*, 1805.

I am looking forward with much pleasure to the letter that will announce to us your return to Halle; how I wish it would come soon! I have lived much with you in thought of late; my heart has often spoken to you, and has felt your loving response; and why I did not afford myself the further pleasure of writing what I felt and thought, I cannot tell. A great many things have been passing through my mind latterly; I feel that my intellect is expanding and is being enriched; it seems to me that I have learnt to understand the world better —the visible and the invisible world—and their mutual relations. Thoughts and feelings come suddenly upon me, which are not indeed quite new to me, but which I seem to have made more my own. It is one of my greatest delights to exchange thoughts with my Ehrenfried upon matters sacred and deep, and yet near to us; he understands me though I cannot fully express what I mean, and he brings light into my confused ideas. Often I long for you, want to write to you, but it seems such a poor means of communication compared with actual presence, when the word goes from heart to heart; and what I want to speak to you about is not sufficiently matured to be written. If you were with us, if I beheld your dear face, that inspires so much confidence—oh, my dear father, we must meet soon again! . . . . How delightfully I picture everything to myself! Sometimes I feel quite alarmed at the thought that after all it may not happen as I expect; but this feeling is only transitory. I know that the best, the eternal, will ever be with me in life, such as I picture it to myself; and as regards the things of this world, I shall ever gain more and more tranquillity. How merciful has God been to us hitherto in this respect also! our life is not disturbed by one discordant tone. . . . . Next spring will bring together many who love each other. I wonder if you will come with the one who is dearest to you of all? Shall we be allowed to shed tears of joy with you? Oh, your rich heart needs not the sunshine of happiness to make it throb with life and warmth! your inner life will be full of energy under all circumstances. . . . .

My soul often craves for a clear consciousness of the nearness of God. He bestows upon me blissful moments, in which I feel joy in Him and love to Him, and strength and energy for every duty; but then, again, I am so often apathetic, and as if inwardly dead. And when I awake from this state, I am very desponding, and feel myself unworthy of yours and Ehrenfried's love and of my happiness. My beloved, oh, *how deeply beloved* Ehrenfried, always raises me up again; when resting on his bosom, my heart feels light again; I am able to smile at my sorrows, to look anew healthily into life, and to resume my activity. . . . .

I have missed the post, and am glad that I have thus an opportunity of adding a few more words. What I said above about the apathy which sometimes overcomes me was, I am afraid, very obscurely expressed. I must tell you something more about it, for, perhaps, you are not aware that I am subject to such fits, and I must not let you think me better than I am in reality. Living such a happy life with my Ehrenfried, possessing such rich treasures, ought I not always to be strong and free, and to receive joyously into my soul the many blessings that are offered to me, happy one, in preference to so many others? And yet, I let so many escape without enjoying them. I know that very often it is physical indisposition that robs me of my freedom and causes my waywardness; but I do not feel as if it were physical; then follows discontent with myself, and I become melancholy and remorseful, until my dear, kind Ehrenfried reconciles me again with myself and exhorts me to have patience with myself. To feel oneself mentally free and healthy in each moment of life must be delightful! Ah! when the heart longs for intimate and true communion with the unseen, and the wish is granted, and we feel ourselves in consequence happy and elevated, then the soul overflows with joy, but also with sorrow for the time that has been allowed to go by without any such uplifting of it—at the thought that this glorious life, this life of life, has been so long dead within us. On these occasions I feel a certainty that a time will come when such a frame of mind shall ever be mine — my feelings are not overwrought, but hushed and tranquil, such as may pervade a whole life. With many people it is different; they appear to me so excited, so passionate in their higher moods, that I cannot conceive them capable of the most exalted spiritual enjoyment, except at rare intervals and during periods of ebullition.

Dear father, I dare say what I have written is **very** confused; but it is right that it should be so, for **many** things are still confused to me, and I may speak to you as your child.

I am full of joy, dear Schleier, for to-morrow, if the weather be good, we are to go to Rügen, to Lotte Kathen. As a wind-up, I shall have a good gambol in the fields with the children. From my childhood I have always been fond of harvest time. . . . .

Schleiermacher to Henrietta Herz.

[CCXLVIII.]   *15th August,* 1805.

Have I already told you that I have also made Goethe's acquaintance? Immediately after my return I saw him first for an hour, at Wolf's; the next day he went to Lauchstädt. The day before yesterday I dined with him and a large party at Wolf's; yesterday they started together on a little excursion; and after their return he will, I believe, remain a fortnight longer here, during which time I hope I shall see him frequently. The first time we met he was already very friendly to me, but a regular talk we have not yet had together; for on that occasion Gall was the topic of the day, and at the party there were too many people present. Steffens has delivered three public lectures against Gall, on which the world will no doubt pass some strange strictures. Do write and tell me if you should hear anything about them in Berlin. Steffens laughs and says that he is sure that my last sermon, which was similar in tendency, will be equally criticized, and give rise to the same vexation of spirit.

[CCXLIX.]   *Halle, 23rd August,* 1805.

. . . . . About Goethe I can tell you no more than I have already said. When Mina Wolf went over to tell him that I was there, he was lying on the bed reading, but said, " Ah, that is a noble friend, I must go to him at once;" and he did come very soon, and treated me as an old acquaintance, and I treated him in like manner; so far you get with him very soon. But the subjects I should like the most to discuss with him, I have not yet been able to broach. The first time he was full of Gall and Schiller, and the second time there were too many persons present to allow of my taking exclusive possession of him. But I hope soon to be able to tell you more, provided I have not displeased him. They say he returned

yesterday with Wolf. All who have known Goethe formerly agree in saying that he has changed very much to
his disadvantage, in the same sense as it may be said of his
works and of his opinions on art. But in like manner as
his works are still glorious productions, so is he also still
one of the noblest and most amiable personages that one can
behold.

[CCL.]   26th.

        Goethe returned last night with Wolf, and to-day
already I have been invited to meet him, and that without
any other company, so that now we shall probably have a
good deal of conversation, and in my next I shall have more
to relate. For the rest, Goethe is not to that extent in favour
of Gall as to make our differing estimate of him a barrier
between us. You may also conceive that I did not make a
direct attack upon Gall from the pulpit, but merely alluded to
the evil sentiments that prevail and that are exhibited in individual matters, and what I said I applied equally to knowledge
of men, to action upon men, and to judgment of men. You
will, perhaps, perceive from this, that no particular part of the
sermon was directed immediately against Gall, but the whole
bore upon him. However, people interpreted certain expressions as being particularly pointed against him, though they
were equally applicable to every physiognomist of the old
school. Had I time I would write down the whole sermon
for you.

[CCLI.]   *No date.*

        . . . . . In regard to Louis Börne * you are partly
in the right and he is partly in the right, and I am not at all

* Ludwig Börne, then still called Louis Baruch, being destined to
follow the medical career, was, on the fervent entreaties of his father,
received into the house of Dr. Herz, there to prosecute his studies.
After the death of Herz the youth, then only seventeen years of age,
conceived so violent a passion for the beautiful widow of his master,
though she was three-and-twenty years his senior, that, finding that

wrong. Kindly inclined towards him I have always been, but he is indifferent to me. How is it possible to take a greater interest in a man than he takes in himself? He undertakes nothing, trifles away his time, neglects his studies, ruins himself by laziness, and takes it all very composedly, merely saying that such is, once for all, his nature, and if he were to force himself into anything else, matters would not be the least better. How is it possible to produce any effect upon a man who thus reasons away his own power of will? I do not know whether he will go to destruction; many characters rescue themselves from this condition; but while he is in it, there can be no question of exercising any influence over him, or taking any interest in him. In addition to this he is affected and false. Thus, for instance, he pretended to me that he was going to Francfort with the greatest reluctance, and that he feared that he should suffer from dreadful *ennui* there; whereas Mrs. Reil assures me that he was as delighted as a child at the thought of going. That he should complain of being melancholy, I can understand; but not that you should pity him for it. What reason has a young man, who has everything he wants, to be melancholy? His melancholy arises out of his idleness, which is enervating him. You may write every word of this to him; indeed, I shall repeat it to him myself when he comes back. Pitied he is to be if he continue in this way, but helped he cannot be unless he helps himself.

[CCLII.]   *No date.*

 Between Louis Börne and me, dear Jette, such as we are, no relations could ever have been established. He loves and pets his own idleness and vanity, and he demands of other

his feelings were not returned, he twice attempted to commit suicide. Henrietta Herz, though reproving with gentle dignity the folly of the youth, continued, nevertheless, ever after to evince a friendly interest in him, and was, therefore, anxious to secure for him the friendship of Schleiermacher. See *Fürst, Henriette Herz, Ihr Leben und ihre Erinnerungen.*—TRANS.

people that they shall likewise pet him, and if they do not, he arrogantly overlooks them. The latter he cannot do in regard to me, and the former I cannot do in regard to him ; for idleness and vanity in young people are disgusting and hateful in my eyes. This is, in fact, what has separated us. An interesting person, if you so choose to call him, he may perhaps be, but more than this I think he will never be ; more especially as I have never discovered in him any real decided talent, on which I might base a hope that it would at last gain the mastery, and work a new spirit in him.

Schleiermacher to E. and H. von Willich.

[CCLIII.]   18*th October*, 1805.

Perhaps you have already heard from Mrs. Herz the dreadful news of the unexpected change that has taken place in Eleanore's feelings. I do not know whether any one can form to themselves an idea of my state ; it is the deepest, most crushing sorrow—the pain will never leave me—the unity of my life is rent asunder ; but whatever can be made of the ruins, I will make of them. . . . .

Anxious about you, dear daughter, I was beforehand, but I have been still more so since this dreadful communication ; I felt as if in every direction one tragic event must follow another. Thank God, our friend Herz has just written to inform me of your happy confinement. In the midst of my misfortune I feel this joy deeply, but I cannot, as yet, find words to express it. Your lovely image, with the sweet babe, will often stand before me and comfort me. Greetings to all—writing is like death to me ; I cannot continue.

[CCLIV.]   28*th October.*

A couple of hours after I had despatched my letter to you, I received yours, dearest friend, with the first glad tidings from yourself. Your second also came, unfortunately, too late ; I did not receive it until the 25th, and could not, therefore, formally present myself among you on the solemn day.

Nevertheless I was surely with you, for I am much with you every day. My tenderest, fatherly love I bestow upon the little being! May this love be numbered among the blessings that meet it on all sides on its entrance into life ; when I shall see it, and trace your united features in its face, and bless it with tears of joy, God only knows! I shall not fear to appear before you. I do not think that my looks will sadden you too much, and I stand greatly in need of seeing all those whom I love; but I do not know how I shall manage it in these sad times, that weigh so heavily on all, and with the pressure of my occupations which, if I would at all keep myself erect, I must lean on for support, holding them sacred and attending to them diligently. Only let me soon have a confirmation of the good news, that you will not be obliged to leave Jette and the child to follow the army. May you be allowed to enjoy your happiness undisturbed !

Within the last .week the lectures have recommenced. According to my own judgment, I am delivering those on ethics in a freer and more lucid manner than formerly, and my audience is pretty numerous. The course of Dogmatics, however, is only attended by a very small number of auditors, but these are very receptive, and I hope to say and to effect much good ; and when I repeat the course, greater numbers will be sure to come. I am also delivering publicly, to an audience of about a hundred persons, a course of exegetical lectures on the Epistle to the Galatians. If but half the number remain to the last, I shall be well pleased. It is most fortunate that these lectures give me so much to do, that the academical church service is at last to commence, and that I have my Nanni here.

Henriette von Willich to Schleiermacher.

[CCLV.]   *October.*

I knew it, beloved father, that even in the midst of your grief you would rejoice at my happiness, and would think of me, and of the innocent babe. From the moment I heard the sorrowful tidings, I longed much for the first words from you, though I did not venture to hope that they would give a less painful idea of your state of mind. Dear father, I know not such grief, yet I can well conceive how deep, how dreadful, yours must be. That we, who love you so tenderly, can give you no comfort, is very distressing! How beautiful it is in you, that your heart is still open to our affection and our joys! Could you but come to us! How I feel when I hold my little daughter in my lap, or lay her to my breast, you will not expect me to describe—how could I? It is such an all-absorbing love, deep, deep in my heart—a longing desire to screen the little creature from every pain, every suffering, and to take all upon myself. Every cry goes through my heart, each look seems to me so touching. One evening, in particular, I felt so strange. I was still somewhat weak; H. B. was playing softly but so sweetly on the piano. I felt as if my whole being was dissolving, and floating towards heaven with the child. It was a very blissful state. . . . . .

[CCLVI.]   *November.*

I cannot allow Ehrenfried's letter to depart without enclosing a few lines. I have had many long and confidential chats with you in thought, but my time has been so much taken up that I have not been able to write. Were it not my babe, that is the chief impediment, I would think it hard. I cannot tell you how glad I am that it is a pleasure to you to get letters from me. I love you so tenderly! Your last words were so kind, but so sad. What a heart is yours! so much love in the midst of so much sorrow! Ah, were you but happy! I feel always as if I must implore you to be so, as if it were in your own power. Ah! do not give yourself up too much to grief; do not renounce joy for your whole life. Dearest, I feel as if a good angel must come to you one day, and plant in your heart new joy and the hope of new happiness, not taking away your pains suddenly, but healing them gently. My dear father, sleep sweetly; I must say good night; I dare not sit up later, though my heart would fain dwell longer in communion with you.

Schleiermacher to E. von Willich.

                    26th November, 1805.

I am quite dismayed, dear friend, when I think that
for very nearly a whole month I have not written to you or
Jette. But it has come so naturally, that I am almost tempted
to say that it is right. The pain at the bottom of my heart
is ever lifting up its voice throughout the day, and I am ever
endeavouring to smother it with more work; but were I to
attempt to write, I should be unable to keep it down, and
should be upset for the rest of the day. In the evening it will
break forth in spite of all; and, however late and fatigued I
may go to my bed, which I dread, I find my grief wide awake;
and, though I extinguish the light, my sorrow will not allow
itself to be enveloped in darkness. You see, dear friend, if I
would live, I must spare myself as long as I am in this state.
Were I, before going to bed, to sharpen the sting, I should
get no sleep at all, and I get little enough as it is; and I
should have a still harder struggle in the morning, to obtain
sufficient mastery over myself to forget my pain, and to
throw myself entirely into my work. Yes, could I write to
you without thinking of myself, how many letters would
you not have received, you, dear friends? But to do this, I
confess, I am still too weak; however, I trust the time will
come.

Now let me tell you of a delightful hour which I spent yesterday. I had preached once more, after a long interval, and
afterwards we dined at Steffens', together with Reichardt.
I had some letters to despatch, and therefore went home after
dinner, accompanied by Steffens. As soon as we found ourselves alone, he thanked me so heartily, and with so much
emotion for my sermon, which he said had produced a very
strengthening effect on himself and his excellent wife, that I
was deeply moved, and felt a kind of mournful happiness steal
over me. He next spoke of the clear and truthful character
of my mind, which nothing could disturb; and I then broke

through my reserve, and told him of my misfortune and my inward desolation. Until then I had seldom seen him alone, and never at an opportune moment for opening my heart to him. It was an elevating hour. Within me the deepest sorrow and the highest joy embraced each other under a transparent veil. Yes, dear brother, I feel distinctly that in myself I am nothing now; but I am the organ of so much that is beautiful and holy—a focus in which all the joys and all the sorrows of my beloved friends are concentrated; and as such I honour myself, and therefore I live. Therefore, also, I must endeavour to prevent the sorrows of my life from spreading over and darkening the double vocation that has fallen to my lot. Therefore, also, I wish to tell you a great deal about my labours; but, after all, what I have to say is simply that they grow and thrive, and afford me much satisfaction.

[CCLVIII.]   *1st December.*

It is very good of you to give me an account of your professional duties also, and I am glad you feel that in my hearty sympathy with your sweetest joys, I do not forget your office and the gladness that you must experience in seeing that a blessing attends it. The present increase of occupation can hardly be pleasant to you. Such separate acts performed among people with whom you can enter into no closer relations, cannot effect much. But to draw ever nearer to the flock that has been intrusted to one, that I consider the prime duty. With the power of so doing, you are especially endowed, and I am sure that even the less cultivated members of your congregation will gradually learn to understand you better. As regards myself, I see clearly that no congregation will ever suit me so well as an academical one; but I shall first have to form it here, and it will never be very numerous. To teach scientific principles from the academical rostrum, and at the same time to place myself in the pulpit within the sphere of an uneducated audience (except it were country people, with whom I believe I could manage it), would be excessively difficult to me. But I have a lively hope that by means of the connection between my sermons and my lectures, I shall be able to bring clearly home to the minds of the students the true relations between speculation and piety, and from both places alike, from the pulpit as from the professor's chair, I trust I shall be able to enlighten their minds and to warm their hearts.

As yet, however, it is, alas, but a hope; for my preaching to the university has not commenced. Through my lectures on doctrinal theology, my views in regard to separate points of Christianity are developing themselves more clearly, but I am persuaded that when, in a couple of years hence, I shall publish a little handbook on the subject, it will be an offence to the Jews, and foolishness to the Greeks. My short exegetical course has been of great use to me in regard to the philology of the New Testament; and as it continues to be numerously attended, I may hope when I begin a regular course, next term, that I shall not lack hearers. But what trouble these two courses do give me ; and it is but too true that I now require two hours to do that which formerly I could do in half an hour. The night is far advanced, and I must conclude.

Schleiermacher to Henriette von Willich.

[CCLIX.] *December 2nd, 1805.*

Dear Jette, if you only knew what a comfort you are to me, and what a soothing image of you is conjured up before me by each word expressive of your joy as a mother, and of your sympathy as a daughter! I see you before me in all your tenderness and with your loveliness, enhanced by the presence of the dear babe in your arms. Nay, with such a daughter, and such friends as you all are to me, I cannot succumb even to the greatest of sorrows—for joy will vindicate its rights. The sorrow does not indeed give way to the joy, but both overspread the entire being ; and in my case I feel distinctly that the joy emanates alone from my friends, and from all the beauty and goodness that beam upon me from the world, for in myself I cannot keep it fresh and living; but I am quite content to live through and in you all. Dear Jette, your words do me so much good, and so also your sweet affection for me. I am so moved that I must cease, but let me embrace you with the tears, in which my sorrow and my joy are streaming forth. Kiss your sweet babe for me, and to your Ehrenfried also give a hearty brotherly embrace.

Schleiermacher to Charlotte von Kathen.

[CCLX.]   *Halle, 2nd December, 1805.*

A long while already, dear kind Charlotte, I have in my possession your letter, through which your friendly, gentle spirit gazes at me as clearly as out of your sweet eyes; and also your dear present, which I so often looked forward to with pleasure, and I have not yet said a word of thanks to you. But it is constantly so with me now: I cannot give utterance to my feelings; they all seem driven back. My grief shrinks, recoils from the sound of its own voice, when I make an attempt to speak it out, and refuses to be expressed except in the faintest tones. Could I but take your hand, dear friend, and press it to my full heart! Ah, I do so even from this distance, and I feel how you strengthen me! You remind me so sweetly of that in which I can rejoice with you, and indicate to me a sacred place of refuge. Yes, dear friend, I will cling to everything beauteous that draws me sympathetically towards itself, and working lovingly and diligently, as best I can, I will gradually use up my life.

In sorrow and in tears the work of your hands, destined for me, was begun and completed. Thank God, that your maternal anxieties have been so happily set at rest, and that you can now press your little darling to your heart with confident hope. . . . .

Would you see me, such as I am in daily life? I would fain conduct myself so that no one should suspect what a

shock my life has sustained ; and as far as men are concerned
I succeed very well: but with women it will not do; they
have too keen a perception of what passes in the heart. On
the very day that I received the painful tidings, a lady friend
of mine from Berlin was here. She had been at my house
the previous evening, and I had spoken with such joyful confidence of my future life. To this friend I first opened my
heart the ensuing day, while accompanying her some miles
on her way back to Berlin. I afterwards returned home on
foot, along the same road that I had trod a fortnight previously—oh, with what different feelings! To my kind
sister I never mention the sad event—just because I see her
every day ; and, happily, I have not been obliged to communicate it to her, as she learnt it from a friend who received
the account as soon as I did. Even with him I rarely touch
upon the subject. Steffens, that loveable, glorious man, is
the only one here to whom I felt as if I must speak ; besides,
his wife, as he told me, had observed that for some time my
face had borne traces of deep grief. I labour a great deal,
but achieve very little. At the writing-table my work is
most irksome to me ; but in the professorial chair and in the
pulpit I feel myself quite free : from those holy places, devoted
directly to a vocation bearing upon society in general, the
sorrow, that touches the individual alone, is excluded—those
are true places of refuge. Every word that comes from a
friend also refreshes and strengthens me. The Willichs have
done a great deal for me; and you also, dear Charlotte, are to
me a supporting angel.

Henriette von Willich to Schleiermacher.

[CCLXI.]   21st *January,* 1806.

. . . . . I should like so much to tell you a great
deal about my Henriette, that you may learn to know her
before you see her, though it may, perhaps, be difficult. She
is just now sleeping sweetly! I am sitting close to her cradle
writing to you—it is such a delight to be near her! I have

just been reading *Valérie*, a French novel. The many delicate pictures which it contains, and which are so simply drawn, have made a lively impression on me ; and one of them, which pleased me more especially, is constantly recurring to my mind. Yes, dear father, my life is very happy ; ever filled with love and care of my babe, to whom almost all my outward activity is devoted. But when she is resting in sweet slumber, then my cares also go to rest, and with my whole free soul, I give myself up to the occupations I like best—to writing, reading, and needlework. But when the little one is awake, I am too restless, too much interrupted—my eyes are always turning towards her; and my desires, and the sweet fancy that she would be more comfortable still in my arms, always take me back to her. . . . .

Ah, I must pour out my complaints to you, and tell you how wretched it is, that in connection with the sweet babe, I discover a great tendency to jealousy in my heart. In regard to Ehrenfried, I have never felt that ; he is so entirely mine. In respect to my friends, I have not either experienced much jealousy, because my estimation of myself makes me feel my inferiority to them, and because I am always hoping and endeavouring to work myself up to a level with them. But in regard to my darling, it is otherwise ; the very thought that she might possibly love some one else better than me, or feel more happy with some one else, if it be not my Ehrenfried, actually makes me feel as if I were suffocating. Alas, this feeling may eventually fill my heart with bitterness ! But, perhaps, it only arises out of my intense longing, in my love for the child, to obtain a sign of its tenderness, of its return of my affection, of its special love for me, while the little innocent still looks at us all with the same eyes, and gives no other preference to her doting mother than she gives to any one that cradles her tenderly and carefully in their arms. Perhaps I shall not have this feeling when the babe learns to stretch out her little arms towards me, and to call me by the sweet name of mother. . . . .

Schleiermacher to Henriette von Willich.

[CCLXII.]   *Halle, February*, 1806.

Pity me a little, dear Jette, because I can never get to write to you all as much as I wish, which would do me more good than you can well conceive.   But so it is, no joy departs alone ; each one takes another along with it, and how much more must not this be the case with the greatest and brightest of all life's joys!   The cause of my not writing is really entirely owing to this.   On the one hand, I feel that I had better be silent about my grief even to you ; on the other hand, the sense of suffering intrudes into all that I have to think of and to do, and keeps everything back.   During the last couple of weeks in particular, I have felt a heartache and a dejection which I cannot describe.   Grief must have a peculiar life of its own, that surges and swells, and has its ebb-tide and its flood ; for I know of nothing outward that can have excited it at this moment, more especially. .   .   .   .

Well, then, I will go to you for strength, and be not uneasy lest the reaction should afterwards be too great; for when I return from my visit to you, I shall have to begin my new course of lectures, and shall enter at once into the busy life which entirely absorbs me, and in connection with which I have already met with a success that has had a very beneficial effect upon me.   Dear child, let me beg you not to be too much saddened when you see me ; do not let it overcome you ; forget that your father is not happy, in order that the sweet image he has formed to himself of his happy daughter may not be dimmed; and try to think that I shall be much pleased, nay truly happy, while among you all.   But, above all things, entreat our friend Herz, who really seems to have economical scruples, to come with me ; we shall otherwise lose so many delights.   I will also once more entreat her to set these aside.

But how will it be, little Jette ?   Will you also be jealous of me if I enter thoroughly into the life of your little daughter, and she is friendly to me, and grows fond of me ? It is a dangerous matter. You know that the love between grandparents and grandchildren is particularly tender. . . . . Ah! dear child, I look forward with indescribable joy to seeing both the little Jettes! Here, I have also a little child, in which I take a great interest, my dear Steffens' little Clara—such is to be her name, for she is not yet christened.

[CCLXIII.]   *28th February.*

Unfortunately, my letters were not sent by the last post, and, in consequence, my fatherly greetings and blessing for your birthday will probably not reach you until the day has past. Beloved and happy daughter, in whose contemplation, in whose affection, I feel so content, whom God has blessed so bountifully—what can I wish for you but that you may retain what you *have?* that you will remain what you *are*, I know, and in this lies the promise that you will also become more than you are, that you will go on steadily developing yourself more independently and more beautifully, and that you will thus also continue to react beneficently on those whom nature has placed around you. Among these I reckon myself ; for just as your little daughter helps to form you, as you must feel, so you contribute to my culture. I thank God that He allowed me to find you, before He took so much away from me, and that you have given yourself to me as a daughter so freely and heartily. The purest and noblest love of my heart pours itself out upon thee, and I feel it, I am to thee all that a father can be to a daughter who is a wife and a mother, in the sense that thou art. Oh! remain ever my joy and my pride, dear child, for I feel that I live in you and in Ehrenfried, and in your noble union. I hope soon to see you in spite of all difficulties, but I reckon upon hearing from you once more in the meanwhile.

Schleiermacher to E. von Willich.

[CCLXIV.] *No date.*

I should have written to you sooner, dear Ehrenfried, had I not been anxious to await the decision in the matter concerning Bremen, which I cannot, however, even now report to you. I take it for granted that you have heard something about it from our friend Charlotte Kathen. Let me now relate to you how I have regarded it from the beginning. You know that divine service in the university church has not yet commenced, because of the repairs required in the organ. In November last the minister was here, and spoke a great deal about pushing on these, but in December the authorities again converted the hardly finished church into a granary. Towards the end of the year the proposition from Bremen was sent to me. The first preliminary inquiries I set aside at once. But they were repeated urgently from various quarters; I heard much good about Bremen, about the piety of the inhabitants and their good-nature, and great love and reverence for their pastors; the life in and for a regular congregation attracted me greatly; in this place I saw that the prospect of war would destroy for an indefinite period my sphere of action as far as preaching was concerned; I reflected upon the fact that if the university had felt any real interest in the matter, the evil might easily have been remedied, and that my academical activity was also hemmed in and impeded by all kinds of paltry obstacles and petty fault-finding; I also took into consideration how heavily and slowly everything progresses that I now work at, and finally I took a decided resolution. I wrote to the minister and also to privy-councillor Beyme, that, although I was upon the whole well pleased here, I should decidedly accept the call to Bremen, if guarantees were not given me that the obstacles in the way of the performance of divine service for the academy should be speedily obviated, and if I were not at once appointed a member of the faculty of theology.

From the character of the reply given to this I conceived that I should be able to judge whether the authorities were sufficiently in earnest regarding the object held in view in appointing me to think it worth their while to exert themselves to keep me here. If not, I should be glad to get away, the sooner the better; whereas, in the contrary case, that is, if everything were as it ought to be, I would never desire any other sphere of influence than my present one. The privy council has now declared itself ready to do everything in its power to satisfy my demands, which it acknowledges to be just. From the minister and the university authorities I have as yet had no communication, and I am, therefore, still in some measure undecided; more especially as I am doubly reluctant to give up my professorship, because I still entertain the hope that I may in time regain my former working powers. In short, I desire very much to remain here, but only on condition that my entire sphere of activity be speedily opened to me. Whether I shall be a gainer, from the pecuniary point of view, by remaining here, is a question. I have put forward no claim in regard to money, because it is against my nature to do so; but it would be nothing more than just if they were to allow me a salary when I enter the faculty, as hitherto I have had none in my quality of professor. Our meeting again, also, in a certain measure, depends upon this; but should I eventually go to Bremen, I should not, at all events, be able to leave this until after the close of the lectures, and in that case the few weeks more which the circuit by way of Stralsund and Rügen would take would be of no importance.

At my lectures I have a good many very regular and attentive hearers. I know that some who attend the lectures on ethics are not afraid of devoting three or four hours to the repetition and discussion of a single lecture, and rejoice at finding the subject becoming ever clearer to them. So also among those who attend the lectures on doctrinal theology, there are several who have, to my great satisfaction, expressed themselves to the effect that it is only now that they understand the true significance of Christianity. This is truly encouraging, and the more so as it is a proof to me that I am more lucid than I thought I was. Poor Plato, on the contrary, would fare far better in Bremen. In regard to this, as to all my other literary undertakings, the prospects here are very unfavourable, more especially if I begin exegesis also, which I must and will do some day. Altogether, I see before me in the next three years a mass of work which will hardly allow me to think of any other undertaking. . . . .

My letters have been so long detained that I am now able to tell you that I have had an answer from the minister, who likewise promises to do all that he can; and it is almost certain that I shall remain here.

[CCLXV.] *Halle, March,* 1806.

. . . . . I know not how much I have written to you about the Bremen affair. The very first answer I received from Berlin rendered it probable that my demands would be acceded to, and soon after the matter was settled. But in the meanwhile the people of Bremen proved themselves so fully in earnest, and showed me from all sides so much confidence and affection, that it was with quite a heavy heart that I wrote to decline their proposal; and since then they have made me munificent offers of an increase of salary to the amount of several hundred dollars. In Berlin I have preferred no claims in regard to money, as I should never think of changing my sphere of action for the sake of money, and, therefore, the present offer from Bremen does not either in the least tempt me. Nevertheless, I hope that the authorities in Berlin will soon think of making an addition to my salary.

. . . . . Reimer has also quite unexpectedly proposed a new edition of the *Discourses,* and also of the *Sermons,* for the Michaelmas fair. Had it not come so suddenly, I would have requested you and other friends to let me have their remarks on particular passages. I have just finished revising the first *Discourse,* and have only altered one passage considerably; but various little corrections always suggest themselves, and these are the most disagreeable. Important alterations I should, in every case, hesitate to make, lest the character of the book should be changed. I shall not, either, this time, put my name on the title-page. It seems to me as if the incognito actually belonged to the style of the book. Any one writing under his own name could not possibly speak thus.

Henriette von Willich to Schleiermacher.

[CCLXVI.]   13*th March*, 1806.

Your dear words reached me on the morning of my birthday, my beloved father. Before your letter arrived, my baby had brought me pretty flowers and other presents from my dear ones. . . . . When I realize to myself that you are really coming, I am out of myself with joy: how delightful it will be! I am always thinking of it. But I must speak to you openly on a certain subject. You know how from my heart the confidential "thou" has flown into my pen when writing to you; and when addressing you in all sincerity of feeling as my father, I cannot speak otherwise. But when you are here, I shall not always be able to address you thus, nor can I always call you father. Therefore, that both ways of addressing you (in the third as well as the second person) may become natural to me, I shall also, in my letters, use the one or the other as it may happen. And you are my friend as well as my father, are you not, dear Schleier? Pray do not laugh at me, for I should really feel very much embarrassed were I to be guilty of a slip of the tongue in the presence of strangers. I should at once become conscious of the difference between us—you the great author, the celebrated professor, and I the little *Pastorinn*, as they often call me.

Schleiermacher to Henrietta Herz.

[CCLXVII.]   14*th March*, 1806.

What Johannes Müller said about the *Christmas Festival** gives me no pleasure : it sounds too much as if he had
calculated upon its being repeated to me. A comparison
with *Plato* is verily too great an honour for that little book ;
that he must reserve until he sees my philosophical dialogues.
But what he says about the conversion of history into alle-
gory, is a misunderstanding which is very disagreeable to me,
but for which, I trust, I am nowise to blame. . . . .

Henriette von Willich to Schleiermacher.

[CCLXVIII.]   *April*, 1806.

I will not attempt to describe to you how sorry I am,
my dear, dear Schleier, to find my glad hope disappointed :
we both know *what* joy we felt in the prospect of meeting
again, which we have now lost. How exultingly I should
have laid my babe in your arms! How full of high significance and deep emotion would the moment have been to me,
when I beheld your eyes resting lovingly and with a blessing
on the little creature! Ah, I cannot tell you what an intense
satisfaction it would be to me, should you learn to love my
child *very* much, should it become one of your favourites
among children. In affection to you, I am sure it will be
like me.

[CCLXIX.]   *Poseritz (in Rügen), May*, 1806.

You must share my joy at the spring, my beloved
father! Since yesterday I live entirely in the delightful feeling that at last it has come to us with its flowers—that my
babe is inhaling its fragrance, and is blossoming forth in it,
and that her existence is intimately interwoven with it—sweet
spring, and sweet baby.

* A little book written by Schleiermacher.

We have been here since yesterday, and to-day the weather is delightful, the air balsamic, and everything is budding and developing itself to the eye. I have been longing very much for bright and genial days, and I should be so glad to spend many such here with my little girl. It seems to me that, like the flowers, she also would bloom more freshly here than shut up within the walls of the town. The beautiful images that surround her cannot pass before her eyes without producing an effect. This morning we put a nosegay in her little hand while she was still asleep; her first look fell lovingly upon the flowers, and when I came in to her again, she was already busily engaged with them. Early in the morning I go into the garden with her, and her eyes rest so seriously and thoughtfully upon every object, that she can hardly find time to play and laugh with me. Dear Schleier, I can think of little else than the child at present.

Schleiermacher to Henriette von Willich.

[CCLXX.]　　　　　　　　　　　　　　　　*No date.*

　　Dear Jette, I know it is a little eternity since any of you heard from me ; but I hope that, since my journey to Berlin, you have had accounts of me from our friend Herz, and that you know at least that I am well. That I have often turned in thought to Stralsund and Rügen, with a heart full of loving yearning towards you all, and particularly towards you, dear child, and your wee, wee Jette, you will believe without my telling you.

You will perceive, dear little *Pastorinn*, that I have already again adopted the familiar *thou*, and shall very likely never get the better of the habit when writing to you. If, therefore, it be not particularly disagreeable to you, let me go on with it.

The journey to Berlin was but poor compensation for the delight I had promised myself among you all. I was wonderfully dissipated, and saw a great many people, which was partly occasioned by my having gone thither in company with my friend Steffens; but I enjoyed very little of the society of my most intimate friends, and did not even show my sister as many of the sights of Berlin as I had desired. I have recently returned from a very different kind of tour, in the Harz Mountains, undertaken with Steffens and some young people, pupils of us both. This will, at least, give you a good standard of measure for my health. In nine days we traversed very nearly fifty miles on foot, wandering through the mountains in all directions, and very frequently along dangerous footpaths ; and I was the briskest of all, ever in advance, above the earth and under it; yet I was able, immediately after our return, to burrow myself into the midst of a heap of work which is daily accumulating. It was a delightful tour. We were very much favoured by the weather, and in addition to the satisfaction of the scientific object we held in view, we enjoyed ourselves gloriously. I dare say there was not another among us through whose mind passed so many strange thoughts as through mine. The quiet of such a pedestrian tour—for I never speak much while walking—enables me to give myself up to all the thoughts that move me most; and as on the occasion in question my inward cogitations were constantly interrupted by the scenes and company around me, the fermentation was never exhausted, but recommenced again at every interval of quiet. Dear child! how much sorrow, how much joy, how much tender melancholy passed through me then! How willingly would I not have ended my life through one of the many little dangers that beset our path! And yet, on the other hand, what love of life I felt, when I became conscious of how I live in you, in all our friends, and in my vocation!

Schleiermacher to Charlotte von Kathen.

[CCLXXI.] *Halle, 20th June,* 1806.

 Is it not very hard, dear Charlotte, that I cannot even by writing compensate myself a little for the disappointed hope of spending some time with you? But I will not begin with complaints. We know, nevertheless, that our lives are connected, and that we are with each other in spirit; and your letter itself consoles me so sweetly for the privation. For what is it that prevents me from writing, but my working for my young friends and pupils; and if they are attached to me, and retain a profound impression of what I teach them, can I desire greater happiness, or pay too highly for it? I have been deeply moved by what you tell me about K——. Give him my very kind regards. I remember him quite well, though I never learnt to know him intimately. I could not then, as now—since my sister has been with me—have a certain evening in the week on which to receive the most zealous and best informed of my young hearers. I do not know which party gains most by this arrangement, the young people or myself. To them, perhaps, many an obscure point is cleared up during our unconstrained conversations, and they gain confidence; but, on my side, I acquire an increased tact for the guidance of my lectures, and learn to know more thoroughly what are the wants, and what are the faculties, of the most superior among my hearers. In this manner, I also gain more courage; and thus, each year the path which I have to tread widens more and more before me.

How kind of you to give me such a detailed account of the two days which I should have liked so much to spend among you—the day of the christening and the birthday. You had, indeed, most kind intentions in regard to me. Thank dear Kathen very heartily for so willingly bestowing upon me this privilege, and for taking upon himself to represent me. And the excellent Mrs. Baier, the venerable lady, towards whom I felt as towards a mother almost from the first moment I saw her—with what pious emotion I unite with her, even from hence, in love, faith, and hope for the little creature. Yes, dear friend, I should have reckoned it among the happiest moments of my life, had I been able to present your dear child with love and prayer to God and Christ. But, even as it is, I press it to my heart with love and prayer, and rejoice in the thought of how it thrives in shelter of your maternal affection.

These lines have been retarded a fortnight, and now another letter from **you**, dear Charlotte, together with others from Stralsund, have arrived. You may see now, by the instance of the *Christmas Festival*, how quietly I can wait for a pleasure, without spoiling it by precipitancy. I wanted to see whether my friends would recognize me in the little work, in which there are various peculiarities, which may make it appear quite unlike any of my other writings. For this reason, I did not myself present it to any one, and let it at first appear here and in Berlin without my name, which accounts for the notices in the newspapers having come so late. My friend Steffens at once guessed my authorship, and so did a couple of the young men who attend my lectures. In Berlin, I do not know how it would have been, had not Jette been so precipitate. But you, I believed, would at once discover me, because no one could describe your sufferings as I could. That I misled you is no matter, if you only recognized yourself such as I see you, and if you be not displeased at beholding some of your traits delineated in that picture. You and your little darling were from the commencement so mixed up with the idea of the whole, that it would have been impossible for me not to introduce you in the narrative. Indeed, my art can do no better than weave together what I have seen revealed in noble souls, and this tale has touched many persons in a peculiar manner. It is, therefore, not a gift that I have offered you, but one which you have bestowed upon me, and which, having confidence in you, I have accepted from you. I have long been anxiously expecting to hear what you thought of it. Have you shown it to the Willichs, and were they pleased with it?

You ask me how I feel in these warlike times? Alas, dear friend, I often think of you all with much anxiety, also of your beautiful country. The causes for this anxiety have varied much within the last months. A war between our two kings I no longer expect; but, it is much to be feared, that the French, who are now evacuating Southern Germany, will soon attack the Swedes. Dear friend, if in that case your king should resolve to make a determined resistance, brace up your courage, and be ready to sacrifice everything in order to gain everything, and reckon everything that is preserved to you for gain. Remember that the individual cannot stand, cannot save himself, if that in which each and all are rooted—German freedom and German feeling—be lost; and it is these that are threatened. Would you desire to be spared any danger, any suffering, at the cost of the conviction of having delivered over future generations to base servitude, and of having exposed them to be inoculated with the despicable sentiments of an utterly corrupted people? Believe me, sooner or later, a great and universal struggle must ensue, the objects of which will be as much our sentiments, our religion, and our mental culture, as our outward liberty and worldly goods —a struggle which must be carried on, not by kings and their hired armies, but by the nations and their kings together— a struggle which will unite sovereign and people by a more beautiful bond than has existed for centuries, and in which every one—every one, without exception—must take the part that the common weal imposes on him. That which seems at present impending over you is, indeed, such a separate matter, and has so little interest for you, that your anxiety for your own special circle may well predominate; but when the great movements draw nigh to you, then the general power of these to awaken courage will also be proved in your case, and you will learn to look even upon the fearful images which your imagination conjures up as something external, and as belonging to the conditions of the movement against which you are bound to struggle. The crisis in Germany (and Germany is, after all, the heart of Europe) stands as distinctly before my eyes as the smaller one to which you allude stands before yours. The air around me is thick and sultry, and I hope that the coming storm will precipitate an explosion; for that it should pass over, I think we can no longer hope.

How can you think that you ever could speak too much to me of your children ? Kiss them all from me, and now farewell.

Henriette von Willich to Schleiermacher.

[CCLXXII.]   *4th August,* 1806.

It is a pleasure to me in my solitude to have to write to you, dear Schleier. Since yesterday noon, I have been alone with my little daughter. You know whither Ehrenfried has gone ; before the end of the week I must not expect him back. To me it is no hardship to be alone—it is not painful to me as to so many others. Ehrenfried is mine, though absent, and I am already rejoicing at the thought of his return.

It is very long since I wrote to you, yet you have often been present to me, and I have frequently upbraided myself for not telling you so. I do not know how it has happened. We ought to see each other face to face again. I cannot quite give myself up to joyful anticipations of seeing you next autumn. Ah ! these are not times of joyfulness—so many dreadful things are happening here. A party of twenty persons have lately been poisoned : one of these, a young Swedish officer, the only joy of his old mother, is already dead ; the rest, almost all of them young people, are past recovery. I feel often so sad at heart when I look at my little Jette, that she should be born at a time when peace and innocence seem departed from the world. I long indescribably for the country—the town becomes every day more disagreeable to me; it is so opposed to the inward life which I live with my Ehrenfried and my child, and it is also opposed to the outward life which I most desire to lead.

Yes, dear Schleier, many of the beautiful thoughts in the *Christmas Festival* have made an impression on me, and I have endeavoured to appropriate them. How could a mother read it, and not be touched by it ? Of the excellent Ernestine, I form to myself a most vivid conception, and such a child as Sophie I have ever had in mind. You have depicted maternal love very truly and very beautifully. I have always felt within myself that this feeling is grounded in the divine love, and that it is a longing to behold all that is holy in the child, and a watching for it. Some day, when I shall have an opportunity of speaking to you, I will tell you all that I feel in regard to your book.

Schleiermacher to E. von Willich.

[CCLXXIII.]   *15th September*, 1806.

Dear Ehrenfried, I send you herewith not only the *Christmas Festival*, but also the sermon with which I opened divine service to the Academy. I cannot say that I am very much pleased with the latter. To deliver a discourse on a particular occasion always has a laming influence on me, and more especially under such conditions as the present. The laming influence is, I think, owing to the fact that one knows that his auditors have not come to listen with unprejudiced minds, but that each one brings with him in his own mind the leading idea of what he expects to hear, and of how the subject ought to be represented. Nevertheless, I have had the discourse printed, as many persons seemed to wish it. The church was tremendously full, and the seven hundred students or thereabouts, who were present, comported themselves with admirable decorum. Since then the church has not indeed been so crowded, but I have a select congregation of academical youths, by no means insignificant in number, and hitherto it has been the best among them that have come the oftenest. I am also pretty well pleased with myself; I have a satisfactory consciousness of the blessing that attends my discourses, and the delivery of these forms, therefore, no slight addition to my happiness. We have, however, already had one interruption, the church having again been taken, or rather voluntarily ceded by the academy, for a corn magazine. I protested with all my might, and with full right I believe (for this step was in open violation of the spirit of the royal command), but in vain. However, the zeal of the students on the occasion gave me very great satisfaction. Some of them immediately assembled, drew up during the night remonstrances to the *Protector* and the general in command, and gathered as many as four hundred signatures, though numbers had already left. So much at least has been attained, that another *locale* has been assigned to us, and that as regards all essentials we are able to go on with the services. But now the church also is to have a vacation in consequence of a proposal of mine, which has been agreed to, and to-day I have preached for the last time. My discourse was especially addressed to those who are about to leave the university, for in my sermons I always hold the academy strictly in view, and I had again to-day most touching proofs of the effect produced by them. Upon the whole, dear friend, I have great reason to be thankful for the success I have had as a teacher, and for the joyful prospects which are opened in regard to the next generation of young theologians. My school may, it is true, easily be counted, and it is indeed rather satisfactory to me that the great mass does not crowd around me ; but I can now point out many a glorious mind and respectable talent among my scholars, who embrace the good cause with zeal and affection, and I even know a couple among them who have, through my lectures, been cured of that hostility to Christianity which philologians more especially are apt to entertain ; and what greater joy could I have than this ?

The *Discourses* (the second edition) are now ready, and in a few weeks they will probably be in your hands. I am very curious to know what you will think of them as they now are. In my opinion they have gained much in lucidity as a whole, while comparatively little of the brilliancy of the first casting has been lost. Much more than this I have not produced this summer, and in spite of all my business I have been heartily lazy. Next winter I shall be obliged to exert myself far more strenuously.

Do tell me how matters are proceeding in your country, what people in general think about the new constitution, and what promises the latter holds out. I exult in the war against the tyrant, which I think is now unavoidable, and am delighted with the courageous spirit which prevails generally here among the troops and among the people. A considerable *corps d'armée* is stationed in our vicinity; the king is expected, and when he arrives, it is hoped a forward movement will be made to fight the French, wherever they be met with. I have often felt a strong desire to speak out upon politics too, if I could but have found leisure. In the pulpit I allude to these matters from time to time, but in a very different way from what I hear others do.

Schleiermacher to Henriette von Willich.

[CCLXXIV.]   *No date.*

Dear little Jette, you ought to have written me a few words in Ehrenfried's letter. In the present times one must seize the opportunities when they offer themselves, and not wait for better ones. Who knows if the post will not be stopped before my letter reaches you. Ah! we have had a bad and a sad interval, and I fully expect that it will be worse still before the balance can again incline towards the good. Say, dear child, will you keep up your courage, even should the war draw nearer to you? Oh, yes, I know you enough to feel sure that you will, and need, in fact, no answer; for the wife and the mother will not be less courageous than I have known the girl to be. Besides, a young mother with a little child, and another in expectation, is even to warriors a sacred object. You see, friend Herz has already betrayed your happy secret to me. Dear child, may the blessing of God attend you! But, I would fain beg you let us have a boy this time; the coming times will require men—men who have seen the light for the first time during this period of dissolution; and sons—such as I think yours and Ehrenfried's will be—full of courage, cheerful in spirit, self-possessed, and with holy sentiments graven deep in their hearts, are a costly treasure. Oh, when I look to the future, I am the more pained at the thought that in this respect I can do nothing for it, that I have only words to bequeathe to it, because, at this moment, the immediate influence of my mind on the cultivation of youth is suspended, and I lead in fact a perfectly passive and useless life.

The close view of the war has made a wonderful impression upon us here. We had plenty of terror and suffering, and yet often we could not help jesting. Steffens' wife, with her child in her arms, was in my house, while the French hussars were plundering it; before they came she was dreadfully terrified, but afterwards she was calm and collected. Upon the whole, the terror that prevailed during the four days, until the army had passed through, gave rise to so many ludicrous incidents that they helped to keep up one's spirit.

The only thing I wish is, that if Stralsund should be besieged and taken by storm, you may not be within its walls; for in such a case the first few hours would, no doubt, be full of horror. And yet I could not blame you if you should refuse to leave your husband for any length of time, on account of this uncertain danger. It would pain me beyond all description to see your lovely, peaceful country, which lies so much beyond the limits of all the great world-transactions, become the theatre of such devastation.

My sister and Steffens' wife behave admirably, and I think few women here have shown as much courage under the same circumstances and with equally dismal prospects before them. It is very strange to live so entirely in the moment, to be so entirely ignorant of what the future is to bring, as we are at present; and, in fact, it might be an excellent lesson, were we not by the same circumstances deprived of so much that is good and beautiful. Farewell, dear child, and, if you are able, write soon. . . . .

Schleiermacher to George Reimer.

[CCLXXV.]   *Halle, 4th November,* 1806.

. . . . The pillage was, indeed, bad enough, yet not so bad as one generally fancies. Immediately after the engagement, the imprudence of the people who live below, enabled several hussars to penetrate into the house and up-stairs into our rooms. Steffens and Gass were just with me; we were all three obliged to give up our watches, and Gass his money; Steffens was already drained, and in my possession they only found a few dollars; but all my shirts, with the exception of five, and all the silver spoons, with the exception of two, they carried off. During the engagement, we were very near getting into danger. Steffens came in the morning to invite us to come to his house, if we wished to witness a fight. From thence we saw the attack upon the bridge very distinctly; but when I perceived that the Prussian cannon were being dismounted, and that the position was about to be lost, I persuaded Steffens to go home with me, as his house was very much exposed. We hastened as much as possible; but Hannah and I had not yet reached my street, when we heard shots behind us in the town, and Steffens, who was in the rear with his child in his arms, had very nearly got hemmed in between the crowd of retiring Prussians and pursuing Frenchmen.

The following days I had a fearful number of soldiers billeted upon me, and the proprietors of our house, poor orphans under the guardianship of a couple of old aunts, had nothing in their pockets, so that I felt very much afraid lest the brutality of the people should be roused, and we all spent a very uncomfortable night in Konopak's room. Subsequently we had officers and privates of the guards quartered in the house, and during two nights I was obliged to admit a secretary of the staff and two other *employés* into my large sitting-room, as there was no place for them down-stairs. The officers who had their quarters there frightened the poor people with all kinds of rumours of the town being given up to plunder and to fire, and made us spend a very tragi-comical night. But the preceding evening a storm, almost as bad as this, had in reality broken out—I mean the order for the dispersion of the students. Allow me to give you an explanation of what this means from the economical point of view, in order that you may form a conception of our position. . . . . If peace be soon concluded, it is not at all probable that Halle will remain Prussian. Should it be handed over to Saxony, perhaps the university will be dissolved, or, at all events, there will be an end to my stay in it, as the Saxons are such very strict Lutherans. If the town fall to the share of a French prince, I, for my part, will not abide in it, as long as there is anywhere a Prussian hole to which I can retire. . . . .

Be not angry with me for troubling you so much about *œconomicis*. Unfortunately it is necessary to take these wretched matters into very serious consideration. For the rest, I am working as industriously at *Plato* as anxiety about public matters as well as my own private concerns will allow.

[CCLXXVI.]   Later, but without date.

Dear friend, let me shake your hand in acknowledgment of your hearty sympathy. Do not be too anxious about our finances. As yet I do not know whether S—— will pay your draft, and I cannot go to him until to-morrow morning. But if he does, then take no more care about me. If you could do anything for Steffens, it would be very desirable, although at the present moment his creditors cannot press hard upon him. The general demoralization is fearful; on all sides yawning abysses of infamy and cowardice stare you in the face. Only a few, and foremost among these the king and the queen, form glorious exceptions. The old evil has broken out in a frightful manner, the remedy is a desperate one; but all hope is not yet lost, and I keep my eyes steadily fixed on Prussia, and northern Germany generally. . . . .

Schleiermacher to Henrietta Herz.

[CCLXXVII.]   *Halle, 4th November,* 1806.

Could I but describe to you my state of mind ! My personal position, in as far as it is purely personal, gives me very little concern; but that I should have brought my good Nanni hither at this unfortunate period grieves me. As for my ruined activity, which will probably never be restored— the sudden destruction of the school which I was in the act of founding here, and which gave such fair promise— the probable dissolution of the entire university, which was beginning to rise so nobly in character—and added to this the precarious state of our fatherland, in which at the side of so many defects there is so much that is excellent—Dearest, you can hardly conceive how this affects me, and yet how calmly I can at times sit down to my *Plato* and to my theological writings, and work to my heart's content, in spite of my constant hankering after the pulpit and the *cathedra.* Sometimes, however, I am in a feverish state, and many days are very unhappy. The thought that it may be my fate for a long time to live only for and by authorship, is very depressing.

In this place I am sure I should not be able long to endure such a state, and I shall, therefore, be impatient to get away as soon as I find that there is no more hope for the university. I shall join you first of all; but as without some public vocation I could not either live in Berlin, I must wander farther, to Prussia or to Rügen; and this is the fairest dream that remains to me in the case in question. Our entire ignorance of the state of affairs since the capture of Potsdam and Berlin is frightful, and quite calculated to damp our courage and to paralyze our last energies. As often in critical moments I knew not what Eleanore was doing, but could only love and hope on; so also now I know not what my country is doing. Will that also be untrue to itself, and pass away from me as she has ? Sometimes I think everything may yet go well, may terminate beautifully and gloriously; but this will require prudence and good luck; and shall we not fail in both? Yesterday rumours were rife of a second battle lost, because delivered precipitately and far too soon: I hope they are without foundation.

Do write me soon how you and other friends have got on. I hope you may not have suffered in any way, and at all events the scarcity and dearness cannot be as great in Berlin as it is here. We are living as frugally as possible, in fact, more frugally than possible, for my health is suffering very much from the privation of wine, and from the almost exclusive vegetable diet, and all my old ailings are returning. Fuel is not to be had: we were burning our last faggot when we obtained half a cord gratis from the French commissary, through the influence of Blanc, who is performing important services at present as interpreter; had it not been for this we should have perished with cold. . . . . Nanni does not as yet feel quite at home in the new combined housekeeping; the measure was, however, imperative, for I had only very little money, which I had borrowed, and Steffens had none at all. Had we divided we should both have been worse off than now; for as it is we save fuel and light, and I dare say various other matters in the housekeeping. . . . .

[CCLXXVIII.] *Halle, 14th November, 1806.*

We have been rescued from the greatest need, as I have obtained part of my salary, and Steffens has got some money from another quarter; and there is some hope at present that our entire salaries will be paid. We are still keeping house together; but I do not know how long this will last, as the ladies are put to great inconvenience by it. Of our going to Berlin, there can hardly be a thought under the present circumstances, for many things have changed since my last letter. The scarcity is, I hear, even greater there than here, and I should also have less quiet for working. Besides, were the hopes entertained by Masson to be realized, I should have the great expense of the double journey on my conscience. The day after to-morrow, thank God, I am once more to preach, for Blanc, who is called upon sometimes to deliver sermons in German. . . . Alexander is there, where alone there is anything to be done for our prostrate fatherland, and whence, perhaps, its salvation may yet come. His young brothers have not yet been in battle ; whether Louis has, I do not know; but, I have not seen the name of his regiment among those engaged. With Wedike, I have often in thought exchanged a smile of satisfaction, on account of the quiet which he still enjoys, he being the only one of our friends who is so well off. . . . .

I have again had an invitation to go to Bremen, but indirectly. But as long as there is a shade of hope that the university may be maintained on its present footing, I shall not allow myself to contemplate anything else. More reluctantly than ever would I now separate from the king, to whom I long most heartily to speak a word of comfort and encouragement, in the midst of the misfortunes which have come upon us, certainly by no fault of his. Even the French themselves say that the Berliners are flattering them in the most contemptible manner. I wish that it may not be true, though I dare not hope it.

Schleiermacher to Gass.*

[CCLXXIX.]   *Halle*, 16th *November*, 1805.

. . . . My personal affairs had in the meantime progressed most favourably. Towards the end of September, Eleanore left her husband's house, and no sooner had her brother learnt this, than he invited her to his house, and undertook to carry on the suit for the divorce himself. I saw her a few days later, and found her quite firm and resolved, and subsequent letters from her husband, and even in-

---

* This extract, giving a fuller relation of the final rupture with Eleanore Grunow than is contained in any of the letters in the present collection in the German edition, has been borrowed from Schleiermacher's correspondence with Gass, a preacher of the Reformed Church at Breslau, published in 1852.—TRANS.

terviews with him, did not make any change herein. Immediately after I left, the suit was laid, and her husband consented to the divorce. The *Decernent* had already decreed the dissolution of the marriage, without raising any difficulties, and the affair was to be brought before the court next session. But the day before this, Eleanore, having been informed that the last decisive measure was at hand, was again seized so violently by her old scruples of conscience, that, after a few hours of severe struggle, she, of her own accord, left her brother's house, and returned to her husband. Immediately after this she sent back to me everything she had received from me, and since then I have not heard from or of her. Unhappy woman! why did she so long deceive herself and me? Happy am I that I have never in any way attempted to bias her convictions in regard to this point. In breaking off all communication and intercourse with me under the circumstances, she has done quite right; it is necessary that it should be so, if she perseveres in her present determination. How hopeless my life is, how utterly annihilated my whole inward being, you can hardly conceive. My labours, the love of my vocation, and my joy in my friends, alone prevent me from falling utterly prostrate; and that I have my sister with me at present is a happiness for which I cannot be sufficiently grateful. . . . . .

Schleiermacher to Henrietta Herz.

[CCLXXX.] *Halle*, 21st *November*, 1806.

. . . . . Though it is late in the evening, I must have a little chat with you. What dreadful birthdays have I had two consecutive years! Shortly before that of last year, I lost everything that I possessed on one side, and now on the other. When the first misfortune came, I clung to my vocation, and in it I found a motive and an object in life; now that this also is destroyed, what shall I cling to? It has not indeed been so irrevocably lost as Eleanore, yet it would be folly to hope confidently in its revival; and if it is not my highest, but only my secondary, wish, that I may find death in struggling for the common cause, this is because of an attachment to old plans and purposes, which, in many cases, I must confess, is childish. Yet, perhaps, sooner than I expect, my other wish will be fulfilled; for if fortune does not take a turn, an onslaught will no doubt soon be made against the detested Protestantism, and then it will be my duty above many others to come forward. No one knows what may be his fate in these days! We may still have martyrs, both religious and scientific.

We are living here in a most feverish state. Every now and then comes a favourable rumour, that holds out a hope from the side of Austria or Russia, and then again we learn that it is unfounded. From our own camp we have no accounts whatsoever: this much only is certain, that as long as the war lasts, there is little likelihood that the university will resume its activity. Yet my going to Bremen looks to me like an act of treason, which I cannot allow myself to be guilty of; and I do not in the least know what to do, and am living in the hope of an inspiration, when the moment shall arrive that I must take a resolution. Napoleon must have a special hatred to Halle. Whether he conceived it during his stay here, or had it previously, I do not know; but to me the first seems most probable. The new philosophy cannot be the cause of it, for publicly it can hardly be said to have issued from Halle; it is more likely that the spirit of freedom, and the open expression of public opinion, for which Halle has always been famous, is at the bottom of it. There have also been numerous spies here during several months, who may have betrayed to him the sentiments of the people. It is said now that the deputation from Leipzig has increased and strengthened his hatred in a most shameful manner. But one ought not to believe in such baseness until it is proved. . . . . May a good genius direct the resolves of our king, and induce him to bear everything rather than to conclude a dishonourable peace ; and to hold fast by Russia, for that is the only way in which we can hope for a favourable change in our fate ! I feel rather confident that he will not act otherwise. . . . .

To write letters is becoming quite a hard task to me, though I do not know why. Willich may, of course, send his wife to Rügen; but in case Stralsund be besieged, he himself ought not to desert his post. Should Stralsund be captured, then, indeed, Rügen also must be considered as lost. The rod of wrath must fall upon every German land; only on this condition can a strong and happy future bloom forth. Happy they who live to see it; but those who die, let them die in faith. . . . .

Can it be true that all the statues, and all the works of art, and all the personal property of Friedrich the Great, are being carried off? A thousand greetings to all friends, and more especially to the Dohnas. I am glad that Fritz has distinguished himself so much. If all had but done the same! Adieu, dear Jette.

Schleiermacher to E. von Willich.

[CCLXXXI.] *Halle, 1st December, 1806.*

Already, some days ago, dear friend, I received the consolatory news from our friend in Berlin that she had heard from you, and now comes your little note to myself. I congratulate you, my dears, that up to the present moment you have not been immediately engaged in the great conflict and surrounded by the thousand horrors that accompany it. Look upon so much time gained as a great good, and enjoy it cheerfully, but be prepared; for if the drama is not to end in a shameful submission, and in the inauguration of a barbarism that will extend its power over many coming generations, you must be drawn into the vortex. I have often thought with delight of going to join you, should my forced inactivity endure for any length of time ; but, even if the prospects to which I have alluded were not before you, I should be obliged to give up this plan, because there would be insuperable difficulties in the way of my transplanting myself to your place, with all the auxiliary means which I require for my writings.

You are aware that Napoleon has driven away our students. The reason for this we are still ignorant of. A few days before the entry of the French, and on receipt of the accounts of new victories, they did, it is true, give a *vivat* for the king, and a *pereat* for Napoleon; and it is even said that they repeated the same during his presence here, while the troops in the market-place were crying, " *Vive l'Empereur!* " a mad proceeding, certainly. A paper was also circulated here, recommending various measures for the benefit of the army, and in which were several hard expressions against the French, and this was signed by the university among others. All this may have worked together to bring about the result.

I have again received a call to Bremen; but I have determined to decline it, because I will remain faithful to Halle as long as there is the slightest hope of the maintenance of the university. Should the king be obliged to conclude an unfavourable peace, and should he retain Halle, though his territories were otherwise greatly reduced, there will be numbers who will prefer leaving to staying, and I will not be among those who set so bad an example. But should the war be protracted, as I hope, I will seek a provisional appointment somewhere else in Prussia, so that I may be at hand immediately when things change. For the influence that an academical teacher may have upon the young generation seems to me more than ever of the highest importance. We must sow seeds, which may not perhaps sprout for a long while, but which will, in consequence, require to be all the more carefully treated and tended. Dear friend, were I to describe to you the utter desolation of my heart when I think of the loss of my pulpit and of my professorial chair, and when it sometimes comes home to me that, after all, my sphere of activity may never be reconstituted, you would hardly be able to understand me. When, however, I look further, and take a more comprehensive view of matters, I become calm again.

The constitution of Germany had become untenable; in the Prussian monarchy there was also a great deal that had become superannuated and that was merely patched together: this has been destroyed. The manner in which the kernel shall save itself from similar destruction will prove whether it be sound or not. I feel certain that Germany, the kernel of Europe, will stand forth again in a new and beautiful form; but when this will take place, and whether the country will not first have to pass through still greater troubles, and to bend for a long time under a heavy yoke, God alone knows. I have no fear, except, sometimes, of a dishonourable peace, which may save the appearance—but only the appearance—of a national existence and freedom. But even in regard to this I feel tranquil; for if the nations submit to it, it will prove that they are not yet ripe for better things; and the severer visitations, amid which they are to mature, will not fail soon to fall upon them. Thus, dear friend, concerning what is personal to me, which is of the least importance, and concerning the national cause, which is of the greatest importance, I feel equally calm, however dreary things may look in respect to both; but the intermediate matters, such as the manner in which each individual may be able to influence the whole, and the way in which the ecclesiastical, the educational, and the scientific institutions may be organized—these fill me with anxiety; the latter more especially, for Napoleon hates Protestantism as much as he hates speculative philosophy. My predictions in the *Discourses* will not, I think, prove false. When it comes to this, dear friend, let us cling to our posts, and fear nought. I wish that I had a wife and child, that I might be on a level with every other man when the sacrifice is called for. I have preached twice within the last twelve days, and, as you may suppose, on both occasions, on the times and the signs of the times, but after my own peculiar fashion, and without fear. I wish I could preach oftener, but opportunities for doing so rarely occur. In my academical church I only preached four or five times, then came the vacations, and now it is de-

stroyed. Of the engagement near Halle, I witnessed the first
act, in which the Prussians defended very badly, and soon lost,
an excellent position, entirely through the incapacity of their
commander. During the second act I was plundered, but
that was a mere joke. . . . .

Should Stralsund be besieged, you will, I suppose, send
your wife and child to Rügen. I hope you will hold out
better than Magdeburg and Küstrin. When you are able, do
write and tell me where Brinkmann is. . . . .

Schleiermacher to Charlotte von Kathen.

[CCLXXXII.]   *Halle, 1st December,* 1806.
    Dear friend, what a fearful time lies between the last
words that we interchanged and the present moment! The
common misfortunes of our fatherland, accompanied by
many humiliating circumstances that I should have thought
impossible. I felt almost certain that we should lose the first
battle; and I therefore trembled with rage at seeing that the
battle-field had not been chosen at a distance; but the fearful
disorganization which followed, and the universal discouragement, with the exception of one glorious example, was more
than I could ever have expected. The king alone, in his
steadfastness, it is gratifying to behold; and I trust, now
that he has got over the capture of his capital and the sur-
render of his fortresses without suing for peace, he will not
think of separating his fate from that of the rest of Europe.
The times have now come, about which I wrote to you some
time ago; and most likely what has as yet taken place is only
the beginning. The conflict must become wider and deeper,
if new life and prosperity are to rise out of the universal
desolation. To this sweet hope I cling; even death shall not
tear it from me, should I not live to see it realized. For the
present, dear friend, I am in as sad a condition as a man can
be—reduced to the miserable, inactive life of a private scholar,
and also to the poverty which seems to belong to the lot of
such individuals; pulpit and *cathedra* lost to me; the uni-

versity, in which so fine a sphere of activity was being opened up to me, dissolved, with little hope of its reconstitution as long as our part of the country is occupied by the enemy; for the great conqueror seems to hold Halle in special detestation; and if the reason be that our youths gave no signs of joy, or even of admiration, when he was here, and that their whole conduct rather indicated the contrary, then I cannot help rejoicing that it should be so. Well, I trust God will help me to another field of activity, for, without such, life loses all its value in my eyes. Oh, dearest Charlotte! what birthdays have I not had these last two years! Before the first came round, all the blossoms had been stripped from my tree of life; before the second, the storm had shaken off all the fruit. What shall we do with the bare trunk?

You may probably have felt anxious about me on many other accounts likewise, as rumour always exaggerates, and after an engagement in a town one generally pictures to oneself a thousand horrors, of which, however, few were perpetrated here.

Ehrenfried writes me that Kathen has lost a brother. Well, he has died the death of his profession, it is true, not only in an unfortunate but in an ill-conducted conflict, in which the blood of thousands was sacrificed by a few incapable men, yet in a conflict for a great cause, in which every one who falls is a costly and holy sacrifice, and not in a vulgar quarrel of princes.

What is your excellent friend Moritz* about? Has he not been advised to take a trip over seas? for certainly he cannot be one of the authors who have gained the good graces of the mighty oppressor. Could we say this of every German it would be easy to provoke him to death; because, free speech is to him the most deadly poison. Do write to me soon, and tell me something about your peaceful, quiet home, which may God long preserve to you!

* G. M. Arndt.

Schleiermacher to Henrietta Herz.

[CCLXXXIII.]   *Halle, 8th December, 1806.*

. . . . In a few days I expect we shall, without fail, have accounts of a battle. If it be favourable to us, it cannot prove very decisive, as he holds too many fortified places. You know, I suppose, that the king's head-quarters are quite near the Dohnas' place. The severity in regard to the officers is, no doubt, owing to the fact that none have presented themselves to enter his new legion. For the rest, I must say it is very good-natured of you to call the devil a spoiled child; and the destruction of a university may very well enter into his projects, even were he not so malevolently revengeful. I am truly glad that they do not sue for mercy. . . . . If you could manage to be much with the Reichardts, it would give me great pleasure. Farewell, my only one; I must hasten from you to that wearisome review of Fichte, which must absolutely be finished.

[CCLXXXIV.]   *Halle, 28th December, 1806.*

I have finally determined not to go to Bremen, and shall write to-morrow to decline. I could not possibly renounce Halle and my academical career as long as matters are so undecided; and I could not either make up my mind to say to Masson, as I once thought of doing, that he should only consider my departure as a leave of absence, and that as soon as Halle was re-established (alas! it is established)—I mean as soon as it was in activity again—I would return; for the more I reflected upon this, the more treacherous it seemed to me towards the people of Bremen, and the more unworthy of their kindness; while, at the same time, I felt it to be treason against my inward vocation to leave this place. Were it not for Nanni I should have little care about money matters. I would live like a student, and my literary work would suffice to support me, however unfavourable the times might be. But Nanni *is* here; nevertheless, I dare say we shall get

on, more especially as Masson must necessarily do something
for the university, or, when spring comes, all the professors
will disperse. At all events, I will not be the first to run
away, rather the last. . . . .

[CCLXXXV.]   *Halle, 2nd February*, 1807.

You must take a grander view of the destinies of
men, dear Jette, and then you will find in the present times
nothing more than what history shows us at all times, viz., that
after enervation comes dissolution, and struggles between life
and death, during which, even if it be but one baseness struggling against another, the creative energies of the goodness
and capacities of the human mind are developed. Throughout history we see the genius of man working in the same
way. The invisible hand of Providence, and the action
of man, is one and the same. If we look too much at par-
ticulars, the smallness of the objects makes us giddy. But
if you cannot help doing this, as is mostly the case with
women, then, at least, lay fast hold of your objects, and you
will perceive that even among these the difference is much less
than it appears when you mistake small things for great ones.
What can have happened to Misere? There is little difference
between her present and her former joys and sorrows. And
this is not only applicable to Misere, but to every human
being. Verbally, I should be better able to demonstrate this
to you; but you may find the fundamental thoughts of what
I should say, in one of my sermons on the justice of God.
This standard may be applied to all times.

Henriette von Willich to Schleiermacher.

[CCLXXXVI.]   *Sagard, 13th March*, 1807.

Schleier! dear Schleier! my beloved friend! my
father! Oh, my God! my God! how shall I tell it to you,
and how shall you be able to hear it! Schleier, I am no
more the happy Jette, whose pure felicity you bore in
your heart, and at which you so tenderly rejoiced. My dear

Schleier, prepare yourself to hear the worst ; the happy Jette
is now a poor, sorrowing, lonely, weeping Jette. Oh, my
Schleier ! let me then at once give utterance to the dreadful
word. My Ehrenfried—my deeply, tenderly beloved Ehrenfried—is with me no more; he lives in another world. Oh,
Schleier ! can you realize it ? Can you conceive that I have
survived it ? I cannot myself understand it, nor the composure with which I have borne it, and with which I still
bear it. How I long to open my whole heart to you ! Yes,
Schleier, you have, indeed, cause to weep over me; but you may,
nevertheless, be without anxiety. God supports me wonderfully.
I do not despair, nor do I despond. I still live in the consciousness of *his* love, and *my* love. I bear him ever in my
heart. I love him with all the energy, all the yearning
tenderness that my soul is capable of. Oh, Schleier! in the
midst of my anguish I have still rapturous moments when I
have a vivid feeling of how we loved each other, and that
this love is eternal, and that God cannot possibly destroy it,
because God himself is love. Schleier, I will bear this life
as long as nature wills it, for I must exert myself for his
and my children; but, O God! with what longing, with what
a presentiment of indescribable rapture, I look forward to the
world in which he lives! What happiness would it not be to
me to die ! Schleier, shall I not find him again? Oh, my
God! I implore you, by all that you love and hold sacred, if
you can, give me the certainty that I shall find him again—
that I shall recognize him ! Tell me your innermost belief in
regard to this, dear Schleier. Alas ! it will be annihilation
to me to lose this faith. In this I live; through this I bear
with resignation and serenity; it is the only thing I look forward to, the only hope that sheds a faint glimmer of light on
my darkened existence—to meet him again, to live again for
him, to make him happy. O God! it is not possible; it cannot
be destroyed, it is only interrupted. I can never again
be happy without him. Oh, Schleier ! speak to my poor
heart; tell me what you believe. Ah ! does he, perhaps, also
long for me, remember me? Is he, perhaps, at times invisibly

near me? Oh, my poor heart, how it is drawn hither and thither by hope and doubt! Yet no, the doubt does not extend beyond my thoughts; this I feel as a never-failing consolation, which can never desert me, that our love was divine, and that death cannot destroy it. Oh, my Schleier! how I long for you! You will be a comfort and a support to me. I feel such unbounded trust in you, I will tell you all that I experience during this time of sorrow. Oh, Schleier! how will not you also grieve for the faithful, beloved friend! Oh, how happy I was! With what joy I looked forward at his side to being once more a mother! Now I shall shed many tears over the little one's cradle.

Only eight days my Ehrenfried was ill of a nervous fever. Alas! I was ever full of hope; I thought it impossible, I nursed him with such tender love, and he was always so gentle to me, so kind, so loving. Alas! the last days the fever was so violent that he was no longer conscious. Oh, bitter memory! and yet not unmixed with sweetness! How his love for me broke through his incoherent ravings! He gave me still sweet names, even after the illness had entirely obscured his mind. The last word that he spoke to me was, when I asked him if he no more knew his Jette: "Yes, Jette, my sweet bride!" Oh, Schleier! how significant and how true! His BRIDE, that I am!—oh! I will strive until I become worthy of being reunited with him, of being again entirely his. . . . . Do you know when I feel my grief most poignantly? When I think that in a future life there will be nothing left of the old, whoever shall be worthiest of him will be nearest to him—oh! and there are many of those that love him that are worthier than I—and when I think that his soul is dissolved, merged in the great All—that the past will not be recognized—that all is over—oh, Schleier! this I cannot bear—oh! speak to me, dear, dear friend!

Farewell, Schleier, I have so much to say to you; and yet, perhaps, I shall not write again for a long time. Nevertheless, you will know from this how I feel. I suffer much; but inward tranquillity and outward composure never fail me entirely.

Your JETTE.

Schleiermacher to Henriette von Willich.

[CCLXXXVII.]   *Halle, 25th March, 1807.*

My poor, dear child! Could I but press thee, poor mourner, to my heart, we would mingle our tears ; for I also am shedding bitter, scalding tears! Oh, to see so sweet a happiness destroyed! You know how my heart exulted in it. But you set me such a beautiful example. Your grief is so pure and so holy ; there is nought in it that your father could wish otherwise. Let us, therefore, count it among the noblest possessions of our lives, and love it as we loved the dear departed, and submit tranquilly, though sorrowfully, to God's eternal order of things. But you appeal to me to settle your doubts. It is, however, only the images of your painfully travailing imagination, which you wish me to confirm. Dear Jette, what can I say to you? Certainty beyond this life is not given to us. Do not misunderstand me. I mean certainty for phantasy, which desires to see everything in distinct images; but, otherwise, there is the greatest certainty—and nothing would be certain if it were not so—that for the soul there is no such thing as death, no annihilation. But personal life is not the essence of spiritual being; it is but an outward presentment thereof. How this is repeated we know not—we can form no conception of it; we can only form poetic visions. But while giving yourself up to your sacred grief, let your loving, pious phantasy shape its visions freely, and restrain it not. It is a pious phantasy; it cannot will what is contrary to the eternal order of Providence; and, therefore, all that it paints will be true, if you leave it but free scope. And thus, I can assure you, that your love will ever attain all that it desires. Surely you cannot now wish that Ehrenfried—O God! the beloved name! with what emotion I write it for the first time!— surely you cannot now wish that he should return to life, for that would be contrary to the eternal order of things, to which we all cling more earnestly than to any of our individual desires. In this life, however, your love desires to bear him in its heart, to preserve his memory ineffaceably, to have his image ever before you as a holy and lifelike presence; and that he thus lives on in you, and lives anew in your sweet children—let this be enough for you. What would, or what ought to satisfy you in a future life, you cannot know; for you know not the order that prevails there. But when you are removed thither, you will know it, and then there, as little as here, you will desire what would be opposed to it, and most assuredly it will afford you as full and rapturous satisfaction.

But if your imagination suggest to you a merging in the great all, let not this, dear child, fill you with bitter, poignant anguish. Do not conceive of it as a lifeless, but as a living commingling—as the highest life. Is not the ideal towards which we are all striving even in this world, though we never reach it—the merging of the life of each in the life of all, and the putting away from us every semblance of a separate existence? If then he lives in God, and you love him eternally in God, as you knew God and loved God in him, can you conceive of anything more glorious or more delightful? Is it not the highest goal which love can reach, compared with which every feeling that clings to the personal life, and springs from that alone, is as nothing? But if you picture to yourself a phenomenal life like the present, and conceive that you may, under such circumstances, be distant from your beloved, and that others may be nearer to him—dear daughter, that is an empty phantom, that you must try to get rid of. Love is the power that attracts spirits—the great and eternal law of their nature. Does any one then love him more than you do? or does he love another better than you? Are you not two halves that complete each other? Oh, as sure as my holy joy in your marriage is one of the dearest sentiments of my heart, you are this, and never in all eternity will any obstacle rise up between you!

The day after to-morrow, it will be the anniversary of the death of Christ. I will preach upon the text, " Except a corn of wheat fall into the ground and die, it abideth alone: but if it die, it bringeth forth much fruit." I will show how death sanctifies all love; how, at his death, the most blessed action of man begins, and that this is true in regard to each human being in like manner as it is true in regard to Christ. Dear Jette, my thoughts will be full of you and the dear departed, and I shall speak with deeply-moved heart. I shall renew with him the bond of true and holy brotherhood. I shall speak comfort to myself—could I but do so to you likewise! In him the Gospel also has lost a faithful teacher, a preacher full of truth and zeal, a soul without guile, which, through its truth and its fidelity, would have worked much good. Let us not forget this in *our* loss, and let us weep for this also.

Dear daughter, by this time you are probably once more a mother. Do let me know soon. Yes, many tears you will shed over your babe. I have a presentiment that you have given birth to a boy—oh, nourish his father's spirit in him, and may God's blessing attend your endeavours, so that he may thrive, and take the place of him whom the world has lost. Oh, dear Jette, could I but be your father in every sense, could I but tend you and support you in your sorrow with fatherly affection, I would do so without concealing from you my own grief. Try, therefore, to conquer all obstacles, and to write to me often. It is a consolation to me to know that you are in Sagard, in the house where your happy bridal days were spent, and I bless your faithful, affectionate brother for it. Yes, you are again his bride;* your love has returned to the period of sweet longings, and an eternal wreath adorns your brow. As such it was that I first named you my daughter, and such you shall remain to me.

* In German, *bride* denotes the period before marriage.—TRANS.

Henriette von Willich to Schleiermacher.

[CCLXXXVIII.]   *April.*

My beloved father, I thank you most heartily for your
letter—oh, how inexpressibly I longed for the first words
from you—it was as if Ehrenfried was once more to speak
comfort to me. You have strengthened like a true father—you
must be my father in the highest sense of the word—you can
be so—I give you my entire filial affection from the innermost impulse of my heart—I lean upon you alone. You will
support and guide your child; you will not desert me in the
drear, drear hours, when grief seizes my heart with its
sharpest fangs. Oh, my father, it is too much—to live, and
to live without my Ehrenfried—it seems such a dreadful contradiction !

My hour of trial is over—a healthy child is in my arms.
Oh, my God, what feelings have passed through my heart on
this occasion !

The poor, dear, little children ! Alas, what can poor I,
with all my love, do for them!—from him I drew all my
strength—he was my light, my sun.

Secretly, I nourished in my heart the thought that I should
die, and almost let it grow into a hope or a foreboding ; but
alas, I am to live! I can write no more—ah, love me, and
speak soon again a few kind words to me. Nothing soothes
me so much as to know that you are weeping with me.

Schleiermacher to Henriette von Willich.

[CCLXXXIX.]   *Halle, 13th April, 1807.*

My letters, which were sent by the same conveyance
that brought me yours, you have, I trust, received, my dear,
my noble daughter. And now I have obtained from Lotte's
letter the happy certainty that I had prophesied right. You
have given birth to a boy ! On the day of the Resurrection,
Heaven bestowed upon you this new life—a restored, a new-

born Ehrenfried. You will call him thus. I am sure you
will give him this earnest, solemn name ;* he brings you
peace now, and will be an honour to you hereafter. Oh, could
I but fold in one embrace the sweet babe, and you, my
daughter, and your little Jette—the son of sorrow and the
daughter of joy ! May I be able in time to help you to bring
up and educate the boy, and to teach him as a man what his
father was, as you will teach it to him as a woman.

Oh, what bitter sweet exultation I feel in you, in your hallowed
affliction, in your inexhaustible grief, in all the glorious things
that I hear about you, but which I need not hear to believe !
For I know you and your love, which was too deep and too
pure to allow of a less pious and beautiful outburst of grief.
I have wept tears of sorrow, but also tears of thankfulness over
you, and have rejoiced that you were my daughter, and have
recognized myself in your suffering ; for I feel that I would
bear in the same manner, outwardly and inwardly, could I
be subjected to a similar trial. Dear daughter, once more I
bless you in your affliction ; though your sorrow will never
vanish, a new life of joy will open up for you in your children.
Your son, the blessed Easter gift, will represent to you him
who has gone before into eternal bliss ; you will form his
image in the boy, and try to bring it forth in ever truer
beauty, and thus it will be the vocation of your widowhood,
to tend and protect as a mother that which you love and hold
sacred as a bride. For a short time, or for a long—how little
does this signify in the world—the highest happiness has been
yours, and is still yours, and, therefore, even in your sorrow
you are, as ever, my happy daughter.

At the hour when you brought the sweet boy so safely into
the world, I must just have been preparing to go to church ;
and I remember that I thought of you at the time. I spoke
of the glorified life of Christ upon earth. May the beautiful,
free, heavenly existence which I painted, be the lot of the
dear child, in like manner as your life and your love are now
truly glorified, and raised above all earthly trials.

* Literally, " honour peace."—TRANS.

Henriette von Willich to Schleiermacher.

[ccxc.]   *28th April.*

How much good your kind words do me! How your affection and your approval comfort me. But, I implore you, do not picture me to yourself in too bright colours, for this makes me uneasy. Deep and pure as was my love for Ehrenfried, so is also my sorrow, and I shall ever strive to become that which the sweet life with him would have made me; for though he is no longer with me, he still lives in me, and continues to mould and form me. But, believe me, I am nevertheless very weak—do not, I beseech you, praise the strength and composure with which I have borne my loss, for my state of mind would only be praiseworthy had I attained to it through hard struggles ; but such is not the case. I have been simply what I could not help being, because such is my nature. As grief came to me, so I have borne it, and that is tranquilly. I should be tormented by the thought that my grief for the matchless and beloved man were not sufficiently acute, did I not ever feel so vividly within me the most unutterable love for him ; were I not ever conscious of the most intimate indissoluble union with him, and of the undying character of my affliction, which has, so to say, become part and parcel of my being. There have been hours, indeed, during which I have learnt to know the deepest human anguish; yet even after this, the certainty that my Ehrenfried could never leave me, has always returned to me, and has given me courage to bear a joyless existence, through help of the blissful hope that I shall once find again in God, that which He has taken away. Ah ! dear father, if I carried out at all times what I recognize as right in hours of ecstasy, and then believe myself capable of—then I should be what you believe me to be, and what you love in me—but alas, the excellence and the beauty which I love and treasure in thought, I so seldom realize in myself or carry out in life; not because I lack good-will, but because I am wanting in inward strength and quick sensibilities. At former periods of my life already I had a painful consciousness of my deficiencies in this respect, and so also now—now that I must strive to attain the *highest,* if I would not lose *all.*

Oh, how easy it was to be good, when I was happy! I could do nothing better than love him, and through him enjoy life in gladness. Ah! why was it to endure so short, that sweet happiness? So young, so new to life, and yet, to be dead to all its joys—alas! am I not deeply to be pitied? Still, how willingly would I not renounce every joy, could I but have kept him; what strength did I not ever feel to bear calmly every human suffering could I but be at his side; with what courage I contemplated the horrors of the war! Ehrenfried often said to me in jest, that he believed I was wishing that the enemy would come, that I might have an opportunity of proving my intrepidity. They did not come— something far more dreadful was to befall me.

But I must speak to you a little of my sweet children. How inexpressibly I love them, you know. Alas, there have, indeed, been moments when I have contemplated their ex- istence with a kind of bitterness and pain, because I felt as if they alone prevented me from following my beloved. But at other times I have felt ever deeper and deeper how God's mercy has been revealed to me through them. My God, what should I be now without them! The darling children! Thanks be to God that I am here to devote my life to them. . . . May He give me strength to rear the tender plants, and by wise nurture to help them put forth the fullest and fairest blossoms. I watch over them with ever-wakeful care, yet how little can I do! I have so little reliance on myself, and yet, on the other hand, I feel that I cannot leave to another what nature has entrusted to the mother—the first guidance of her children. To you I may confide, that I am often troubled by the fear that kind and loving indivi- duals of my family may feel themselves called upon to inter- fere on this point, because they think that so young a mother is hardly mature enough for the task. But perhaps I do them injustice, and I will, therefore, endeavour to discard the thought. Should they do so, it will at all events be from pure affection. Oh, my dear father, I need not tell you what a joyful prospect it would be to me could I hope that you would once serve my boy as model and example. But the future is dark, and I can only wish and hope. My heart is often sorely oppressed. It would be a great comfort to me could I see you soon; but I suppose it is vain to hope for this. It seems to me as if I had so much to say to you. The children occupy me all the day; they draw me necessarily and irresistibly into the midst of life, and I can already quite well skip about with little Jette and play with her, though inwardly my heart weeps the while for my Ehrenfried. When I am quite alone with Ehrenfried's letters, I seek comfort and strength in tears and prayer. There is no more joy for me than what may come to me through the happiness and the improvement of the children—to myself directly, the source is for ever closed.

Schleiermacher to Henriette von Willich.

[ccxci.] *Halle, 8th May,* 1807.

How may you and your little ones be getting on? I cannot help hoping that you are all well, and that the smiles of your infant, and the innocent playfulness of your first-born, in her unconsciousness of her great loss, as also the soothing charms of nature, have by this time calmed your sacred sorrow and deprived it of its bitterness, while they have enhanced the sweetness which it contains, and which you have also already tasted. Dear, mourning daughter, you are, nevertheless, a blessed woman. For over such love as yours death has no power, it is but a false appearance, which will vanish more and more. You will attain ever greater and more lively certainty that Ehrenfried lives in you and in the children, and in every case in which formerly you would have looked up to him for guidance, he will now also afford it to you; and every experience that you may acquire, every new energy of love that arises within you, you will feel comes from him. Therefore, also, you may be assured that you will be to his and your children all that you ought to be, and able to do for them all that you ought to do—you alone, with your treasure of love, and that unclouded understanding, that has its source in a pure heart. Oh! could I also, now and in future, be something to your sweet children, so as to be able to exercise over them the rights of a father, which you again so delightfully concede to me as regards yourself. You know how indifferent life had become to me; but now that the dear friend has left us, who, humanly speaking, ought to have far outlived me, life lays again a firm hold on me. I have now a dear daughter who wants the support of her father; and her son, the heir of the beloved name, will be glad on entering life to find a faithful fatherly friend to guide him. See, dearest daughter, for this let us live, and live willingly, I implore you, though I think it quite natural that you should have wished to die. God bless you, and comfort you, and strengthen you !

Henriette von Willich to Schleiermacher.

[ccxcii.]   *No date.*

How I get on, dear father? Ah! could I but tell you, could I but understand myself. Grief and calm reign alternately in my bosom—calm, when I am surrounded by my relatives, or when I am actively engaged with or for the children; but when no one sees and hears me, grief takes possession of me. Then the murmurs so long restrained burst forth—then the oppressed heart seeks relief in tears and sobs. I do not weep much nor often, but when relieving tears come, they are scalding tears, and well up from the innermost depths of my being; and then I feel that God sees them, and that they are not wept in vain. Oh, my dear father, the sweet comfort that you speak to me I have just experienced in another way. I have just come from church ; could I but describe to you how I feel when I give myself up entirely to God, when my spirit is absorbed in Him, when, without a wish and without a murmur, satisfied in all ways, it demands nothing better than to melt away with the tones of the hymn that sets forth His praise—when thought ceases, and solemn light and darkness seem at one and the same time to veil my eyes, and when I feel Ehrenfried's presence so vividly, and that God will never take him from me, because our love is His most beautiful law, and because God dwells in him, and also draws me ever nearer and nearer to Himself. How glorious it is to feel that I am a child of God, that I have freed myself from the world, that it has no more power over me, that it can give me nothing and can take nothing away!

I have thought much of you to-day, and have felt how true it is that I am your daughter. Indeed, I often feel how much I resemble you, and how I shall grow ever more and more like you.

The first time I went to church after the birth of my little Ehrenfried, I took the communion. Oh, what moments were those! How my soul travailed and prayed for a real, true life in God, and for that true composure which does not exclude the most lively grief, and for deliverance from that dead tranquillity which is not tranquillity, but torpor. At such moments I feel as if I had in me the strength to attain to all that my soul beholds in its visions; and to you I may say it, that when I examine my heart, I find no desire, no interest in me that would interpose itself between me and my goal, and lead me away from the latter. But nature has not endowed me with the quick sensibilities and lively emotions which I see in others, and which even in early youth I prayed for as a heavenly gift, the deficiency of which I felt bitterly. I know, had I this, I could do much; it would be like a sacred flame, and would attune to a higher pitch the eternal chords of humanity within me.

Ehrenfried would never allow that I had any right to make this complaint; but I know that it is true, and will prove it to you. See, dear father, while in others I perceive that on given occasions their feelings are intensified to such a degree, that they are obliged to struggle hard with them, and that their whole being seems violently agitated—in regard to myself, I hardly know what such a struggle is. I believe that no elevated or beautiful sentiment is quite unknown to me, but, with the *degree* in which I experience them, I have surely often reason to be dissatisfied. Even in my present position, I have rarely experienced such frenzied, despairing anguish that seems almost to annihilate all clear consciousness, and yet mine is an affliction that cannot be exceeded—yea, an affliction even unto death. My beloved father, I wish so much that you should know me exactly as I am!

You say that Ehrenfried lives in me and in the children. Yes, dear father, I also feel this. I feel that he never refuses to be with me, when I call to him with earnest longing; I cannot fail to recognize that he diffuses a heavenly blessing through my soul. But then, oh, God! as he must also live another independent life besides this in us, I cannot help indulging my heart in the blessed hope that I shall one day participate more thoroughly in that life. It seems to me that it is only this hope that gives truth and strength to the continued mental life with him as long as I am on this earth. It would be intensely painful to me were I to conceive of the beautiful relations between human beings as merely evanescent, for in that case they would be only subordinate means. How delightful it is, on the contrary, to think of them as continuous, and as gradually expanding into ever greater beauty as man himself reaches, step by step, a higher perfection! Dear father, I entreat you, give me your mind on this subject. How much do I not also wish to hear explained, better than I am able to do so for myself, how the spiritual in us is separated from the material, or, rather, that which is immortal from that which is perishable. To me it seems as if with life the images of life also must vanish, though they are, indeed, taken in by the mind; yet, again, that self-consciousness must necessarily continue, and that this cannot be possible without remembrance of the past.

If I speak confusedly, have patience with me. Thank God, you are my father, and I need have no fear of you. If Ehrenfried is able to think of me and the children, I know exactly how he thinks of us; and, oh, what emotion it causes me when I dwell on this! This evening, again, I have felt such inexpressible longing for my beloved. It is a lovely summer evening. A little girl told me that her mother was lying under the mound in the churchyard. I went aside and wept bitterly at the thought that he also lies there—he who was everything to me; and at the thought that I can enjoy nothing now with a light heart, not even a lovely summer's day.

[ccxciii.] *Poseritz, October 12th.*

Our dear Rügen is sighing under a heavy yoke, and no one knows how it will end. Alas! how I wish the strangers would go back again to their homes, after which they are longing so much! Though I do not suffer in regard to external circumstances, yet, as you know, every individual suffers much in various other ways during such times. All bonds are dissevered, all enlivening social intercourse impeded. I often feel so unutterably lonely, I can neither see my sisters and brothers, nor any other friends. . . . Nature is carrying her beauties to the grave; she speaks no longer to me with cheerful prophetic voice—no longer breathes the spirit of love and joy; around me and within me all is dark and dismal. The dear children are my only occupation and my only solace. Reading and writing I am seldom able to indulge in. I cannot deny that sometimes I feel the privation rather bitterly, and it seems to me that I ought not entirely to submit to it. Ah! dear father, you will not misunderstand me, you will not take as a complaint that which I disclose merely to give you a true picture of my life. I have at all times present to me that I am nothing but an instrument to promote the well-being of the dear children, to nurse and to tend them. It is not as if I lived a life of my own, and in this sense I may say that I often forget myself and my fate entirely; but when I awake to greater consciousness, I am terrified at the misery

and emptiness of the life that is left to me. Months go by
without my having an opportunity of hearing one forcible,
elevating thought—one deep and striking truth from the lips
of a cultivated man; and yet for me there is no higher enjoyment than to strive after light and truth, in as far as my
powers will admit.

Schleiermacher to Henriette von Willich.

[CCXCIV.]   *No date.*

At last I am able to write a few words to you, my dearly
beloved daughter, with the assurance that they will reach you
safely. The uncertainty in which I was hitherto in regard to
this, has deterred me from writing, and I have lived with you
in silent, uncommunicated thought only. You, also, have
kept back much that you would otherwise have communicated. Perhaps hereafter the usual means of communication
will be open—though from such distressing causes that I
would far rather it should not be so—and then we shall often
interchange words, until the time comes when I hope I shall
be able to go to you and seek sad but sweet solace in your
company and that of your little ones.

For the present, I know not where to begin, as I would
fain avail myself of this opportunity to say all that I wish to
say. First of all, then, let me express what has given me
most pleasure, that you continue to call yourself my daughter,
and that you feel how much you resemble me. Yes, it is so,
my dear child; and it is a consolation and a great happiness
to me in my lonesome life. But let me tell you, even in
regard to those points in yourself of which you complain, you
resemble me; and as I thoroughly understand myself, and
have the power of looking calmly into myself, I cannot admit
the validity of your complaints. You cannot but feel that
that of which you complain is not a deficiency arising out
of the neglected culture of your nature, but your nature
itself. And how can you venture to complain of that which
is the immediate creation of God, for as such one nature

must be as good as another. That which you look up to
in others as greater and more excellent, is simply *different*,
and you must see that you also reveal to them noble elements
which they do not find in themselves. Against this, indeed,
you humbly contend, and maintain that you have not attained
to what you are through struggles, but that it has come of
itself. But, dear child, that is just the way that all that
is most beautiful comes. What can man do more than
develop and purify his nature more and more through the
work of the spirit? Force he need never use, unless where
he has previously allowed his nature to be violated by some
evil influence. Otherwise the work of divine grace in man
is a silent, quiet work; and the more completely it is carried
out, the more natural it seems, and the more natural it is in
reality. Only that virtue which conquers faults is a struggle;
that virtue through which each one of us evinces his own
peculiar perfection in the sense and spirit of God is nothing
more than calm action. Why should you, therefore, deplore
that you rarely feel distracting grief? Do not you, even you,
because it is your nature, feel in your gentle sorrow more of
the divine and the beautiful influences, in which the beloved
of your heart reveals himself, than you are conscious of in
the moments of your more impassioned grief? The perfection of those dispositions, in whom you admire the higher
degree of life and sensibility, is one, yours and mine is
another. The former embrace, indeed, in their existence a
greater variety of the emotions that may arise in man, and in
so far they are richer, but they are at the same time more
dependent on surrounding circumstances, more confused, and
more subject to irregular impulses. You are more equable,
and therefore a more immediate image of the eternal; and
you possess yourself in a higher degree, you are more uni-
formly in harmony with all the conditions amid which you
are placed, because you do not in a one-sided manner now
seize upon them in one way and now in another, but always
comprehend each in its entirety. That state which you call
torpor is also well known to me; it is the natural defect of

such dispositions as ours, and it always makes its appearance when they have been excited beyond their usual measure. In the deepest anguish, when my whole being has been the most convulsed, I have felt this torpor more than at any other time. But you will no doubt always find, either in pious and tranquil self-communion, or in active occupation, the means of restoring the clear consciousness of your inner being. In one thing I beg you never to relax, and that is in your endeavours to maintain the perfect independence of your maternal relation to your children. This is due to you, and is also necessary for you; and in like manner as you are persuaded that it would only be affection that would prompt any interference with you on this point, so will you find the right mode of evading it without giving offence. . . . .

Henriette von Willich to Schleiermacher.

[ccxcv.]   *No date.*

Your last letter has given me great pleasure, my beloved father; I had been looking forward to it with intense longing. Oh, dear friend, let us never again be so long separated! To me this separation has been very painful —do you not know that no one in the world can strengthen me as you do? ——, I intreat you let me often have a loving word from your full heart, an elevating word from the depths of your faith, that my faith may strengthen and refresh itself therewith. Alas, dear father! why is there so much suffering in the world? A few days ago my beloved brother bore his third child to the grave. Such tender parents they were, whose happiness centred in their children, and they have lost three babes one after the other. My brother's misfortune touches my heart very nearly; he was of a gay and cheerful temperament, his married life began so happily, and now—all its young buds are prematurely nipped. My youngest sister S. has also been deprived by this of her greatest delight in life. She is staying with my brother, and to be with the children was her highest

happiness, and exercised a most beneficial influence on her.
I think I have never yet spoken to you about her, though
I am very fond of her. I believe she is by no means
mentally insignificant. But her fate has been the same as
mine, and must no doubt bear the blame of the crushed
blossoms of cheerfulness, of the absence of openness and
animation. We were in childhood left much to ourselves,
with the exception of a short period, during which we were
under the guidance of an excellent man, who died just as I
was beginning to cling to him with strong affection, and to
devote myself with great zeal to the mental occupations which
he had opened up to me.

Permit me, dear father, to put a question to you regarding
one observation in your letter which I do not quite understand. You say that one nature is as good as another—that
I do not understand. It seems to me that there is very great
difference between men, that some are born with higher, more
celestial, others with more earthly natures — that some are
called to lead a life so glorious and heavenly, that others dare
not even strive towards it, because it lies so entirely beyond
the limits of their powers. Now, when the latter become
conscious of their limitations, I think it is but natural and
allowable that they should be filled with sadness, though I
believe, and have indeed experienced it, that every murmur
dies away when we resign ourselves entirely to God, and a
certain contentment takes possession of the heart, together
with the hope that through the grace of God we may perhaps
one day obtain that for which we pine.

You say, also, that our nature is the *immediate* creation of
God. But do we not frequently inherit from our parents the
defects and deficiencies of their natures? Do you not believe
that many children are born in sin, and can only, subsequently, purify themselves by conflict and repentance? Allow
me to ask you, you dear father, do you believe that God
exercises direct action here below, independently of his
being in man and *in everything that is?* and do you
recognize in individual events, only the natural course of

things, following each other 'as cause and effect, which must, indeed, also depend upon God — or a distinct willing and working of the Highest? Forgive me, dear friend, if I do not always express clearly what I mean. . . . . May I continue to chat with you in this way about any subject that occurs to me?

Schleiermacher to Charlotte von Kathen.

[CCXCVI.]   *Berlin (no date).*

Dearest Charlotte, what a time it is since I have written to you, though I have repeatedly received welcome and friendly lines from you. Want of safe means of conveyance has deterred me, and, besides this, my writing letters always depends upon my enjoying a certain amount of quiet, which at the present period I can rarely command. I cannot now think of Rügen, and more especially of you, without anxiety, as the roar of battle is likely soon to be heard in your vicinity. But you are courageous and prudent, and in your Kathen you have a strong and faithful supporter such as few have. I do not wonder that you feel yourself bound to him more closely than ever, but I rejoice heartily at it. The present, though a period of dissolution, in many ways tightens the bonds of union between those who are closely related, and also affords uncommon opportunities for the revelation of inward capacity and of the strength of affection. And it is thus, no doubt, that you two have been able to gain a deeper insight into each other's hearts, from which you have derived new joy in each other. I should like to know what view Kathen takes of the position of your lovely country, and what are his hopes and his wishes in regard to it, though it is true that no hope can be entertained for any country separately, but all must depend upon the effect of these convulsions on our common German fatherland. We must look far into the future, and learn to discern with some certainty what it promises, if we would not lose all courage and all joy in life. My endeavours to do this absorb so much of my time and strength, that I have little left (perhaps less than I ought to have) for those matters which used to occupy me the most, and which come most immediately within my sphere. But as regards my own very uncertain, and at this moment apparently utterly ruined prospects, I am even more composed and indifferent than I expected to be. In view of the great spectacle that is unrolling itself, the little separate interests of life entirely disappear. The least that I might be able to effect in regard to the former, would, at this moment, give me infinitely more pleasure than the greatest that I could effect in my own circle. . . . .

I am longing to get back to my books and papers, so as to make amends in winter for the sins of the summer, and to be able once more to enjoy with my sister the society of our friends in Halle. But not even a few weeks in advance, is it possible at present to make any plans; the peace, for which we bear no blame, is even more uncertain than was the war. One determination only I hold fast, and that is, to follow the fortunes of my immediate fatherland, Prussia, as long as it continues to exist, and does not prove itself quite unworthy of this resolve. Should it entirely succumb, then I will, as long as it is feasible, seek the German fatherland wherever a Protestant can live, and a German governs. In this way, I shall always be able to accomplish, in some measure, the duties of my vocation. Such must be the consolation of those who cannot bear arms. Ah! take care that your boys grow up strong, and powerful, and firm, and defiant, and warlike, yet gentle and affectionate.

Do write soon again.

[CCXCVII.] *Berlin, 31st December,* 1807.

Dearest Charlotte, I am delighted with the glorious thought that has been discussed since I wrote to you. I watched with great anxiety the plans of emigration projected by our friend Herz,* and I did all that I could to upset

* At her husband's death, already, a great change had taken place in the pecuniary position of Henrietta Herz, who was, in consequence,

them or to delay their execution, and to devise means for her awaiting here the final result of affairs. But to know that she is with you is even more satisfactory to me than to have her here, although I shall lose so much by it. It is long since anything has pleased me so much as this, and I can now contemplate with so much greater serenity my own unsettled and, as to the future, most uncertain position. You must have been in some error regarding this matter, dear friend, when, during my stay here last summer, you wrote that you would rather wish me back in my wonted sphere of activity in Halle. This was and is destroyed; the university is provisionally dissolved, and only a peace favourable to Prussia could have rendered its re-establishment possible. The new Westphalian government does, indeed, hold out a hope of its reconstitution; but I cannot submit to that government, and as long as there be a German prince, under such I must live. For to operations which are directed straightways towards the destruction of German sentiment and German spirit, I cannot give even the support which my presence would imply. During the last two months of my stay in Halle, I felt under great restraint, and after prayers had been ordered in the churches for the king and queen of Westphalia, it was no longer possible for me to stand up in the pulpit. In short, I have not heart to teach there, and I have therefore left

obliged, in a great measure, to renounce that sociable life which had been to her the source of the greatest enjoyment, because, in intercourse with all the brightest spirits of the day, she felt that she was not only a recipient, but also a diffuser of moral and intellectual life. Subsequently, the political convulsions which disturbed the finances of the country further reduced the resources of this excellent and distinguished woman, who was the sole support of her blind mother and unmarried sister, and she found it necessary to look around for some means of making a livelihood. Having, at the entreaty of her friends, and more especially of Wilhelm von Humboldt, declined to accept brilliant offers made to her abroad to undertake the education of princely scions, she ultimately determined to remove to Rügen, and there took up her domicile with Charlotte von Kathen, and became the instructress of her children.—See *Fürst, Henriette Herz, Ihr Leben, &c.*—TRANS.

the place entirely, and I should have left, even had I not had
the firm conviction that a French government cannot possibly
allow a German university to go on undisturbed. I came
here in the summer to deliver some lectures, and thus to sub-
stitute something similar for my ruined sphere of activity.
At present I hold the same object in view, if I can but find
auditors. The government has, besides, declared its intention to found a university here instead of the one that has
been lost, and, as one of the preliminaries, my appointment
to it has been talked of. I shall, therefore, settle here for the
present to see whether circumstances will favour the execution of this plan. Here I may still preach without feeling
my heart oppressed ; and this, with a little leisure and my
daily bread, is all that I strictly require.

The year that ends to-day has taken much from us all ; so
much that I heartily rejoice to think of friends who have
only shared some individual loss or other with me, or have
only suffered such themselves. My welfare has on all sides
been shaken to its very foundations, yet I see nothing that
promises an entire change for the better. To keep up my
courage and be steadfast, to enjoy cheerfully what is left, to
look hopefully forward to what I shall not live to witness,
that is all that remains to me. Give my hearty, most hearty
greetings to dear Kathen. How rejoiced I am at the importance he attaches to having our friend with you ! How
delighted I shall be if I am able this summer to go to you,
and to find us all again united, with the exception of one who
is gone before us!

1 hope soon to be more settled here, and to be able to write
to you oftener.

Henriette von Willich to Schleiermacher.

[ccxcviii.]   *30th January,* 1808.

        . . . . Ah ! you know what memories are stirring
in me in these days—what painful scenes are passing before
me—how I sat at the bedside of my suffering husband and
felt myself so forlorn—how I listened to every breath—how I

watched every gentle movement, in earnest expectation that some sign of improvement would soon show itself. Alas! I waited and waited.

How often I lose myself in contemplation of the wonderful guidance of our destiny! how darkness closes around me when I venture to look deeper into its mysterious concatenations! But ever more and more clear is my faith in the relation between the individual and his fate; ever more clearly I understand those words of Novalis: " Destiny and character (*gemüth*) are only two different names for the same idea," which long dwelt in my memory without my understanding them. It is certain that in early youth already, a vague presentiment of my present fate was shadowed forth in the dreams of the girl. Wide-spread and cheerful activity in the midst of the world was never included in the pictures of life which accompanied my steps up its ascent; quiet retirement from the world and its affairs—renunciation of the sweetest joys of life—longing looks towards heaven, seeking for love *there* —high enjoyment in spiritual intercourse with the living and the dead—such were the tendencies early developed in me, and most in accordance with my nature. It was no surprise to me when I found love, but when enduring earthly happiness was opened up to me, then I was surprised. And to me, in the depths of my pain, it seemed neither strange nor unexpected when it vanished.

Dear father, you do not know how much good you do me, you more than any one else, by your confidence in me. How I wish I could adequately thank you for it! and yet again, it depresses me, because I always feel so little worthy of it! I often see distinctly how you carry over upon me the sweet image, which you bear within yourself, of a daughter such as would be worthy of you; and as there is indeed some resemblance between me and the beloved image, you overlook the great dissimilarities that are concealed beneath it. Alas! I have often such violent attacks of this morbid self-distrust, that I feel as if I must tear myself away from all those who cling to me, because they see me in a deceptive light, and it is denied to me to become that which they believe me to be. You know that this state is but transitory, but a lasting discontent, nevertheless, dwells in me, and because it is lasting I know that it cannot be unfounded. Ah! dear friend, I shall never be healed while here; the source is deeper—ah! how shall I express to you what I believe it is? *want of love*, narrowness of heart—I believe it is that. Kind father, withdraw not thy hand from me, when one day thou shalt become aware that I am speaking the truth.

[ccxcix.]   *2nd February.*

Calm sorrow dwells in me on this anniversary of the most painful parting, and serene and solemn joy, that he, the dear one, is gone into a higher life and to higher joys. This day will be celebrated by those spirits with whom the glorious soul entered into closer bonds when he took leave of this life.

Just as this morning a bright sunbeam fell upon me, so also *on that morning* the sun shone out after many gloomy days, and its brightness made an indescribable impression on me. The preceding night had been full of terror, being the first in which total hopelessness had taken possession of me—but then I could pray, I could hope again; and, full of new strength, I went in to the beloved patient, to devote myself anew to nursing him. But, alas! when the symptoms of the malady became so terrific that I could not maintain my composure, my friends led me away, and I never saw him again alive! It has pained me greatly, and I have often deeply regretted, that I did not hold his hand at the last moment; but a certain anxiety about myself and desire to spare myself in the state I then was, induced me to yield to the entreaties of my friends to keep away from his room. Ah! would that I had not yielded! How indescribably I longed, and in memory still long, for one moment only of clear consciousness, for one loving word at parting? Oh! why was this happiness denied to me? Surely I would have been strong, and such words would have been for ever after a source of infinite comfort to me. Oh, how beautiful was the death of my mother! When she had expressed with full certainty that death was approaching, the pious, sorrowing old father, who was seated at her bedside, asked her if he should read to her out of the Bible or the hymn-book. "No, dear father," she answered, "I need not that; I have long been prepared for this hour. Now call together our children; I wish once more to see and to speak to them all." She took most affectionate leave of us, and then calmly fell asleep. . . . .

With what fervour I have to-day consecrated my life anew to the dear children—*his children*. . . . .

Believe me, dear father, there are dissonances in me of which you have no suspicion. I would not give expression to them in distinct words; but believe me, and detract something from the sweet image of me, which you bear in your heart. One thing that pacifies me in regard to myself is, that there is one point in which I feel that I can concentrate all that is best in me—my motherhood. Yes, dear father, I promise you, I will be a good mother; for this I feel strength and capacity, and not only good will. You shall never have reason to upbraid me with weakness, or with motherly vanity; only when reproach would be unjust—when the limits of my nature forbid me to be more—only then will you find me fail.

Henriette von Willich to Schleiermacher.[*]

[ccc.]   *5th August*, 1808.

How is it that my heart is overflowing, and yet I can say nothing that you knew not full well already? Or would you like to hear it again and again, how unutterably I love you, how indescribably happy I am! Could I but once fully express how deep veneration, heartfelt gratitude, and childlike love are blended in the one sentiment, which now dwells in me, complete, and definite and pure—how I long to live entirely for you—what an insatiable desire I have to

---

[*] Written after Schleiermacher had been to Rügen, and they were betrothed. No letters relating to the interval of six months between this event and the preceding letter have been found.

see you happy—a desire that makes me feel that I would
gladly sacrifice myself for you, could that make you happy!
O God! it often seems to me that I can hardly bear the
blissful thought that it is to me that you will devote your
life, your holy love. How grateful I feel to you, dearest, for
the beautiful delicacy with which you gradually drew nearer
to me—which did me so much good, and which awakened
corresponding sentiments in me sooner than would have been
the case had you at once revealed to me the fulness of your
love and demanded mine in return, before I had found the
way to link together my past and my present happiness.

Tell me, my beloved father, are you really pleased to see
me give myself up so entirely to joy and happiness? When
I think of our dear Ehrenfried, and a gentle breath of sorrow
passes through my soul, I ask myself whether I ought not,
perhaps, to bear otherwise the new mercy of God bestowed
upon me through you? Whether it is right and proper that I
should enter life again with such youthful freshness, and open
my heart so entirely to joy, when not long ago I prayed that
undying sorrow might follow the widow through life? Oh,
I need not tell you how Ehrenfried lives in the depth of my
soul—how sacred to me is every remembrance of him; you
know it. Yet I am now so completely happy through you—
as happy as I possibly can be.

With what pleasure I look forward to your first letter, I
cannot describe to you, my dear, dear Ernst. Ah! am I still
so dear to you as when you were here—when you called me
your sweet heart? I never now for a moment doubt your
love; but I do ask myself sometimes, Will he then really wish
to share with me all that is dearest and most sacred to him?
But herein also you shall ever follow your own bent, only
remembering that you will be conferring indescribable happiness on me whenever you impart to me any of your treasures. However, you may be assured that I shall never, even
through the faintest betrayal of sensitiveness, restrain you in
regard to what you may wish to be to, or to share with, your
friends of either sex. Not to be able to understand, will

always pain me; but I will not allow a shadow of ill-humour to arise in me in consequence, and I will wait patiently till you turn again to your simple little wife. My dearly beloved Ernst, farewell! Do write me soon a few affectionate words, and tell me also if there be anything in me that you do not approve of, if it be ever so trifling a matter, I implore you.

You dear, excellent soul, may you be truly happy, and pray you also for me, that God will pour his blessings into my heart, and make it rich in love and piety, and in all gifts, without which I cannot make you happy.

Schleiermacher to Henriette von Willich.

[CCCI.]   *Berlin, 7th August, 1808.*

Dear, only beloved Jette, in Prenzlau I could not find a moment to write to you, and I was not sufficiently anxious to force one into my service. What gratification could a few lines have given you, which could only have told you that we had got so far safely? We have been back here since five o'clock on Friday evening, and although I have not as yet done any work, I hope to commence with a thorough good-will to-morrow, or, at the latest, the day after. Be not surprised, dear heart, that I commence with this; it is the most important in regard to my well-being here, which can only be secured by a great deal of work. Trinity Church was one of the first objects which I could clearly distinguish, and thus I had at once before my eyes the consolatory and delightful object for the attainment of which I must first of all strive.

Thanks be to God, who has given thee to me, and has bestowed upon me the hope of the blessed life which we will prepare for each other, and the delicious repose which upholds and encircles our union, and the firm consciousness that that which has developed itself so purely and so equably in us, is the loveliest and the best He could bestow. Accept a tender and grateful embrace, my sweet beloved bride, and be entirely mine, and hope for a blessed fulfilment of our wishes, without fear of anything, for all will be well at last.

To my dear sister Lotte, I wrote a few words yesterday, to announce my happiness. If your heart approves, then send me soon a few affectionate lines for her; it will give her so much pleasure to hear from you.

During the short period since my return, I have already met with much affection and confidence in various new and important quarters, and have also seen significant portents of what I predicted, viz., that great convulsions would soon take place in Germany, and I feel now even an increase of that pleasurable emotion which I told you it caused me to think that our fate is intimately interwoven with that of our country. Should it happen—which I do not, indeed, as yet foresee, but which may nevertheless come to pass—that I should be much mixed up with these commotions, then keep up your courage, and remember that fatherland, you, and the children, are my watchwords. But let us write very diligently to each other as long as it is feasible; so that when the time of privation comes, we may already have a nice little collection of tokens of remembrance from the first period of our union. You are, I trust, still as content in heart—as content, as happy, as full of trust—as I am. Jette, my heart's beloved, I know it cannot be otherwise, because in you and in me it is the same, and has grown in the same way; but, nevertheless, do not give up repeating it to me, it is so delightful to hear. Think also frequently of all the sweet, happy moments which that blessed time bestowed upon us in such rich measure, and let us continue them as well as we can during our separation. Every word of endearment is a kiss; and at each outburst of your feelings, I hear the throbbings of your gentle, loving heart!

While at Stralsund, I visited Ehrenfried's grave, and with undoubting confidence I held out my brotherly hand to him in the other world, in token of the new tie between us. His spirit is surely with us! Greet and kiss the children from me, for my heart clings to them. God bless and watch over you, my dear beloved child, and remember that I am ever with you in spirit.

[CCCII.]   *10th August*, 1808.

Here I sit, darling Jette, in my former solitude, without being able as yet to feel quite at home in it. My work is not entirely to my taste, because so many other things are running in my head. A thousand times a day I bewail that I have not you and the children here. Just now, again, while we were at breakfast, I was whimpering to Nanni about what a pity it was that we did not take a right view of the matter, and come to a more bold decision. At a pinch, we might all very well have found room ; and that we should want bread, such a silly weak fear never entered my mind, and surely not either yours. You would have come with entire confidence, had you seen that I was equally confident.

Am I not sinning against you, my sweet beloved, more especially as I know that you are courageous and strong, in leaving so long unfulfilled the duties towards you and our children, which I have, in fact, already taken upon myself? Believe me, dear heart, it is not passionate impatience, not morbid longing, but only a correct and profound appreciation of the character of our times, in which nothing, absolutely nothing, is secure beyond the present moment. Had I seen this as clearly while in your tranquil, lovely island as I do here, I believe we would have managed to take better measures to bring everything to a conclusion, and to unite us all sooner. Here, again, you are without blame, but am I so likewise ? Do I not, in fact, deserve that the sweet hope which I did not know how to secure and to change into reality by the strength of my will, should vanish, and that fate should snatch me away before I can call you entirely my own ? And should it turn out even better than we expect, shall I not, on the other hand, be a thousand times more happy than I deserve to be ? It is true, if I were at this moment to resolve to conquer all obstacles, and to bring you home this autumn already, I should not know how to accomplish it; but, while I was with you yonder, had we pondered in common, I believe we should have hit upon some good and feasible plan. However, our life, during the coming winter, might have begun with much anxiety and suffering; and this is, in fact, the reason why I left you behind in safety under the protection of kind friends. But as I am sure that if you were my wife, you would not leave me in times of need and danger, so I think you would willingly have become mine at once, to share them with me. But why am I telling you all this, as it cannot otherwise than make you sad, and, perhaps, also perplex you ? Because I want you to know exactly my state of mind; for these feelings are not merely the result of a transitory mood, but will dwell in me, and be more or less apparent, until at length the happy hour arrives. Also, because I do not wish you to think me better than I am, and that you may see the weakness of character that reveals itself herein. For does it not seem to you, also, as if I had not been brave enough, not manly enough, to set aside what was merely an empty phantom? And now, dearest Jette, I will endeavour to get the better of this repining and this longing, and throw myself into the arms of sleep, and to-morrow I will add a few words.

Ah ! dearest, say, do you also long very much for me ? Do you know and do you feel thoroughly what you are to me, and how much richer and more glorious my life would be if I had you here ? Does it trouble you that, now that we are separated, my love seems less serene than during the delightful time we spent together ? Never mind this; it is nevertheless always the same love, and, after all, serenity is its fundamental character. Therefore, also, I become ever more calm, more tranquilly joyful, the more vividly I bring you before my mind's eye.

Quick ! let me wish you and the children an affectionate good morning. Towards morning I dreamt a great deal about your being here, and, in consequence, I have already been very diligent, almost for the first time since my return, and I shall see how far I can get on to-day. In fact, according to my nature, I ought at present to feel a strong impulse to work well and diligently; for, under such circumstances, I live most heartily and most intimately with my friends, and with you

above all others. If you would do me a great service, commission Nanni to greet me in your name, whenever she thinks
I require it most, or it would be most wholesome.

Dear Jette, how joyful I am in my heart of hearts ! I
have found the precious treasure, and I feel inclined to give
up everything else, and to invite the whole world to come and
partake of our glorious life. I feel also less and less repugnant to take you away from your lovely Rügen; for, where-
ever we settle, we will create a little paradise of our own. Dear
sweet, wherever you are there is love and healthy life ! A
thousand kisses for yourself and for the children. Take care
that they do not forget me.

Schleiermacher to Charlotte von Kathen.

[ccciii.]   11*th August*, 1808.

My most hearty greetings to you, beloved friend and
dear sister, in remembrance of the happy time that we spent
with each other in such pure and heartfelt affection and joy.
Such rich fruit as it has borne to me, no others indeed can have
reaped; but on all it must, nevertheless, have acted like a refreshing restorative, and your friendship will know how to
appropriate a share even in that happiness, which has fallen
more exclusively to my lot, as indeed everything must ever
be and remain common among us. Were I not deeply impressed with this conviction, I should feel ashamed of being
the one who from all sides received the most and the
best. You saw me as you had seen me and known me
before, only for a longer time, and perhaps under less con-
straint. But, although I had also known you previously, I
had never before been an immediate witness of your home-
life, and this is a great thing. Not until then did I acquire
a clear and definite conception of your manner of living with
your children, with Kathen, in your household, and now I
can follow your life even from a distance, in all its details.
Therefore, let me now reap all the fruits of this, by keeping
me ever informed of the consecutive events of your life, dear

Lotte; so that everything that touches you nearly may also touch me, and that I may know in what measure you are made to taste of the sweets and bitters of life. At present, I follow you in thought through the labours of the harvest, and wish that the joy which the gathering in of these blessed gifts always occasions may be reflected in your heart and sweeten the trouble. On our journey home we found that the harvest had already begun in Anklam, and that nearer home it was almost over; but the nearer we drew to the great city the more my interest in the harvest vanished, because it has so little to do with life here. Believe me that, from this point of view also, though you may probably not have felt it, the time I spent with you was most beneficent to me, in as far as I was once more brought into immediate contact with, and had an opportunity of rejoicing in, man's labour in connection with nature, this groundwork of all other activity and of all well-being. Just as the simple, strengthening fragrance of the blooming corn-fields and meadows act upon my senses, so does the sight of these labours act upon my mind.

Above all things, keep me informed of the progress of your children; the longer I was with them the more, I may say, I lived myself into their life, and rejoiced in them. I mean the elder ones, for of the younger ones I saw, unfortunately, too little. For the latter you ought to have a sensible nurse, who should at the same time be a woman of some education. This would save you a great deal of trouble and many petty annoyances. Dearest Lotte, had I but already such a home-life to present to you, and to invite you to come and witness! In a certain measure you may form a picture of what it will be, from my life in Götemitz and my manner of being with Jettchen, with Nanni, and with the children; and you will, therefore, probably be less impatient than I am. Dearest Lotte, I am afraid my impatience will go on increasing; but I have determined to behave very well, and to be mindful of my health, to take everything easy, if possible, and, at all events, to encounter with fresh courage those matters which cannot be taken easily, so that I may get well through the winter, and find myself in full vigour on the arrival of the lovely spring which is to be the happiest in my life. I do not know whether any one can entirely realize the peculiar state of my present feelings. I believe that the combination is a very unusual one, and to give full utterance to it, I must be a poet. But, perhaps, every betrothed says the same. Be it so! Nevertheless, I believe I am right. The sorrow on which our love is based, and which will ever be an inherent element in it, my previous relation to Jettchen, and the mode in which the world claims my innermost being and my whole heart at this very moment, when I would fain retire completely within myself—such a state of things cannot be common. God bless you and strengthen you!

Schleiermacher to Henriette von Willich.

[ccciv.]   *Halle, 18th August, 1808.*

On Monday, just four weeks after we had pledged ourselves so joyfully to each other, I received your first letter, my sweet Jette. My God! how much hast Thou bestowed upon me in this short time! with what a completion has my agitated life been crowned! But I am no longer in that state that I feel inclined to question whether it be really true. I have already lived myself into it; I possess it and enjoy it every day and every hour. When I think of you and of the children, it is as when an absent husband and father thinks of his dear ones. I am sure you must feel the same; you must think of me as if I were absent on a journey, and were soon to return, and that we were then to move into a new dwelling. It cannot be otherwise. Longing for you, and the sweet, tranquil certainty that you are mine, are blended into one feeling. But, dearest Jette, what of this gratitude that you say you feel towards me? Do you know, that if I am to tell you everything that displeases me in you, I should like to begin with this. You mean, no doubt, something very beautiful, though I do not exactly know what; but look well at it, and do not give it this name ; for gratitude refers to benefaction, and of such there cannot possibly be a question between you and me. Can a person bestow benefits on himself? Can the right hand do this to the left, the head to the heart, the nerves to the muscles? Can a father give charity to his child? It also seems to me that I could only feel gratitude towards a person who was otherwise indifferent to me, towards a patron of exalted rank, or some such; and yet, when we look closely at it, we see that it is nought. Your veneration for me makes me a little ashamed of myself ; but we will leave that as it is. Each one of us has some advantage which has claim to the veneration of the other; and, on my side, I shall not fail in reverence towards you. But your childlike love ! Yes, sweet heart, that I accept; for that sweet relation between us, and our common love for our dear Ehrenfried and for all that belongs to him, is the groundwork of the love we now feel for each other and of our great happiness. My dear heart, that you were pleased with the manner in which I approached you gratifies me, and I find it very natural ; but, I beg you, do not attribute this to me as a merit, and do not suppose that it was in the very least precalculated, or that I concealed anything until the opportune moment. No, dear Jette, I gave utterance to everything that was clear to myself; all the rest was, no doubt, vaguely present, but just because it was vague, it could not develop itself, until that which was clear and definite had found utterance, and could only be unconsciously expressed in the first gentle whisperings, which are, in fact, not speech. And did not, in the same way, a vague feeling of what was coming and what was in my heart steal into yours before full consciousness came? The first that became quite clear to me was, that our lives belonged to each other; that I could never give up the children and yourself; and that you could never lean so confidently on any one as on me ; and this I expressed to you, and then I felt that I had nothing further to look for in life, that everything that I could wish would be mine in full measure if *we* were to each other all that, with the full consent of our hearts, we might be; and thus, you see, that I truly imparted to you each feeling as it was in me, and that full and entire love was already in my heart and in yours, though it could only enter our consciousness by degrees. Therefore, also, it is clear to me that our feelings in regard to each other have come into existence in a truly divine manner, working themselves forward from the innermost depths of our being, attaching themselves by what is highest in them to our entire existence, springing from nothing partial, and consequently neither one-sided nor wavering. Why, therefore, should you not give yourself up freely to the joy which this new revelation of God in you causes you? Your mind is fresh and young, and why should you not enter life thus? Is it not this very youthful freshness in you that I love? Is not this exactly what I require? Is it not this which, during the whole course of our acquaintance, has had a determining influence on us both? Think of it as a sweet possession which we hold in common; think of it as mine as well as yours. Be ever willingly the youthful mother of your dear children—the youthful, youth-imparting, daughterly wife of your Ernst, your dear old father.

Dear, sweet Jette, I clasp you to my heart, and with the tenderest caresses invoke a blessing upon you, that you may ever retain this lovely freshness. Sorrow you no longer need; Ehrenfried will no longer fail you. In the same measure as we feel certain of our happiness, we must feel certain of *his* joy, and his *joy* must and ought to dispel your grief. But if we were ever to cease to live with him, and to let him live with us, then also we should cease to love each other with the same love as now. But this cannot be; and, therefore, the fluctuations which you so naturally experience will gradually cease, and the past and the present will blend into one.

What happiness it is to me, my dear, sweet life, that you have such confidence in me in regard to the children also! I have the same; but try to feel that all this is not mine only, but belongs to us in common. Formerly I had no liking for very young children, and did not in the least understand them.

It is only through our children that I have come to this; and the talent thus developed is to me part of our love, its first sweet fruit, growing out of the peculiar happiness of becoming at one and the same time lover and father.

You must now look upon yourself as fully initiated into my entire life; there is nothing in it which does not belong to you, which you have not a right to share, and which it will not be a gratification to me to open up to you. As to your not understanding, there is no fear of that, in regard to anything that is essential to you. There is nothing in my life, or in what I am striving for, the *spirit* of which you will not be able fully to comprehend; otherwise, indeed, you would not be able to understand myself, and would not be fully mine. On the contrary, it is in the nature of things, that you will ever be the first to understand, because you will be the one to whom my whole life and my whole being will ever first and most immediately reveal itself, and the will to understand will not be wanting. I know you too well to fear that. It would, indeed, grieve me should there ever be anything that was important to me, which could not, in its essentials, have an interest for you. But as regards matters of detail, and worldly affairs, there others are in advance of you, and in relation to these you must be guided and controlled by the amount of leisure you can command, by your inclination, and by the natural bias of your talents.

In what is at present occupying me and agitating me, you must also take part; and should Henrietta Herz not have communicated to you what I wrote in my last—which she may not have done, because of her unwillingness to disturb your first joy by anxieties—then request her to do so. I depend upon your courage and upon your confidence in me. I have no foreboding of danger, therefore be you also without fear; I shall tread no other path than that of my vocation, and moderation and prudence neither fail me nor those who are to direct my special undertakings. The part that I have to play is worthy, beautiful, and blameless; and what can be more gratifying than to feel that I am actively helping to direct and prepare the state of things on which depends the happiness of our lives ? Heaven grant that things may but take such a course as to render possible the execution of what has been planned, which ought not to be attempted except under conditions that render failure almost impossible!* Pray that God will guide me, bless me and protect me, as I pray that He will strengthen your courage and your energies. Do everything for yourself and the children for my sake, and be assured that for your sake I will take proper care of myself, and that, amid all occupations, cares, and labours, you will ever be in me and with me.

One thing more. It may be that I shall have to go to Königsberg. However, though I wish much that this may take place, it is as yet uncertain. Longer than three weeks I shall hardly be absent. Should I be obliged to start soon, Nanni shall immediately inform you.

Henriette von Willich to Schleiermacher.

[cccv.]   *22nd August.*
My beloved Ernst, a thousand thanks for your dear letters—but I am so full of anxiety. . . . Try to conceive all that I would fain say to you—how dreadful I feel since I can no longer look with undoubting certainty towards the fulfilment of our sweet hope—how, in the midst of the most cheerful anticipations and the sweetest dreams, I am startled by that thought which opens such a wide field for the gloomiest forebodings, to which I do not, as you know, abandon myself, but which, nevertheless, make it impossible to go on picturing to myself with certainty our future life. My beloved Ernst, must you then do this? Alas, if you feel that you must, then I have nothing to say, then I dare not implore, dare not hold you back, and then also I know that it would be of no avail to attempt it. My dear, dear Ernst! Ah, were I but near you —I have never longed so much for this, as since I know that you may be exposed to danger. Ah, what would I not share

* What undertakings are here alluded to, is not known.

with you ! and yet I am to share nothing, shall not even have accounts of you. Oh, my Ernst, God grant that it may not come to this—may a merciful Providence soon send a change!

However delightful it would be to be with you already, I nevertheless find it quite natural, that it was not thus resolved at the time, and indeed I do not know that I should willingly have consented, as there was then no question of necessity, and it seemed probable that next spring we should be able to begin our life in peace and quiet. Without some predominant reason, such as I admit that of a long period of uncertainty is, but which you did not then foresee, I should hardly have been willing to leave my relatives here so suddenly. No, dear Ernst, I do not think that this very natural delay can be considered a weakness on your part. You wanted to prepare everything so nicely for our happy life, you dear love. Though you may feel pained at my not being near you now —as it also pains me—do not reproach yourself, you have no reason to do so. My Ernst, your letter has not perplexed me, for I also see but too clearly what you have not ventured openly to express, and what, in spite of any heroism that I may possess, is terrible for me to contemplate. . . . When I reperuse your letters, I rejoice at every word from your heart which assures me of your love. Yes, I am entirely yours. Oh, dearest, endeavour to feel, as I do, how blessed I am at this moment in the full certainty that you really love me, in the holy and unbounded trust with which I give myself up to you. I fancy myself seated beside you stroking your cheek and kissing your dear forehead and eyes. Ah, and I cannot believe that we are not really soon to be united. Yes, my Ernst, nothing on my side shall prevent my being yours as early as it may be possible. Write to me without delay, and if you can, say something reassuring, but only in case you really feel it yourself.

As punishment for my naughtiness, I will confess to you that I had filled some sheets of paper for you, principally with retrospective glimpses of my past life; but that I had not the courage to send them out into the wide world to seek for you, nor did I like to keep them, so I have burnt them. Forgive me, for I am already sufficiently punished by having failed to impart to you what I would so willingly share with you. How happy I have been since we met, I cannot prove to you better, than by telling you that with me it is always a proof of the presence of an unclouded, cheerful state of mind when I sing much, and that of late I have been constantly singing with all my heart, sacred melodies as well as others. Upon the whole I am very brisk and lively after my fashion, and have cut off some of my sleep, in the hope that I shall at last get accustomed to need very little. Oh, my beloved, if I may but make you truly happy! One hearty kiss, and then good night!

23rd.

This morning I am far more tranquil than last night. It seems so unnatural to me to think of you surrounded by danger; besides, on consideration, you write with so much calm confidence about our living together, as you could not possibly do, I think, were matters such as I imagined. My Ernst, were I but safely and tranquilly in your arms, or even if not safely and tranquilly, were I but with you! Were it not for the dear children, nothing should prevent me from joining you, just because of the suffering we might have to go through. As it is, however, I see that it is better that you should stand alone, than that you should have double cares upon you.

Farewell, my dearly beloved Ernst; God protect you in all that you undertake. Remember how my whole heart clings to you.

[cccvi.] 24th August.

My beloved Ernst, does it give you a little pleasure to get a letter from me unexpectedly? The whole week through I am longing for the day that is to bring me a letter from you. I meant not to have written until next post-day, but I long so to chat with you, that in spite of all obstacles I am determined to do so. Do you know how I manage to live constantly with you in thought, and to become ever more familiar with your mind? I have been reading once more your *Monologues*, and with renewed love and renewed interest, now that the glorious soul that reveals itself therein is mine. Oh, Ernst, dare I really say mine? Is it really love that has made you mine? Yes, my feeling tells me that it is so, but my thought cannot comprehend it when I consider what I am, and I am ready to weep bitter tears at the emptiness of my mind and the poverty of my heart. I see clearly what a woman should be, to be worthy of being your wife; but, alas! not only do I feel myself far from this perfection, but many of the traits in the picture have been so utterly denied to me, that it would even be useless and wrong in me to struggle to obtain them.

When I have a quiet hour to myself, I read one of your sermons, and I cannot describe to you the pleasure which I experience, when I find that that which you explain so well and so beautifully, is entirely in accordance with the views on the subject which I entertained previously—when I see that I have found the truth for myself, and that through you it becomes thoroughly clear to me. I read yesterday the sermon: "The wholesome advice to possess as though we did not possess." I did not know beforehand what it contained, and how far it might be applicable to my state. It has strengthened me very much, and has made me feel that my love to you is of the right kind, and that even if it were to cost my whole happiness and my life, I could not wish that you should do otherwise than your holy zeal impels you to do. I have thought with anxiety that my former letter might, perhaps, have seemed to you to convey a different feeling. But it was not so; I only meant to express to you a solicitude which is not incompatible with joy in you and in your noble undertaking.

Oh, my Ernst, how deeply do I feel that for no price would I miss the least particle of the beauty of your soul! How happy it makes me to think of what a glorious being you are! . . . . Should the felicity really be reserved for me, when all suffering and danger lie behind us, and our fatherland has been resuscitated, to live tranquilly at your side, beloved by you and yours—oh! my God, it will be something unutterably great! When the sweetness of such a life appears before me in its small details, I feel as if I could, indeed, make you happy, as if my love, the entire devotion of my being, which will never wish for more than to live for you and for the dear children, might bring joy into your life. My dear little father, I press your hand to my bosom and cover it with the tenderest kisses.

Do you know, dearest, what my relations accuse me of?—that I idealize my friends so much at first, that I must necessarily in the end lower my tone a little, and thus cause them pain. I do not believe it is so, dearest; do you? In reference to you, it is true no one ever said so. I confess that the beautiful always affects me at first somewhat passionately; but when that from which such an impression is received is in truth beautiful, there is, I think, no reason to fear that the love it inspires will be evanescent. There have been times, for instance, when the intimate interchange of thought between myself and Lotte Kathen and P——— has ceased; but I always come round again. Nay, at times I do, indeed, even grow cold towards my friends; but I am conscious all the while, that this is only a passing state, and in reality my previous enthusiasm soon returns in all its pristine freshness. . . . .

Schleiermacher to Henriette von Willich.

[cccvii.]   *Königsberg, 29th August.*
Since Thursday evening I have been staying with my excellent Wedike, who is the same in all his ways and manners, in spite of the great change from a country life to a town life, and his removal into a far wider sphere of activity. The joy that he and his wife evinced when I arrived, dropping down from the clouds as it were, you can hardly picture

to yourself. At first I was really painfully affected by it, because it was so evident that they attributed my coming entirely to the wish to see them, while I was conscious of being brought hither by business which I should be obliged to conceal from them, and which I must now manage to transact as well as possible without awakening attention, though it will take up much of my time. But as it cannot be otherwise, I must leave matters as they are. Another family from Halle, who had been participators in all the misery there, was so rejoiced at seeing me again, that the wife, contrary to her usual reserve, fell upon my neck, and she and her daughter well nigh wept for joy. In addition to these friends, I have seen the royal children, and to my great delight have found them in good health and going on well. I have also learnt to know some of the leading men, on whom the hopes of my country rest, and I expect to have a good deal of intercourse with them. But I ever return with renewed pleasure to the home of my dear friends, and thoroughly enjoy every quiet hour that I spend with them, anticipating with delight, while witnessing their happy life, what *ours* will be in future. In this house rules a spirit of love, of cheerfulness, of calm contentment, of indifference to the world in general, and of hearty friendliness towards every one who draws nigh of himself—in short, it is a little heaven on earth. To me this home-life appears even more complete and more pleasing than formerly, now that Wedike has a sphere of activity more suited to his capacities, and exercises a greater influence on the world. But I think he is not sufficiently interested in his vocation, and the heaven he dreams of and longs for is still a kind of Arcadian life. However, this is only a tribute that he pays to his weakness and to his want of interest in the great affairs of the world; all that he has to do, he, nevertheless, does well and ably, and even with a relish, when the nature of his work will admit of it. I shall hardly have an opportunity of hearing him preach, which I much regret; it was not his turn yesterday, and next Sunday the people want me to preach for him, which will give me no pleasure, except in as far as regards the court and a few other persons. . . . .

Do you know, my own Jette, that it seems to me an eternity since I heard from you? It is true it is only a fortnight; but when such unwonted events take place, as this journey is to me, and one is removed out of one's usual sphere, time always seems long. I still continue to count the Mondays, and to-day I have celebrated the sixth since I entered upon a new life. This life came into being at the moment that you placed your hand in mine; but I also recall to mind with heartfelt joy and gratitude the previous happy moments, during which I revelled in the presentiment of what was coming. The same composure, the same feeling of security and of inward happiness which dwelt in my heart, when I led you out of the summer-house and along the path that day, and which would probably have prevented any one from perceiving that something great and extraordinary had just happened to me, still pervades my heart; and so, likewise, the same yearnings, the same passionate exultation, and the same mournful remembrance of our dear departed, but also the same happy consciousness of his approval and his blessing.

Darling child, here I witness daily what a glorious thing wedded life is — a happiness with which no other can be compared. And you will prepare this life for me, you will bestow upon me the happiness I had long ceased to hope for. I see my way so clearly through all the storms which may perhaps beset us before the spring, that they do not cause me even the slightest anxiety; and you, my brave heart, I do not doubt feel as I do. Heaven will be with us, as it is in us and around us. . . . .

Henriette von Willich to Schleiermacher.

[cccviii.]   *No date.*

. . . . . What a joy to receive your dear, glorious letter! But, seriously, I feel slightly hurt at your making so little of my gratitude, though in doing this you would indeed be quite justified, had I meant it as you have understood it. I do not remember having said that I felt great gratitude towards you ; but that this feeling had been absorbed in the one great sentiment of love, which has made all that is yours mine, and all that is mine yours. . . . . My Ernst, I never believed either, that you concealed anything from me, or that there was anything pre-calculated in your conduct. At the moment that your manner spoke to me of real love, this love developed itself in me, and so it was at all times. My heart ever re-echoed what was passing in thine ; and so it will ever be. Oh, my Ernst, I am indescribably happy ! Yes, truly, Ehrenfried will ever live with us and in us. How often you remind me of him, even without calling up any distinct thought of him, for his image, dear never-to-be-forgotten man, lives deep in my heart. I am also quite reassured now as to the happiness I feel, and give myself up to it without restraint. . . . .

[CCCIX.] *4th September.*

Dear Ernst, so you are now really in Königsberg ? Believe me, I am quite alive to the grandeur of the thought that our fate is so intimately linked with that of our country—I feel myself great in you. My entire being is elevated through you. Oh, dearest, how proud I am of you ! Jette is right when she says that even to perish in such an undertaking is sublime. I would, therefore, wait calmly for the issue without complaining, could I but say: " Where thou art, there will I be ; and whithersoever thou goest, thither will I go." But if that, which is too dreadful to think of, should befall you, I should be obliged to continue to drag on a miserable existence: for could I follow you and leave the children alone ? But why dwell on a thought that my mind shrinks from ? God be with you, my Ernst, as my prayers are with you. The consciousness that you are mine, that you love me, makes me so happy, that it will enable me to bear a great deal. My feelings are in a state of strange fermentation ; the past is again drawing nearer to me, and all its memories are awakening with renewed strength. You know how significant to me is the 5th of September. I have again, as it were, drawn closer to Ehrenfried; I feel deeply that I could not exist without keeping his image alive within me, without keeping my remembrance of him ever fresh; yes, how necessary it is for my happiness that I should ever be sure of his love and his approval.

I must confess to you that his image has not at all times been thus interwoven with the feelings you have awakened in me; not unfrequently I have quite forgotten him, or a fleeting thought of him has merely glanced through my mind, when I have felt so indescribably happy in the present. But in moments of calm quietude I pray to him as to a patron saint, and thus it is I live with him. It is not always, however, that I enjoy such equanimity of feeling as at present, for I am just now calmly happy in all my relations — in my relation to Ehrenfried, to you, to my children, to my sisters and brothers, and to my friends. . . . . .

[cccx.]   *13th September.*

Dear Ernst, Ehrenfried's sisters and brothers all rejoice sincerely in my happiness, and, indeed, how could they do otherwise? and, yet, though not a soul has ever uttered anything of the kind to me, I have often a vague fear that they and his nearest friends must feel hurt and surprised at my attaching myself to you so soon after his loss. Yea, sometimes even the doubt arises in me whether Ehrenfried himself, of whose approval I feel upon the whole so assured, and who, I believe, looks down upon us with a blessing, might not wish this to have been otherwise; and why is it that I cannot always feel free and happy, but am oppressed, as if I had not acted rightly? At this moment, however, I feel quite happy, and press you with indescribable love to my heart. Oh, Ernst, I often think that I love you even more than you love me; say, is it really so?

Dearest, forgive my begging you, if you should ever find

anything in my letters which you think deserves reproof, to administer it as gently and in as kindly a tone as possible. I am very sensitive, therefore promise me this.

14th September.

Dear Ernst, look upon that which I wrote last night as nothing more than the product of a passing mood. To-day I feel so light, and everything in me and around me is bright; but, nevertheless, I do not wish to withhold those pages from you, for I want you to know everything in me, that which is not good as well as that which is good. . . . . The transition from the previous delightful relation between us to the still more intimate and tender one, was so imperceptible that I could not say how or when the change took place ; and, in reality, it is now, as before, filial love that I feel for you, only infinitely increased. You may be right in saying that it is out of filial love that I devote my life to you; but do not call it a sacrifice, for this love is in itself my highest and my only happiness.

Although my joy in the happiness of the children by far outweighs my joy in my own, I believe, nevertheless, that no prudential considerations for their weal would have induced me to lay my hand in yours, had not my whole heart followed it.

Schleiermacher to Henriette von Willich.

[cccxi.] *Königsberg, 11th September, 1808.*

Yes, my heart's own Jette, your last letter caused me great and unexpected pleasure. You are indeed most kind to have stolen the time for writing it, and to have written so circumstantially about our little daughter. That I had not misconstrued your former letter, you will by this time have learnt from my last . . . . That which first drew my heart towards you, four years ago, was the beautiful combination of sweetness and deep feeling with cheerful lightheartedness, strength, and courage. Could I but describe to you what passed within me when I saw you for the first time at Götemitz, and when we were strolling on the sea-shore at Stubbenkammer. I felt such delight in you, and in your love to Ehrenfried, that my whole being seemed absorbed in it; I attached myself to you in a peculiar manner, and with a feeling that you belonged to me also, though in a very different sense from that in which you belonged to Ehrenfried. The tenderness which I felt for you was that of a friend, a father, and yet no other love could have exceeded this feeling in intensity; and ever when I was most conscious of my affection for you, it was your moral strength and courage which stood most vividly before me, and in which I rejoiced the most. And it was these qualities in you that comforted me the most when I first heard of our dear Ehrenfried's illness, and when I anticipated, and ultimately heard of, his death. You were ever my own strong daughter, strong in the Lord, and in the power of your noble life. In like manner you are now my strong and courageous betrothed; and in your expressions I have seen naught but the utterances of your love taken by surprise. I knew at once that your courage would not fail you, and that you would soon recognize that I could not act otherwise than I have done, and that you would not wish to see me animated by different sentiments, or adopt any other principle of action. This it is that makes you mine, entirely mine; and it is because I am what I am—because I take possession of a different side of your nature from that which Ehrenfried's character and career rendered it possible for him to touch—that you can love me after him, as you do love me, sweet dear.

But now tell me, have you full confidence in my prudence and my discretion? do you feel that, from what you know of my actions in daily life, you can judge of how I will act on more important occasions, and relative to greater undertakings? For if so, you must feel assured that I will not foolishly or unnecessarily increase the dangers which I am exposed to. You will require to have this assurance, dear Jette; but it seems to me that, if you will but think of my love for you and for our little ones, you must feel certain that this love alone would suffice to inspire me with the requisite amount of prudence and circumspection. I have no misgivings; and the coincidence between these outward circumstances and our union gives me a feeling of exultant happiness which I cannot describe. Each acts upon the other, and establishes the proper relation between the two. Were I not able to carry through that in which I am now engaged, and which I am so confident that I can carry through, I should not feel so certain that I had a right to claim you as my own, to take possession of your entire existence and of your children. And, on the other hand, were you not mine, I should not have felt so conscious of how true is my patriotism and my courage. As it is, however, I know that I may place myself on a level with whomsoever it may be, that I am worthy of having a country I can call my own, and that I am worthy of being a husband and a father. Therefore, keep alive courage and hope, my sweet pet, as I do, and rely upon it, that that which does us inwardly so much good, will also outwardly succeed. Be ever assured that I am not withholding anything from you, and that I will not fail to inform you as soon as cause arises for well-founded alarm.

What I find more especially delicious in your letter is, that no sooner have you made some strange assertion about yourself, than by your own words you refute it: thus you tell me about the poverty of your heart and mind, and of the riches of mine, and yet, the next moment, you show me that all my views were yours, even before I expressed them, though they did not appear to you in so clear a light. Now, this is just my vocation—to represent more clearly that which dwells in all true human beings, and to bring it home to their consciousness. But between you and me there must be greater agreement than between me and others, because were not that wherein consists my real individuality familiar and perfectly comprehensible to you, you could not be mine as you are. Let it then be so, and place yourself on a level with me, as it beseems man and wife, and be perfectly assured that you make me surpassingly happy, and that your love satisfies all my wishes and all my yearnings. This need not prevent you from admiring in me that which belongs more especially to man—the independent light of knowledge, and the controlling and formative power ; just as I admire in you all that is most peculiar to woman—the native and undimmed purity of feeling, the self-sacrificing, tender, nurturing skill, that brings forth and develops. And thus we shall ever be as one, and will not inquire if or why the one is superior or inferior to the other.

Schleiermacher to Charlotte von Kathen.

[cccxii.] *Königsberg, 15th September, 1808.*

Dearest, best of friends, it is, in fact, not very long since I parted from you; yet it seems to me a little eternity, and I feel painfully the almost total silence that has been maintained between us during this interval. You know, indeed, how I am getting on, as, upon the whole, I also know how your life proceeds; but it was such a delight to me, when with you, to sit on the sofa, and have an hour's cozy chat with you alone, that it has become quite a necessity to me to renew these conversations from time to time. If you can find leisure, do pour out your heart a little to me. As yet, you have not, perhaps, got through the bustle of the harvest. I do not know how it has turned out; but I hope that Kathen's and your own joy at the new blessing promised to you, will make every burden and trouble light. However, I remember that you have told me that you are seldom in good spirits during these periods, and this makes me anxious. I envy our friend and L—— the sweet privilege of helping you to bear and endeavouring to cheer you, and most sincerely wish that I could share in it. And when I then think that the time will soon come when I may experience these joys and devote myself to these cares in my own home, in connection with my beloved Jette, dearest sister, I cannot tell you in what an atmosphere of rapture and hope I live, and I can feel naught but this, though I know that fearful storms may arise before I am able to run into port. At all times I see the sweet happiness before my eyes, and feel it in my heart, and it is to me as if I must pour out my inward joy and bliss on every one who knows of it, or who ought to know of it. Dearest Lotte, pray keep up your spirits, and, when you feel depressed, inspire some draughts of our atmosphere of hope, and place before your eyes the picture of my happiness and that of your beloved sister, and refresh yourself with the sight.

In as far as regards my impatience—for I plead guilty to a certain amount of this—the change caused by my journey hither has been a relief; but, on the other hand, I regret that the increase of power and energy, which I feel within myself, should not at once be brought to bear on some regular sphere of activity. I have some hope that my coming hither may prove of advantage to you also. A young man, who, during the period of his academical studies, was an inmate in the family of my friend Wedike, seems not disinclined to join you.

About my remembrance of the delightful time I spent in Rügen, and how I thank God for what He allowed me to find there, I shall say nothing. I become daily more familiar with the thought of my happiness, and everything and everybody that is connected with it becomes dearer to me, and all are welded together in my heart into one inseparable whole. In like measure as I long for Jette, I long for the sweet children and for the paternal life I shall lead with them. Not a shadow of fear or misgiving dims my joy, but, on the contrary, I look forward with the greatest confidence to next spring as the unfailing commencement of my true life. God be with you, dear Lotte! Let me soon have a few cheering lines from you.

Henriette von Willich to Schleiermacher.

[cccxiii.]   *18th September.*

My heartiest thanks for your letter of the 5th. Ah, if you but knew what joy these letters are to me—how I dwell upon each word of endearment—how I feel your love—how it thrills through me even as if you were sitting by my side! My sweet Ernst, with what devotion I cling to you, and how my being is stirred when it comes home to me so forcibly how truly you love me! I never doubted it, and yet it is as if each day brought me greater certainty.

How is it that each time I write to you, I seem to love you better, and to want to address you in new terms of endearment, and yet I can find none? For my heart is already so entirely thine, that it has nothing more to give. But I know that when we meet again, I shall be able to interchange thought and feeling more freely with you than when you were here last. How delightful it is that love's sweet action can continue so undisturbed, even from afar!

Dear Ernst, how gloriously all the ideals which I dreamt of in early youth have been realized, and even more than realized! How often I used to think, Is it, then, not possible that life might be as beautiful as I figured it to myself? Now I know that it can be so. Happy, most happy, my life was already with my dear Ehrenfried; but with you, it will be richer still in beauty. To you, I may say this; for you know how truly attached I was to the never-to-be-forgotten departed, and how I still cling to his memory.

Schleiermacher to Henriette von Willich.

[cccxiv.]   *Königsberg, 18th September,* 1808.
          .   .   .   .   . I was a changed being directly after the receipt of your unhoped-for letter. Fresh life and gladness streamed through me; for it is a glorious thing to get a letter from you, my darling Jette. If it were possible, I might say, that every word that you utter makes you dearer

to me; but I knew beforehand that you would soon learn to regard our whole position with more composure, as, altogether, there is nothing that may occur in our future life, in respect to which I do not confidently anticipate that you will ever do, and be, what is right and good. But to see the reality face to face, in addition to this inward knowledge, this firm faith, what more can life bestow?

It is hardly possible, dear child, that a human being can at all times live consciously in that state of happy balance of mind that arises occasionally when his whole nature is powerfully stirred, and each relation of his life is felt and enjoyed; these are exceptional moments, during which heaven indwells in the heart, and time embraces eternity; but it has given me great satisfaction to find that you can confess, without any sign of dissatisfaction, that you are not always in this state of equipoise. I trust that your fits of discontent with yourself will become of ever rarer recurrence, and that you will ultimately cease to feel disheartened in reference to what you desire to be, and ought to be, in the happy future.

This reminds me of what might, in fact, cause me some discouragement. I mean what the others say about your tendency to idealize your friends; for if they do not accuse you of it in reference to me, this is only because in this case they are themselves labouring under the same malady. This is owing to the *Monologues*, in which I idealized myself, and now the kind creatures think that I am in reality what I therein represent myself to be. And, in fact, so I am; for what I express in that book, are my innermost sentiments, my true spirit. But the innermost being is never clearly manifested in phenomenal life, but always appears veiled in obscurity in this imperfect world; whereas this obscuration is not reproduced in the *Monologues*. Therefore, pray beg Henrietta Herz to tell you all the evil she can about me— she knows a good deal, and has suffered under it—and then reflect, that you will have to bear it all. I am telling you this so honestly, as it appears; and yet not only sincerity, but also the vanity, or rather the flattering hope of love is concealed behind it.   The fact is, I imagine, that after all, you will not think it so bad; and that you will see that your love and our marriage will be the very best means for working out and bringing forth my true nature in an ever purer form. Should you, therefore, in reality find that I am not so bad as Henrietta Herz depicts me, when she is very eloquent on my odious qualities, then look upon the improvement as your work. For the rest, I must tell you that I never heard any complaint of your tendency to idealize, though I have heard something about your tendency, when your heart is full of one friend, to forget and abandon another. But I have always felt just as assured that this was only an appearance, only an evanescent mood, as you expressed yourself to be when you wrote to me about it recently. It is just the same as with the various occupations which we are called upon to attend to in life, and which we really do attend to, though at one time we take very energetically hold of one, and then pass on to another, without, therefore, having forgotten or abandoned the previous one.

[cccxv.]   *Berlin, 1st October,* 1808.

Here I am again since yesterday morning, dearest Jette, having already rested well after the fatiguing journey, having provisionally communicated with my friends, and having feasted on the letters which I found awaiting my return. Yes, verily, the life of love goes on fresh and undisturbed in spite of distance; it breathes its own ever new life into the dead letter, and imparts light and colour to it. How vividly you stand before me, while I am reading your letters; I see you playing with the dear children, and every word recalls to me your sweet voice, which thrilled through me in so peculiar a manner the very first time I heard it. Yes, verily, ours will be a glorious life; my greatest trouble is, that I must in full earnest begin to break myself of the laziness, which is one of my principal vices; how shall I otherwise find time to enjoy all that there will be to enjoy, and to do all that there will be to do ! For if my dreams and my presentiments do not prove false, a very active, and I trust, with God's help, a very useful life lies before me. And you will enter into it all, will share in it all, and whatever I effect will be your work. Yes, from this point of view, my beloved, it may be that your new life will be even richer than your former life. Do you feel distinctly, are you quite conscious of how entirely you enter into all my being and doing? In every relation in life I stand forward at present with greater freedom and with greater power.

Henriette von Willich to Schleiermacher.

[cccxvi.]   *3rd October.*

Oh, dear Ernst, how much delight you have bestowed upon me! no less than two dear, sweet letters I have from you. I suppose Jette has before this written to you about the enclosure which was added to one of your letters; and probably she has also told you that all my letters have arrived *cut open,* but that none have come open by chance, and that *no one,* except Jette and myself, is acquainted with your secret. Dear Ernst, upon the whole I am tranquil, and always full of unbounded confidence in you in *every* respect. But you may conceive how very easily even an insignificant circumstance upsets this tranquillity. However, I thank you heartily for not concealing anything from me; for it is an inexpressible comfort to me to know everything concerning you . . .

I feel with you how much satisfaction you must derive from the extensive sphere of your activity, more especially as you are so confident of success. I am now so closely bound to you, that everything that moves you goes over into my being also. The intensified feeling of life, awakened in you by the consciousness of the greatness of the results which you will, in some measure, be instrumental in bringing about, reacts upon me, and I feel myself of greater significance. Oh, my Ernst! now that you love me, and that I am one with you, I am so proud, and feel myself of so much importance, in spite of the deep humility which still dwells in me, and which I never can or ought to renounce.

I had still a kind of vague feeling, as if it were not so much that you were thoroughly happy through me, as that you desired to make me and the children happy; but now your dear letters have given me the blissful assurance that you really love me with all your heart. This feeling is too delightful! See, during the whole of our acquaintance I have ever felt as if I ought not to attribute to myself the peculiar love which you bore to me, for that it was in reality the beautiful relations and circumstances amid which I lived, and which you longed to behold, that attracted you towards me. I never could believe that my simple self could be so dear and so interesting to you. . . . . .

Yes, my Ernst, most willingly would I have been at your side during the period of tumult and danger, and I felt it a privation not to share all with you. But as this cannot be, let us wait patiently for the time when you will be able to make the necessary arrangements without exerting yourself overmuch, and be assured that the sweet hope in my heart restrains all impatience, and that, though parted from you, I shall feel quite content here, while I live through your life with you, and enjoy in advance all the delights of the future. Do not understand what I have said as arising out of anxiety lest you might be imprudent in this respect, but merely out of the desire that you should not exert yourself to hasten our union more than you would otherwise have done, because of the longing I expressed. I would not have written this, had I not promised my sympathizing sisters to advise you not to do anything precipitately. I, for my part, know how unnecessary this is, and there is not a thing regarding which I have not the most unbounded confidence in your prudence and your judgment.

[cccxvii.]   *7th October.*

. . . . . How Jette and I have laughed at your odious qualities, with which she was to make me acquainted!

As yet I have not been able to get anything out of her, and if it be nothing more than what I have sometimes heard others complain of, namely, your quickness of temper and the short way in which you answer when any one says anything that you disapprove of, I look upon this as one of my little delights; for in real earnest you never can be angry with me, and in real earnest I can never be hurt by what you say, but I shall pretend to be so, and then will follow a reconciliation in the grandest style, and that will be delicious. . . . .

I often think of Eleanore with deep emotion. The thought that your whole heart was given to her moves me strangely, and you will readily believe that everything which at that time constituted your deepest life, and filled your whole soul, is very sacred to me. It sometimes occurs to me that you must feel that the happiness which you look forward to in union with me cannot be so great as that which you would have enjoyed had she become yours at that time; and though it would be a far greater delight to me had you not this feeling, nevertheless, should it in reality exist, it will not distress me. I do not know how it is, but I have a firm conviction, which makes me thoroughly happy, that *at present* no one is nearer and dearer to you than I am. I feel as if Eleanore would not have belonged more entirely to you than I do, but you loved her with the fire of youth, and with an ardent desire to save her.

[cccxviii.]   *17th October.*

. . . . . I cannot express to you what pleasure you give me by what you say of your love for the children. Oh, I can quite conceive it, for I feel how I should love your child, had you one—and how I love our children, more especially because they are Ehrenfried's, and because in them only he still lives to us! What a felicity that you are to be their father! but how can you speak of thankfulness towards me? what shall I, then, do with all the thanks with which my heart is overflowing, and which you refuse to accept?

. . . . Oh, Ernst, what overwhelming maternal anxieties I should feel, were it not for you!

It is so delightful to hear you say that I already contribute my share to all that is beautiful and excellent that emanates from you, and I take it quietly, feeling that I can accept it in all humility and without contradiction, because it is not to me personally that it is owing, but to that which is really divine in our love. Yes, Ernst, I will take a deep interest in everything that occupies you as soon as I am able to comprehend it.

I received yesterday a few very hearty lines from Hermann Baier. He said that he could not return the greeting I had sent him through his mother, without a feeling of reverence for the providential manner in which my life had been guided, and that the serenity and composure which had borne me through all my trials must have been more than what the world calls faith and prayer. Dear Ernst, I do not exactly understand what he means by more than faith and prayer. Does it not seem as if he were speaking of an immediate working of God in the soul, of strength and tranquillity *given*, not in the manner in which they are given to every pious, yearning soul, but as if actually let down into the heart from on high? Perhaps what I am saying is somewhat confused, but I am determined not to be diffident any more in speaking to you. Do tell me if you think he can have meant that, and if you also believe in such workings of grace, not as a general benefit open to all, but as a special gift bestowed upon a few? . . . . .

Schleiermacher to Charlotte von Kathen.

[cccxix.]   *Berlin, 20th October,* 1808.

Dearest Lotte, just as you picture to yourself my life, happy and beautiful as it will be in future, without the distance in time impeding you, so also, I believe, I can take a correct view of yours, without being misled by the fluctuations which occur in it. I fully understand that these have in reality their immediate source in your nature and in your position, and I agree with the opinion that, although the evil may be mitigated, it cannot be cured. But for this very reason, dear Lotte (I am sure you will not misconstrue what I am about to say), although I sincerely sympathize in all your pains and troubles, I have never, in thinking of you, said to myself, "poor Lotte," except in regard to those matters which might really be improved, and which, I believe, you have now improved, as you have given the care of your house-keeping into other hands. When we subtract these and other such cares, dear friend, you are to me with all your woes—of which, indeed, a sufficient number remain—a new proof of the fact, which I have often observed in general, and which is constantly being confirmed by special experiences, that the fate of each individual, when we take a comprehensive view of it, is in immediate harmonious relation with his inner, most individual being; and I should not, therefore, wish it to be otherwise in your case. To all those who are capable of understanding you, your entire nature develops itself most beautifully in the position in which you are placed, and I, for instance, can very well imagine you placed in different circumstances in which I should not have learnt to know you so thoroughly as I do now. But, above all things, do not lose patience, more particularly not with yourself, and begin as early as possible to carry out your prudent resolution to spare yourself.

About myself I have nothing to tell you, except that I am full of joy and happiness. I feel every day more and more what felicity is mine now, and will be mine in future; and in regard to all outward matters, I entertain the most perfect confidence and trust. I have never complained : as soon as I had recovered from the first heavy blow, I felt, thanks to all you dear ones, that my life was still very rich in blessings ; but what were they compared to what I now possess! And how many times multiplied is not my present happiness, by the satisfaction with which it is regarded by all who love us. Yet when I think of all that I ought to do, all that **may** be expected of me, now that a happiness has been bestowed upon me, so far beyond my deserts, and so much greater than I had ever hoped for, then, indeed, I am a little alarmed. But not much: for, in reality, I feel more vigorous and energetic than ever, and it seems to me that everything I undertake must succeed. To think that it is already a quarter of a year since, and that another half year must still elapse! Since this new epoch in my lifetime seems to fly doubly as quick as before, and I can quite fancy that when Jette and I have grown old and gray, we will still feel as if only a few days had gone by. Dear, precious sister, you will derive much joy from witnessing our life, not only in case, as I look forward to with confiding faith, God showers blessings and grace upon us, but also, should life now and then turn its shadowy side towards us. Care and sorrow also belong to life. Indeed, did I not begin by giving Jette anxiety? Causeless anxiety, it is true, but it was delightful to see how she bore it; and now I know as well as if we had lived through all kinds of troubles together, what she will be to me in every trial and every emergency. . . . . You have, by this time, provided well for all your elder children, dear friend; that is capital! and you may now give yourself up the more freely to the little ones. Regards to your whole house, from your

SCHLEIER.

Schleiermacher to Henrietta Herz.

[cccxx.]   *Berlin, 20th October, 1808.*

. . . . The little excursion proved very pleasant, though undertaken without the ladies. At first Reimer and I determined to go on foot; but as a Mr. Von Lützow, a friend of Fritz Dohna, and a delightful man, joined our party, and he had luggage with him, which we could not possibly carry with us when on foot, we took a carriage. Steffens and Blanc we met in Dessau already, and you may suppose that our joy was great. Steffens was more lively and in better health than he had been for a long while, and he had left his wife and child in equally good health. We were just the same to each other as ever, and rejoiced at the prospect of living near each other in future, and talked over all that we would do if necessary, to promote the plan. We spent a whole day very pleasantly in Wörlitz, though it rained : on the way thither I told Steffens about Jettchen. You know him, and can therefore picture to yourself his heartfelt satisfaction. He also thought that it was the happiest thing that could have befallen me, and that it had come about just in the right way. We traversed the garden in all directions, and in spite of the rain, we much regretted that we had not all those that we loved gathered together in that beautiful spot. Lützow, who had business to transact with the hereditary prince, and also other matters to attend to, could not be with us the whole time, but, to my great delight, he has fallen over head and ears in love with Steffens. We could get no private carriage to take us back again, and I did not venture to undertake the journey on foot in the bad weather, as I was to preach early on Sunday morning, and under the most favourable circumstances, we could not in that way reach home until late on Saturday evening. We were in consequence obliged to travel post in an open *calèche*, and during a very cold night. From Potsdam we continued the way on foot, in order to get ourselves warm again, and thus we arrived half a day earlier than we had expected. Poor Nanni had looked forward with great pleasure to this journey, yet she bore the disappointment beautifully. I am pleased to find that she has made so much progress in your affection; she is in truth developing herself more satisfactorily every day, and her inner being would certainly never have been brought out in this way in Pless. We get on admirably together, but more especially since our visit to Rügen, which has given a new impetus, as it were, to everything that is good and beautiful. . . . . But tell me, my most precious old lady, is it not also owing to Jettchen, and because since my engagement to her I have been taken more especially into your good graces, that you value my odious qualities so very lightly? Have you forgotten the black looks which you all used to accuse me of, and my levity in regard to economical matters, and many other defects ? But now let me read you a lesson, dear Jette, in reference to what I find very strange, namely, that you should think that I was doing you injustice, when I said that you discerned my foibles more clearly than any one else. Must not the most intimate friendship lead to the most intimate knowledge, and is it not one of its great advantages, that a friend loves a friend with all his faults, whereas by others he may be loved merely because the faults have not been discovered? What a strange impression it makes upon me, dear Jette, to hear you call me *great*, I cannot describe. You know that I hate so-called modesty, and that I know pretty well what I am worth; but greatness I must confess I cannot discover in myself. . . . .

I wonder whether I shall show any talent for educating children—I, who know not in the least how to educate myself or to make anything out of myself! I trust exclusively in God and in love, which are but one. Yes, if God keeps His promise in regard to me also, and gives me understanding with the office, the children will be the joy of our lives— these children—and, perhaps, others. Shall I confess to you, dear Jette, that I cannot get rid of the strange presentiment that I shall never have other children than these? A thousand times I have repeated to myself that this presentiment originates in my old habit of looking upon my union with Eleanore as one that would be childless. A hundred times I have laughed at myself for entertaining it, and yet I cannot get rid of it. Can you picture to yourself a little Schleiermacher? Sometimes when I succeed in doing so, I am ready to go crazy with joy. . . .

Schleiermacher to Henriette von Willich.

[cccxxi.]   *Berlin, 22nd October,* 1808.
       It is rather late, yet I must chat away the midnight hour with you. Scold you I will not; indeed, I feel more inclined to tell you, that were it possible, your last two letters

would have made you even dearer to me than before, because of the beautiful manner in which you have given expression to the essential nature of love, and have shown how the greatest and the smallest, the most solemn earnestness and the sweetest sportiveness, are therein blended; and how each mood—the devout, and the pious, and the self-devoted, in which one would willingly encounter death for the other, or both would willingly die together—bears at the same time in itself the full consciousness of all the sweet delights that have been enjoyed during the brightest and most light-hearted moments of life; just as, during the latter, we feel with unmixed earnestness all the energy, the fulness, and the depth of existence. Yet after all, my glorious Jette, there is no truth in this having made you dearer to me, for I always knew that these feelings dwelt in you. Nevertheless, each new revelation of your life is to me a new addition to my life, my joy and my happiness; and the same, I trust, you will feel as regards me, only in a different way. Do not, therefore, imagine that our blessed married life is to be all in all to *you*, but that it cannot be so to *me*, because science also has claims upon me. Herein you are quite mistaken. My life, in connection with science and with the Church, and, if God gives His blessing, as I trust He will, also in connection with the State, must not be separated from your life or be foreign to you; but you will and ought to take the greatest interest in it. Where this is not the case there is no true marriage. This will not, however, necessitate your understanding all the sciences and the terms belonging to them; but my endeavours and the results of them you will always be able not only to witness and to understand, but also to share in, so that it may be said that nothing has succeeded without you, nothing has been completed without you, that you have borne your part in all that I have accomplished; and thus you will be able to rejoice at my activity in the world as if it were your own. You will witness and feel, how at times I am more, and at others less, successful; how sometimes thoughts well forth in abundance; how, at other periods, indolence holds me spell-bound. You will quicken and refresh my slumbering soul, and I will let it flow into yours and fill you with its abundance. For this reason, I should be much pleased if I could manage to have my study and your sitting-room contiguous and communicating by a door, so that we could always be near to each other.

Shall I begin from the present to give you from time to time an account of what I am doing? At this moment matters are proceeding rather irregularly; on one side I get on pretty well; on another, very badly. I have just finished the translation of a dialogue in Plato, and am engaged in revising it, and in smoothing and polishing particular passages. This is a wretched business; for I seem to have worked with less attention than usual, chiefly because of the many interruptions that occurred, and which prevented me from keeping the preceding parts sufficiently clearly before me. And now the correction goes on very slowly, because I find it so tiresome, and I must take care not to sit at it too long at a time, lest I should do the work negligently. This arises from the fact that I have never known, and never shall know, how to exert myself as energetically as other people in my position do. In addition to this, I feel at present specially called upon to elucidate and complete for my own satisfaction my thoughts and views relative to the state and the social community in general. These thoughts are, therefore, for ever commingling with my other occupations, and give me a glorious consciousness of life and productiveness. I also feel a strong inward inducement to deliver lectures upon this subject; this is always my first resource; for in so doing, the entire matter presents itself most distinctly before me, and gradually works itself out; and I will, therefore, make arrangements to commence the lectures in three or four weeks. Then I shall be again in such full activity in the cathedra as I delight in, and you will see how well I shall get on. As yet I have only preached here once, but in future I believe I shall do so more frequently. . . . . I have a strong presentiment that I shall remain in this place; and under such conditions as I expect soon to see established, I should much prefer it. I picture everything to myself in very rosy colours, though I will not deny that I can imagine something more delightful still; but, perhaps, that also will come by-and-by. . . .

I dare say Hermann Baier meant no more by what he wrote to you, than that it was something higher than what the world calls faith and prayer; for can there be anything higher than true faith and prayer? It is true the divine dwells in man in very various ways; in some individuals it manifests itself more spontaneously and energetically than in others; and even in its highest and most glorious manifestations it appears very differently under different circumstances, sometimes rather as induced, at other times more as immediately given; but even that which is immediately given must always be based upon what the individual has spontaneously created in himself; it is the blessing that attends faith and prayer. Everything divine is the common good of all mankind; but to some it comes through others, and to all it comes at one time differently from another. Any other distinction I do not know. But we will speak a good deal about these matters on future occasions, my sweet daughter, and your father will explain to you as much as he himself knows and feels.

Have you given Hermann Baier a very friendly message from me? I cannot tell you how much I like him. He pleases me very much, and I have taken him completely into my heart. I do not know whether he feels the same towards me; but never mind, a little fond of me, I dare say he is, and I look forward with great pleasure to a letter from him, if he will be true to his word. In regard to dear old Mrs. B——, I have no doubt you will know how to take my place, for you are aware of how much I love and honour her. The bond that exists between us is a peculiar one, and has been knit without our having interchanged many words; I might almost say there is something inexplicable and mysterious in it. . . . .

I am at present full of hope, feeling as if it would be given to me to effect a great deal, and as if my outward life also would be full of pleasantness and sweetness. This is, because I believe that with you I shall obtain every blessing that Heaven can bestow upon me, and because I cannot picture to myself your sweet nature and my life with you, as in any way troubled. Sweet heart, how I shall dote upon you, how I shall carry you on my hands, and yet, how full of earnestness our life shall be! Do you not also think, dear Jette—*I* am proud to think so—that never have children been given into the hands of a second father with greater confidence and more sincere joy? Oh, how happy I am through you! how beautifully the whole of our new life is based upon love and friendship! And Ehrenfried's love and friendship are its first and firmest foundation.

A short while ago I passed a hearse; and all at once I thought of my own funeral. In imagination I saw you once more as a widow; but I was not distressed; I felt more vividly than ever the hearty sympathy of my many excellent friends. I knew that you would have the consciousness of having made me thoroughly happy, and that I had fallen asleep satiated with all the good that earth can bestow, and I knew that this feeling would comfort you. It seemed to me that though sad, you must feel inwardly rich and content, while possessing the memory and the many mementos of the happy life we had led together. Have you not also thought of death, since our engagement, and in the same way? . . . .

[cccxxii.]   *Berlin, 29th October, 1808.*

Dearest Jette, I have just been reperusing some of your letters. Tea was over, I had read a couple of songs of the Iliad to Nanni; and in what more delightful manner could I conclude the week? Strange to say, on this reperusal several of the passages seemed to me quite new: how can this be, as I have certainly never been guilty of overlooking anything in your letters? It is true, that the same happens to me in regard to the books I like the best; each time I read them over again the chief impression which I receive is determined by some special passage or other, and the rest remains as it were in the background.   I had thus quite forgotten that at one time, poor child, you were troubled by bad dreams about me. . . . Dreaming is a pleasure which I hardly know; it is as if I had barely vivacity and fancy enough for my waking life, and must not therefore draw upon the store when asleep.   I ever fall asleep with your sweet image in my mind, but in dreams it does not appear to me; however, as soon as I awake I find it there again.   I was also struck by what you wrote about your different states of mind, during the periods when you bore your children under your heart.   No doubt the ruling state of mind of the mother, and the peculiar disposition which is being formed in the child, must in a great measure be identical, and herein, partly, lies the truth of the idea of hereditary sin, which for this very reason is made to descend originally from the mother and not from the father: but of criminality and blame there can hardly be a question in any case, and at all events in yours most certainly not.   For consider, it is as yet by no means determined whether it is not as much the nature that is being formed in the child which is the cause of the mood of the mother, as the latter, that is the cause of the former.   These moods seem sometimes quite foreign to the mother's nature, or at least mental conditions which have appeared very rarely and very vaguely, assume suddenly a predominant character—or a state of mind which had not been experienced for years and had been quite forgotten, suddenly reappears.   A woman in this condition is placed, in a very immediate manner, under the sway and the care of infinitely plastic nature.   Nature cannot indeed oppose her freedom, can force nothing upon her which is in reality foreign to her; but, during this period, it rules with wonderful power over the combinations and relations between the various energies and tendencies, and probably little more is left to the mother than to introduce, as it were, a genial temperature into the state that has been assigned to her, and to keep pure the note that has been struck, and carry it through harmoniously by the aid of reason.   Thus from the very beginning self-culture and education are identical, and in regard to neither is it ever permitted to use force; thus from the very commencement, energetic reciprocal action is established, in which each part has but to observe itself exclusively, and for the rest to let holy nature rule.

Shall I tell you in what light your special case appears to me? If you were in reality so violent and self-willed a child as you describe, you must be resigned if it has pleased nature to develop this germ anew in your child. But do not reproach yourself for this. Who would not shrink back in fear from the thought of becoming father or mother, if nature could be supposed to single out some one particular quality in the parent's character and isolate it in the child; and, alas! my dearest Jette, I, in whom dwells every corruption without exception, would, above all others, have reason to fear to be a father; and the more you loved me and the more thoroughly you adopted my being into yours, the more reason I should have to fear. This would, indeed, be the most fearful way in which God could visit the sins of the fathers on the children; but it would not be just, except in those cases in which nature can derive nothing but sin from the essential being of the parents. Therefore you cannot impute any guilt to yourself; for you cannot but see that there are also in your child some of those elements in virtue of which you are the sweetest, loveliest, most charming of beings. . . . .

The above are some points in my deepest conceptions of love and marriage; but I have never seen the matter as clearly as now, that I look upon your children as my own, and that I live in the sweetest, most blissful hopes.

Henriette von Willich to Schleiermacher.

[cccxxiii.]   *1st November.*

. . . . . It is quite curious how free I feel in regard to you; I could speak to you about anything and everything. You are not to me as a man, but like a delicate maiden, so innocent, so like a child, and this is to me a delicious feeling.

How delightful it is that you are living in the midst of such activity, and that you feel sufficient energy to undertake still more; and what a dear you are to wish me to take part in it all! Could I but express to you how I feel all the good that is flowing in upon me through you. What new life dawns upon me each time I receive a letter from you! These last days I have been again rather depressed and dissatisfied with myself; but no sooner had I read your letter than the mist vanished, and all became clear and serene in my heart.

Sometimes I feel overwhelmed when I think of all the greatness and all the delights that await me in my new life. Although it gives me infinite satisfaction to see that you are neither proud nor vain of what you are, I am, nevertheless, not a little so; and I anticipate with no little pleasure being the wife of a celebrated man. If only it were not damped by my fear of the figure I shall cut under the circumstances. . . . . Yes, my darling Ernst, if my room could be next to yours, that would be charming. I shall always come in very softly, and look over your shoulder at ·what you are writing, without disturbing you, and kiss the hand with which you are not writing, so as not to interrupt you. Is it quite decided now that the university is to be in Berlin? I must confess that the beautiful royal residence has great attractions for me; and when I think of the glorious concerts and operas and other such things! Music has an extraordinary effect upon me, and is most soothing to my nature. My Ernst, how much that is delightful you bestow upon me, in addition to the best of all, yourself! . . . . Do not either forget the historical book. I have been reading Anacharsis's *Travels in Greece.* What an indescribable enjoyment it is to catch such glimpses of the ancient world! I grasp quite greedily at everything calculated to enlighten me on the subject.

———

Schleiermacher to Henriette von Willich.

[cccxxiv.]   *Berlin, 4th November, 1808.*

A full fortnight you have not, after all, allowed me
to pine, darling; for to-day, after dinner, just as I was indulging in a lounge on the sofa, your little letter arrived.
It has amused me very much, though it might as well
have given rise to very serious reflections; for only conceive, it has suddenly disclosed to me a very important
difference existing between us. I also, it is true, hope that
the time between this and April will pass swiftly; but, nevertheless, it seems to me tremendously long, and I feel so impatient that I would fain spur it on with vigorous deeds and
sweet, loving words, to make it speed more swiftly still—and
to you April seems so near! Nanni—who was just standing
behind me, and to whom I said that I would write and
tell you, as I do by the present, that I supposed it was
because the time seemed so short to you, that your letter
also was so short—made a very serious face and said, " If
her letters become short there will be reason to fear that her.
love also will gradually vanish, and then the best of the
whole will be lost, even before you ever come together."
But then, again, she said that she was sure it was because
she had preached so much to you about all that must be got
ready first.

Oh, you darling women, how happy you are with your
spinning and weaving, and linen chests, and with your
thoughts of all the tables and chairs, &c. that have to be
rubbed down, which makes time seem so short to you, that
you fear the joiner will never get through all the polish
and that your pretty little fingers will never get through all
the stitching until the bells are ringing for the wedding!
However, do not despair; I dare say you will get ready!
But, on the other hand, think of me. I know that before I
shall be able to call you mine, I shall have time to deliver
two long courses of lectures, to make myself master of a new

science, and to translate the whole of a thick volume of *Plato*, besides to preach numerous sermons, and, perhaps, if the spirit comes over me, to write some other book. And with all this you expect that the time is not to seem long to me? I entreat you, my own Jette, consider what an amount of life and mental activity is consumed in all these occupations, and share in my feeling! or if this be not enough for you, consider that if we should live together for a period only twenty times as long as the time between this and our marriage, you will have a husband more than half a century old. Now, my child, I am sure this must make an impression! You may suppose what effect was produced upon me when I read your entreaties not to hurry on matters, if it should cause me great exertion or anxiety; and how I rejoiced at your patience —rejoiced in real earnest, not in joke nor in mockery; for what a delicious combination will it not be—your patience and my impatience!

My sweet Jette, you do not as yet know the extent of my indolence, you do not know that I never over-exert myself. Never, by any chance, do I work more or less than exactly suits me at the time, than the spirit moves me or the work spurs me on; and anxiety I know not. But life is short, and time is noble, and we ought to lose as little as possible. All this stirred in my heart, while I was lounging on the sofa. . . . .

For the rest, when I tell you that I feel more secure, and that I see more clearly the more freely you open your mind to me, I do not mean thereby to say that I had previously found anything wanting, or felt that there was anything obscure in you; it is nothing but the ever-increasing fulness of the life of love, another phase of the ever-renewed feeling of happiness! . . . .

Have you also read aloud to Lotte passages from those letters in which there is no poetic sentiment? I hope you do not wish me to write poetry to you. . . . . Upon the whole, place before me the letters of ten loving couples, and without looking at them I will venture to wager that nine of the ten are nothing to be compared to ours. On these latter I place a very high value, and am fond of revelling in my half of the riches; and when a woman, like our excellent P——, tells me, that she has listened to you with emotion, I believe her, and rejoice at it, and yet I am sure there is no sentimental piping in it, but nothing but what is simple, fresh, straightforward, devotional, tender, in a word, everything like love itself, and expressed without reserve, just as the pen runs, and as the tongue would run. I have, as yet, seen no one here to whom I could have the heart to read any parts of your letters. I am somewhat avaricious of them, and would rather lose, I know not what, than risk throwing away one of your dear words on an auditor, through whose heart they would fail to flash like joy and happiness, because he was thinking of God knows what, while I was reading.

And now, good night! You see that my hour for writing to you is always a late one, in accordance with the old proverb, " After labour rest is sweet;" for to me it is the most delicious rest to lean against you, though only in spirit, and to breathe thy fragrance, sweet blossom of my heart.

Schleiermacher to Henrietta Herz.

[cccxxv.]　　　　　　　　　*Berlin, 5th November*, 1808.

Happy beyond measure I am, that is quite true, I feel it; but whether a great talent would have been lost, had this happiness not befallen me, that is not yet quite decided, dear Jette. As regards my relations to my wife, I believe it; for I see clearly that there will be a vigour, a purity, and a completeness in our married life which it will be well worth witnessing, and to which, I trust, I shall be able to boast of having contributed my part. But whether I shall show any talent in regard to the children, I know not as yet; in great matters, perhaps, yes; but, as far as concerns the petty details of life, I feel still very deficient in skill and very timid, although it seems to me that I am daily acquiring new light in reference to the subject.

Schleiermacher to Henriette Von Willich.

[cccxxvi.]   *9th November*, 1808.

. . . . It is very extraordinary, and at the same time very delightful, that our thoughts so often meet at the same moment on the same subject. When you wrote to me to beg me write to W——, my letter to him had just been sent off; and now you write to me about your taking the communion, and I mentioned the same subject in my last to you. However, I may boast of having managed the matter better than you, for I have informed you beforehand. This time, I suppose in vain, for probably you will not like to commune so soon again as the 27th, though I do not see why you should shrink from so doing. Should you object, we must fix some other day later; for we ought, during this period of sweet expectation, to perform on the same day this most touching and sublime religious act, that our thoughts may dwell with each other the while. Upon the whole, I trust our married life will be as pious as it will be serene; and during breakfast, or at any other time when we can manage it, we will often read together in the Holy Scriptures, or on them. What you tell me in connection herewith regarding our friend Herz is a matter of great interest to me; but we can do nothing but let her follow her own bent. I am convinced she feels herself the want of this beautiful community.* I have often seen her painfully moved when the subject has been touched upon. I do not know why; but I have long had a presentiment that it will be in Rügen that she will take the final resolution. So much is to be said in favour of the presentiment, that here many outward circumstances would render the step more difficult. However, let us wait patiently for the issue.

In regard to our little Henriette, it will certainly be of the utmost importance that we should early develop the germ of piety in her, which will be the best way of producing inward

* The community of the Christian Church.

equanimity, and, in consequence, outward gentleness. Yes, dearest Jette, if God's blessing be not withdrawn—and why should it?—we will lead a life that will be edifying and strengthening to many, and a joy to all who shall witness it. . . . .

I preached to-day in the cathedral with great fire, and entirely to my own satisfaction, which is by no means always the case. Do you know, darling, when we are married, you must not always go to my church, but also sometimes to hear others. As a general rule, I shall be able to tell you pretty correctly beforehand whether or not you will lose anything by not hearing me. But when you are present, you must be prepared to give me your impression of the sermon, to tell me whether it has pleased you or not, and to point out whatever may have struck you especially. It is a great gratification to me to hear such remarks; for if nothing is said about my sermon, I am apt to think that I have preached badly. However, when you are here, I trust I shall never do that; for you will always inspire me in some way, and the increased happiness of my life will not fail to make my sermons more animated. . . .

Henriette von Willich to Schleiermacher.

[cccxxvii.]   15*th November.*

. . . . . I cannot tell you what a strange state of mind I was in while at church; how vividly you were present to me, although my whole soul was full of devotion; how, in the moments of profoundest worship in the sanctuary, I was so conscious of my love for you, that the feeling of the divine character of this love penetrated me anew, and filled me with rapture. One doubt, however, arose in my mind, and I determined to speak to you at once about it. It is whether I am wrong in calling those feelings religious which are awakened in me by the music in church? For I must confess that I feel quite differently when the service is not accompanied by music. I cannot describe to you how my soul is borne aloft, as it were, by the tones; what a feeling of freedom is developed in me, what a consciousness of the holy and the infinite seems to pervade me. That oppressive weight, of which I lately complained to you, and which I told you made me feel as if my physical being held the spiritual in bondage, and prevented it from pouring itself out in tears and sentiments—that weight seems to be gently lifted off, and my soul moves in unrestrained freedom. And images of the eternal and the infinite, and love to the dear souls whom God has given to me, fill my mind. With what tears and solemn promises I fold, at such moments, our children to my heart! But tell me, my Ernst, is it in accordance with pure Christian feeling, that anything *external* should produce such a powerful religious effect on me—that I require an *external* agency to enable me to lose myself in God? . . . .

Let me tell you, dear Ernst, that I do not quite know what face to make to your question as to whether I wish you to write me poetical letters; I must confess to you that I feel a little hurt at your telling me thus outright, that you believe I place some value on fine phrases and nonsense. . . . . About my letters you say afterwards many delightful things. You, dear man, how can they be so valuable to you? to me it seems each time I am putting one in a cover, that it is hardly worth sending, and then, also, I regret not having worded my thoughts more elegantly, and written more neatly. But no; the spontaneous outpouring of my thought, such as it communicates itself to the pen, is after all the best, when I am writing to you; and indeed I could not write otherwise. And as regards the elegance and neatness, that is only a joke—that is of very little importance; but that many a thought is so imperfectly expressed, that I must console myself with the idea that you know me already so thoroughly that you will be able to supplement what is wanting—I am often quite aware of, but I do not fret at it. . . . .

Can you quite understand me when I tell you that I am sometimes really alarmed when I think of the many allurements in the great royal city? That I fear they may exer-

cise too great a power of attraction over me, because of
the novelty to me, and because I have in reality great taste
for such pleasures as the capital affords? Many things which
we might otherwise enjoy together, I shall be obliged, as far
as I am concerned, to forego, on account of the children. I
can fancy, for instance, when some interesting men are assembled around you in our home, and you are conversing together on such subjects as I am able to understand, how difficult
it will be for me to tear myself away, when the hour strikes
that I ought to go to the children. I have already experienced this on various occasions, and have been obliged to
make a tremendous effort to bring my mind into the com-
placent state in which it ought always to be when I am with
the children.

[cccxxviii.]   *Thursday.*
        .   .   .   . Ah, dear Ernst, in regard to the children,
I am sure I feel the delay even more than you do. I can
often hardly bear to think that the dear little creatures are
held back so long from their father and from the salutary life
they would lead with him. No anxiety can possibly exceed
that felt by a mother, lest she might injure her children!
The sweetest image I can picture to myself is, the children
clinging to you with loving reverence, seated on your knee,
or folded in your arms. Yes, my Ernst, I entirely agree with
you that the religious feeling ought to be early developed in
little Jette. How well I know from my own experience that
a new life, as it were, may spring from this, and I dare say
most people have experienced something of the kind. I was
a very insignificant child, dull, and without sentiments of
affection. But I remember with strange delight the growth
of my first love—love to the invisible Father; and how I
seemed as if born anew, and my feelings were so unerringly
directed towards what is good and true, that even now when
I recall to mind what was then stirring within me, I can find
nothing with which I do not agree, or which I would reject as
false. I felt that the higher life that was born within me was

a gift of the grace of God. I clung to God with indescribable love and yearning, and I often shed the most delicious tears over a simple hymn of Gellert's, or when singing to an andante or an adagio on the piano words of my own composition, which were always of a religious character. As often as I laid bare to God my heart and my life, I never offered up any other prayer than that He would purify my heart, and inspire it with new treasures of love. I was so entirely resigned to His will, that I would have received with equal joy the promise of a life of suffering as of one of happiness. And how strangely secret and mysterious this inner life was! for there was not a soul who would have cared to share it with me. I have often thought of late, how would it have been had you then already been my dear father?

. . . . I fancy the house must be very pretty, and am not a little pleased at this, and I already enjoy in imagination the delight with which I shall enter your room, either for a little chat, or to dust your books, merely for the sake of being about you. For you must try to have all the books in the room. Why should you not line all the walls with shelves? In the study of a scholar, it seems to me, that there can never be too many books. And then I picture to myself the twilight hour, when you will have the children on your knees, and will be telling them stories, and instructing, while amusing, them. And then the evening, when everybody else has retired, and you live for me alone, and we sit a good while longer in confidential chat, you telling me about former times, before I knew you.

Upon the whole, I think everything so well arranged, that nothing is left for me to wish. On the subject of the doubts you all entertain of my talent for housekeeping, I have had a long talk with Jette Herz, and have done what I could to remove hers. For, indeed, she does me injustice; and should you have felt any little uneasiness on this head, let my earnest assurance that it is groundless comfort you. But there is one defect in me, that may seem to you intolerable, if I do not succeed in gradually conquering it, and that is, my dreadful

forgetfulness.   It *is* abominable, and I give you leave to
punish me whenever you detect it.   .   .   .   .

Schleiermacher to Henriette von Willich.

[CCCXXIX.]   *21st November*, 1808.
      I have commenced my birthday, my own dear Jette,
with earnest prayer that it may please God to fulfil the sweet
promise of happiness held out to me, and to continue it to me
when it has in reality become mine, and to purify and sanctify
me through and through, so that I may worthily enjoy it and
use it!   I have lifted up my heart to Him with deep-felt gratitude for the wonderful way in which He has guided me
through bitter suffering, and through periods of hopelessness,
to the purest and highest bliss!   And, with profound humility,
I have felt that I am far too unworthy of the mercy which
the Lord has shown unto me. You see that you were included
in my thanksgiving and in my prayer, for how could I thank
and pray except with you, and for you, my treasure, my price-
less jewel!   I have sought support in you to-day as I shall
seek it in you the whole of my life.   On your bosom I have
wept the sweetest and most pious tears!   .   .   .   .   When
subsequently I went in to breakfast, Nanni brought me, from
the other room, the beautiful presents on a little table, the
whole being wreathed round with the lovely garland.   I
cannot tell you how fresh it was, and how prettily the little
immortelles peeped forth from the moss; and they were
gathered at the *Brunnenau*, in the traces, as it were, of the
first footsteps of our love.   Yes, everything that shall grow
out of this shall ever be to us as immortal flowers.
      You wish to know what I am doing : ah, dearest, this time
I am a little ashamed to answer your question; I am doing
little or nothing, and have, perhaps, more reason to be displeased with myself than you have.   It grieves me that you
should again have had one of these fits of despondency; but
it gives me great pleasure and great hope for the future, that
you attribute to my letters the power of banishing them.

How much more effectually shall I not exercise the power when I have you here ! When you feel depressed, come to me at once, and I will comfort and cheer you. But to return to myself—I have to complain of the fact that the new connections I have formed rob me of an amount of time which is out of proportion to the little good I can effect, though I do indeed often keep matters straight, and prevent many a precipitate step. In addition to these occupations, I shall now have the lectures. As regards these, you will have many opportunities of observing how much time they rob me of, when they first begin and before I have got into the vein, though, in fact, the time is not spent upon them, but is wasted in irresolution as to the plan to be followed. But the further I advance in the exposition of my subject, the more secure I feel, and afterwards everything seems to go of itself. In *Plato* I have not for a long time done anything worth speaking of, and the other matters which I intended to take in hand have also remained in abeyance. But things shall not be left long in this state. However, follow my example, and do not despond. It is not given to everybody to be equally full of energy, and to have the same freshness of feeling at all times ; and more especially it is not given to a man who is still single. I know that in regard to myself, also, many things will be improved as soon as you shall be here. But tell me, why do you demand that religious emotion should always express itself in flowing tears? Dearest Jette, I like better the tears that merely suffuse the eye. . . . .

Do you often kiss the children for me? Do you tell them under what circumstances I shall love them best, and under what others I shall be displeased with them? . . . .

Schleiermacher to Henrietta Herz.

[cccxxx.]   *Berlin, 21st November, 1808.*
     Not until now, that all have gone, and the day has reached its utmost limit, have I been able to sit down to write a few hearty words to you, my dear, faithful old friend, and

to thank you for your affectionate remembrance. Yes, in
truth, I did wake up in a very different mood, and have felt
very differently the whole day from what I ever did before.
Such sweet and such certain hope, that it is in fact as good as
delightful reality ; such firm trust, such a rich and full life :
dear Jette, how shall I render myself worthy of it ? and
what account shall I be able to give of it to God and men ?
Well, I will do my best ; it is to be hoped that a door will
soon be opened to me for new and extensive activity : and
then there are the sweet children whom God has confided to
me, and to whom I hope to be a loving and rational guide ;
and then I have all of you, my friends, whose lives I am to
help to make easy and happy, and with whom I am to share
the rich treasures of my life. In short, if God's grace be not
withdrawn from me, I shall be one of the richest of mortals.
And you are right : I may, with thankful and devout humility,
accept the paradise God has opened to me, as something to
which I have a claim. I have taught so much about the
beauty and holiness of family life, that I ought to have an
opportunity of showing that what I have taught has been to
me more than empty words, and that the doctrine has in truth
sprung from my deepest feelings and from my inward energy.
And this I have more especially to show, that wedded life,
such as it ought to be, interferes with no duty, does not prevent friendship, devotion to science, or the most self-sacrificing
life for the fatherland. What a magnificent opportunity do
not the existing circumstances afford me for showing this, and
how beautifully Jette acquiesces in my views and helps me to
carry them out !

Schleiermacher to Henriette von Willich.

[cccxxxi.]   *Berlin, 27th November, 1808.*
        You have not, I suppose, been able to take the com-
munion to-day, dear heart ? Well, at all events, I was united
with you in spirit, and thought of you most tenderly. I
prayed for us both, and was in a very devout and exalted

mood. I had preached upon the Song of Praise to the Virgin Mary, and very much to my own satisfaction, although I had hardly had time to prepare myself until the morning. But very frequently I am most successful under such circumstances, provided there be not any inward drawback. Dearest Jette, I look forward with intense satisfaction to the time when you will receive the Holy Communion from my hands; for the regulations here will not allow of our partaking it together. The latter would, indeed, also be very delightful; for in this performance of the holy act in common, the wedded union is more distinctly expressed. But it will, no doubt, make a peculiar impression on you, when you see me standing before you as the proclaimer of the grace of God. . . . .

I have been much touched by a letter from Steffens, in which he speaks of the prospect there is of his living near us, and of participating in our life. I have spoken to you about Steffens, and of the great love I bear to him ; but you can hardly be aware of what importance he is to me in regard to my whole sphere of activity, and how, in regard to the young people whose minds we have to work upon, he and I seem necessarily to belong to each other, and how he stimulates me and carries me forward, more than any other man I know. . . . .

[cccxxxii.]   *Wednesday Evening.*

Though I have not been able to write, my thoughts have been constantly occupied with you. I have been sitting for my portrait at the request of a friend. Before me, as the point of direction for my eyes, I had a very good copy of Raphael's glorious picture of *John the Baptist in the Wilderness.* The picture inspired me with earnest and devotional feeling; and as this made me think of what you wrote to me about the vivifying effect of art on the religious sentiment, you were brought very vividly before my mind. Dearest, be not over anxious, and do not try to separate what God himself has intimately united. Religion and art belong together as soul and body. When your inward feelings are strongly moved and seek an outward expression, they, no doubt, pour themselves out in song, in consequence of your natural talent for music; and so also in the church, music and singing are the common bond between, and the proof of the emotions stirring, in all, and this community of feeling again heightens the emotions of each individual. I should be quite sorry if you were indifferent to the music and the singing in the church, and if you believed that the same feelings could be awakened without their help. The organ, more especially, is an invention that entirely belongs to Christianity; so much so, indeed, that it is hardly used for any other service. In the church in which I am to preach in future, the organ has unhappily been destroyed by the French, and the accompaniment to the singing is at present merely played upon a little hand-organ. It has always been one of my dearest wishes to have a hand-organ in my house, so as to be able to play choral hymns morning and evening. As regards paintings, I am very sorry that they have been in so great a measure banished from our churches; but the time for restoring them has gone by, and we must resign ourselves to the fact. It is true that through art, feelings may even be awakened in such persons as are not in the least pious, and which they are, nevertheless, deceived into believing truly devotional; but the heightened feeling with which they inspire the pious, is, no doubt, really religious. To those who are receptive for their influences, there must be something truly divine in them; for it is the innermost living spirit of nature that speaks through them. And when you rejoice at the thought of the concerts at the Singing Academy, you may do so doubly, because they perform almost exclusively grand, sacred music. I go there every Tuesday with great pleasure; so, on those evenings, between six and seven o'clock, you may always know where to send your thoughts in quest of me. . .

I had a great deal more to say to you; but what happened? A carriage stopped at the door, a French officer alighted, came up, and requested me to accompany him to Marshal

Davoust.   I found two other gentlemen in the carriage before me, and the upshot of the whole was that the Marshal made a speech to us, in which he informed us that we had been marked as fiery heads and provokers of disorder, and more of the same kind.   To me, it all seemed very amusing; but, though obliged to play the part of interpreter for the others, I behaved with proper decorum.   Do not be alarmed, for the whole affair is a mere nothing.   The other men were perfect strangers to me, and are in no way connected with my friends; the latter, happily, are quite unknown; and it is merely some silly rumour about my sermons that I have to thank for the honour of having been called up.

Berlin, 4th December, 1808.

[cccxxxiii.]

I am vexed with myself for allowing myself to be so absorbed by outward matters, when I have so much to say to you that is far more important.   Yet, in saying this, I feel again as if I ought to make an *amende honorable* to the external things; so true it is, that when one is initiated in the secrets of love and marriage, one gets quite a new feeling of respect for them.   The whole house, with everything that is in it, becomes a sanctuary.   Chairs and tables, all participate in the life that surrounds them—you sit upon the former, you work at the latter, in the wardrobes are the clothes in which your beloved person is clad, and then the sofa on which we are to sit and sulk; in short, before I go further, I desire, in consideration of all this, to make the most ample apologies to the outward matters.

You say you like so much to know what I am doing.   I am sorry to have to answer that at present I am doing very little, and I am longing heartily for a more regular state of things.   I am so often interrupted, particularly by the men engaged in the undertaking you know of, that I find that I made a tremendously false calculation when I reckoned upon finishing a volume of *Plato* before the close of the year.   My lectures, however, are already giving me great satisfaction. With the first two or three of the series, it is true, I am rarely pleased (and this time made no exception), as also I am seldom pleased with the exordiums to my sermons. But, by this time, I have got well into my subject, and so have my auditors; and the whole is taking more distinct form in my mind; and the truth having thus seized me, my task becomes more and more easy; so that sometimes, in the midst of a lecture, some special matter suggests itself to me unexpectedly, without my having previously thought of it, and in this way I myself almost invariably leave the lecture-room with increased knowledge and insight. I cannot describe to you what a delight it is to feel this; and in addition to this, the subjects that I am treating of are so exalted. To explain to the young men the nature of Christianity and of the state, is, in fact, to give them all that they need to elevate the future above the past. Dearest Jette, when hereafter I shall come from the lectures so full of joy at my success, and fly into your arms, so different from when I left home, absorbed in speculation, with wrinkled brow and doleful look, I am sure you will feel delighted. But does it not strike you, as it does me, in connection with what I have just said, that all my beginnings are bad? Now, suppose this should be the case with my married life also? Yes, sweetheart, I cannot guarantee that it will not be; but, if so, do not allow yourself to be alarmed, but feel sure that a better state of things will follow. Displeased we may at times be with each other, just as we are sometimes displeased with ourselves. But this cannot, I think, be expressed in any other way than either by my laughing heartily at your misdeeds, or, if I see that this seriously annoys you, by my laying your little head upon my bosom, and coaxing you and pitying you. How you will treat me under the circumstances I do not know, but discord between us there can never be. . . .

Is it not strange that, as a child, I was exactly as you describe yourself to have been? Without affection, and without sensibility. Love and religion are indeed identical, 'and, therefore, to me also they both came at once, though I cannot exactly say how; and even subsequently I experienced great fluctuations, having fallen back into my original obtuseness for long periods at a time. Strong in my own experience on this point, I have often been able to console parents whose children have lived on in this seeming insensibility, with the assurance that the good would at length awake in them, and hitherto my prediction has always been verified. Our children must, at bottom, be of noble nature, and where this is the case, the life of piety and love which surrounds them, must sooner or later awaken sentiments in accordance with itself. . . . .

[cccxxxiv.]   *Berlin, 15th December*, 1808.

. . . . . That you cling to me with all your heart, that you have such unbounded confidence in me, I cannot hear too often, dearest Jette; and each time you repeat it, I am filled with new joy and delight, and with new gratitude towards God. Were you but already here, that I might share each moment of gladness and of sorrow with you, and seek refuge in your bosom against every trouble ! I stand sadly in need of this just now. There are moments, at present, when I long for you with a very different longing from that which I have felt heretofore—with a longing to pour out my griefs and anxieties to you. I am very much depressed by various matters, not concerning my own affairs, but those of the nation. Our good king has allowed himself to be taken by surprise by a contemptible party, and to be led into a step which will again bring matters out of the safe direction in which they were progressing. It is true, there are still excellent men at the head of affairs ; but who knows how long they will be able to maintain their position against the assaults of the despicable individuals who have again ensnared the king in their meshes ? and thus the country may a second time be brought to the brink of an abyss from which it may not be possible for the well disposed to save it, without having recourse to measures of a very perilous nature. Even were I quite secure against all accidents, it would not be possible for me to communicate these matters

in detail in writing; but I feel the need of speaking to you
in general of everything that weighs heavily upon my heart.
For some days these thoughts have absorbed almost the whole
of my time ; and morning and evening, when undisturbed in
bed, I do nothing but pour out my complaints to you.   All
my occupations are upset, for I am constantly involuntarily
interrupting myself to reflect upon the present state of affairs
and upon means for ameliorating it.   In the pulpit and the
cathedra, alone, I do my duty properly.   Nevertheless, I do
not consider the time devoted to these reflections as lost, for 1
hope my brooding will result in clear and correct views, and
will, perhaps, lead to the development of some useful and permanent activity.   You must not, however, picture things to yourself in too dark colours, my heart's beloved!   Never, I trust,
shall you be pained by seeing me utterly dejected and desponding.   That would, it seems to me, be the worst that could
happen to you, for it could not fail to diminish your esteem
for me, and this, I hope, I shall secure for ever.   My present
anxieties and my present grief have by no means assumed the
character of hopelessness ; on the contrary, I am greatly excited,
and do not only appear full of life and animation wherever I
show myself, but I am so in reality.   And if I were able to
talk matters over with you, I am sure your looks and your
sympathy would inspire me with even greater courage.   You
see, dearest Jette, that it would not be possible for me ever
to keep anything secret from you.   It is essential to me
that you should know all that is passing in me, all that is
stirring my feelings ; and I cannot help pitying those poor
fellows who feel themselves obliged to keep many things
from their wives; their marriage seems to me not to be a
true one.   But it is, in truth, folly to say that women cannot
be depended upon for silence.   I shall trust implicitly in
yours whenever I recommend it to you, and I feel convinced that no fear would wring a secret from you that
I had confided to you.   But just because it is a necessity
of my nature to confide and communicate everything, I
require such a strong, energetic, courageous, and trustworthy

wife as you will be. Thus ought all German women to be, and such the best among them have ever been. . . . .

. . . . In my choice of a historical work for you, I was guided by the very lively interest I once heard you express in the history of antiquity. It is the oldest work on history from that period; and, I trust, that the more you read of it, the better you will like it; and I reckon upon our reading many passages of it together some day. Upon the whole, we will dwell much in antiquity, which is nearer, as it were, to us Germans than to any other nation. Should the civil community around us be organized in the admirable way that I looked forward to a short time ago with more hope than at present, then the comparisons we may institute will be still more interesting. Should matters take a different turn, then the contemplation of antiquity will afford us the best and the noblest consolation. This reminds me that you had begun to read Plato with Ehrenfried. How far did you get? In the volume which is about to appear, the Phædon will strike you as inexpressibly beautiful; it is just suited for such a meditative nature as yours. This delightful work will continue long through our wedded life.

. . . . . I cannot write much more to-day, yet must give myself time to scold a little, because you do yourself such abominable injustice, in saying that you cannot express in your letters all the fondness that you feel. My own Jette, your religious feeling and your tenderness, and the intimate connection between both, which is the most beautiful thing in the world, speak out so bewitchingly in your sweet words, that in reading them I can never help feeling that you cannot possibly derive the same satisfaction from my letters as I do from yours. Altogether, women are the true letter-writers; we men are mere bunglers in the art. And as for writing love, what man can do this as women can, and how few women even can do it as you do, love; so pure, so deep, so lively, and so sweet ! . . . .

Henriette von Willich to Schleiermacher.

[cccxxxv.]   19*th December*, 1808.

     .   .   .   .   How I shall feel when I have been forget-
ful and you laugh at me, I cannot as yet say—but that I shall
not feel hurt, that I know—though I may be vexed with
myself even unto tears. But I must tell you I am not so bad
as to forget something every day. Probably you will only
have occasion to enjoy your laugh about once a week.

It must indeed be a glorious enjoyment to feel as you
do, that you are gaining knowledge and insight for yourself
while imparting it to others. I shall most heartily participate in it, and I know that a share of all that is great and
beautiful in you will always devolve upon me. Dear Ernst,
with what tenderness your wife will receive you when you
return home, and how the little ones will cling around you!
God grant that I may ever on these occasions be able to read
in your eyes, that it is happiness to be with wife and children
—but how could it be otherwise?

Ah! my Ernst, words seem ever poorer, and less capable
of expressing how very dear you are to me.

Schleiermacher to Henriette von Willich.

[cccxxxvi.]   *Berlin*, 25*th December*, 1808.

     Last night, at Reimers, in the midst of the Christmas
festivities and joy, I was seized with dreadful cramps in the
stomach, which kept me in torture all night; I got up this
morning with a remnant of pain, and very exhausted and
miserable, and went thus into the pulpit: but nevertheless, I
preached very much to my own satisfaction, whether equally
so to that of my hearers, I cannot say, for the one does not
always follow from the other. When I had finished, I was,
however, so ill that I should have liked above all things to
go to bed. I can endure great pain without being so far
overcome as to be unfit for society, or for work; but in

consequence of the resistance which I make, I become more exhausted than most people . . . .

I am writing to you in the midst of a state of confusion, which will no doubt be very striking to you when you experience it for the first time here. It is near upon two o'clock of the night, the watchman is blowing his horn with all his might, the drums are beating, and from my window I can see the reflection of a great fire. The arrangements for extinguishing fires are very good, and the damage done is therefore seldom great, for which reason I can give myself up to the glorious impression of the fury of the element, and the victorious struggle which human ingenuity and activity are waging against it. I wish such a fire would break out once in my neighbourhood, so as to necessitate my taking measures of safety, for I should like to know how much presence of mind I should show on such occasions, as I have never yet been tried; and before my happy life with you is to begin, I should like to know how far my capacities go, and what I am worth, in all directions. Upon the whole I have pretty much confidence in myself, yet as long as I have not been tried, I cannot know whether this confidence is well founded. This is another reason why I rejoice at having been, in a certain measure at least, called to combat in a new arena before my union with you; and should I now be so fortunate as to be invited to take part in state affairs, if only temporarily, there will be nothing left for me to wish. Church and science, state and family—these comprise all that concerns a man in this world, and I, happy one, shall be among the favoured few who have had a share in each. It is true it is only in our modern days, when men are separating and dividing all things, that such a combination has become of rare occurrence; formerly every able man might be called upon to act in each of these departments, and thus it must be again in future : it is for this that we are striving. People who rise above the common herd, all seem to rejoice so much at the thought of gaining an undying name in history. I do not know how it is, but I cannot feel that this is worth striving for. The way in which kings, merely because they are such, secure a name for themselves for a couple of centuries at least, is certainly not to be envied. The action of men in the state is always a common action, and we are not just when we ascribe any great result to a single individual. Of science this is still more true, and the coming generation will consist of very poor fellows indeed, if fifty years hence they have not acquired much greater knowledge of all things, than even the foremost of us has in the present day. The artist alone can become immortal in this way, but I am once for all not an artist.

[cccxxxvii.] *Saturday Evening, 31st December, 1808.*

The last day in the year I must end as I hope to begin every day of the most blessed half of the next, with a little chat with you. You have been grieving on my account—that must not be. I would fain see you as cheerful and serene as I am myself. No, dearest, so depressed I could not be by an evil impending, it is true, but not inevitable, as to awake in low spirits. I trust I shall never despair of my country, I have too firm a faith in it, too firm a conviction of its being an instrument in the hand of God, and that we are a chosen people of God. It is possible that all our efforts may prove vain, and that for the present we shall have to submit to hard times; but the country will after a while come forth renewed from its trials. But even this possible failure there is not so much reason to fear now, as when I last wrote to you; but should it be otherwise, you need not fear to find me melancholy and dejected, though vexed and indignant at the gross follies committed you may see me sometimes, and also speculating upon the best means of counteracting and retrieving these follies and mistakes, or upon the measures to be adopted in future should the false step be taken. For the rest I am not as yet decided what path to follow, as the matters that are to determine me are by no means settled. But whatever may happen, I trust that nothing shall keep us separated longer than at first determined. I have pictured to myself

with true delight, how, living in a time pregnant with great
events, I shall ever have you at my side, or know that you
are there, eager to welcome me back when I return home
after having attended to some business or other which has
roused and called for the exercise of all my energies. To live
in times like these is a thing to thank God for; for all goodness is felt more deeply, and the power of representing it in
all its beauty and all its glory is much enhanced. Yes, even
looking only to the pure enjoyments of love, I would rather
introduce you into such circumstances than into a retired
idyllic life. For nothing can be more exalting to love, than
thus to draw within its sphere all that is great in the world
around it. Therefore let us meet cheerfully and blissfully
all that may come.

[cccxxxviii.]   1st *January*, 1809.

    Your letter has come to me as a new-year's gift.
Dear heart, you seem to have felt such joy at the receipt of
the picture, and to have regarded it with such deep and holy
emotions, that I almost regret having written to you so playfully about it. I am afraid you are actually guilty of a kind
of idol-worship in regard to it, my sweet bride; and yet how
can I help rejoicing at this? I am but too well pleased to see
how the eye of love beautifies what it looks at, and I cannot tell
you how much I have been moved by it. But I must seriously
entreat you not to form to yourself an image of me from the
picture, which you may not afterwards recognize in the original. There may be something peculiar and characteristic
about my forehead, but beautiful it is by no means; and as
for my eyes, the artist has not been able to say more for them
than I can. You know how I have ever complained of their
immovable, glassy appearance, and of their being rather blinds
behind which my soul is concealed, than windows through
which it looks out; and how provoked I am at their expressing so little of what there is in me. But you know also there
is a saying—very likely not entirely without foundation—that
when a married couple live long and happily together, they

grow like each other; so it is for you to try what you can make out of these dim eyes.

. . . . Your tea was tried for the first time yesterday, in honour of a very nice fellow, little T——, from Anclam, who was one of my earliest and most faithful pupils in Halle, and between whom and myself there exists great mutual regard. I invited him, together with some other of my former pupils, and among these I always feel thoroughly happy. I used to say formerly, that the time I spent in Halle was the most delightful period of my life, and one that would never return. If I do still say this sometimes to such persons as know nothing of my new happiness, I always punish myself inwardly for telling an untruth; yet there is one feature of that period which I can hardly hope to see repeated, namely, the healthy and hearty manner in which I lived with the young people; for here circumstances will not be exactly the same. However, what can be done in this direction we will do; and I am sure it will give you true pleasure to see me draw the youths around me, and to witness their affection for me.

[cccxxxix.]   *Berlin, 7th January,* 1809.

. . . . . I am glad that the letter containing the so-called confessions has not been so long retarded, as I am thus able to answer it at once. But I should like to seat you first on the sofa, and place myself on a stool or on the floor at your feet, so that I might look up the while into your glorious eyes; and then I would fain assure you, that I do not in the least picture you to myself otherwise than you really are, and that I am altogether incapable of entertaining such preference for one good quality above another, as to exaggerate the one in imagination and to depreciate the other. And as for what you denominate your want of feeling, my own Jette, how long have I not known that? how much have we not already written to each other upon that subject? how often have I not conceded to you as much as I thought was true, and endeavoured to make you comprehend yourself more clearly? This time, let me try whether I cannot make more impression, by representing the matter to you from another side. Real, true feeling is nothing more than the transition from the impression which man receives from without, to action. He who is so strongly affected by the outward events, connected with the ideas which ought to be the guides of man and to constitute his true and higher life, as to adopt the right in action with full consciousness and with confident energy and delight, he feels strongly and truly. Such an individual will—even where immediate action is impossible or not called for—be stirred by emotions and desires which will, so to say, typify right action, and thus give expression to the inward disposition. In this highest sense you cannot possibly say that your feelings are blunt ; you need but question your life and your actions, and they will contradict you. That you are not always so conscious of your feelings as others may be, that is possible, because this consciousness is, in fact, only acquired by the passive excitement of the feelings, by memory or sympathy, or such like, and such excitements are usually rare in persons who lead a healthy active life,—in short, it is not in strength, but in softness of feeling, that you may be slightly deficient. As the two are very seldom found in perfect equilibrium, you have no right to maintain that those natures in which the former preponderates and the latter is held in subjection, are the least noble. At all events, if you be right, I may tell you at once, that you condemn me as well as yourself, for I am exactly like you in this respect ; and in Stralsund, as amid the bustle of the fair, I should, as little as yourself, have experienced grief and deep sadness if, like yourself, I had had some active business to occupy me; for, under such circumstances, passive emotions are not easily roused in dispositions like yours and mine. And when you tell me, that even when you are not occupied or otherwise drawn off by the circumstances of life, you are at times quite incapable of such feelings, because of your inward emptiness and dryness —for I know you will say all this—I reply, that the reason is always the same, though in these cases it is more distant and less apparent. For the rest, I do exactly the same as you. I also speak a great deal about my own coldness, and also sometimes call it want of feeling, though more in sport than in earnest, and people resolutely refuse to believe me, because they think me an excellent man, and they are conscious that their own virtue and piety consist mostly in these passive emotions. But, dear child, I do believe you, only I cannot allow you to call it want of feeling, and to mistrust your own strength, because you suppose it to be connected herewith. Nay, I can no longer resist! I must seat myself by your side, and press you to my heart, and coax and comfort you, after all the torture you have inflicted on yourself. But I cannot help you: it must remain as it was. I can, once for all, not see you otherwise than you are, and I cannot withdraw even one atom of my love from you. . . . . Were I in earnest to reproach you for anything, it would be for failing somewhat in true faith; but even this is only a passing condition, for the prevailing state of your consciousness is, I am sure, that of cheerful, serene, and trusting love. You cannot either seriously think that you are incapable of sharing with me all that is noble, good, and holy; for even should I at times be more strongly affected than you, at other times the reverse will be the case, and more especially as regards your beautiful outbursts of veneration for myself, and we will therefore faithfully help each other. Or do you think that I never feel apathetic, and good for nothing, and indolent? Yet I do not therefore say that I am not worthy of you, but I will ever, on such occasions, seek to strengthen and refresh myself in communion with you.

[CCCXL.]　　　　　　　　　　　　　　　　*Sunday.*

I have been preaching on the blessedness of early piety; but I do not know how I have preached, for no one ever says a word to me about it. I am aware that I touched upon matters, which it is right and good to mention, but how I expressed them I do not in the least know. This I know, however, that the sermon was very long, and that in spite of the mild weather I felt colder than I often do in the severest frost; from which fact a somewhat unfavourable inference may be drawn. Were you here, my own Jette, I should be better informed. Continue to love me with all your heart until we meet, and be as happy as you can.

[CCCXLI.]   *Berlin, 21st January,* 1809.

  I forgot in my last to answer L⸺'s question as to how far we had got in the *Odyssey.* We read yesterday the 17th and the 18th books, and I dwelt with particular emphasis and conviction on the lines :—

    "No cunning shift the stomach's rage can still,
    That rueful source of many a human ill."

Not because of the starvation, which I have never experienced, but because of the cramps, which Homer never experienced. However, it was rather the remembrance than the actual pain that affected me so strongly ; for although I had several severe attacks in the beginning of the week after the catarrhal fever, I believe that I am now really convalescent. We have enough of Homer left for three evenings more, for I always read two books at tea ; when this is finished, I propose to read the *Æneid* to Nanni in Voss's translation, and then I think she will have had enough of ancient poetry for the present. I cannot tell you what a charm Homer has exercised over me again after four and twenty years—only think, longer than you have lived!—for so long it is since I read him regularly through, though in the interval I have occasionally conned over certain passages. The sweet simplicity, the fresh and lively mode of presentation, and the healthy tone of life, that prevail throughout, are most delightful. As I said lately to some one, were I called upon to save three works of antiquity only, not including the Bible, they should be no other than Homer, Herodotus, and Plato. I am always particularly pleased when we are at home in the evening and able to " Homerize." . . . .

 . . . . I have to-day been preparing communicants. This reminds me, that as in future it will of course not be proper that I should take the communion in any other church than my own, I may now make a definite arrangement with you relative to this matter, for besides to-morrow there will only be twice communion there, viz.: on the 5th of March and on the 16th of April. Pray inquire whether you will be able to attend the Lord's table on either of those days; it would be very gratifying to me if it could be so. . . .

[CCCXLII.]   *Wednesday, 25th January*, 1809.

. . . . . I am at present occupied with a very difficult task, namely, the introduction to the Phædon. As yet it refuses to take shape on paper; I am in consequence in a very sad state, such as you will probably have frequent occasions of witnessing in future, and I may, therefore, as well describe it to you beforehand. The matter which I am to produce is not inwardly ripe; something is wanting, but I do not exactly know what. As long as I feel this I cannot possibly begin to write, and I can as little make up my mind to take hold of anything else, and thus the subject that troubles me always remains on the order of the day, without anything essential being done to forward it, though much time is spent in cogitating and turning it over and over. This continues until suddenly I feel inspired and a new light dawns upon me. And only think, I have still eight such introductions to write, which I shall have the same difficulty in producing. But when this is done, then all the work laid out to be finished before my joining you, will be accomplished.

. . . . . I have just received a letter from my sister Lotte, who seems to have had great pleasure in reading your letters to me and also mine to you. She confesses that she is quite in love with you, and that she wishes very much that we could pay our visit to her in Silesia this year already, as she has all kinds of strange doubts as to what may happen next year. For my part, however, I have no presentiment of anything likely to prevent us, either good or evil. She writes that she is despatching a large packet to the island (of Rügen); you will, therefore, soon receive a letter from her without its passing through me, and you will thus be placed on an independent footing in regard to each other, and may in future make as many remarks about me as you like. . . . . .

I shall not be able to devote much time to you to-day, but shall write a few lines not to lose my reputation for answering without delay. The persecution directed against Stein has by no means surprised me. I had, indeed, not anticipated it; yet when it came, it seemed to me like something well known to me, and that I had expected. One thing only has given me pain, and that is, that he has departed in such great haste, which was not at all necessary; I am also sorry that I was not able to see him before. I have sent him word that I congratulate him, for to be declared an enemy of the "great nation," is the highest honour that could befall a public man in our day. If I have not for a long while spoken to you about public affairs, it is merely because things seem sunk in a state of sullen brooding and suspense, which may last some weeks longer. Be not alarmed, for even if I would, I could not remain silent to you, and therefore as soon as a crisis comes on you shall be informed of how far I am affected by it; but do not think that matters are always so serious as I may represent them in the first moment of excitement.

As far as I have been able to learn, Dohna is getting on admirably. He keeps me in tremendous activity. He wishes to have the most circumstantial letters from me every post day, and I can hardly help yielding to his wishes, as I write to him on matters concerning the internal administration, which are exceedingly interesting to myself. That you have read yourself so deeply into the most sorrowful period of my life,* and have sympathized so heartily with me, is a great satisfaction to me. Yes, dear heart, I shall be very happy in future, and you would be astonished if you knew how calm I feel in regard to that period, though I cannot conceive why it should have formed an essential part of my life, if it were not that I learnt then to think more correctly on various points connected with married life; and thus you also, my beloved,

* He had given her his correspondence with Eleanore to read.

have been benefited by it.　From one point of view, you are right in what you say about the unequal relation between husband and wife.　The connection of men with science and art and all the affairs of the community, and the capacity they show in these various spheres of activity, seem so much more important than the avocations in connection with which women develop their talents, that in cases where the husband exhibits great capability, it appears as if the wife must of necessity feel herself subordinate to him ; and the relation can hardly be a good one, when the wife is greatly superior to her husband in mental capacity and strength of character.　But if a wife understands her husband, as true love will always teach her to understand him, and if she is mother and wife in the true sense of the words, the feeling of her husband towards her cannot be other than one of perfect equality; and as, if she be not possessed by vanity, she may in many respects keep herself more pure and unstained by contact with the world than a man can; this gives her on the other side a superiority over her husband, and allows him to place her above himself, without any risk of disturbing the true relation between them. As a general rule, you are more innocent than we ; and I am sure that, upon reflection, you will not object to this superiority ;　and thus you will find that nature has after all regulated the matter well and beautifully.　.　.　.　.

.　.　.　.　.　The devotional feeling aroused in you by my picture, has again made me see distinctly how it was possible for the belief in miraculous pictures to have taken birth, at a time when the art of painting had attained its highest development, and when the faith in the holy legends was still a living faith.　For it is wonderful what life, what transparency and animation there is in a picture when it is executed, and also viewed, in the right spirit.　.　.　.　...

[cccxliv.]　　　　　　　　　*Berlin*, 28*th January*, 1809.

.　.　.　.　.　I have been to the play for the first time for a very long while.　Nanni wished so much to go some evening, and I had heard that they were to give a new piece

by Kotzebue, in which Iffland and Mrs. Bethmann were
said to perform admirably. If I thought that you had read
the play, I would give you my opinion of the performance—
that Kotzebue is in truth an infamous fellow. He has not the
slightest conception of true morality; and when he attempts to
represent noble characters, he defaces them in the most vulgar
and disgusting way, so that one is actually ashamed and
vexed with oneself for being carried away and moved by the
events of the piece, which happens from time to time to an
honest dog like myself. . . . . .

[cccxlv.]   *Tuesday Evening.*
          . . . . . Then came your letter this afternoon, just
as I was about to start for the lecture-room; and I am delighted to find that I had been anxious without reason.

But, alas, I am saying all this, as if matters were still as
they used to be. You will understand this; you know how
difficult it is, when a great change has taken place, always to
remember it. But I would rather confess to you at once,
honestly and openly, as we have ever treated each other,
that your letter has made an extraordinary impression upon
me. To think that you have not one spark of wit, it is too
bad! Deep feeling you are also wanting in—but that is the
old story—and even your much vaunted strength, is not real
strength! I cannot conceive how I came to love you! It
is as if a veil had fallen from my eyes, and it seems to me
a most unfortunate affair, which I ought to get out of as
speedily as possible. Come quick, dearest Jette, throw yourself into my arms, and forgive the stupid joke that my pen
has been guilty of. Look through my eyes into my heart,
and read there how entirely we are made for each other, how
little I should wish you to be otherwise than you are, and
that, after all, I must be a much better judge than you are
of how much wit, how much feeling, and how much strength
you have. Yes, and I can tell you to a tittle how much you
have of each; only as regards your wit and fancy, I must
have time to reflect; for hitherto, I must confess, I have given

little attention to such special qualities in you, but have loved you in bulk. But seriously, it would be a pity should you not have a vein of wit and fancy in you. Pray do try and discover one, if you have to dig ever so deeply for it, because in our house you will most likely have to furnish the whole supply. I can assure you that I do not possess an atom of it. Have you ever, in myself or in my writings, met with a single brilliant sally, startling turn, or striking and unexpected combination? Yet this is what is generally understood by wit. Reflect a little, and you will find that all that I have written is tremendously consistent (at least, so I flatter myself); but, at the same time, as bald as necessity would have it, and, therefore, also dry and monotonous. And should you, on some exceptional occasion, find that I am really witty, you may feel assured that I am not myself at that moment, and that it is only my mimetic talent that is exhibiting itself; some witty friend will probably be before my mind's eye at such moments, and in imitation of him, I speak, even though sometimes *par anticipation*. If, therefore, you value wit so very highly, I shall have more reason to be afraid of Steffens, of Brinkmann, and of many others, than you will have to fear Caroline, Wilhelmine, and Hannah, and I do not know whom. In reviews, I am, indeed, always said to be rich in wit and fancy; but if the people that say so knew what wit and fancy are, they would hardly be reviewers. Listen to me, Jette! We will make a contract with each other, by which, as is right and proper, we will both be gainers, and which we will honestly keep: we will never compare ourselves with others; there is nothing to be gained by that; and if any one were to expect me to describe you by comparison, I should really not know what to say, if it were not, "To tell the truth, your ladyship, she is not as amiable as you are, not so witty as another, not as sensible as a third, not so loving as a fourth, not so well-informed as a fifth, not so pretty as a sixth, but, taken altogether, she is the only one whom I love." Could you do otherwise in regard to me? But for all this, I remain an extraordinary being, and so do you. And now, dearest, do not be vexed with me because of my sauciness.

As for the acquisition of knowledge, that is a subject on which a great deal may be said; but it is very natural that men should not be willing to come to your aid in this matter, and, therefore, you must not put an evil construction on it. Only consider how their entire education, from their earliest youth, is directed towards the attainment of knowledge, how they must toil for it the whole of their life, that those among them, who really know something, have devoted their time exclusively to this object, and yet feel that they have attained but little. And then, further, consider that, knowing no other way than the one they have themselves trodden, it is but natural that they should despair of being able to help you to knowledge. Now, there is, indeed, another way, but that can only be known to those in whom science and feeling are so intimately blended as you rarely see them. For my own part, I have a kind of vague presentiment of how we ought to proceed in the matter; and, I believe, I shall be able to aid you in acquiring such knowledge as is best suited to women. The only thing that I fear I shall be wanting in is sufficient familiarity with all the details of the subjects that are likely to interest you the most, and which you will desire to become acquainted with. In my opinion, all knowledge must, in the case of women, be given in a religious form, and, at the same time, also in a sensuous form; the first, I might be able to accomplish, but in attempting the latter, I should often fail for want of details—at least, when endeavouring to impart instruction in unpremeditated and animated conversation. I have always obstinately refused to deliver lectures to a mixed audience of men and women; but to women alone—that is to say, to women with whom I am intimately acquainted—I should like very much to deliver a course, and I trust we shall be able to manage to have a regular evening hour for such entertainment. The power of penetrating deeply into the inner nature of things I may tell you at once, that you possess, but in attaining a thorough knowledge of details, I think you will not be so successful as our friend Herz. That you did not avail yourself of the first year of your marriage with Ehrenfried to extend your knowledge, is very natural; but, in reality, you were on the way to it. You know you read my *Discourses* with him, and also began *Plato;* and though it was beginning with the most difficult, it was, nevertheless, a step in the right direction: and then, Ehrenfried had not time to instruct you, otherwise than through books. Be quite easy, we shall manage all this, and I will never allow myself to be so hampered with business as to be unable to devote a great deal of my life to you in regard to these matters also.

[CCCXLVI.]   *5th February*, 1809.

Your letter is before me, and the first thing that catches my eye, is again that offensive inequality between thine and mine. Hear me, child, this is not to be borne, and I must try to drive every vestige of it out of you. Good God, what shall I do to make you feel how entirely I am yours? . . . . But one thing more is required for this, which will appear to you rather paradoxical, and for this very reason it is meet that I should tell it to you; this is, that you must not aspire to be more than is right. Otherwise equality cannot be established. What I have said to you about married life and about society, applies to you as well as to me. In society you must allow free scope to your individuality, be to each what you can be to him or her, and take from each what you can get, feeling all the while that whatever enjoyment you receive or afford, is mine as well as yours, because you yourself are so entirely mine. Until you have lived in society in this free and simple manner, you cannot in fact know whether you possess wit and fancy, and whether you are interesting; for in our intercourse with each other these qualities cannot manifest themselves separately and distinctly, because in the true life of love all these secondary matters are so insignificant that they are not noticed. Do you not feel that it would be ridiculous, if, at any time, when you and I had been discussing the most interesting subjects together, either with much animation or with deep earnestness, you were to say to yourself that I had shown much wit and fancy, and that I had been very interesting?   I am sure such a thought would never strike you.   .   .   .   .

This evening I have something very tiresome in prospect. I am to spend it in the society of a number of men, not one of whom is good enough for me.   They have all low views, and will, no doubt, talk no end of nonsense about the present state of affairs.   Under such circumstances I do one of three or four things.   Either I give utterance to the bitterest sarcasms, and thus close the people's mouths, or I turn everything into a joke, or I remain perfectly silent, or I adapt myself entirely to their views, bantering them the while so slily, that they remain to the last in doubt as to what my real meaning is.   According as I am influenced by the spirit of the society, I adopt one or another of these expedients, and remain faithful to it the whole evening.   In every case the people feel uneasy and wish me at the devil, and afterwards, of course, cut me up most unmercifully; but I cannot help it.   Why are they such miserable wights?

[CCCXLVII.]   12th *February*, 1809.

Again our thoughts have met in memory of our dear departed.   You are right; in silence I prefer to fold you with your sorrow to my bosom, feeling one with you in love and holy remembrance of him.   It must be a delightful and tranquillizing thought to you, that you took so much part in his life in his last days, so that you may look upon that period as the real consummation of your beautiful union—at least on your side.   One thing, however, always impresses me most painfully, when I revert to Ehrenfried's death, viz., that he was not allowed to retain his consciousness, and to recognize you to the last; but on calm reflection I always console myself with what I have expressed in one of my sermons, that the last moment of full consciousness is in reality the last moment of life.   Judging from my knowledge of my own physical constitution, I think that I shall most likely enjoy the privilege which I wish so much had been granted to our beloved friend. Yes, dear Jette, the anniversary of his death shall always be a time of hallowed mourning and remembrance in our house ; and it precedes so beautifully Passion week, the general period of mournful remembrance. Our children, also, shall learn as early as possible to unite love for their departed parent with affection for their living father. But, dear child, do not overstep the limits which God has marked out for us; do not wish that Ehrenfried should give us any other token of his sanction and remembrance than that which dwells in our hearts, in the beautiful blending of our love for each other and our remembrance of him, in the commingling of our joy and our sorrow, when, on the anniversary of his death, you repose silently on my bosom, and I kiss away the tears from your sad eyes; and also that other beautiful outward token, that we have an image of him in our children, and that it is our highest wish to bring them up to be worthy of him. Could we have more delightful tokens than these? Could we contemplate in a more worthy image, the eternal existence of our departed friend ?

One word more only to-day. You are always desirous of knowing in what state of mind I am, and the rumours of impending convulsions which have probably reached you may have made you more anxious than ever. I may assure you that I am in a state of perfect and blissful calmness. I see distinctly that in a few months we must either have gained everything or lost everything, according as the government may resolve, and as yet it is very dubious what it will resolve. I know, however, that I have done everything, and ever will do everything that is in my power, to promote a better state of things; and, therefore, I am quite easy, and entertain a profound conviction, that however things may turn out, my life with you will not fail me. Endeavour to participate in my tranquillity, dearest heart; I think that nothing can rob me of it. . . . .

[cccxlviii.]   13*th February*, 1809.

Your letter has given me very great pleasure. You chat most delightfully, my heart's own Ernst, although at the same time you treat me most unmercifully. But wait a little : since my meekness makes you so saucy, I will take my revenge by adopting a pride and presumption that shall make you wish the meekness back again.

But let me tell you, my beloved, that I believe, nevertheless, that you possess wit and fancy, and that some evidence of it may even be traced in your writings, although what you say about consistency and necessity is quite true. I believe that you have afforded many a reader pleasure by unexpected turns of thought, and have caused much vexation to the foolish, who would fain continue in the beaten tracks, by the new ways of life you have opened up. But slap my mouth, for venturing to prate about your works—in short, it is my opinion that you have wit, and that in me there is not the slightest vein of it. But I must once more commence a lamentation at your so unmercifully placing before me all that I am not! Never mind, take the kiss of reconciliation, dear love—I am so entirely thine, and my heart embraces you with the ever-increasing consciousness that you are mine, entirely mine, and that I am really the right wife for you. Ah, your manner of repeating it is ever so indescribably sweet! *My* Ernst, I am too happy!

[cccxlix.]   19*th February*.

. . . . . What you say about your manner of treating men is interesting enough; but to speak seriously, would it not be worth your while to show them the truth? may there not be some among them who would hold out their hand to goodness, if they did but recognize it, but who are too weak to find it by their own unaided efforts? Here, in Rügen even, repeated complaints have been made of the manner in

which you avoid entering upon higher topics in society.
Many persons were much disappointed on finding that, when
they broached a subject of the kind, with the hope that you
would throw some further light upon it, you either remained
quite silent or entered into their opinion without expressing
yourself on the matter at any length, or with any interest—
in short, as you describe it. In this way you can hardly fail
sometimes to hurt those, who would really have been willing
to adopt higher views. . . . .

Schleiermacher to Henriette von Willich.

[CCCL.]   21*st February*, 1809.

  Last Sunday I preached in the church that is to be
mine in future. It was, as you know, the beginning of Lent,
during which I always feel particularly devout, and speak
accordingly. I was rather pleased with my sermon, though
I had had very little time to prepare it properly ; but the
whole of the rest of the day I was not myself. . . . .
 . . . . I have repeatedly upbraided myself for never
having answered your question relative to Alexander Dohna,
as you might so easily misunderstand my silence. But it is
very difficult to speak about him to any one who does not
know him ; and I cannot undertake to answer for your not
getting a false impression of him through me. I believe you
would learn to know him better from a single letter of his
than from any description of him that I can give you. My
relation to him is not either easy to describe. As regards
essentials there is an intimate bond between us ; each knows
everything of importance that regards the other, we have unbounded confidence in each other, and when we are discussing any subject, each speaks out his meaning without reserve.
In addition to this, we are personally much attached to each
other, we find pleasure in each other's society, and there
is nothing in either that is decidedly repugnant to the other.
At bottom, we are thus essentially friends; but, nevertheless,
this does not appear on the surface, as much as it does in my

intercourse with other friends. Not that his rank, or his own valuation of this, raises any barrier between us—far from it! Of anything of this kind there is not the slightest question. But, on the other hand, there is an entire side of my nature, which never appears in my intercourse with Alexander— namely, the light, merry, humorous side; but here, again, it is not that he would be offended by this, but his manner does not invite the expression of it, and he does not enter into it, and respond to it, because there is nothing of the kind in his nature, and therefore I prefer to give him that in me which he likes better—in short, gravity always predominates in our manner towards each other, and our intercourse is ever of a serious nature; and when I place this thus distinctly before myself, I always feel as if something was wanting. On the other hand, Alexander entertains for me a kind of respect, which is sometimes quite oppressive to me. More particularly when there is anything in me that he does not quite approve of, he would never speak to me about it, unless under very particular circumstances; as for instance, if it were in connection with public affairs, or if it belonged to the far past; otherwise he would not have the courage to do so. Such are the limits of our intimacy; within these we are perfectly open and confidential, and sure of each other.

[CCCLI.] *3rd March*, 1809.

 . . . . And now to your last letter. I ought not to have treated your expressions seriously, and yet I did so; but not because I was not quite aware of how much was said in playfulness and how much in earnest, and that in regard to essential matters there was, in fact, nothing to be cleared up between us. But my name would not be Ernest, if it were not part and parcel of my nature to turn suddenly and unexpectedly from playfulness to earnestness? I have already played you this trick more than once, and in each case as also in the present, it has been the slight degree of earnestness concealed in your expressions that has called forth the great amount in mine—and I was induced to show you, by the manner which I adopted, how thoroughly we are one in all essentials—just to make you say afterwards, that you entirely agreed with me. Another time I may, most probably, in like manner turn serious matters into sport; you know this, do you not? and you belong to the few women who are able to understand it, and with whom, therefore, I can venture upon it; for not unfrequently it has caused me to be called hard-hearted, sarcastic, and irreligious. Who knows if L——'s and S——'s suspicions, of my not being quite free from worldly principles, may not have been caused by something of this kind. Had they addressed themselves to myself on the subject of their doubts and notions respecting the relations to which you allude, I should certainly have felt myself called upon to do everything in my power to make them understand those matters better, and also my feelings in regard to them; and should you at any future period be able to afford me an opportunity for so doing, you will oblige me much. In such cases, I am always most willing to enter into explanations; but with men, dearest Jette, I am tremendously cautious. Not, however, when I am alone with one or two men, and when I perceive that any one is really and earnestly anxious to talk over his opinions and mine; and when I think such discussion may lead to some result, I never fail to seek an opportunity of being alone with him. But in society, there is nothing I hate more, and more studiously avoid, than an approach to anything like a discussion. For the first, I cannot dispute, without going to such depths in the matter as are not compatible with the light and agreeable tone which ought always to prevail in general society; and for this reason, I always take up the least important side of the ques-tion, break off, or give it a playful turn, so that it may not become too serious. Secondly, if I hear a disputant put forward vulgar or nonsensical arguments, or such as give evidence of a low mind, I cannot answer for what degree of bitterness and asperity my manner may assume. I should like to know who it is in Rügen, who has complained of me in this respect; and if it be feasible, I will try to set matters right again. Frequently, however, my repugnance to entering fully upon a subject, arises from the feeling that I should not be able to do so without becoming prolix and tiresome; and this feeling of shyness comes over me much oftener than you think. . . . .

Here, the larks have already begun to sing, and we have had the loveliest spring days. Dearest Jette, how my heart beats with joy when I think of how fast the time is approaching when I am to start on my journey! how near at hand is the new, happy, glorious life on which I am to enter! I am already familiar with its every detail, and often a smile, which no one can understand, plays round my lips when I picture to myself some little circumstance, some little piece of playfulness, or some short delicious moment, belonging to it. I am so glad that everybody knows what is going to happen, so that I may speak freely about it; and I am always talking about wife and children, as a man who has grown suddenly rich is always talking about his thousands.

Henriette von Willich to Schleiermacher.

[CCCLII.]   *3rd March*, 1809.

    Since L—— has been in Götemitz, I have again lived more with the children, which always makes me very happy. I do not speak much or often to you about the maternal feeling in me, but I feel sure, nevertheless, that you know it, and in what full and deep measure I possess it, and how tranquil happiness and secret anxiety alternate in my bosom in regard to the children. But the anxiety will cease when your fatherly eye watches over them, dearest! Never are Ehrenfried's and your image so intimately and touchingly blended in my soul, as when I hear the little creatures call you father.

After I had sent away my last letter, I felt for a moment uneasy as to what impression my constant dwelling on my own imperfections might make upon you. I have often been struck by the great monotony of my letters arising from this cause, yet I am always impelled to lay bare before you my deficiencies and defects. How greatly would not even my present happiness be enhanced, could I once learn to understand myself thoroughly, to be contented with my own nature, and to live with you and the children, without heeding myself. Oh, my beloved Ernst, when the great happiness shall be realized, when, pressed heart to heart, I shall feel that you are in reality mine—shall I also feel that all your sweet prophesyings about me are being fulfilled, or will the sentiment of my own unworthiness follow me even then, and still leave something to be wished for in the midst of our otherwise perfect felicity?   .   .   .

Schleiermacher to Henriette von Willich.

[CCCLIII.]   *No date.*

I wish to adorn you on your birthday, dearest Jette, and pearls are the ornaments I like best. I would fain have sent you real ones; for in our life everything must, as far as possible, be real. Pray do not fancy that they signify tears, for this only holds good in regard to dreaming of them. They signify, on the contrary, the most precious product of a quiet, unobtrusive life.

At whatever hour you receive these lines and the accompanying little present, you may feel sure that my whole heart is with you at that moment, for it will be so throughout the day, and the longing for you that never leaves me will be more intense than ever on that day, which will in future always find us united in gratitude and joy. God be with you, my darling. I kiss your forehead and your lovely eyes, and bless you. Let the image of your Ernst be with you throughout the day, when you dwell with thankful heart on the manner in which Providence has guided us. I also will praise God and thank Him on that day, for having given you to me, for the glorious life that we are about to enter upon, and I will pray for strength and power to render each of your days more happy and more bright! I wish that I could communicate to all who take part in the sweet happiness of our hearts, the deep emotion and jubilant gladness that fills my being. God bless you. Enjoy in richer measure than ever the present in common with the children and with your dear friends, and in remembrance of me, and of the never-to-be-forgotten happy past, and the future so full of hope; and go on longing to share with me everything that moves your heart, though even as it is, you know that I feel all with you, that your being is merged in mine and mine in yours.

[CCCLIV.]   *12th March.*

I have spent the greater part of the forenoon in arranging in my head an introduction to one of Plato's dialogues. I would willingly have discarded the subject and sat down at once to chat with you, but I felt that I ought not to do so. Most people think me an extraordinary being who can do everything that he wills to do, and whenever he wills to do it. Were I in reality such, I would do ten times as much as I do, and my productions would be very superior to what they are, alas! But the fact is, that my case is exactly the contrary. I can do nothing, absolutely nothing, by mere force of will, but must await the favourable moment. Therefore, when it comes I should consider myself very culpable were I to let it pass without availing myself of it. . . . .

And now let me thank you a thousand times for what you tell me about your birthday—about your feeling so happy and so willing to commence your new course of life at my side, and about the first thoughts of pious love devoted to me in the morning. You will, I trust, as you say, be happier even next year than this; yet I cannot say that our present and our future stand in the same relation to each other as hope and reality. For have we not already the reality? Do we not already belong to each other, and do we not constitute each other's happiness even now? Has not each penetrated deeply into the life and the soul of the other? Still, it is true, something more than this even is actual presence, and the power of sharing immediately with each other everything that moves the heart, and of acting together on the sweet children, on all who love us, and on the great and beautiful world that surrounds us. And this blissful present is drawing ever nearer! . . . .

Henrietta Herz, as well as yourself, writes me that the sermon could not have been understood by the uneducated. Do you think, then, that my other printed sermons would be understood by the uneducated? You will, indeed, find very few uneducated persons in my church—only a small but select congregation. On the other hand, however, I know that a few simple citizens who come pretty frequently to hear me, understand me very well, and would probably also have understood the sermon in question. But when I am properly installed in the church, I will always compose the afternoon sermon with a special view to the uneducated.

Henriette von Willich to Schleiermacher.

[CCCLV.]   *17th March.*

S——'s and L——'s suspicions of a slight intermixture of worldliness in your principles (if that be not too strong an expression), arise solely from the fact that they cannot see your relation to Eleanore in other than a reprehensible light, and so also your sanctioning in other cases attachments between persons, one of whom is already bound by marriage. You will hardly be able to make S—— understand how love can be more exalted than a bond, which, though bearing a sacred name, in the cases in question, is not a holy one, and ought, therefore, not to exist. For with exceeding trouble she has worked herself into a kind of love for her husband, and now thinks that every woman may love her husband if he be not a thoroughly bad man. Should you, however, desire to explain yourself on this subject in her presence, I shall try to make an opportunity when you are here, and I will myself listen to you with much satisfaction. However, I cannot help feeling that it is a dangerous experiment to open up the true and higher life to such persons as S———. For were they really to understand it, the greater part of what has hitherto upheld them would give way under their feet; and yet they would not have the energy to recommence life in a new spirit. . . . .

I know my names now—Sophie Charlotte. But though I would willingly do you the service to be twenty-two years old, I am in reality but twenty-one. But let me be young— it is my only consolation when I think of my ignorance.

[CCCLVI.]   28th March, 1809.

Though it is very late, I must give a few minutes to you, dear Jette. At tea-time I read a tragedy of Sophocles to Nanni, and since then I have been occupied in thinking over my Easter sermon, so that I may be able to-morrow morning at breakfast to look out the hymns which are always called for on Wednesday, though they are not to be used until Sunday. I am, therefore, now so far prepared that I need not think of my sermon again until Saturday. It is a real gratification to me, dearest, to think that you look forward with pleasure to my sermons! Now already I always think of you while composing them, and calculate the weeks that must pass before you can hear them. Three weeks more and I shall most likely be on the way to you. Yes, you are right, you cannot fail to take an interest in my activity, when you see with what pleasure I carry it on, and that it is not without a blessing. At first it will, indeed, be the sermons that you will be best able to enjoy with me, but the lectures also, I think, you will enter into, when you have witnessed my manner of living with the young men; and in my labours as an author you will also become interested, provided you visit me frequently while they are going on. If, as the most people hope, it is settled that the university is to be opened at Michaelmas, you will see me at work upon a little book this summer already—but only a little academical hand-book.

I am sure you will often think of me in church during the holidays. . . . .

Henriette von Willich to Schleiermacher.

[CCCLVII.]   *30th March*, 1809.

Yesterday it was our Friedchen's birthday. I wished so much to write to you, dear father of my little orphans, to express to you my gratitude and my joy, to place our beloved babe in your arms ; and to thank God in unison with you, for the child and for having given you to him as a father. How vividly I recalled to mind the hour, two years ago, when he was born, and how even then the physical suffering did not deaden the grief in my heart, and how conscious I was throughout of my unhappy position, yet how free from discontent, and how my tears flowed when the child was first laid in my arms. But they were not only tears of sorrow—ah, no! had my feelings been expressed in words, they would have been words of joy and of thankfulness for the child—my own, dearly loved, fatherless child ! . . . .

Good Friday Morning.

How I long for you to-day, my Ernst ! Oh, could I but be in your church, and celebrate with you this inexpressibly touching and holy day. I cannot tell you what an impression this day always makes upon me—with what love and sadness it fills my heart—how the image of the Holy One is present to my soul—how my spirit hovers round his grave in sweet melancholy, and round the hour of his death. Oh, that I were with you ! That my tears could be mingled with those of the pious among your congregation ! That I could hear the words that will flow from your great heart ! But I sit here solitary, in front of your picture, thrown back upon my own feelings alone, and the day will go by without my participating in any solemnization of the sacred festival of sorrow. But

... be with me in spirit, and will allow your love
... me to blend with your pious sentiments, as mine do in
regard to you. . . . .

2nd April.

. . . . Our friend will be understood by few persons
here—thoroughly understood perhaps by none. Of such extraordinary delicacy and conscientiousness as reigns here in
the better circles, I think the world in general can have
no conception. Even the men possess the same. On first
acquaintance I thought it very attractive, but on looking
deeper into it, it gives me an impression of great hollowness,
—I mean in as far as it exceeds true, natural delicacy, and
seems to me to be the result of the narrow limits within which
they live, and perhaps also of a defective education. Verbally
I shall be better able to explain to you what I mean, and when
I do this, you must tell me exactly what you think. . .

Schleiermacher to Henriette von Willich.

[CCCLVIII.]   *10th April, 1809.*

A cloud is drawing up over our immediate future,
through which I cannot as yet see. Dohna writes to me that
the erection of the University here has again become uncertain in consequence of the objections raised by certain parties,
who consider the measure dangerous, or the success doubtful.
My foreboding that we should not remain long in the Cannoneer House,* seems therefore likely to come true ; for if no
university is erected here, it is possible that we may sooner or
later go to Francfort, because under the circumstances, I should
neither be able to find a proper sphere of activity here, nor
to secure a sufficient income. For the moment, at all events,
this uncertainty places me in a great economical predicament.
One thing, however, I have firmly resolved, and that is, that
neither economical nor political difficulties shall make me
defer our union even a day. I am sure you will think as I
do in regard to this, and that you feel the same perfect confi-

* Schleiermacher was then living in Cannoneer Street.

dence that the necessities of life will not fail us.   It is just possible that Humboldt, who has gone to Königsberg, may set the matter going again.   Had I known sooner of the great uncertainty relative to the University, I would have refrained from many expenses connected with our future home, and now you must be prepared for my being as economical as possible, and for the house being for the present very imperfectly furnished.   But I trust, dear Jette, that your entrance into it will not be the less joyful, because of the want of these earthly matters; this will not trouble our pure sense of happiness.   As lightly and as gaily as I saw you the first time we met, skipping about and culling flowers, on the brink of the precipice at Stubbenkammer, you will, I am sure, skip about on the brink of the dark times before us, culling as many flowers as it offers.   Thus you stand before me, my precious one, and I embrace you with the truest affection and the most joyful confidence.   You, and you alone can be my companion through life.   But you have already long been asleep.   I have been writing to Dohna, and in the meanwhile the night has advanced.

Be not uneasy, dear Jette, about the opinions entertained of me by people in general.   To me this is nothing new, and is not of the slightest importance.   It cannot be otherwise than that a great many persons must misunderstand me, that some must dislike me, and that to others I must be a thorn in the flesh.   To alter this, it would be necessary that my innermost being should alter, and surely you would not have this. In consequence of these misunderstandings, a number of calumnies and idle gossipings, baseless stories and false surmises, and other such like, are set afloat from time to time, but I go on my way undisturbed, without looking to the right or to the left.   I am best pleased when I hear nothing about them; but when they do reach my ears, I do not heed them.   They very seldom trouble me for more than an instant; for, on the one hand, I have a great talent for forgetting, and on the other, I feel myself so far above these matters, that even when I know and remember that a person has been saying all kinds of ill-natured and foolish things about me, it does not in the slightest degree influence my conduct towards him; and, upon the whole, I have as little tendency to vindictiveness as to jealousy. The calm manner in which I take it, indeed, often causes a storm to blow over, but not always before it has sown the seeds of a new one. Such has been my way of proceeding during fifteen years—first in a smaller and now in a wider sphere,—and I cannot say that it has in any way interfered with my activity; at all events, not half so much as if I had been less independent and had sacrificed any of my natural characteristics, and had thus from the very commencement lamed my own powers. I do not know what it can be that is rendering Alexander so anxious at the present moment, except it be some false reports that have reached the ears of his colleagues, or perhaps even of the king, and which may be interfering with some of his projects in regard to me. But perhaps it is all the better that it should be so. Nevertheless, I should be very sorry were the king in any way to misjudge me in this instance, when he may so easily see the truth. I should, however, regard it as a simple, natural event, and let it pass by as such. . . . . .

. . . . . Something in one of your last letters which gave me great pleasure has just recurred to my mind, I do not know why. I mean the purely objective view which you are able to take of certain peculiarities in the people who surround you, without allowing yourself to be influenced by them. I think these peculiarities are not so much a fault of education in their case, as the result of their limited experience, and their consequent ignorance of many ways in which human nature may develop itself, which renders them incapable of appreciating many of the more beautiful sides of this, which they, on the contrary, confound with sentiments and actions which they have always been accustomed to see connected with a certain amount of grossness. I had previously discovered numerous similarities between England and Rügen. This is another and a very striking one, at least so far as the women are concerned.

I cannot possibly abstain from writing to you, dearly beloved soul, for I partook communion a few hours ago, and although various worldly matters have obtruded themselves in the interval, in sitting down to write to you the solemn impression returns to my mind. With prayer I have consecrated our union as a Christian marriage. I have prayed that throughout life we may be filled with true piety, and holy, divine love; that our thoughts and our actions may ever be directed towards all that is good, and that we may ever seek this for ourselves and for our children. In this spirit, I have laid our hearts before God as an offering, and have commended ourselves to Him; and it was an inexpressible blessing to know that you were united with me, at the same hour, in similar feelings and prayers.

Oh, how we shall share in future every such holy emotion!— no pious moment enjoyed by the one will be lost to the other!

The publishing of my own banns went off capitally; but Nanni says she was in a tremendous fright the whole time. She and I went afterwards into the garden, where the rose-bushes are already beginning to bud, and marked out the grass plot for the children to gambol upon. The gambolling will indeed be restricted within somewhat narrow bounds, for the whole garden is not as large as half the house at Poscritz, and, for the present, we have marked out one-quarter of it only for grass, another for strawberries, a third for flowers, and the fourth for pot-herbs and other such things. In addition to this, the garden contains two fruit trees and one acacia and a-half, which form an arbour. . . . . .

. . . . . With what joy I announce to you that this will be my last letter; but I must break off abruptly, merely adding that I am very well, and that you must, once for all, dispense with my taking care of myself. It would kill me, were I to do so; and when you have seen how unnaturally prudence sits upon me, I am sure you will give up recommending it.

War has at length broken out, thank God ! but in our own country I am afraid everything will remain more tranquil than is to be desired, and anything that will interfere with our journey I do not in the least anticipate. And afterwards, come what will, you will be mine, my beloved, my only one ! For ever and entirely thine !

PART IV.

———✧———

FROM SCHLEIERMACHER'S MARRIAGE IN MAY, 1809, UNTIL HIS DEATH, 12TH FEBRUARY, 1834.

FROM the time of his marriage until his death, Schleiermacher resided permanently in Berlin, in which place, while pursuing a laborious career of wide-spreading public activity and usefulness, he became the centre of a most happy and exemplary domestic life, and of a large and interesting social circle, and to many, far and near, the object of a devoted affection, which he returned in full measure. The pulpit, the professional chair, the academy of sciences, extensive literary undertakings, participation (at least for a time) in the administration of the State, his duties as a member of the Poorlaw Directory, and other public offices, in addition to the claims of family and social life, fully occupied his time, and in consequence, as before observed, such consecutive and circumstantial records of his internal life, as his previous correspondence affords, do not exist in regard to this period, except in his written works. As early even as the year 1810 we find him, in a letter to Charlotte von Kathen, excusing himself for writing so seldom, as compared to formerly, with the fact that he was no longer a *single* individual, and that when his wife wrote it was the same as if he wrote himself.

Schleiermacher used to travel every autumn, mostly with his wife and children: sometimes, however, these vacation rambles or journeys in quest of health, were undertaken alone, or in company with other friends, and sometimes he remained at home, while wife and children went abroad. Retaining, after his marriage as before, that irrepressible desire for constant communication of thought and feeling to those he loved best, which had given rise to his earlier correspondence, the separations caused by these various journeyings each time called forth anew the activity of Schleiermacher's pen in correspondence with his wife. However, there was but seldom occasion to enter minutely in these letters into questions regarding his outward or his inward life, and the contents have mostly no further interest than such as is connected with a cursory description of the little events of the journey, and the impressions received from the countries visited. They afford, nevertheless, in a certain measure, a consecutive picture of Schleiermacher's life with his wife and children, and give an idea of the spirit that pervaded his home; and for this reason these unpretending letters, among which are included a few to other friends, as also extracts from the parents to the eldest son (Ehrenfried von Willich)* when

---

* Nearly all of these being from the mother, and containing merely motherly admonitions and expressions of affection, the greater number have been excluded by the translator as having no bearing upon Schleiermacher's life, and only such have been retained as contain descriptions of the events of home life in which he is concerned. These

absent at school or at the university, are here given, in order in some measure to fill up the gap which this work would otherwise present.

[Respecting Schleiermacher's taste for social intercourse, we learn from Henrietta Herz,* who returned to Berlin after an improvement had taken place in her pecuniary position, and who was a constant member of Schleiermacher's circle, that " the lovingness and sociableness of his nature was so great, that although intellectually-inciting conversation was most agreeable to him, he nevertheless also found great pleasure in intercourse with individuals who were not in point of mind on a level with him, and who were even mentally insignificant, the heart and the disposition alone being always sufficient to attract him. In consequence his social relations were very numerous, and took up a great deal of his time, and perhaps, indeed, were chiefly the cause of his not having had leisure during his lifetime to prepare his lectures for publication. It is true that he had the power of working at any time, his mind being always sufficiently collected for the purpose; but for this very reason he was ever inclined to think that he should be able to accomplish more than proved actually to be the case. He very rarely refused an invitation, and also saw a great deal of company at his own house; but frequently after the most luxurious

eliminations, as also various curtailments in the wife's letters to her husband, have been made with the greater confidence, as the extracts that remain, suffice to show the development or changes that have taken place in her character.

* *Leben und Erinnerungen.*

and hilarious dinner-party or supper-party, he would sit down to his writing-table, in a moment be absorbed in the deepest speculations, and work far into the night. When it so happened that he had to preach the next day, and his drawing-room was full of company, he would draw aside for about a quarter of an hour, taking up his stand close to the stove, and looking thoughtfully straight before him. His more intimate friends were aware that at such moments he was reflecting on his sermon, and took care that he should not be disturbed. In a short while he was again a lively participator in the conversation going on; but in the interval he had jotted down a few notes with pencil on a slip of paper, and this was all that was ever written of his sermons before they were preached; yet I have frequently heard him the next morning, after a preparation seemingly so insufficient, deliver the most deeply-reflected and deeply-felt discourse."

Relative to this mode of composing his sermons, which, as is shown in his letters to his father, he had adopted very early in life, Lücke says:* "It is well known that Schleiermacher never wrote his sermons before delivering them. All those that have been published were taken down during delivery. While I was a constant hearer of his, two young friends were always engaged in this work. Those persons who were aware of this felt higher admiration for the great gifts of the man. The sermon could not be said to have come into existence in the pulpit, in as far as it was generally conceived in his mind several days previously, and left as

* *Erinnerungen an Schleiermacher. Studien und Kritiken,* 1834.

it were to mature there until the moment of delivery.
But no part of it was committed to paper while I lived
with him, except the text and the theme, which was noted
down on Saturday evening, and at the most, in addition
to this, the heads of the divisions of the latter. This he
called writing his slip, and thus prepared he entered the
pulpit. Here the sermon took definite form, the mode
of representation and the detailed execution being the
living product, not only of the preceding reflection, but
also of the animating impression produced by the assembled congregation, and of the never-failing power of
his mind over the order of his thoughts, and his equally
unfailing command of language. Those who knew the
secret could follow the growth of the artistic structure
of his discourse. They perceived how, at first, he spoke
slowly and deliberately, somewhat in the ordinary tone
of conversation, as if gathering and marshalling his
thoughts; then, after awhile, when he had, as it were,
spread out and again drawn together the entire net of
his thoughts, his words flowed faster, the discourse became more animated, and the nearer he drew towards
the encouraging or admonishing peroration, the fuller
and the richer flowed the stream. He was ever the
same and always equally attractive by the original
manner in which he treated his text, by the novelty
and freshness of his thoughts, by the order and clear-
ness of his mode of representation, and the fluency of
his delivery. When your attention was not too much
engaged with the thoughts, you might often have an
opportunity of admiring how, though giving way to
that liking for complicated periods, which rendered his

style so peculiar, he, even in the midst of the most complicated, ever found the most appropriate term, and never lost the clue which led him with certainty to the conclusion. He had modes of expression peculiar to himself, and also a sphere of thought peculiar to himself. But the richness of his mind and the fulness of Christian life in him never allowed any of the ordinary defects of extemporary preaching to be apparent in his sermons, and caused one to contemplate with unalloyed pleasure his wonderful mastery of the homiletic art and the rich fruits that it bore. A person who only heard Schleiermacher preach once, might fear that his manner was not popular enough, and that he would not be easily understood by the less cultivated among his congregation. But when you heard him consecutively this fear vanished. It is true he expected a good deal from his hearers, yet in reality no more than attention and familiarity with the Scriptures; and as he knew how to rivet the attention of the less educated by the freshness and vivacity of his mode of delivery, and by his constant application of even the deepest Christian ideas to practical life, and to the actual conditions of the Church, of family life and of the fatherland, this explains how it was that, although his congregation mostly belonged to the educated classes, persons of the lower ranks, and even belonging to other congregations, were constantly seen in his church. I believe that this portion of his congregation steadily increased, for just as his whole system of theology was ever in living progression, so also the fervour and Christian simplicity of his mode of preaching increased year

[illegible]

[illegible]

[illegible] from the [illegible] [illegible]. "The [illegible] are [illegible] [illegible] [illegible] [illegible] [illegible] [illegible] [illegible] has to [illegible] [illegible], and [illegible] it seems to me [illegible] to be [illegible] [illegible] to [illegible] the [illegible] that we might [illegible] to be [illegible] [illegible], and that we might [illegible] to [illegible] the [illegible] [illegible] [illegible] [illegible] and [illegible] [illegible] that we have [illegible] [illegible] the [illegible]."

The [illegible] of [illegible] [illegible] [illegible] [illegible] [illegible] [illegible] [illegible] [illegible] [illegible] a [illegible] [illegible] [illegible] [illegible] [illegible] is [illegible] to [illegible] [illegible] [illegible]. [illegible]

---

* [illegible]
* [illegible]

of proud aristocratism, and in the dead forms of bureau-
cratism, struck down like thunder and lightning, and
the subsequent elevation of the heart to God on the
wings of solemn devotion, was like harp-tones from a
higher world. The discourse proceeded in an uninter-
rupted stream, and every word was *from* the times and
for the times. And when, at last, with the full fire
of enthusiasm, he addressed the noble youths already
equipped for battle, and next turning to their mothers,
the greater number of whom were present, he concluded
with the words : ' Blessed is the womb that has borne
such a son, blessed the breast that has nourished such
a babe,'—a thrill of deep emotion ran through the
assembly, and amid loud sobs and weeping, Schleiermacher pronounced the conclusive Amen."

Wilhelm von Humboldt, also, in his well-known letters
to a female friend, bears testimony to Schleiermacher's
wonderful power in the pulpit. " Of Schleiermacher,"
he says, " it may be said, as of the greater number of
very distinguished persons, but in an incomparably
higher degree, that their speaking exceeded their
writings in power. Those, therefore, who may have
read his numerous writings ever so diligently, but who
have never heard him speak, must nevertheless remain
unacquainted with the most rare power and the most
remarkable qualities of the man. His strength lay in
the deeply penetrative character of his words, when
preaching or engaged in any other of his ecclesiastical
functions. It would be wrong to call it rhetoric, for
it was so entirely free from art. It was the persua-
sive, penetrative, kindling effusion of a feeling, which

:emed not so much to be enlightened by one of the
irest intellects, as to move side by side with it in
erfect unison."

Schleiermacher's activity in church matters was in
ccordance with the whole tendency of his religious
haracter. He took a lively part in the proposed reform,
vhich was to give to the church of Prussia a synodal
onstitution in lieu of the existing bureaucratic abso-
itism. The principles on which he acted in regard to
his question,* are expressed as follows in a paper on the
ubject written by him in 1817: " As in a truly free
tate-constitution, which necessarily depends upon the
eal and affection of the citizens, everything is based on
i free and living communal system, from which springs
ll true interest in the legislation, and in which the
xecutive finds its best support and its greatest strength;
io also it would be vain to attempt to touch and to im-
rove the constitution of the clergy, if the reform to be
introduced be not founded on a well-organized Christian
presbyterian system. The Protestant Church consists,
in truth, of the totality of the Protestant communities,
and the clergy are only their servants. . . . . If
we be in reality in earnest in our desire to exercise our
office in the most blessed way, we churchmen ought to
wish for nothing more sincerely or more urgently than
the institution of rather extensive assemblies of elders,
based upon the free election of the community, which
would draw closer the bonds between us and the com_
munity, which would enable the latter to gain a deeper

---

* *Gutachten über die für die Protestantische Kirche des Preussischen
Staates einzurichtende Synodal Verfassung.*

insight into the tendency and character of our office, and would put us in a position to correct their judgment of us in an unconstrained manner, and to counteract prejudice and fickleness ; which would further enable us to render intelligible to them and to explain the grounds of such matters as may be determined in the ecclesiastical synods, and to awaken their zeal in favour hereof, as also to prove to the world that much that we have long wished for in vain, in regard to the dignity of public worship, to the upholding of ecclesiastical freedom, and in reference to certain unchristian acts and relations, is not only our wish, but that of the Christian communities themselves, which have hitherto only wanted a recognized and legal form through which to make themselves known."

In another question, of still greater importance to his country, Schleiermacher took an active and very decisive part—namely, the question of the union of the Lutheran and Reformed Churches in Prussia, which had been a favourite idea of his long before it was proposed by the king. His views on this subject are expressed in a compendious form, in the subjoined passage, from a pamphlet addressed by him to Dr. Ammon, in reference to the opposition raised against the union by the original Lutheran clergyman, Claus Harms, in Kiel, who had republished, on the occasion, Luther's famous ninety-five theses, with the addition of ninety-five of his own, and who declared the union to be an apostacy from Lutheranism and from Christianity.

" Harms," says Schleiermacher, " regards the subject from a point of view, from which Lutheranism appears

to him as identical with Evangelical Protestantism and
Christianity. But Luther and Melancthon, Calvin and
Zwingle, and their various fellow-labourers, were not
creators of a new state of things, but merely instru-
ments in the hands of divine Providence, and it is, and
ever will be their highest glory that they were found
worthy to be such. They produced nothing new, but
merely cleansed the old doctrine from the rubbish that
had been heaped upon it, so that it could appear again
in its pristine purity, and commend itself thus to men.
The work of the Reformation was not, therefore, to
found a Lutheran Church—against which, indeed, no
one protested more warmly than Luther himself—nor
was it to found a Reformed Church, but to bring forth
in renewed glory the Evangelical Church, which is
guided and governed by its founder, Jesus Christ, the
eternal Son of God. He is the quickening centre of
the Church; from Him comes all, to Him all returns:
He is Beginning and End: in Him we believe, and
through Him alone we are blessed. . . . We ought
not, therefore, to call ourselves Lutheran nor Reformed,
but we ought to call ourselves *Evangelical* Christians,
after His name and His holy evangel; for in our name
our faith and our confession ought to be made known."

The same liberal principles that guided Schleiermacher, in regard to the ecclesiastical matters already
mentioned, led him strenuously to oppose the proposal
which was being mooted in high governmental circles,
to make subscription to the confession of the Evangelical Church compulsory and binding, though at the
same time he expressed a wish that a form might be

adopted according to which every Evangelical Christian should, on ordination, declare his concurrence in the condemnation of the tenets of the Roman Church, contained in the symbolical books of the Church.

In the question of the reform of the liturgy and of the hymn-book, which, though less important, caused as great excitement at the time as any of the foregoing, Schleiermacher also took a prominent part, and in addition to the sharp polemical warfare, and the numerous enmities resulting from this, to which these various questions gave rise, Schleiermacher was in this later period of his life subjected to many other annoyances, which never, however, disturbed the equanimity of his mind, or troubled that happiness which he drew from a source far deeper than those whence these annoyances sprung. When, after the glorious war of liberation in 1813–15 the reaction set in, Schleiermacher became an object of suspicion in the highest circles, like most of the men who had infused into the nation the spirit which had driven the foreigner out of the land, but which was now to be quelled, lest it might insist with too much vigour on the fulfilment of the promises made by the sovereign in the hour of need. Having been denounced to the king for some expressions used in a circle of what he supposed to be confidential friends, he remained for a long time under apprehensions that he might lose his position as professor at the university, like Arndt and De Wette, and many others, who, in consequence of the prevailing system of espionage and denunciation, were either suspended or dismissed. In a letter dated March, 1820, to Arndt, who in 1827 had married his sister Nanni, he says: "For the last fortnight the city has again been full of the rumour of my dismissal. The fact upon which this is based, is that the State-chancellor has demanded to see the documents of the faculty referring to De Wette's dismissal, and that thereupon Schulz has made many inquiries as to what toasts I had proposed on the 9th, at the festival in honour of the general arming, celebrated by the students. Certain expressions of well-informed men which have come to my ears, give me reason to think that hostile intentions towards me have really been seriously entertained; but I have been told by the same persons, within the last few days, that the matter may now be considered as having blown over, and thus it seems that this time at least grace has triumphed over disgrace. However, the documents have not yet been returned, so I must not sing pæans too soon." And again in 1823 he writes: "The projected journey is more especially important to me, because I wish to look out for a spot in Germany where it would be possible to live, in case of matters going wrong. For though as regards yourself, you may be quite right in thinking of England, I would be of no earthly use beyond the limits of Germany, and within these, I should prefer above all others a constitutional country in which the two Confessions are united."* It was these and various other annoyances that induced him to think of retiring ultimately to some quiet country parsonage, as frequently alluded to in his letters, and also to the contemplation of possible poverty, which is hinted at therein. However, his real

* *E. M. Arndt. Nothgedrungener Bericht aus meinem Leben.*

devotion to the king, which went hand in hand with devotion to constitutional liberty, seems at last to have been recognized, and in 1831 the order of the Red Eagle was bestowed upon Schleiermacher.

In 1829, however, an affliction for which there is no earthly consolation, fell upon Schleiermacher. His only and dearly beloved son, Nathanael, was taken away by death in that year, when only nine years old. This event, which is not mentioned in any of the letters included in the present collection, is touchingly alluded to in the following extract of a letter from Schleiermacher to his friend, Gass, which also proves him to be possessed in old age of the same calm power of self-command, that distinguished him in the strength of manhood: —" I am very thankful to Ohl," he says, " for having taken upon himself to convey to you the first accounts of the heavy calamity that has fallen upon us. . . . Since the boy had begun to attend the gymnasium, I looked upon it as my special vocation to take him under my more particular guidance. Ultimately I had arranged it so that he studied in my room, and thus I may say there was no hour in the day in which I did not think of the boy, and occupy myself with him, and now in consequence I miss him every hour. But there is nothing to be done but to resign myself, and to labour to transform the character of my grief. For struggle against it I will not and cannot, and give myself up to it I know I must not. On the day of his burial already, I began to attend to all my duties as previously, and life goes on in its old grooves, but more slowly and more heavily. My health seems not to have suffered. My wife also, who, from the Monday until his death (it is a fortnight since to-day) never moved from his bed, has kept up wonderfully."* And then he passes on to speak of other matters with his usual interest, and to enter into the joys of his friends with his usual sympathy. The discourse pronounced over the child's grave is one of his most celebrated. In addition to this son, Schleiermacher's wife had borne him two daughters, and the family was further increased by the adoption of a child of one of his half-sisters who died in Gallicia, and the child of a friend, both of whom, as also the two children of his wife by her former marriage, were cherished and educated by him as his own. His sister Nanni's place was, after her marriage, taken by the elder sister Charlotte, the early friend of his boyhood and youth.]†

Schleiermacher to Charlotte von Kathen.

[CCCLX.] *Berlin, 3rd August, 1809.*
It is all the delights of our new life that prevent Jette and myself from writing. We are much together, and besides this, each has his and her own occupations. I have my professional duties to attend to, with a host of disagreeable petty matters, which are quite new to me, besides a volume of Plato that is going through the press; and Jette is still busy with various household arrangements. In addition to this, we are endeavouring to enjoy as much of the summer as we can, at least in the Thiergarten. Yesterday we were for the

---

* *Schleiermacher's Briefwechsel mit T. C. Gass.*

† The parts inserted between brackets are not included in the German edition, but have been added by the translator as a feeble attempt to supplement what the last section of the letters leaves to be desired.

first time a whole day in the country with the children, and romped to our hearts' content. To-day the whole city has been in a state of intense bustle from the early morn, it being the king's birthday. Your heart, dear sister, is full of joyful hope for the fate of the world ; in mine this hope has almost been quenched as regards the immediate future, and to-day the thought has frequently forced itself upon me, that this may be the last festival of the kind that we shall celebrate. Should it not be so, and matters turn out more favourably than I expect, then my worldly position will also very soon be satisfactorily settled.

That our dear friend Herz has gone to Prenzlau for a few days, you will no doubt learn from herself. We miss her much in every way, and the lectures I delivered to the three ladies have in consequence been interrupted. What you write to me, dearest sister, about communicating the letters of friends too generally to other friends, was probably written with a special view to her. You are, however, mistaken on this point, and even the *Monologues* might have enlightened you on the subject ; I feel exactly as you do, that perfect friendship must in every case be a strictly personal relationship; and although it is very delightful to make one's friends acquainted with each other, there is of course a natural limit which ought not to be overstepped. And this limit I am sure we both equally recognize in the present case, for I know full well how far you have got with Henrietta Herz, and what distance still separates you, and I do not believe that I should ever communicate to her any parts of your letters that you would disapprove of. But if you mean that you might say things to me, which you would not wish me to communicate to my wife, you must write to me more explicitly about this; for although I can conceive the possibility of this being the case, I should not have the proper tact in the matter, without your direct guidance. However, I should certainly act in accordance with your wishes, and allow your words to reach no other ear than my own, as long as such should be your pleasure. For your unbounded confidence is of infinite value to me,

and I would not forfeit it for a great deal, even independently
of the beneficial effect I know it has upon yourself.   Yes,
dearest Lotte, let this sweet confidence continue undisturbed;
be assured that I shall ever guard it as a precious treasure.

Your faithful Brother.

[CCCLXI.]   *Berlin, 4th November*, 1809.

Accept my sincere thanks, dear sister, for your little
note, and a little note also in return this time; for I can
only steal a moment from my necessary occupations which are
daily increasing.   I cannot describe to you what a pleasure it
has been to me to make Jette and the children acquainted
with my relatives, and to show her my beautiful native
country; and I still congratulate myself upon having seized
the opportunity that offered, though it may have been a little
imprudent from the economical point of view.   The enjoyment
we have derived from the journey will be a lasting one, and
the toll which was levied upon us in the shape of mishaps
and disappointments, was so slight compared to the length of
time, that we may in fact consider ourselves as having come
off scot-free.   In regard to the university—the accounts of
the proposed erection of which I received just after our arrival
in Gnadenfrei—I still fear to give myself up to my joy.   It
does not at all seem clear to me that our present tranquillity
will remain undisturbed, and that the existing order of things
will be maintained.

Your little note has saved you from a serious scolding that
I was about to give you because, just as you had settled the
conditions of the most unconstrained and thorough-going correspondence between us, you ceased to write altogether.

Farewell, sister of my heart, and write soon.   Greet and
kiss all the children from me, remember me to grandmamma,
and say to all who care for me, that I had long been silent,
but that I shall soon begin to write again.

[CCCLXII.]   *Berlin, 26th April*, 1810.

You are right, dearest sister.   I have postponed writing
far too long, and you will do me a great service by not asking

how this has happened. I saw one day that Jette was giving you a little sketch of our life, and more particularly of my doings, and this is all the excuse I have to offer. Formerly, it is true, I was equally busy, and yet I found time for writing ; but then I was still a single man. That is in fact the great point, which you will know how to explain to yourself in detail, taking into consideration among other things, that when Jette writes it is the same as if I had written, only that I am sure she does it much better than I should. If I could but describe to you how entirely I am absorbed in my work, and in my home. It is an inexpressible happiness, but also a great misery. Home and business stand hostilely arrayed against each other, and interfere very much with each other ; for in the midst of my work the thought of Jette and the children will intrude, and on the other hand, when I am with the latter the thought of my work will come into my head. In short, I retain my motto : " Man is a troubled individual." . . . .

Your birthday we celebrated in the most beautiful manner. We took the Communion on that day, and afterwards Henrietta Herz dined with us, and we drank your health. Continue to remember us with affection.

[CCCLXIII.]   27th December, 1810.

Dearest sister, the longed-for happiness has come, and come so gloriously ! On Christmas Eve Jette was still quite brisk, was making preparations for young and old, and went with me to the Reimers to witness the Christmas joys there. Towards nine o'clock we returned home, and before midnight the little girl was happily ushered into the world, strong and healthy, and with its little head covered with thick dark hair. I was to preach on Christmas-day, and I had all along felt very uneasy lest I should be disturbed by the event ; but with what a bounding, joyful, deeply moved heart I could now preach, and after the sermon offer up my thanksgiving for the happy delivery. It is not, indeed, customary to do so here; but I could not refrain; I felt the need to pray for

wisdom and understanding, and to feel that others were joining in my prayer. Many persons present guessed by my
manner that it was my own wife I was alluding to.

Forgive my not writing more at present, dearest Lotte.
I am deeply moved by the sincere sympathy of all my friends.
It must be true, that there are few men so blessed as I am.
May God also grant me grace and faithfulness to enjoy and to
use profitably what he bestows so bounteously. Unite your
prayers with mine, you dear, true-hearted sister, and let us
soon have a word of gladness from you.

[CCCLXIV.]   *7th March*, 1811.

    I am getting on very badly with my letter-writing
just now, dearest sister; and partly, I believe, because I am
also otherwise not getting on very well. Since the beginning
of last month I have again been suffering from cramps in the
stomach, and at times so violently, that for weeks together I
have been obliged to lie down on the sofa in perfect idleness as soon as I returned from the lectures. I ought at
present to be in a state of intense activity, in order to be
prepared for the next term, but I am so exhausted by the
pain that I can do little or nothing. And when I sit down to
write letters my conscience pricks me, because I feel that if I
do anything at all, I ought to do that which is more pressing.
Even my enjoyment of the two delightful days which we have
just celebrated—the day of the christening, and Jette's birthday yesterday—was disturbed by the pains. On the first of
these days, more especially, I am sure you were with us in
spirit, in like manner as we bore in mind your sincere and
faithful affection. It was a solemn day to me. May I never
forget what I felt when performing the sacred rite! May
it more particularly be present to me should I ever be on
the point of acting towards the child in a spirit contrary
to Christian paternal wisdom. I believe there was not an
individual present, who did not, in his own way, feel with me.
Dearest sister, I think few persons are so favoured by God as
Jette and myself; and we both fully recognize it, and are pre-

pared for everything that time may bring as a counterpoise to our rare happiness. You, poor dear, have again had to suffer a great deal, and now, I dare say, you feel grateful that the cup has once more been taken from your lips, and that you have still your little flock entire and gathered around you. Anxiety for our loved ones has also its noble influences on our lives, and is an element that we cannot do without, and which we ought not to wish to be exempt from.

[CCCLXV.]   *September*, 1811.

    . . . . Your whole position seems to me very gloomy. If it could help you, I would describe how very much worse even matters look in many parts of our state, and more particularly in the province of Prussia. We must be resigned to give up all outward prosperity, and feel assured that, as far as this is concerned, no improvement can take place until after the most dreadful convulsions and devastations; and we must only endeavour to work upon the minds of people, so that when the evil comes it may be borne with fortitude, and be brought to a happy issue. I do this to the utmost of my powers in every direction that is open to me; how long I shall still be able to do so God only knows. But I would fain have spoken to you about the blessing which I think attends my efforts in this respect, and about the seeds which I think I see germinating, and have shown you how I enjoy to the full the rare happiness, which this hope, and my life with Jette and the children afford me, though I am at the same time quite alive to the fact that the cup which contains it is but of fragile nature. Everything else is as nothing to this. I am not either then to be an eye-witness of your present delightful life, and shall not be able to make you feel how entirely, and with what pure enjoyment I enter into it! Well, it cannot be otherwise, and must therefore be right. I only wish that my image stood so vividly before you as yours stands before me at this moment. Ah! it is a great pity that we shall not be able to go to you!

In the autumn of 1811 Schleiermacher undertook a journey through Silesia, with a political object in view, as appears from his letters; but the precise nature of this object cannot now be ascertained. The following letters date from the period of his absence.

Henriette Schleiermacher to her Husband.

[CCCLXVI.]   *Berlin, Monday (No date).*

Can you guess, my heart's own, what I have been doing? I have been transporting Schlegel and hanging your picture opposite to my bed instead of his. Last night, as I was walking to and fro in the room, in somewhat melancholy mood, and full of various thoughts and of longing after you, my eyes fell upon Schlegel, and I felt quite enraged to think that a stranger's picture was hanging there, and not yours; and I would willingly have effected the change at once.

Tuesday.

I was interrupted in my writing yesterday morning, and calculated upon going on in the evening, but Harscher remained until eleven o'clock, and then I was so fatigued, in consequence of having been disturbed by the children the previous night, that I heard you say quite distinctly, "wife, go to bed," and I obeyed.

I am sometimes a little weak, my dear husband; at all times and in all places I miss you; and there are moments when I would fain creep into a corner and cry for you from my full heart. Yes, dearest life, without you there is no happiness for me, and it is a hard trial to me that your absence is so protracted. Do you also sometimes miss me a little? I know that I am but a worm; but love me, nevertheless, above all measure, and try not to find out as yet that you could very well do without me. Ah! I ought not to have seated myself here at your writing-desk, where we have so often been sitting, two on one chair, and where the feeling of my present desolateness overcomes me more than anywhere else. As far as outward matters are concerned, I can assure you that great care is taken that I shall not have time to give myself up to my longings. There is always something to be done, and so many little diversions are proposed, that there is neither time for injurious inertness nor beneficial repose. . . . .

Friede got his first smacking to-day. He was as quiet as a mouse, and did not give any signs of pain, but to me it was dreadful pain. As for Elsbetchen, you do not know how sweet it was to see her looking for you in the bed, the first morning; it made me feel quite sad. You can hardly be surprised, dear husband, that that child exercises an immense power over me; only by looking at me, with her bright, cheerful, loving eyes, she can make me rapturously happy whenever she will. Dearest Ernst, if God has so ordained it that we are to live long together, cheerfully and happy in the midst of our children, ah, then! surely all the good that we now enjoy will go on ever increasing!

There can be nothing more precious than a number of dear, well-favoured children; and I cannot tell you with what emotion I contemplate the picture of a sweet, quiet, domestic life, such as ours will be. It is a pious emotion, and my heart is at the same time full of hope that God will increase my powers, so that everything may become clearer and more living in me, and that my good will may express itself more effectually in action. Ah! and you always form the brightest point in the picture, round which everything else turns, and to which everything has reference. Only pray to God, that He will in no way destroy this life. From His hand only could a real destruction of it come; for the thousand evils which emanate from the world, and which many look upon as a destruction of their happiness, would to us only be a call to exert our powers in manifold ways. My dear husband, if God keep his hand over you and preserve your health, and preserve our sweet children to us, then whatever may be the

day's work allotted to me, I will ever at eve lay my head
upon your bosom with a feeling of true contentment, and
thank the Lord for my happiness by my happiness. I kiss
your hands with tenderest love, my dearest life,

Your JETTE.

Schleiermacher to his Wife.

[CCCLXVII.] *Hirschberg, 20th September,* 1811.

I received your letter yesterday morning, just as we*
were going to take a drive. I only glanced cursorily at it
then to see how matters stood, but afterwards read it properly
through while seated close to the Kochelfall, and thanked
God with tears, dearest wife, that you are mine. How could
I make myself believe that I could do without you? The
life that I am now leading seems to me so empty, although
I know that I am working for a noble object, and although
these days have been rich in enjoyments. But the sweetest
part even of these was the remembrance of the time when I
revelled in the contemplation of these natural beauties with
you. And not only on these occasions, but at all times, I am
ever living in thought with you and the dear children in our
little home. It is to me like a bright, sunny spot in a
beautiful landscape, in the background of which, however,
a terrific thunder-storm is gathering. That the storm will
prove utterly destructive, I do not anticipate, but much
devastation it cannot fail to cause, and we must not hope to
enjoy the bright effulgence of the setting sun, until it has
passed over. It is the beautiful country that surrounds me,
that has given this picturesque turn to my thoughts. Yesterday and to-day I have gone over again the most lovely parts
of our tour in Silesia. . . . .

I cannot tell you how delighted I am with everything that
you write. I had my doubts as to whether Elizabeth would

---

* Schleiermacher was accompanied by a sister-in-law of his wife,
L. von Willich, whom he afterwards left with her brother who lived
in Prenzlau.

look for me, and am, therefore, the more rejoiced to hear that she did. But she will necessarily have forgotten me before I return, and in her relation to me, this journey will be like a wound, which may indeed be easily healed, but which will, nevertheless, leave a scar. Her consciousness of me is interrupted, and will have to be created anew. . . . . We will look cheerfully and courageously towards the future, for you are right; ruin it cannot bring to us. Even from God, such cannot come—when you except that which comes by death, which is always equally near and equally distant— and the devil has no claim upon us.

Farewell, dear heart, I embrace you most tenderly,

Your ever-faithful ERNST.

[CCCLXVIII.]   *Breslau, 25th September*, 1811.

Here I am, dear Jette, in the city of my birth, since four o'clock this morning. Since I wrote last, I have altered the plan of my journey, because I missed some people in the neighbourhood of Schmiedeberg, with whom I must communicate. Sunday, at noon, I was still in Hirschberg and on the Cavalier mountain. On Monday morning, Count Gessler, who had arrived the day before, paid me a long visit. He must have been recently in Halle, for he told me a great deal about Steffens and Blanc. At ten o'clock in the evening I started for Gnadenfrei, where we caused Lotte a delightful surprise the next forenoon. This morning I arrived here, and have now taken up my abode with Gass, after having enjoyed a few hours' sleep at the inn. As yet I know very little about the people here, and do not either count much upon them. . . . . This place makes a strange impression on me; the sight of the streets and the houses gradually recall to my mind the memories of my earliest childhood, and when I think of how God has guided me since then, a feeling of tranquil confidence comes over me, which I am sure you will share with me. For the rest, Breslau pleases me much more than I expected, though it is very little altered, except by the last siege.

Henriette Schleiermacher to her Husband.

[CCCLXIX.]   *Berlin, 23rd September.*

Thanks for your short letter, dearest heart! It was all too short; but I am truly glad to know that you are in good health and have met with no mishaps. Here all is well and going on so entirely in the old way that I have, in fact, nothing to tell; nevertheless you must allow me to chat a little with you. Little Elizabeth seems to be thinking seriously of getting her teeth, but she is quite well. She has such a pretty fashion now of stretching her little head forward, and putting it on one side, and looking fixedly at you, until you are forced to look at her in return, when her wee face quite brightens up. She is a darling! God grant that I may have the joy to see the child grow up so gentle and loveable as she is now; that her sweet tenderness for me may ever remain the same; and that I may never have to stand opposed to her in any struggle. Ah, Ernst! I often feel very sorrowful at the thought, that in my life with the two other children, something sweet and beautiful, and which I fear can never be restored, has been lost. I could weep for ever over it. I am sure you must feel and understand what I mean. They do not seek refuge in their mother's bosom; they do not rejoice in my affection; I cannot see my way to establish a rule of love over them; my constant, cold reprimands have killed sweet confidence; the icy crust around their mother's heart has chilled the tender babes. Ernst, do not say that I am fancying something that does not exist; I implore you, believe me, that I may not lose my faith in your power of insight. It is entirely true, I am deeply penetrated by it, and I see distinctly to the very bottom of it, and can trace its source; I know with how many other things it is connected, and more especially with the cause of my being generally so little loved in this world, that, with the exception of yourself, there is not one among the many whom I know, to whom I could point as to one who feels true affection for me, of whom I could say, She is my friend.

. . . . I know that I have made a fearful accusation against myself, but I feel the necessity of giving vent to my sorrows to-day, and of showing you what is passing in me. But do not suppose that all this has come suddenly upon me. Give me your hand, husband, that I may press it to my eyes and to my heart, you most faithful one! Let me rest upon your bosom while I pray to God that, for the sake of our children, for the sake of the one still unborn, it may not be made to suffer for its mother's sins. Oh, husband! how my soul is swayed to and fro between bitter suffering and inexpressible bliss! . . . .

Yes, beloved husband, were it not that from the hidden depths of my heart there ever uprises a sense of pain, which never quits me, but is now more keen, and now more dull, and follows me through every phase of my life, I should be the happiest woman on earth; but as it is, I oscillate between sublime moments, when my happiness is quite present to me, and I have the power to quaff it in full measure, and those periods of torpor, when my outward life seems to drag on slowly and sullenly, and my inward life seems sunk in profound sleep, and which again give way to hours of deep humiliation and contrition. Could I but lead a really pious life, I think I would be cured. It seems to me that I am pious, but that I do not live piously. I feel that the element of piety is deeply rooted in me, but it is so rarely active. How often have I not been on the point of asking you whether I could consider myself pious, when I can live so long without prayer and without the feeling of the presence of God, and I only turn to Him on extraordinary occasions, when human prudence and human consolation are insufficient; or in those hours of deeper self-consciousness, when I fly to Him for salvation. Dear, beloved husband, should even these outpourings be very foreign to your present thoughts and occupations, you will, I trust, nevertheless give them a willing ear, and I will therefore not allow shyness to tempt me to keep them back. . . . .

Schleiermacher to his Wife.

[CCCLXX.] *Friday, 27th September.*

Dearest wife, you complain so gently and so sadly of the shortness of my letter, that I was quite moved by it. Yet I shall hardly be able to write longer letters during this journey, as I can never find any peace or quiet. And it is not only that my letters are short, but I feel with regret that they must seem very dry to you. It is unfortunate with me that when I am tossed about in this way, nothing is to be got out of me, however distinct and clear all my impressions may be. But fancy that I am leaning my wearied head on your dear bosom, and that all will soon be well again.

In what you say about yourself and the children, dearest Jette, there may be some truth, but it is by no means so bad as you fancy it, nor is the cause such as you believe. The whole is but a transitory state, and as yet nothing has been lost. You and the children needed to pass through a severe school, in order to acquire stability and the habit of bringing regularity into your life, which in your former circumstances it was impossible for you to acquire. To a man it is natural to regard this point as of the utmost importance, and it is I who have been the first to introduce the severe tone. It is, also, quite natural that during these endeavours earnestness of manner has predominated and tenderness has been thrown into the background. But by this time I think the point has been gained, and the period at which the children will begin to enter into relations of obedience with other people, also, will gradually and of itself work a change without our doing anything decidedly towards it. Your maternal heart has never been estranged from the children, and your love for them has not grown cold. My darling Jette, anything so unnatural could never enter into our being and action. Even I have a strong conviction that the children love me sincerely and heartily, and nothing will disturb my faith in this; yet I strongly suspect that they do not miss me at present—as you say not a word about it—and that you are at great pains to keep the remembrance of me alive in them; nevertheless, I am sure affection for me is deeply rooted in their hearts, and will develop itself more and more. Try to have the same faith in regard to yourself—it will not deceive you; and do not allow outward cares and occupations and transitory moods to rob you of the precious moments in which you can fully seize it. And how can you say that you are not loved? Nay, dear heart, you have been taking far too gloomy a view of things. I am glad, however, that you wrote to me during that mood also.

The evening before last the Heindorffs took us by surprise while we were at tea, remained the whole evening, and were very cheerful. Yesterday morning I allowed myself to be persuaded to preach next Sunday in the Reformed church, situated in the neighbourhood of the house in which my first days were spent. I did not know how to refuse, though I can hardly hope that it will go off very well in the midst of the tumult in which I am living. In the afternoon I paid a very long visit to President Merkel. We remained in the garden until seven o'clock, it was so deliciously warm.

In the spring of 1813 Schleiermacher found the state of Berlin so dangerous that he considered it right to send his wife and children into Silesia, where he hoped they might be in safety. The following letters were interchanged during this period of separation.

Schleiermacher to his Wife.

[CCCLXXI.] *Berlin, 13th May,* 1813.

I was glad to find you gone when I came back from Göschen's, and then I was quite startled to discover that I did feel glad. But I had no time to reflect; the deputation was already assembled, and over and above this a violation of our authority had taken place. Süvern was out of himself, he wanted to resign his command; I had enough to do to calm him down (but with his whole heart he will never enter into these matters), and afterwards I was obliged to hasten to the committee to get the affair sifted and settled. Nicolovius met me in the street, and confirmed the news of the dissolution of the department. Schuckmann has already started for Silesia to represent it there, and Nicolovius is to leave to-morrow for Pomerania or Prussia on a similar errand. Whether we are to conclude from this that the entire province, between the Elbe and the Oder, is in a condition to call for the embodiment of the *Landsturm*, I do not know; indeed I know nothing, for nothing is communicated.

In the midst of all this I have thought a thousand times of you, dearest, incomparable wife, and of our parting and our separation, and the many possibilities that may intervene to prolong the latter. Towards seven o'clock I was at last at liberty to come out here and to gather my thoughts. On the road I was overtaken by the Solgers, who came to present themselves for the first time as man and wife. They went in with me, and we enjoyed a few pleasant cheerful moments. In the evening I read a little in your *Lavater;* many passages pleased me and many strengthened me; but one section, addressed to a widower, I turned over without reading.

I have had my bed made upstairs, have written a few lines to B——, and these to you, and now I will go to rest. I wonder if you have got safely as far as Francfort. I hardly venture to hope so. And I wonder whether you will be able to do anything there? Ah, if I could but know!

Dearest Jette, how shall I be able to do without you and the dear children, and the sweet habitude of taking care of you all and of sharing everything with you! Instead of your dear presence, I have now nothing but wavering, indistinct pictures of you. In addition to this I have already had many disagreeable moments. The business which I have undertaken, and which I perform with the utmost fidelity, is becoming very irksome to me; not that anything very disagreeable occurs within our immediate sphere, but because it seems to me that the superior authorities are not doing their duty properly, and that the scheme will lead to no results, though there are excellent and powerful elements among the masses. You see that I stand sadly in need of the prayers which I have begged you to send up for me.

The candle is nearly burnt down, and it is high time I should get to bed: the nightingales and the gnats have, up to this moment, been contending for the mastery over me. Good-night, my darling wife! Alas! how disturbed may you not be at this moment, and how uncomfortably bedded! May the magic power of our dreams, at least, unite us.

[CCCLXXII.] *14th May.*

I got up very late this morning, so as to be obliged to hurry away to get to the college in time. And what a confused, busy, and yet empty day it has been! When returning from the college I heard some good news, which almost made me regret having sent you away; but then, again, I thought of how many moments would come when I should be glad of having done so, and indeed they have not been long in coming, for this evening Pistor has again received bad news; but, then, he sees everything in the worst light! The whole story about Torgau is said to be fictitious. The Crown Prince of Sweden has really arrived; the English and the Spaniards mean to make an irruption into France with one hundred and sixty thousand men; such are the most favourable accounts that we have, and also that the Danes are helping to defend Hamburg. On the other hand, it is said that the French have really crossed the Elbe, somewhere between Wittenberg and Torgau, with the intention of marching upon this place, but no one knows where they are, and in what force. Bonaparte himself, they say, is to cross near Pirna, in order to offer battle to the combined armies, which, it is supposed, the latter will not accept, but retire farther into the land that is overflowing — not with milk and honey, but with *Landsturm.* The king himself has given orders that, in case of need, Berlin is to be defended; and they are beginning now to throw up entrenchments all along the *Schafgraben,* from the Köpnick Gate to the Potsdam Gate. Princess Wilhelm is still here—there is all the news for you in a lump.

After the lecture there was to be a conference of the defence committee at my house; they kept me waiting very nearly an hour, and I was glad that I had the church accounts to make up in the meanwhile. I dined at a little past twelve, and in the intervals between the soup and the vegetables, and the coffee, I went on with the church accounts. You know how furiously zealous I am in such matters, when once I have begun. From two to five there was a meeting of the *Landsturm*; at six there was a *presbyterium* at my house, and just as it was about to commence, I received an order to deliver a consecration sermon in the court in front of the university building, for the battalion of the *Landwehr*, which is to leave to-morrow morning; it is the one in which Reimer serves. As soon as the conference was over, I was, therefore, obliged to throw on my gown, and to resort to the court, where an eternal buzzing went on until eight o'clock, when the discourse was delivered, and thereupon the oath was taken. With what delight I look forward to a quiet morning to-morrow. I will not go to town* until dinner-time, for I am to dine with Reimer, who will remain the day over. At tea-time I again read a little in *Lavater*. Why I have described to you the whole of this hurry-skurry day, I am sure I do not know. Very likely you may have spent an equally disagreeable one; I have a foreboding that to-day you are crawling on somewhere between Ziebingen and Francfort. Poor dear, to think of your being so forlorn! May the children but keep well, and may you thus escape the worst troubles that might befall you. Dear heart, do write to me as often as the bustle of the journey will allow, and be not abashed at what you may think too great dulness,

---

* As long as he inhabited the official residence in the Cannoncer Street, Schleiermacher used to live in summer in a small house near the *Schafgraben*, outside the Potsdam Gate, the large garden attached to which bordered on the *Thiergarten*; but the greater part of his business he transacted in town.

for you see I set you an excellent example in writing uninteresting letters.

As you like to know everything, I must inform you that I have reported to Boyen what a very bad effect is produced on the public, by the silence which is maintained respecting the position of the armies. Unfortunately, I can hardly hope that any good will result from the step I have taken, for there is not a man among them who feels himself skilful enough to place indifferent news before the public in a form that shall not be too discouraging. For the rest, dearest heart, the fact that the king himself has given orders that Berlin shall be defended, has contributed very much to raise my spirits. Good-night, my own heart ; God be with you !

[CCCLXXIII.]   15*th May.*

   . . . . Your dear face is before me in all its moods; and when sadness is the predominant expression, I do so wish I could stroke your hair and forehead, and kiss away the suppressed tears and sighs ! May God take you and the dear children under His holy protection !

Yesterday evening I spent with the Schedes in their garden. But already on the way thither, I was seized with a pretty severe attack of my cramps, which tormented me for a couple of hours. I have now written to Wolfart to make arrangements for being mesmerized, as often as I can find leisure. But according to the accounts received, we may expect to-day or to-morrow an engagement between Bulow and the French, who have crossed the Elbe ; and this will, probably, decide the immediate fate of Berlin. Do not, however, be anxious about me, dear heart. The means of defence will hardly have been sufficiently expedited by that time to allow of any resistance on this point, and probably the *Landsturm* will only be called out to evacuate the town. I shall then do so likewise, and will follow you slowly.

I feel, at this moment, that it is very foolish in me to be writing you this, as my letter cannot leave until the day after to-morrow, and by that time I shall be able to tell you how it has all passed off; but I hug my folly in this instance, because it makes me feel as if you were reading while I am writing, and thus annihilates the time and space that separate us.   I had just sat down once again to compose a sermon in a regular manner, when Twesten brought me the news, which threw me anew into a state of excitement. In the city I heard afterwards, that the entire *Landsturm* is to march out to the Templo-berg to-morrow morning at half-past five.   Only fancy my consternation, as it is Sunday, and I had no ammunition.   Our section had not, however, received any orders.   I hurried, in consequence, to the committee, and found that there was no truth in the report.   But I shall not fail to get some ammunition to-morrow, that I may not be put publicly to shame.   Yesterday evening I found two more letters from Countess Voss awaiting me; one was to you, asking for letters of introduction for Stralsund, whither she intends to proceed should matters turn out badly. . . . .

In addition to the fright which I got about the ammunition this morning, on hearing of the sudden marching orders, I was also greatly alarmed at the thought that I might not find time to send you one word of farewell.   Indeed, how easily may this not happen!   Let me therefore do so at once. But what more can I do than press you to my heart with the tenderest love, and pray for blessings on your head for all that is good and lovely in my life, which I owe to you, then endeavour to impress deep upon your heart my image, with all its imperfections, but also with the feeling of how much you have contributed to renew, and to embellish, and to purify it!   And I would fain also give you the most lively assurance that I take you with me, in like manner as I remain with you.   Yes, I feel that I shall also dwell in you as a good spirit.   Oh, my matchless, tenderly beloved wife, may you be sweetly reposing at this moment, and could I breathe into you a heavenly dream!

[CCCLXXIV.]   *17th, Evening.*

To-day I have put my house in order, have paid up
the servants, who, however, still remain, have purchased a
powder-flask and a canteen, have mended and packed Röder's
green mantlesack, and have changed my paper-money into
gold. My most important papers, your letters and Henrietta
Herz's parcel, I have given into the keeping of Pischon; the
linen and your books are put into the cellar.

These preparations, dearest, have been caused by the bad
news which was spread this morning. It was said that Bulow
was sorely pressed by a very superior force, and was retreat-
ing with the utmost speed. This evening, on the contrary,
tranquillizing accounts have been received from him; he
believes that Berlin has nothing to fear; and intends, as soon
as he has received reinforcements, to move forwards again,
and to assume the offensive; and now the excitable population has again exaggerated these accounts into news of
a victory. For the present I will do no more than rejoice
that I shall have an opportunity to-morrow of making some
further preparations.

[CCCLXXV.]   *18th, Noon.*

I have been running about so much, and am so tired,
dear Jette, that I can hardly write; and, in addition to this,
I have again an attack of the cramps—the first since last
Saturday. As long as matters remain quiet I shall continue
to be mesmerized daily by Wolfart, at his house, and hope
soon to be better in consequence. To-day is the anniversary
of our wedding-day. In my heart it is the day of our
betrothal, when you gave me your sweet "Yes" on the
bench, that is the chief day of rejoicing; but this day also
reminds me specially of a new life begun with you, and of all
that we have both become through it—but also of how much
more I could and ought to have been to **you**, and of how
many a suffering of various kinds I might **have** spared you.
May God grant us an opportunity of leading in future also a

life of-ever increasing purity, beauty, and fulness, and may
we be allowed to celebrate this day together next year,
feeling that the struggles of the times lay entirely, or at least,
in great measure, behind us.   Embrace the children most
tenderly for me.   God bless and preserve you, my darling.
My prayers accompany you all, but you above all others.

[CCCLXXVI.]   18*th, Evening.*

Dearest wife, what an unexpected delight was the
receipt of your little note!   Thanks be to God for having
guided you safely so far.   .   .   .   .

Here we have heard nothing about the defection of Austria
(Saxony only is said to have declared decidedly in favour of
France); on the contrary, it is confidently asserted that the
alliance is quite settled, but nothing relating to it has been
made public; and, until this takes place, I shall not believe
it.   The cause of the delay is, no doubt, to be sought in
selfish negotiations which are still being carried on.   As
regards our position here in Berlin, I have not the courage
to repeat the rumours that vary with every hour.   I only
rejoice when evening arrives, and I can come quietly out
here, where the nightingales never fail to greet me, and
where I feel at home, and where my spirit can dwell undisturbed with you, for the house in town is hateful to me
under the present circumstances.   In the daytime, however,
I am always in town, because there is always something to be
done in the defence committee, and also because I am not yet
quite equipped for the march.   I have offered Savigny and
Eichhorn to help them in the committee; and shall perhaps
begin my labours to-morrow already; for, as for regular
study, that is not to be thought of until the immediate crisis
is over.   I am continuing my lectures; but I believe I am
the only professor who does so.   One thing only you may
be assured of, dearest wife, in the midst of these fluctuations,
and that is, that the sooner we are attacked here by the
French the less reason you will have to fear for my life; for,
in case of their speedy arrival, no attempt will be made to

defend the city; the longer they defer coming, the better prepared we shall be.   In the first case, the only cause for anxiety would be that we might possibly not be able to make good our retreat towards Silesia, but be obliged to move towards Pomerania. This would be very hard upon us, as, under those circumstances, we might be separated for an indefinite period.

Dear heart, I feel pretty sure that, under all circumstances, or at least as long as the prevailing confusion be not too overwhelming, I shall act with judgment and presence of mind. Nevertheless, continue to pray for me, more especially in regard to this point. I rejoice at the courage with which you proceed.   God hold his hand over you and the little tribe, in future also.

[CCCLXXVII.]   20*th, Evening.*

I would willingly have chatted a little longer with you yesterday, but on my arrival here, somewhat later than usual, I found H—— waiting for me. After he had thoroughly discussed himself, he took hold of me, spoke a great deal about what was enigmatic in me, and of his intense desire to learn to know me thoroughly, and of how necessary this was for the completion of his culture and his views. You know how I detest everything of this kind, and I really could not help telling him in a very friendly way, but at the same time very curtly, that I was surprised at his difficulty, for that any one might learn to know me through and through in three days, because everything in me sprang from very simple motives, and that besides it did not seem to me to be worth any one's while to seek to construe every individual trait in each individual mind. While giving you such a full account of H——'s visit, the feeling of the dreadful solitude in which I live, quite overwhelms me. Nevertheless, every interruption of this solitude in the evening is a real loss to me; for it is then that I give myself up to the sweet remembrance of our former life here, and to thoughts of the many enjoyments which you have procured for us, by establishing us out here.

I have also been calculating, that if the danger, which at the present moment seems entirely to have withdrawn from Berlin, should not approach again, and a fortunate battle should remove the war into Saxony, and I should win the great prize in the lottery on the 1st of June, I would buy an excellent travelling carriage and set off to fetch you back. Such is in fact the reward I ought to have for the privations I am undergoing. You may well laugh at me, dear heart, but you must learn to know my follies also. . . . .

Süvern has resigned his command on account of some unpleasantness during drill. This is a very disagreeable affair, and I am doing my best to set matters right again. In short, I am behaving so well, that I am sure you would be delighted with me, could you witness it. . . . .

[CCCLXXVIII.] *21st, Evening.*

What will be the end of it, dear heart, if I go on in this way writing to you for ever? I should like to know how the distance between us affects you—it increases my longing for you every day; but now that I have brought my occupations into better order, and that we are not so tormented with rumours, I am again able to work. However, I am obliged to take hold of such a variety of things, that I cannot continue any one subject long enough to feel that I am getting thoroughly into it. The interruption of the sweet habit of sharing everything with you, which was enjoying in such full measure just before you left, I now feel most keenly. The intense love I have conceived for the garden, arises out of nothing but this. I hardly ever walk in it, I only sit and look at it from the window, and I am nowhere so happy as here. I look upon the place as a sweet gift from you, which I must ever have by me to gaze at. At present I have no dark forebodings whatsoever. I am only thinking of our speedy reunion, and of how I shall celebrate it and enjoy it. But even this hope is founded rather in my wishes than in any particular conjuncture of events ; for until a battle has been won in Lusatia, or some other event has transplanted the war

entirely to the other side of the Elbe, there can be no security
for us. . . . .

. . . . . To-day I have received my increased salary
for the ensuing month, so that all likelihood of immediate
starvation is again postponed; and after all, I dare say, we
shall not run any very great danger in this respect, or be
very hard bestead. Well, if it is not to be, I suppose we
must bear it; and our separation is, alas! quite enough to
have to endure. Good night; try and keep the children as
regularly to work as you can: but it is easy enough for me to
talk; perhaps you will find it much more difficult to execute.

[CCCLXXIX.]   *22nd.*

. . . . . The only rumour prevalent here at present
is, that Ney's corps is still retiring, and Bulow's pursuing him.
The most people are therefore quite easy. Nevertheless, everything depends upon the next battle. The Austrian alliance
is, it is said, placed beyond all doubt, but officially we hear
nothing on the subject.

Only think, that at court and in the aristocratic circles, it
is asserted that I have gone off. I suppose it is P——, who
got your passport for you, that is mostly to blame in the matter.
For it has also been reported to the place-major. Mrs. Von
Hazfeld, more especially, has done her best to spread the
rumour, and in consequence my first feeling was a desire to
take a little revenge on her. Indeed, I had no peace until I
had indited a very sharp note to her. You know my ways,
but I thought it not worth my while to send it off—for the
fable will very soon disprove itself.

In the morning, one meets troops of people with spades and
shovels, going to work at the entrenchments, and in the evening one sees companies of the *Landsturm*, exercising in all the
great squares. The two redoubts near our *Schafgraben* are
very neat, and when they are manned and armed, I am sure
the enemy will not get in until they have been battered down
and the cannon have been dismounted. When we consider
that there are about thirty to forty thousand men belonging

to the *Landsturm* here (though the latter number is probably exaggerated), and that these will be supported by about fifteen thousand regular troops, there is every reason to suppose that, if matters are conducted with proper skill, Berlin will be able to hold out even against a very superior force, provided the latter be not aided by very heavy artillery.

Embrace the children most heartily for me, and tell them to behave so that you may have good accounts to write to me of them. The sermon which I had commenced before you left, is still incomplete, but in addition to this I have been studying the New Testament, and taking notes, and have also been delivering my lectures very regularly. I always feel that I must give you an account of what I am doing, for that helps to spur me on. To-morrow I am to preach for the first time without you, only your empty seat opposite to me—it will be very hard. May God soon unite us again, my beloved, my precious wife! I embrace you in spirit and press you close to my heart. God be with you all!

[CCCLXXX.]   *22nd, Evening.*

My joy at the receipt of your letter was so great, so overwhelming, that it made me neglect the parade, and now I have qualms of conscience in consequence. . . . . I have further to think of my sermon, which is by no means ready; but I fear that I shall neither be in the proper mood for thinking of it to-day, nor for delivering it to-morrow. To-day at noon arrived a courier with the news of the successful engagement on the 19th. However, as he left the field of battle during the engagement, though our troops had then the advantage on every point, everybody is now very anxious to learn what the ultimate result has been. The people ought to be spared this sort of suspense, they have not strength to bear it; even we find it difficult. You, poor dear, have no doubt a good deal more to bear than you have allowed me to know, and I dare say it is only your bravery that makes you feel so pleased with the journey. I can only love you and praise you the more for it, and beg you be assured that I feel how much reliance can be placed in you, my heroic, energetic wife.

Since I wrote the above, I have got my sermon into proper order, and I will now say good night. I ought, perhaps, to be in a state of great excitement regarding the decision of the battle; but I am not so. I have a firm conviction that the affair will not terminate in one day; for a total rout of our army is not to be feared, as it had already gained great advantages, and the spirit of the troops was excellent, and the command conducted with great prudence. Neither do I think it likely that Bonaparte will be thoroughly defeated; he is far too strong and skilful for that. Even the decision as to whether or not we are soon to meet again, seems to me to depend upon other events. It is what will take place in Austria, or on the Lower Elbe, that can alone induce him to fall back so far as to allow us to feel secure again.

[CCCLXXXI.]   *24th, Forenoon, in the city.*

I was not able to write to you yesterday; I could only remain a moment at the garden-house in the evening, for I was good for nothing, thoroughly knocked up by the cramps, and obliged to have recourse to *magic*, during which I read your letter once more. Afterwards, though still suffering a good deal, I went to Reimer's—he was here for the day, but started again for Potsdam in the night—where I met Eichhorn and Bardeleben, and Schele (who has of course been obliged to give up all attempts at administration on the other side of the Elbe, and is about to join Bulow), and Arndt, who is here again, and Bothmer, who has arrived from Hamburg, and who means to join Wallmoden. I have commissioned the latter to inquire about Marwitz, and to induce him to write. I was anything but animated, for I was not only suffering much from the cramps, but I had been reflecting the whole day with much grief upon the defective manner in which public affairs are conducted, and the conversation at Reimer's only served to increase this. I returned home towards midnight, quite knocked up, and was obliged to go to bed immediately.

My sermon would perhaps have seemed to you rather forced in the beginning, as on a former occasion; it was a characterization of the Apostle Peter, applied to the present times, and the conclusion was spirited, and I hope effective, and contained a recommendation to watch over the weak, and to inspire them with faith and courage. I discovered a great many gaps among my auditors, and the sight of your empty pew (Pischon alone was in it) brought the tears to my eyes. I am so glad, dear heart, that in this respect you are better off than I am, for you have the children to fill out your life, and are in the midst of new, pleasing, and diverting circumstances. Your longing for me can hardly assume the character which mine for you often has.

Savigny tells me that people are beginning to fly from Hirschberg, but do not allow this to disturb you: remain quietly where you are, until you hear that the *Landsturm* has been called out; should this take place, then proceed as speedily as possible to the nearest town in Bohemia. I shall give you no directions for other cases that may occur, but shall depend entirely upon you and Carl.* The German legion is said to have arrived on the Oder at last, and Stülpnagel is expected here on Friday already, so I suppose I shall soon hear something about Fritz and Helvetius Dohna. The wish that the legion might require my services, has repeatedly passed through my mind; I would most gladly join it. . . .

[CCCLXXXII.] *Evening.*

I cannot conclude my evening out here without a little further chat with you. . . . . .

. . . . . As for the removal of the state officials, I cannot say how it stands; no one has as yet seen the royal order. In every case at first it only had reference to the chiefs of departments, and each of these did as he liked ; one took his councillors with him, another left them behind, and those

* Schleiermacher's brother Carl was then established as an apothecary in Schmiedeberg, where he was much respected as an able pharmaceutist and chemist.

councillors who have received no distinct orders have also acted according to their own discretion. In our department,* no one has as yet left, except Nicolovius, who has been sent by Von Schuckmann to the other province, and Ancillon, who has probably gone to join the crown prince. It is to be hoped that the downright cowards, whether among the royal servants, or among the citizens—for a great many private persons, and more particularly a great many rich Jews, are said to have fled—will get their deserts. . . . . And now good night, dear heart. Ah! it is a melancholy going to bed up yonder in the coffin, without you and the children.

[CLXXXIII.]   *27th. Evening.*

It is with a heavy heart that I address you to-day, dearest. As I was absent the whole day yesterday, and was occupied the whole forenoon to-day in the church, the news of the great, and, as it seems, rather precipitate retreat of the army, has taken me quite by surprise. I may say, that to-day I have for the first time really repented having sent you away, as you will now be quite near the theatre of war, while we shall be perfectly quiet here: and I think, in addition to this, of your being surrounded by so many bewildered and helpless people, and to feel that by the time this letter reaches Schmiedeberg, you may no longer be there, or that, perhaps, by the day after to-morrow, the postal communication with that place may already have ceased. How I shall be able to bear our separation under these aggravated circumstances, without being consumed by my longing for you and the children, I do not know! Since noon, I have been tormenting myself with thoughts of what a state of indecision you must be in, and of how likely it is that we may be still further cut off from each other, if the present retreat continues. . . . . Only think, in a little note which I have received from L——, she actually upbraids me

---

* Schleiermacher was at that time member of the department for Public Instruction, under the Ministry of the Interior, which was presided over by the minister Von Shuckmann.

for having sent you away, and says that husband and wife ought to share good and evil with each other, even unto death—as if you were not sharing it with me. On that point I am quite easy, and shall be able to set her right also: for she has not the least idea what our *Landsturm* edict means. But that you should now be deprived of the immediate protection of my arm, that is very, very hard; and I reproach myself bitterly for the feeling of helplessness which made me fear that I should not be able to take the necessary measures for your safety at the last moment. Tell me honestly, dear heart, has the thought that I was rather precipitate in sending you away, also occurred to you?—that is to say, judging, not by the present state of things, but according to the circumstances at the time?—do, pray, tell me quite candidly. . . . . My sermon to-day was certainly less popular than usual, but there were good things in it. Ah, dearest, I miss you in everything, even in regard to my sermons and my preaching, as, indeed, upon the whole, you influence me for more than you are aware of. I, on the contrary, have always known it, and could well dispense with the proof derived from my present privation. May God protect you: I lay me down to-night with a heavy heart.

[CCCLXXXIV.]   *28th. Evening.*

I have had a pretty quiet day to-day—I mean I have had less to do in connection with the *Landsturm*, but I shall have to pay for this to-morrow. I have, therefore, done more literary work than usual, having written a good bit of a sermon, and laboured through several prize essays submitted to the Academy, besides other reading, and I was able to come out here as early as four o'clock. In the evening, as I was seated quietly at my tea, Twesten came in, so loaves and cakes had to be hunted out of all corners, and we had hardly had time to chat a little together, before in came Savigny, and Eichhorn, and Schele, and Arndt. After the foraging had been successfully got through (luckily there was a sausage in the house), and I had informed them that they must all use the same tea-spoon, we were very merry, and a glass of wine made amends for all that was wanting. Savigny alone seemed depressed, and I strongly suspect that he held *in petto* either some bad account or some evil foreboding, which he would not divulge. . . . .

Only a few hurried words to-night, dear heart, before I go to bed. I was placed in a singular position to-day. Eichhorn and Savigny proposed to me to accept a mission from the committee to head-quarters, to arrange various matters of great importance. Only think what a temptation! I might, in that case, so easily have seen you all, and have brought you back with me, or, at all events, have united my fate with yours again. For one moment, I indulged in the most lovely and romantic visions, but, happily, I withstood all the allurements, as I did not consider the undertaking advisable. But do not attribute too much virtue to me; for the fact is, I have not altogether thrown the proposal overboard, but have made conditions which would give the matter a different appearance, and which may very likely not be agreed to. This and the *Landsturm* business gave me work for the whole day, but in the intervals, I thought much and devoutly of the great public cause, which has, indeed, occupied my mind during all these latter days.

[CCCLXXXV.]　　　　　　　　　　　　　*30th May.*

　　I could write no more to you yesterday than the little note which I took at once to the post. I dined in the Sunday Society, where I met Klewitz, who returned from Breslau a few days ago. I had a good deal of conversation with him, and was much pleased with the excellent sentiments he expressed. He also said that the battle of Bauzen would most certainly have been gained, had the reserves been brought into action; but that the king himself had given contrary orders, because he feared that Bonaparte would then, according to his usual custom, throw large masses forward, to whom we should have no troops to oppose. But Bonaparte had no such large masses at command. This may be called being over-cautious; and if this principle is to be carried out, we ought never to fight except when we know ourselves to be superior in number. Indeed, it does seem to be the principle followed at present, all action being postponed until we shall have the Austrians behind us; for Klewitz also says that at head-quarters they are quite sure that the Austrians are coming. He speaks very highly of the confidence of the king in ultimate success, and also of the courage of the army. Twesten came in the evening, and only learnt from me that the shamefully treacherous Danes had let the French into Hamburg. I hope that in return the English will set fire to Copenhagen. After Twesten had left me, I could not sit down to write to you, because I was obliged to think of my sermon, which did not, however, turn out very well, partly because I was somewhat inattentive then, and partly because of a very strange paroxysm, which came over me in the vestry, previous to my going into the pulpit, and which I must relate to you. All of a sudden, I do not know by what concatenation of thought, such a dread took hold of me that I should be overcome by fear on the approach of death, that it actually brought on a kind of physical depression, which must have had a perceptible influence on my sermon. You know I have repeatedly mentioned to you that I did not feel quite sure that I should not fear death when it came, but the thought never before overwhelmed me in that manner. But all this is owing to the solitude in which I live; were you here, the thought would never have entered my head. I had a faint hope that I should have a letter from you in the afternoon, but I was disappointed. However, I will not, therefore, allow myself to believe that the French are in Schmiedeberg, and you in one of the frontier villages. I walked out, and found that it was raining; and, however fertilizing and welcome the rain might be, on me it had a saddening effect. I next forced myself to work, and succeeded; for I wrote good part of a sermon, almost as much as would make half a sheet in print, and, what is more, I was satisfied with it; but whenever I made a pause and went to the window, the feeling of sadness again assailed me. Ultimately, I was rescued from it in a most agreeable manner by the arrival of Mina Reimer, who came with the two girls and Arndt. Afterwards Dreist joined us, and we were all very merry.

And now, good night. It strikes me that I gossip too much about the petty events of the day, and I will avoid this in future.

[CCCLXXXVI.]   *31st May.*

 To-day I have given myself a treat which I have never before enjoyed ; I took a walk through the garden at half-past five o'clock in the morning. It had rained in the night, the air was delicious, and the roses were very much refreshed ; they give promise of a second bloom. At what o'clock do you rise, dearest ? Do you enjoy the glories of the early morn, and do you on first awaking think of me and long for me, as I do for you most tenderly and truly, the first thing in the morning and the last thing at night ? I look at the beautiful flowers in the garden with a feeling of regret, because, supposing matters to proceed ever so favourably, they will have faded before you can be back. This morning, Pischon baptized his child, and I was godfather. I was much impressed by the beautiful sense in which he understands Christianity, and also his own vocation, which came out so distinctly in his discourse. The whole ceremony was very touching and pleasing to me ; it reminded me of some of the most delightful moments of our life and of the sweet paternal joys which I owe to you ; and a sincere thanksgiving poured forth from my heart, which yearned more than ever for you. The calm, secure happiness of the young couple also moved me deeply, and from a full heart I prayed for such blessings on the child as are most essential to a girl.

Now, dearest wife, everything considered, I do not know why I should postpone any longer giving you orders to return home. For the present there is not the slightest danger to be feared here, whereas where you are you may be exposed to such in a week, should both armies have recruited their strength sufficiently to deliver battle. Therefore, let us venture it in God's name, and let me beg you to set off as soon after the receipt of this letter as you shall deem the road safe, that is to say, as soon as you hear that our armies are on the other side of the roads.

Dear heart, I am penetrated with joy at the thought of our meeting again. Oh, how sincerely I shall thank God when I hold you again in my arms, when I press the dear little people again to my heart! God grant that there may be no difficulty on your side ; here everything will no doubt remain quiet. It is even said that the Princess Wilhelm, who had gone no further than Francfort, is about to return. . . . .

With what an oppressed heart I sit down to write to you, dearest wife, whom I have perhaps now lost for a long, long time! Will you ever receive these lines ? and when and how will the time come when we shall meet again ? Good God ! yesterday I wrote to you so full of glad hope to beg you come back ; we had not then heard of the retreat of the army into Silesia ; and to-day we have received news of the brilliant action near Hagenau ! It has struck me like a thunderbolt ! In what state of mind may you be, and where may you be ? Have you sought refuge in some corner of Bohemia, or are you still in Schmiedeberg, full of fear that you may have to fly at any moment ? And I, who ought to be your counsellor and your support, I am here ! I reproach myself most bitterly for having been so foolish as to send you away ! O God ! it is a heavy, heavy trial, and I do not know how I shall bear it. Sweet heart, have I not sinned grievously against thee and the children ? Have I not wantonly precipitated that hardest of fates, which ought only to have been brought about by the most important events ? Are you not already as lonely and forlorn as if you were a widow ? Everything around me looks indescribably gloomy, and I begin even to despair of the public cause. These repeated retreats will necessarily damp the courage of the people and bring everything into confusion. From Austria we hear nothing. The crown prince of Sweden is also holding back, it is said because the conditions are not fulfilled which Russia and Prussia promised. And the people ? Good God, can we reckon on it ? How many are they who are really animated by patriotism ? It is possible that Hamburgh may fall in a few days. O God ! my beloved, what can individuals hope for, under such circumstances, but a noble death ! Sweet wife, you whose destiny I have bound up with mine, had I but your hand in mine, could I but gaze into your eyes, could we but seek new strength and courage heart pressed to heart ! My tender love for you and the children is the only happy feeling I have left—or rather my love for you, for I confess it at this moment the children are very secondary in my eyes, because as yet they have not the consciousness of what is going on around them; but at the bottom of my heart there is an immeasurable love for them also, which might at any moment be converted into a lion's love. But I must cease, I must tear myself away, I am too excited.

[CCCLXXXVII.]   2nd June, Afternoon.

About an hour ago, dear heart, I received your letter of the 25th. I am sincerely rejoiced that you have so happily got over the first fright and difficulties, and that I can fully approve of all that you have done and planned.

Alas ! that I can do nothing, either for the great cause of our country or for you, except wish and pray, and devote to both a passive love ! Oh, to be separated under such circumstances is too dreadful ! What you say so kindly, dear love, about feeling consoled at the thought of my being in quiet and safety, has cut me to the heart ; and when you write, "the happy ones, who remained,"—ah, my darling wife, it drives me to despair to think that I sent you away !

In one respect, you are far better off than I. You suffer, but at the same time you are called upon to act. But I can only look on, while my heart is being torn to pieces; and then to feel that, as far as you are concerned, I have brought this upon myself ! Ah ! I shall never be at peace until I hold you again in my arms, and then I shall hardly feel myself worthy of folding you to my bosom. .   .   .   . But I will force myself to go to work, that I may not fall into a morbid state.

[CCCLXXXVIII.]   8th June, Noon.

Everybody here feels as if fallen from the clouds at the news of the armistice ; as yet we know too little about the details to allow me to pass any judgment upon it, and I will not join those who are precipitate in abusing it. Things look dangerous indeed, yet I will not yield to the fear that this may lead to an unfavourable peace. With God's help, at all events, it shall lead to our reunion, and I am out of myself with joy when I think of it. .   .   .   . Never again, dearest Jette, will we thus separate, should even, as I hope, the *Landsturm* edict remain a permanent law—never again, until the most urgent necessity is at the door, will I send you away from me.

[CCCLXXXIX.]   10th, *Evening.*

.   .   .   . It is four weeks to-day since you left, and I hope that only one week more will elapse before you are back again, for I can hold it out no longer. At moments I feel as if I were transported back into my old days of bachelorhood, and as if it were only a dream that I had ever changed my condition, and a shudder of horror comes over me. Then again, when I bring you and the children vividly before my imagination, and the old presentiment returns that you will not keep me long, an indescribable sadness steals over me, at the thought of all that is precious and all that is vain in life, of all that is good and noble which, by the grace of God, has been developed in me, and of so much that is unworthy and contemptible that is mixed up with this,—I feel as if I would fain fold you to my heart, impress upon you once more how tenderly I love you, bless you, and then die. Come, dearest, hasten to join me, to fill out my life again, and to save me, by your sweet presence, from this dreamy state, which solitary work at the writing-desk does not suffice to conquer. .   .   .   .

[cccxc.]   *Tuesday morning.*

I took a delightful stroll in the garden, as early as a quarter before five. I was thinking whether it would be possible to induce you sometimes to slip out of bed so early, and to come and enjoy with me the freshness and fragrance of the morning. At rare intervals it must be, however, because to rise early is, in fact, contrary to your nature. What I occupied myself with?—with you. The anniversaries of the most important epochs of our lives are drawing near—the day on which I saw you for the first time, when you gave me a touching impression of a pious, gentle girl, under the influence of a first and holy love, such as I had never before witnessed. How tenderly attached to you I was! I looked upon it as the highest happiness left to me, to be near you and to witness and to bless your wedded life. Then again, the time when I felt such an irresistible desire to see you again as a sorrowing widow, and when gradually a deeper love still was developed. Yes, Jette, it was Divine guidance that led me to you; and I feel it now as deeply as ever, I could never have loved any other woman as I love you. I press your dear head to my bosom, imprint a kiss on your forehead, and once more promise to guide and support you through this chequered life, with all the strength of my love and my whole being, and to pour upon you all the good that wells up in my own heart, as also all that I can gather in the world around me.

[cccxci.]   *21st, Evening.*

With foolish, youthful thoughtlessness, I had almost given up writing; and now the nearer the post-day approaches the more anxiously my heart beats, lest it may bring a bitter disappointment.

To-day I have begun to write an essay, which I am to read to the Academy on Thursday next, on the various methods of translation.* It may prove interesting, if I be allowed proper leisure.

* It may be found in Schleiermacher's *Works*, sect. 3, vol. ii., p. 207.

[cccxcii.]   *24th, Evening.*

I was unable to write to you yesterday, because I was so very busy with the essay, which I have read to the Academy to-day. It is, in fact, trivial enough, but for that very reason people thought it very clever and interesting, and have requested me to read it at the next public sitting. I did not like to refuse, because as yet I have never read a paper in public, and they might have thought that it was affectation. The essay treats of translation, and contains some home-thrusts at Wolf's system; but I do not know if any one noticed them. Who do you think sat opposite to me, listening with great attention?—Kotzebue; he is the very man we saw in the box at the theatre.

Dear love, how very little, in fact, I have done since you have been away! Four sermons only, and this essay, besides a few insignificant researches, and the current business, and yet I am not at all intent on improvement, but, on the contrary, am speculating upon how I shall manage to save time to devote to you. My chief hope is based upon the probability that the mesmerizing will soon become unnecessary, and that I shall then not be obliged to go to town in the afternoon. God knows, however, whether I shall really be able to manage this, as I have determined to undertake the editorship of the *Correspondent.* I could not do otherwise, for, in the contrary case, the paper must have ceased to appear, and it is a matter of too great importance to Reimer. It will entail a good deal of worry on me, I know; work to which I am not accustomed, and which I shall not at first know how to set about, and quarrels with the Government and the silly censorship. And who knows as yet what Niebuhr will say to it? However, I console myself with the thought that I am doing it from the most disinterested motives, and at a great sacrifice. . . . .

Schleiermacher to Georg Reimer.

[cccxciii.]   *Berlin, 24th July,* 1813.

In regard to the *Correspondent,* dear friend, matters go on only so so. I receive very little assistance except from R——, who is pretty industrious; but as long as he remains in Wolgast, I am afraid his contributions will always come too late, as has hitherto been the case with his most important articles. However, he writes that he is about to proceed to Stralsund, and then, I dare say, he will be of greater use to us. A few days ago, Niebuhr sent for the first time a contribution, which was but of slight importance; but he promises something better shortly. We shall see if he keeps his word. The persons acquainted with the court and others also are negligent, and the Government seems to be displeased, and does not even forward official notices. It is to be hoped, however, that now that the Chancellor has left, this will be corrected; for Sack, I think, is well inclined. I have no doubt that this displeasure is connected with the persecution to which I have been subjected, in consequence of the well-known article in No. 60 ; and this, again, with the dissolution of the *Landsturm,* and with Bärensprung's transportation to Pillau. All these matters hang on one string, and this is what is called a decisive victory over Stein's party. Such are the first-fruits of Scharnhorst's death ; but, never mind, the good cause will, nevertheless, be triumphant. My mishap has only served to amuse me ; it is too absurd to cause me any real annoyance. Schuckmann, who had received a cabinet order to give me a severe reprimand, and to threaten me with dismissal, should I repeat the offence, began in the most angry and savage tone, and even accused me of high treason ; but concluded with repeated assurances that he considered me a most upright man and sincere well-wisher to my country, and with a very quiet conversation about how far liberty of the press should go in regard to newspapers. My imperturbable self-possession, and the explanation of a misunder-

standing in connection with an old affair in which he believed
I had personally insulted him, produced a very evident effect on
him. I reserved to myself the right of delivering in a written
defence ; I dare say he will consign it to the record office, but
I will take care that it shall become known to the public.

It is very desirable, in respect to the *Correspondent*, that
you should come yourself, and put everything in order. The
Landsturm being now dissolved, Göschen might, indeed, find
time to attend to it ; but, for the first, I should not like to
retire immediately after this affair ; and for the second, I fear
that Göschen would draw back within the former limits,
which would not at all be good for the paper. Therefore, if
no better person can be found, I will continue the editorship as
well as I can during the next quarter, after the lapse of which,
I hope some other plan may be devised. For should I be
obliged in winter to carry on the lecturing business more seriously than at present, it would be impossible for me to continue.

As regards public matters, I trust you will not lose courage.
The rumours of peace are gradually dying away ; but, on the
other hand, it is to be supposed that, if Austria joins the alliance, the Russians will play a more secondary part, and will,
perhaps, only have to carry on the siege. Mendelssohn, who
has been here long enough to be able to tell you everything,
will probably do so ; and I will, therefore, not spend time in
pondering upon what might be most interesting to you to
know. Farewell, may God preserve your health and courage!
Eichhorn is said to be seeking an appointment in the army. I
hope it is not true ; but if he could get a high appointment in
the *commissarium*, I should be very glad. However, I suppose that is not to be thought of.

Schleiermacher to Charlotte von Kathen.

[cccxciv.]   *4th April*, 1814.

It is very long since I have written to you, dear
Charlotte ; but Jette, I know, has from time to time kept you

informed of my health and of our entire life. Lured by the fine weather, we are again happily established in the garden-house ; and my first enterprise in the morning is a walk, I may truly say, amid the verdure, for everything is budding and bursting into leaf, and in a few days, the alders will be in blossom. My work, on the contrary, does not progress so well ; but for this, the world-events are more to blame than nature. Good God! how much blood is again being shed, all because of misapplied magnanimity, and how long may it not be before we can hope for peace! Yet God's finger is too evident, throughout our present history, to allow of our doubting that, though it may be through severe trials, it will, ultimately, lead to that consummation which we have hitherto hoped for in vain. Half of what ought to have been accomplished during the former war, in regard to external as well as internal matters, has still to be done ; and even should the measures be carried out at present, we may believe that it would not have taken place under any other circumstances; in like manner, as many persons would never have been able to see through the baseness of the French, had it not been for what has now occurred. Our domestic life, however, will, I think, not be exposed to the same interruptions as during the last years ; and I shall hardly be induced to separate myself again from wife and children, although we may be placing a secret enemy in our rear, by allowing the King of Saxony to be reinstated at Dresden. But fearful things will and must still take place on other points. . . . . .

I hope you will see our Arndt often, and that you will derive much pleasure from his society. You will, I am sure, find his mind and heart as fresh as ever. Among you, I dare say, he is even more thoroughly in his element than here. I only wish that he could obtain a settled position in life—although I do not see how it is to be accomplished—and then, what is more, a domestic circle of his own. After all, dearest Lotte, this is and ever will be the most important thing in life, and I thank God daily for my Jette and the children. However, the thought that they will most likely not have me long with them, sometimes makes me very sad.

Give my heartiest regards to all your people.

[cccxcv.]   *No date.*

Dear sister, I do not know whether I shall have time to write more than a few words, and I will, therefore, begin with the most important. It relates to your boys. I can by no means agree in your views, when you speak of keeping them under your own roof until they are seventeen; and I earnestly wish that I could give you the lively conviction which I myself entertain, that the very opposite is right. Unfortunately, these matters can only be thoroughly discussed face to face, when each has an opportunity of expressing himself fully. But I am firmly persuaded that a boy ought by all means from his fourteenth year already to be brought up in a large community, and to enjoy public instruction, which is always conducted on a much grander scale than it is possible to attain to at home. Boys who live in large cities are indeed best off, as they may combine these advantages with home life. But when that is not possible, I am convinced that all the benefits which are supposed to be derived from a longer stay under the parental roof cannot by any means outweigh the disadvantages. First of all as regards the acquisition of knowledge, it has been sufficiently proved that at home the strict order and regularity which rules in schools can never prevail. Secondly, the very best of tutors cannot accomplish as much as is accomplished in even a moderately good school, where the various branches of instruction are judiciously divided among several teachers, who work into each other's hands. And if between the ages of fourteen and seventeen a solid foundation be not laid, and a certain extent of knowledge acquired, what has thus been lost can never be regained. Viewed from this side, indeed, the matter is self-evident and beyond dispute; but, perhaps, it will be less evident to you that the same holds good in regard to the formation of character. It is believed that in their homes boys are better secured against temptation, and are made more religious. As far as regards religion, you need not be alarmed. Even without having done much towards it directly, you must have laid a foundation of piety in your children, and even at a distance your influence in this direction will continue, and may indeed be greater if the boys feel themselves leading a life conducive to their progress, and consequently most satisfactory to you, than it would be at home if they felt themselves out of place there. One invaluable advantage afforded by schools is, that there the sense of right is developed, and the boy acquires a feeling of self-dependence. It is these two qualities that make the man. And observe, that almost all men who have remained too long in the paternal home prove themselves in some way or other wanting in manliness—they are either irresolute, or incapable, or deficient in public spirit. Now at seventeen it is too late to acquire the two qualities in question; at that age the youth will always feel himself a stranger among those who have gone through this schooling at an earlier age, and will also be deprived of that support, which early intimacies and friendships would afford him. . . . . .

In August, 1816, Schleiermacher's wife and daughters went to Pomerania and Rügen, on a visit to Mrs. Schleiermacher's brothers and sisters, and somewhat later he himself made a trip to Hamburgh, Kiel, &c., and ultimately to Rügen, to bring back wife and children. The following letters are from this period:—

Schleiermacher to his Wife.

[cccxcvi.] *Berlin, 18th August, 1816.*

. . . . . I have had two bad days, and suffered much, especially yesterday evening, when I had a severe attack on my way hither from town. It is to be hoped that F——'s * prophecy has thus been fulfilled; but I know with certainty that I have not neglected any one of her precautions.

I have given up the hope now of escaping all attacks during my travels; nevertheless, I shall enjoy the latter, and if I can only be thrown into the magnetic sleep when we return, I shall soon be better. Pray do not fancy me worse than I am; I am by no means broken down and miserable, only not quite as well as when at the best. Ehrenfried goes about wailing at the dull life without mother and sisters. As for myself, dear heart, I do not say much about it, but I feel it the more, and I become more and more conscious of what a lively influence you and the children exercise over me. It is fortunate that I have got through my ethics, for at present I should not be able to do anything. Our outward life, also, is rather dull. I have been obliged each day to work during tea-time, and it has, therefore, passed off in perfect silence. Yesterday the Savignys went out to the garden-house, but did not stay to tea, and were gone before I arrived, and these

* This friend of the family, a confirmed invalid, had become clairvoyante, in consequence of a long course of mesmeric treatment. During her states of lucidity she was in the habit of indicating (under the guidance of a medical man) what she thought might be good for persons suffering under various ailments. She had given much attention to the case of Schleiermacher also, who had for years been subject to violent attacks of cramps in the stomach, which had baffled all the skill of the physicians, and threatened to put an early limit to his life. Even independently of their practical bearings, the mesmeric and clairvoyante states, which were mostly connected with a deeply religious spirit, exercised great attraction over Schleiermacher's wife, whose enthusiastic mind was deeply imbued with mysticism and a love of the marvellous, and who saw in these states the possibility for man to place himself in immediate connection with the Holiest and the Highest. Schleiermacher has expressed his views of mesmerism and its various phenomena in a letter to Charlotte von Kathen, which will appear in the sequel. Through the mesmeric treatment he was ultimately entirely cured of the painful hereditary disease under which he suffered for so many years, and never had a return of it during the latter part of his life.

are the only evening visitors we have had. I give my hearty regards to all. I must go off now to a meeting of the faculty; when that is over, I shall work quietly at my sermon, and then probably dine at Bergs.

[cccxcvii.]   *Saturday Evening, 24th August.*

At last, dearest heart, a letter from you has arrived. I received it yesterday afternoon. The time seemed very long to me while waiting for it. Thanks be to God that it contains nothing but good accounts of you and the children. Ah! and even that you are a little anxious about me, does my heart good. Yesterday I was thinking a great deal of that day three years ago. It was a noble time, with all its anxieties. Nevertheless, I am not sorry that it is over, and that I am able in undisturbed activity and calm affection to gather strength for the new times that are to come, if, indeed, I should live to see them. I feel deeply convinced, dearest, that we shall be able to bear anything with each other, and that you will come forth more nobly from every new trial. . . . . Sleep well, dear heart; I must go to bed, or you will chide me, for it is eleven o'clock. From a true heart I commend you to God, and pray for his blessing upon you, my only consolation, for whom I thank Him daily, when you are with me and when you are absent. Kiss all the little people for me.

[cccxcviii.]   *Tuesday, 27th, Evening.*

I was delighted, dear heart, that your second letter also arrived on one of my good days, when I could thoroughly enjoy it. . . . . . F—— has prescribed a number of rules for me, and seems upon the whole to be without any anxiety about my journey, although she said once, with some appearance of alarm, "If they could but wait until Friday!" The worst of it is with this kind of prophets, that they are so apt to mislead you. However, it is not in my character to allow myself to be detained by anything of the kind, for she said nothing distinctly, and it would entirely have upset our plan.

Hitherto, indeed, everything seems very favourable. The weather has improved very much since yesterday, and as I shall be provided with numerous amulets, and still more rules and prescriptions, I trust everything will go on well. To-day I have retired from the rectorship, having employed the last hours of it in a kind of examination. The sermons have been placed in safety, but all the other papers remain in the greatest confusion, and *Plato* has not been finished. But never mind, my trunk is packed, and to-morrow morning at five we start. I am going to meet you, it is true, dearest heart, and yet it seems to me that my temporary widowerhood is only now beginning, as hereafter I shall have very little chance of hearing from you. Ah, write away as rapidly as you can, those letters are always the best. Why should my enjoyment in reading them be spoilt by the thought that they had cost you trouble? From eight o'clock until noon I have been sitting still writing, while Nanni has been running about packing. Thank God that I can feel so easy about you and the children. Kiss the dear mites for me, and greet all friends heartily. I am longing very much once more to mix in their life; but you do not say a word to make me think that they care to see me. Adieu. A thousand kisses.

[cccxcix.]   *Hamburgh, Saturday Evening, 31st.*

Oh, had I not to write with thick tavern ink! But this is one of the petty miseries of life which it is difficult to conquer. My pen, also, is not of the best, as I have mended it by candlelight, and my narrative will no doubt bear the traces of both evils. You may judge from these preliminary complaints, dear heart, that nothing very important has occurred. . . . .

I have not as yet seen many people, except Louisa Reichardt, D. Sieveking, and the family Perthes. To-morrow, however, we are to dine at Flotbek with the Sieveking circle, which is said to comprise many interesting persons. To-day we have been running about in the city, on the exchange, and in the harbour. Hamburgh gives one an impression of great animation and great commercial activity. In this point it seems grander than Francfort, but on the other hand it has not so antique and historical a character.

Schleiermacher to Charlotte von Kathen.

[cccc.] *Berlin, 9th January,* 1817.

Dearest sister, I cannot resist the temptation to intervene in your and Jette's discussions upon mesmerism and its various phenomena, more particularly as my case in relation to these is so frequently referred to by you both. Not that I would endeavour to shake the resolution that you have taken, to have nothing to do with it, though at one time you seemed so greatly attracted by it; but under existing circumstances I look upon it as a duty, which I owe to you and to the friends surrounding you, to explain my views on the subject as far as this is possible without writing a whole essay. Partly that you may not be attributing to me opinions and beliefs which I do not entertain, partly also because you all seem to me to look at the subject from a wrong point of view. Through scientific experiments the phenomenon which we designate by the name of animal magnetism, has gradually been discovered. Again, that aspect of it that relates to the nervous system, and through this to the whole animal economy of man, has been introduced into medical practice after a series of experiences very nearly as complete as that which any other curative system has been subjected to, and I cannot therefore acknowledge that there is any moral objection to the use of mesmerism more than to the use of any other medicine. There are other curative means as well, in regard to which it cannot either be ascertained with exactness beforehand what secondary effects they may produce upon the body or even upon the mind, as for instance, quicksilver, cantharides, belladonna, and many other poisons. As in regard to these the patient depends upon the judgment of his physician, so also in regard to mesmerism; and on the physician devolves the duty of observing in each case what relation the secondary effects bear to the primary, and of acting accordingly.

If, however, an individual should say, I will rather die than allow myself to be cured in this way—this is a matter which every one must settle with his own conscience, but he must not make his decision a rule for others. The same holds good in regard to the secondary effects of magnetism. The so-called lucid states are mostly temporary and entirely limited to the period of sleep, are quite disconnected, and exercise no influence over the rest of the patient's life. For a phenomenon such as F——,* is quite exceptional. I cannot see therefore why any one should hesitate to avail himself of this means of cure, when recommended by his physician, because he might possibly fall into these temporary states, which, if he so chooses, may be allowed to pass by without in any way being used. As for what has been said of the mental dependence in which the patient is brought to the magnetizer, this is in the most cases untrue, and where it does exist, it will probably be found to be nothing more than the affection and confidence which other patients feel for a highly valued family doctor.

I have not yet seen Schubert's new book. . . . . He is quite right not to undertake any magnetic cures, and ought never to have allowed himself to do so, as he is not a doctor, and would never think of undertaking other cures. He cannot, therefore, have had the same feeling of confidence, and as a matter of course the secondary effects produced under his treatment must have assumed a distinct character, because he stood in a very different relation to the persons practised upon from that of a regular physician. If therefore his experiences were such as to alarm him and warn him not to continue, he may attribute this to himself. In fine, I would never hesitate to allow any person who is dear to me to be magnetized on the recommendation of a physician, and by a duly qualified person; but I would keep a watchful eye on the secondary effects produced, in like manner as I would were they subjected to any other drastic remedy.

* In her case this limitation did not exist.

Further, as regards the medical advice given by persons in the mesmeric state, when their attention is directed towards the ailments of others, I do not see why a physician should be denied the right to ask this advice and to turn it to account. It is a use which he makes of a state which he has himself called forth, and a use in immediate connection with his profession. It seems to me to be nothing more than when he takes the lymph from a person whom he has inoculated with the cow-pox, to vaccinate another person. As for the confidence to be placed in the advice given, that is a matter for the physician's own judgment; and for this very reason a man who knows nothing of medicine ought not to seek such advice, because he has not the means of judging of its value, and because, moreover, the answer given to a person ignorant of the art will no doubt be very different to that given to a man that has studied it.

I should never have asked F——— to turn her attention to my case, and, indeed, I did not even approve of Wolfart's doing so, as I was totally unknown to her, and it seemed to me to be an act of indiscretion. However, that was his affair, not mine; and I have only followed the advice given in as far as Meier, who is my regular medical attendant, approved of it, or, at least, declared it to be innocuous; contrary to the desire of my doctor I would never have used it. Thus, also, it has been in the case of the drops, as I hereby repeat for the tranquillization of all those who have seen me use them, and who have witnessed their beneficial effects. From the very beginning Meier limited me in the use of them, in so far that he told me I must cease to take them as soon as I perceived that they caused loss of appetite or nausea; F——— had fixed a limit of time. I saw that Jette was very desirous that I should adhere to the directions of the latter; but I would hardly have done this under any circumstances, or had I done so it would have been contrary to my own convictions and merely for the sake of making her easy—for which purpose I may, and do sometimes, either wholly or partially give up my own convictions—had not the nausea and the loss of appetite come on previous to the expiration of the time.

Respecting the mental phenomena of mesmerism, my opinion is this: I would by no means consider it sinful if any one allowed himself to be magnetized by a man well acquainted with the art, for the purpose of instituting experiments in regard to the phenomena. And why? Because we are called upon to make ourselves acquainted with all the phenomena of nature. Forgive me for saying so, but it does seem to me very strange that the men who surround you should tell you that magnetism is an unfathomable thing; for how can we know this until we have examined into it, except in as far as all things are unfathomable? but this ought not to prevent us from trying to penetrate into them as deeply as we can. As it is, we have not, indeed, gained any very deep insight into the power in question, because, judging from all experiments hitherto made, magnetism produces no effects on a healthy body. It is, therefore, only sick persons that are mesmerized, and these, of course, are to will nothing but to be well, as also their physician is to be intent on nothing but to make them well. And even in invalids the physician cannot arbitrarily produce the higher phenomena, nor can the patient do so. This has been fully proved by the cases of various patients who have ardently desired to be thrown into the state of somnambulism without having been able to effect it.

On the other hand, there are many mesmerizers who believe that it depends upon their will to produce the state of clairvoyance; however, this has by no means been established as a fact: but when the higher phenomena—such as the power of seeing at a distance, or into the future—do appear, I should not either consider it sinful of the patient to allow his physician, or any other scientific man, to ask questions of him, while in the lucid state, which might conduce to throw light upon the nature of the phenomena, provided these questionings did not interfere with the progress of the cure. But though I should not consider it sinful, I believe it would be useless; for such experiments could never lead to any satisfactory result, as the state of the patient would be disturbed by outward influences. However, to make use of the somnambulic state of a patient for such experiments, without his consent, that I would consider sinful, because we have no right to make any human being the object of an experiment without his own consent, or, in other words, we have no right to reduce him to the level of a lifeless thing.

As to whether or not we are allowed to make ourselves acquainted with these higher phenomena, I would not undertake to lay down any general rule, except in as far as our duties towards the sick may be concerned. Many persons have reason to keep themselves aloof from everything that may over-excite them ; and such would doubtless do best not to fill their heads with these matters. Others would derive nothing better from it than the useless satisfaction of their idle curiosity, and such I would never allow to approach a patient of this kind ; for we ought never to make an idle spectacle of a human being. But any one who stood beforehand in a personal relation to a mesmeric patient, as, for instance, Jette to F——, or any one who has a serious purpose in endeavouring to make himself more thoroughly acquainted with the phenomena, why should he not seek to become a witness of them ? I would always admit physicians, naturalists, and philosophers into the presence of clairvoyant patients (provided the latter did not object to it, and there was no fear of its being injurious to them), even when in their most ecstatic states; although sick persons (and, if we would judge correctly, we must not forget that clairvoyants are always in a sickly state) can, of course, never be regarded as public characters, and their mental activity does not, therefore, belong to the sphere of public life.

My opinion in regard to the nature of these mental phenomena, and to their truth, is this: any distinction between the natural and the supernatural, between the comprehensible and the incomprehensible, I do not, upon the whole, recognize. Everything is in one sense natural, and in another supernatural. Even that the Son of God was made man must, in a *higher* sense, be natural.

In what category the magnetic phenomena are to be placed is still a subject of inquiry ; but, in order to obtain to a knowledge of this, we must observe them. It may be said, in general, that by changes introduced in the physical conditions, certain limits to which the mind is usually subject are for a time removed. To the removal of such limitations, indeed, we owe all that is sublime and divine in the ancient prophecies ; for, otherwise, the men would not have been men during the period of prophesying or of inspiration, but would have been some other kind of beings. The greatest interest attaching to the higher phenomena of mesmerism is exactly this—that, when well understood, they will tend to throw new light on the original and essential range of the mental capacities of man; and in connection with this, no doubt, also on many points relating to the dark ages and sacred history of all nations. Finally, as regards the amount of truth in these phenomena, and the amount of credence to be attached to them, I can only say that in human affairs there is no more absolute distinction between the true and the false than there is between the natural and the supernatural. There is no error, even of the most pernicious kind, which has not an admixture of truth or which is not connected with some truth, and there is no truth that does not include the possibility of error. This holds good even of the old prophets. For, firstly, in believing that God specially called upon them to prophesy, they were as liable to be mistaken as other men ; secondly, the Bible itself shows cases in which they resisted the voice of God; and, thirdly, they beheld events in images; and when they translated these into words, the ecstatic state had already ceased, and their representations might therefore contain errors or misunderstandings. The same is the case with people in the mesmeric state. They also behold almost everything in visions ; the putting of these into words is no longer part of the original superior activity, during which the usual limitations are removed, but is in a great measure an interpretation of the visions rendered through means of the ordinary human faculties; and, therefore, error is more likely to attach to the interpretations than to the visions themselves. I even anticipate that it will ultimately be possible to ascertain and determine, by close observation of somnambulists, on whose good faith one may implicitly rely, which visions they can explain and interpret with the greatest correctness, and which with the least. But if the original and increased activity be really owing to the removal of limitations otherwise existing, it follows that, in as far as truth is the essence of the human mind in all its branches of activity, the higher activity must necessarily embrace a greater amount of truth than the lower; but only on condition that the state induced be left undisturbed. For this reason every distinct question put is, in a manner, a violation of the mesmeric state (and herein consisted the offence of the heathens in regard to the ancient oracles), which, if a pure result is to be obtained, must be left entirely undisturbed, to work it out of itself. Indeed, he who cannot approach a spirit thus liberated and elevated, without such arbitrary interference, should rather stay away altogether. But, on the other hand, I cannot understand the great reluctance to approach persons in this state ; and I do not see why the mesmerized patient, who is besides a suffering individual, should be further punished by being deprived of all friendly relations with others. This reluctance seems to me either to arise from weakness or cowardice. It is true there may be individuals who have a special repugnance to witness such states, and they ought to be exempted; but it ought not, therefore, to be considered a proof of unusual morality and piety, when a person gives way to this repugnance even under circumstances that would render it natural that he should be present during the phenomena. F—— falls asleep each time I come in to her, and give her my hand. Now if, in consequence of such repugnance as I have mentioned, I should refuse to see a person in such friendly relations with my wife, I should not by any means consider the refusal praiseworthy.

But I am shocked to find that I have written a whole volume, and I pity you who are to read it. I began by candle-light, and could not find a pen to suit me. One thing more I must add : I cannot in the least understand, and must beg you once more to explain, what you mean when you say you fear that the contemplation of such phenomena may render people unfit for the ordinary avocations of human life.

And now a few words on other subjects. My health is, thank God, progressing as favourably as I have any right to expect; I have, at times, slight reminiscences of the evil, but very rarely, and I feel more brisk and animated than I have been for a long while, for which reason I am also as industrious as circumstances will allow. We must strike the iron while it is hot; but as I do not believe in a complete cure, but anticipate relapses, I am careful not to overwork myself, lest I may thereby accelerate a return of the paroxysms. Jette has written to you about our hopes, which I am sure have contributed not a little to renovate my life. I acknowledge it with gratitude and feel very happy ! God grant it may go off well ! This also gives you a delightful object for your visit to us. Do not come until the late autumn, when I shall have returned from the vacation ramble which I shall probably take, and when Jette will be quite well again ; that is to say, about the beginning of October. By that time the expected little one will be in its third month, and old enough to afford you pleasure as a plaything. I am of opinion that we ought to send our Jette to you this summer, and I dare say my wife will eventually make up her mind to it. Your Lotte is a much prized guest among us, and her tone of voice, movements, and expression of countenance often remind me of you in a most pleasing manner.

Being in very ill-health, Schleiermacher undertook, in August, 1817, a tour of recreation in Thuringia, during which he wrote the subjoined letters to his wife.

Schleiermacher to his Wife.

[cccci.]   *Dessau, Saturday Evening, August,* 1817.

From Potsdam and Belitz I might have written the most charming letters : since then I have grown more and more lazy, and am now so thoroughly incrustated that I look upon my present act of writing as one of great heroism. I have now only a faint recollection of how sad and yet how happy and grateful I felt then under the beautiful vault of heaven, with the heavy rain-clouds near the horizon from which burst forth flashes of lightning from time to time, while over my head the stars shone out brightly. But I seemed quite ridiculous in my own eyes, indeed almost wicked, when I thought of how, without any real object in view, but merely following a blind instinct, I had torn myself away from you all and thrown myself into the carriage. What I remember best of all is a funny misadventure in consequence of which I might have been safely and soundly lodged with you again this morning. The driver from Berlin, being unacquainted with the post station at Belitz, drove in at the wrong end of the shed, so that the horses' heads were turned towards Potsdam and Berlin. Fortunately, just as I was about to get into the carriage again, I remembered the story of the Jew from Lissa who was going to Leipzig, and I cried out to the postilion : " Take care and don't drive me to Potsdam." He stared, and answered : "Not to Potsdam ! to what place then ? " In short, the whole expedition had been made out for Potsdam, and all the entries had to be made over again.

This little land, Dessau, has made the usual delightful impression upon me; but at the present moment it appears to me like an orphan, because of the old duke's death. I shall proceed farther at once, and hope to get some hours' sleep in Halle. After that I shall be more brisk, but by that time the mail will have left, and I have therefore preferred to write these lines from this place. God preserve you, my only beloved, and the whole house. Continue to love your roving husband.

[cccch.]   *Gotha, 27th August,* 1817.

Dearest wife, I found your two letters of 19th and 23rd instant awaiting me here. I could not refrain from tears on reading them; but they were unmixed tears of joy; for they did not begin to flow until, having finished perusing your letter, I began to read those from the young ones. Dear heart! how blessed are we in every way, and how full of joyful thankfulness we ought to be. Afterwards, I felt a little sad again in thinking of the special matters mentioned by you. Previously all my thoughts of you had been cheerful, because at a distance we only see things as a whole, and I felt assured that no evil would befall you and the little folks. The lower sphere of the servants never came into my mind. . . . .

When writing to you from Dessau, dear heart, I was really quite conscious of all my love for you; but you know how driving stupefies me. How much drier still must not my other letters have seemed to you! I only hope that they have not made you sad. If so, you have done me great injustice. Though not exactly exhausted, I arrived at each place in a state of great depression, and the want of rest and the absence of outward comfort in the inns, in addition to this, has no doubt caused me to be so unlike myself. I felt, indeed, that my letters were nothing more than bulletins of my health and notices of my places of rest, and I hoped that you would not expect more from them. . . . .

We have now accomplished the largest portion of our tour, and since last Wednesday at noon, until to-day at noon, *i.e.* exactly seven days, we have been constantly in motion, and have certainly travelled upwards of thirty miles. I reserve all details for verbal communication, and will now only tell you, that the journey has in every respect been profitable to me, and I rejoice more especially in the feeling of health that I have derived from it. For I have tried every-thing, fatigue, thorough wetting, evening air, and constant changes of diet, and I have borne it all well. Blanc, who is full of health and cheerfulness, has never had his patience tried by me, and I have not once felt my stomach, though I have put it to severe trials. Sometimes this has inspired me with the foolish thought that perhaps mental labours are no longer suited for my age and my bodily powers, and that it is time that I should think of a country parsonage, where I could live more amid nature and for myself.* But then again, when I reflect upon all that I have still to do, and which I think it is my duty to do, I give up the thought, and hope that, even in spite of mental labours, I shall be able, with care, to preserve my health some time longer.

Embrace the children for me, and tell them that the long walks in the mountains make father so tired that he can only write to mother.

[CCCCIII.] *Ebersdorff, 30th August,* 1817.

Read out this name at once to old Lotte,† dear heart, that she may rejoice to know me in one of the establishments of the congregation. We have come into quarters in very good time, and this gives me a little leisure for writing, but not much, for I want to pay a visit to the pastor, who is no doubt an old fellow-student from Barby, and we intend to go to a meeting, and have besides to make entries in our mine-ralogical diaries and to study for to-morrow.

Yesterday we made a long tour from Saalfeld to the top of the mountain ridge. The valley of the Saale is lovely indeed, and also very interesting from the mineralogical point of view, but the farther we left this behind us, and the higher we mounted, the more sterile and the less beautiful nature be-came, and the people had no longer the same true-hearted, frank, and cheerful manners that had pleased us so much in the inhabitants of the lower parts of the mountains. . . . . .

* This plan of eventually retiring to a country parsonage, was often mooted by Schleiermacher.

† His sister Charlotte, who was then living in his house.

My state of mind while amid a congregation of the United Brethren is always very peculiar. The greater part of my youth and the decisive moment in regard to the entire development of my life, are forcibly recalled to my mind. This point of transition, however casual it may appear on the one hand, seems to me on the other to have been so strictly necessary, that I cannot at all conceive myself without it. And though it would be quite impossible for me to live within the timid limitations of a congregation of brethren, the quiet simple life that reigns there makes such a refreshing impression on me, when contrasted with the noisy vanities of the world, that I cannot help feeling and thinking, that were these communities to be reorganized and modified in accordance with the spirit of the times, they might be converted into delightful and most enviable places of abode. . . . .

It almost vexes me that I have not written you more really descriptive letters, not that I care to depict the landscapes to you, but that I might have recorded my impressions, and have shown you how in each case a remembrance of you was in some way or other awakened. But, in truth, I was not able to do so, because time and the necessary materials (which in the present case, also, are of the very worst description) were almost always wanting.

This forenoon we were in Lobenstein, the residence of a Prince of Reuss, who was a comrade of mine at Niesky and Barby. I meant to call upon him, but he was absent from home. When we were at college together, his prospects of coming to the government were very uncertain, and we often teased him about it. He has now attained what was then the highest object of his wishes; but he is already married a second time, and is childless; and I could not help thinking how much happier a man I am than he. Were I but again at your side, and all the distracting festivities over, and our quiet winter life begun! Dear heart, there can hardly be happier people in the world than we may ever be, if we can but keep sufficiently aloof from the world, and learn to bear cheerfully the petty annoyances of life. And I trust we shall day by day succeed better in so doing. When I consider how much wiser we have already grown, and how much better I have become through you, I despair of nothing that may still lie before us. God bless you and strengthen you. . . . .

[cccciv.]   *Rudolstadt, Sunday, 31st, Evening.*

We arrived here after a delightful, though rather warm walk. . . . . God grant that I may find you and every one else so well and full of life on my return, as I hope to be; for the journey seems to do me a great deal of good. Perhaps you may have heard of me through F——, if she has succeeded in seeing me in her visions, as I have often wished and secretly hoped.

. . . . Only two days more I shall be moving farther away from you; after that I shall daily be drawing nearer to you again. This morning again I awoke in the midst of a dream about you, my dear heart. May you have enjoyed many happy hours together with the pledges of our love ! My own beloved wife, how thankful I ever feel to you for being mine ! I fold you to my heart in imagination, and cover your hand with innumerable kisses. Embrace the little people for me, and give them many hearty messages. Tell Lotte that I am bringing her some poems by Albertini, which I have not myself read as yet. A thousand farewells !

In the autumn of 1818, Schleiermacher again made a tour with Georg Reimer and Leopold von Plehwe (then an officer in the guards in Berlin), to the country around Salzburg, the Tyrol, Munich, &c.; during which the following letters were written :—

[ccccv.]   *Linz, 19th September, 1818.*

. . . . . We were unfortunately detained a few hours in Töplitz, and could not even avail ourselves of these to look about us, because we were told every instant that the horses were coming; thus we only arrived in Prague at nine o'clock on Sunday morning, after having travelled all through the night. The very first view one gets of the city, with its numberless towers, is very imposing; but it is from the Hradschin that it appears in its greatest splendour. The people seem to be quite indifferent to all the beautiful monuments that surround them, and to all the great memories that are attached to them, and appear to be utterly unconscious that, with their Protestantism and their religious liberty, they lost all their dignity. Many of the churches are in ruin, and, with the exception of the old cathedral, those that are the most accessible are from the later period when the Jesuits ruled, and are consequently in a tasteless style. The cathedral is a noble, but unfinished edifice, in Gothic style, with a few good paintings; beneath it the history of Bohemia lies interred. The church music that we heard was in the style of modern opera music, but not bad of its kind. The voices were beautiful, the execution on the organ, as well as the organ itself, very fine. We saw some rather good works of art in the Ständisch Gallery, which owes its origin to a noble idea, and which is to me a proof that the Bohemian nobles stand far above the British. Friedrich* told us that the environs of Dresden were on a very small scale, when compared to those of Prague; and although the view from the bridge at Dresden is in itself more beautiful than that from the bridge at Prague, and the Moldau bridge itself is not more beautiful, though more splendid than that of Dresden, I cannot but agree with him, because of the view from the Hradschin, and the imposing effect produced by the buildings. I was actually seized with a shudder—a religious shudder—at the sight of the immense Jesuit college, and with a political shudder at the equally gigantic palace of Wallenstein. The palaces of the other magnates are on a smaller scale, but yet grand, in the old style. But what shall I say of the ruinous state of churches and convents? Protestantism has been wrenched from the

* The great landscape painter.

people with unheard-of cruelty, but Catholicism they cannot prevent from rotting among them.

On Monday morning at ten o'clock we left Prague. The country in the vicinity is no more than pleasantly undulating; not until we reached Budweis, a really white town, with a large market-place out of all proportion to its size, did the high hills begin to reappear, and not until the next morning did we find ourselves again completely among the mountains, which here separate the territories of the Elbe from those of the Danube, and which are more and more beautiful the farther you advance. . . . The more beautiful the mountains became towards morning, the more beautiful also became the weather, and we crossed the Danube and made our entry into this stately city under a bright sun. We have taken up our abode in the market-place, which is surrounded by four-storied houses with Italian roofs, and has a colossal fountain in the middle, but which is never lighted up by the sun, that seems never to rise above the saints on the house-tops. Compared to the Danube, the Elbe near Dresden is a very child.

How I am longing for the first accounts from my dear ones I cannot describe. . . . .

Frankenmarkt, on the road from Linz to Salzburg,

[ccccvi.]   *Friday*, 11*th*, *Evening*.

. . . . . To-day we have only travelled twelve short miles, but we took a circuitous route to see the Traunfall, and spent two hours in contemplation of this glorious spectacle, which art and nature have combined to make most interesting, and from which we could with difficulty tear ourselves away, so that we did not reach our night quarters here until eight o'clock in the evening, when we made our entry to the sound of a very pretty tune, performed by our postilion on his posthorn. The country on this side of the Danube is even more beautiful than on the other. While in the mountains we traversed the finest pine forests, with which those of Silesia cannot even be compared : the valleys were covered with lovely and abundantly watered meadow lands ; the hills, with rich arable soil ; potato fields were remarkably scarce ; the winter seed, in some parts, already sown, in others, already sprouting ; cherry-trees as large as oaks ; and everywhere a blessed abundance of apples, pears, plums, and grapes. During our trip on the river, near Linz, we bought twenty large peaches for two-and-a-half groschen of our currency. The population are very good-natured, and we have met with several pretty hostesses in the inns, who seemed really virtuous. In the outward appearance of the people, more especially of the women, great variety prevails ; some are slim and graceful, others square and vigorous. Near Linz, you see these slender, graceful figures carrying fruit and vegetables to market on their heads, in large flat baskets, covered with the whitest cloths. The men, also, are a frank, good-natured, sturdy race. Everything connected with material life is good and handsome : the peasant houses, in the villages and hamlets, are well built, and roofed with shingles, and have green Venetian blinds in the windows ; the smaller cottages are like the châlets in the Alps. Manufactures are utterly neglected ; even the splendid Styrian iron is excessively badly treated. . . . . The administration of the country seems to me even far more oppressive, annoying, and unwise than at home, as I will prove to you by various amusing anecdotes when we meet. Taking all these things together, one cannot help feeling here an immense longing for the introduction of greater unity in Germany, in order that this glorious land also might imbibe the spirit that pervades the whole, and be regenerated by it. Catholicism, in these parts, seems to me to be of a lukewarm kind: there are not by far so many images of saints, so many pilgrimages, nor so much bigotry, as in Bohemia ; and our Protestantism, which we are at no pains to conceal in public, when visiting churches or otherwise, appears neither to alarm nor to provoke the people. In Prague, on the contrary, they sometimes scowled at us, when we omitted to dip our fingers in the holy water, or to cross ourselves.

From our sail on the Danube, I have still a few gleanings to communicate. On account of the weather we were obliged to divide it into two parts. In the morning we sailed up the river from the city. Whether the Danube be here much broader than that part of the Rhine we visited together, I cannot say; but, upon the whole, the stream is more rapid, and the breadth more uniform throughout, but the banks less interesting. Our goal was a monastery, which was founded about six hundred years ago by two childless brothers, and endowed with their entire landed estates. But during these six hundred years, not a single remarkable man has ever issued from this convent. The most that can be said of the most renowned of its prelates is, that he was so fortunate as to survive a great many misfortunes. In the afternoon we sailed down the river below the city, and here the Danube soon becomes much broader than the Rhine, and, with the many islands on its bosom, appears in all its peculiar majesty. The banks here, for about two miles, are mountainous on the one side only. A few pistol shots were fired, which I thought would hardly reach the opposite bank, but I was mistaken, and they produced, moreover, a splendid echo.

Forgive the disconnected manner in which I jot down all this. I wish, as you cannot be here to enjoy with me, that I could place everything vividly before you; but I know that description is not my forte, and therefore it would be much better if you could travel, and I remain at home. I can hardly hope to find a letter from you to-morrow, though I have an inexpressible longing for one. God grant that all may be well at home! I do not in the least fear that anything very serious has happened; but my thoughts about home always take the form of the most fervent prayer, and of the liveliest feeling, that my life and my happiness are locked up in you and the children. Good-night, it is high time for me to go to bed, as we are to start to-morrow morning at four o'clock.

[CCCCVII.]   *Berchtesgaden, Tuesday, 15th, Evening.*

. . . . The time spent in Salzburg was not thrown away. The people with whom we came most in contact there, were the family of a bookseller, by name Z——. The husband perished in the great fire, and the family lost almost everything. Reimer had rendered them great services by collecting considerable sums for them, and he was, in consequence, received with profound regard. On Saturday morning we took a walk with the son through the city, which is built in the form of a half-moon on each side of the river, and is surrounded by mountains, but at a greater distance than at Heidelberg. The public buildings are in the grand old style of the ecclesiastical princes; the churches also are grand, but not in good taste, yet not over-laden with ornamentation. Everywhere there are traces of former well-being, but present decay, and on all sides great dissatisfaction with the Austrian Government, which very coolly and unconsciously, as it were, allows the parts to go to destruction for the sake of the whole.

The evening previous to our starting for the mountains, we invited a schoolmaster, who is well acquainted with them, and who is a good botanist, to be our guide, and in company with him we broke up at two o'clock in the afternoon, and proceeded towards this place. During the first hour we were soaked through and through by the clouds, which lay thick and dense in the ravines and on the mountain tops, but I did my best to keep the company in good humour. Subsequently the sky cleared, and we arrived here in the finest weather. The road was very beautiful. The snowclad giant mountains appeared before us in succession; we walked along the banks of a rushing mountain stream, beheld the loveliest Alpine pastures on all the slopes, covered with happy, well-fed cattle, and Leopold was for ever firing off his pistols, and producing the finest echoes. This morning we awoke under the happy auspices of a blue sky and an unclouded sunrise, and started at seven o'clock for the Königsee, the beautiful dark green waters of which are shut up between high mountains, which rise so immediately and so perpendicularly out of the lake, that there are but few spots on which one can land. Our road took us towards the further extremity of the lake, where we were received in a huntsman's lodge, which is attached to a monastery, and whence we proceeded afterwards, accompanied by the huntsman, on a little Alpine ramble, which proved most satisfactory; for we saw about ten chamois, also saw and heard half a dozen small avalanches, and towards the end of our ramble came upon a little glacier; and thus during a good hour's walk, we had learnt to know all the features of Alpine scenery. To me the ramble was made still further interesting by the presence of a botanizing gardener, who knew, and with practised eye detected, many plants that were unknown to me. In the middle of the lake there is a spot (the only one on which it is allowed to fire a shot) where there is a very fine echo, which was not on this occasion allowed to sleep. It rolls around you like thunder; and when the first ceases, the second takes up the sound still louder, until after a time it gradually dies away. The lake, surrounded by steep rock walls, and with the snow-capped mountains mirroring themselves in its 160 fathom deep but tranquil waters, spread out like a glass in the bright sunshine, afforded a spectacle of unique beauty. While sailing on its bosom, we sang hymns from the hymn-book, not very correctly, but not, therefore, the less to the edification of all present. On our return to this place, I had a very interesting mineralogical conversation with Professor Kaiser from Norway, whom I had seen in Berlin, and who had inquired for me in Salzburg, and followed me hither. Our schoolmaster and the gardener having left us to return home, we afterwards inspected a curious depôt of articles of bone and wood, made in the locality, where we purchased some trifles for the children. Subsequently we received a visit from a Catholic ecclesiastic, who pleased me so much, that we parted from each other with a brotherly kiss and with tearful eyes. It is a lovely, fresh, moonlight night, and I have the best hopes of the weather to-morrow. Every evening we drink to the health of No. 37,

Wilhelms Street,* and do not in the least mind, should even Mr. von B——- and H. L—— get their share.

[CCCCVIII.]   *Sunday, 20th.*

. . . . Our Wednesday tour was glorious, not only as regards our final goal, but as regards the whole route thither. How often I have deplored that none of us can draw! Snow and forest-covered mountains, rock walls, Alpine meadows, waterfalls, ever new and ever greater beauties, now narrow valleys, now broad ones, in which we found ourselves surrounded by a circle of mountains, and where the pistol shots called forth splendid echoes. Leopold looked quite idyllic, with an Alpine nosegay in his button-hole and another in his cap, with his pistol in his girdle, and his powder-flask at his side. We travelled ten *Stunden*, about seven of our miles, that day, and all bore it very well. On the Thursday we meant to have travelled fourteen *Stunden*, as far as Gastein, had the weather been favourable. But after the first three *Stunden*, it began to rain ; and this not only upset our plan, but also in a great measure spoilt our pleasure on the road, which lay through similar and even more beautiful scenes than those of the day before, more especially the views up the Pinzgau, a mountain valley, the upper part of which stretches as far as the frontiers of the Tyrol. Perhaps you know it by name from a song which is sung a great deal in Berlin—*The Pinzgauers were going a Pilgrimage*. In this song the people are described as coarse and rude ; but such we have not found them. On Thursday, after six hours' march in the rain, we were obliged to stop in a little market town, on the borders of the Pinzgau, to dry ourselves. At the table in the inn, we found among others a regular Pinzgauer, with beer and brandy before him. He entered into conversation with us, and asked many questions ; and no

* Where Schleiermacher then lived in the Sack Palace, which had been purchased by Georg Reimer, and which, being surrounded by a large parklike garden, obviated the necessity of Schleiermacher's removal to the Thiergarten in summer.

sooner had he discovered that we were Prussians, than he broke out into praise of Prussia, and spoke out freely, giving utterance to very sound political notions, expressing very great contempt for the Austrian Government, and constantly alluding to Prussia and Bavaria as the two pillars of Germany. He was a fine, vigorous fellow, tall and broad shouldered, with a Roman nose, clear blue eyes, and a healthy, manly colour. When we got outside, he fell upon Leopold's neck and kissed him. We proceeded two *Stunden* further, and were again obliged to turn in somewhere to dry ourselves; and as the rain never ceased, and we could get no horses to take us on to Gastein, we were obliged to go into quarters. A meal was prepared for us; and at half-past eight o'clock I said: " Children, it is very late, we must go to bed," and the motion was agreed to *nem. con.* The next morning, having secured horses, we drove two miles further, through a beautiful wild ravine, down which the Gasteinbach rushed foaming to meet us. As the rain had ceased, we walked the last miles towards the bathing-place, engaged lodgings, and then immediately proceeded to visit the mines. To reach these we had to mount during three hours; by that time we were some hundred feet higher than the *Schneekoppe;* but to reach the summit of the mountain, which is more than 8,000 feet high, we would have been obliged to mount during two hours more. Reimer did not enter the mine with us, and I had the pleasure of being the first to introduce the mining operations to Leopold. We had waded a considerable part of our way up through snow; and when we came out of the galleries, it was snowing very hard. Further down it was raining, and the heavens looked so very little propitious, that we gave up the hope of carrying out our plan. Early on Saturday morning, after having feasted our eyes on the spectacle of the Gastein waterfall, we recommenced our wanderings on foot; but after having accomplished one mile, we were again obliged to have recourse to a post-chaise.

It will soon be three weeks since I left you, and as yet I have not had a word from you. These are the bitters of travelling.　Greet the whole dear tribe of children, old Lotte, P—— and K——, and all friends, not forgetting my honest Winkel.*　As regards my remembrance of you, there can be no question of more or less, for you are *ever* present to me.

[ccccix.]　　　　　　　*Nürnberg, Friday, 2nd October.*

Your second letter, dear heart, I found in Munich; but, though we prolonged our stay there four days, I could not find a moment to write to you, so constantly was I handed over from one person to another, and it would have been still worse had I not so studiously avoided the grandees.　For the rest, one cannot help feeling respect for Munich.　The city has a stately appearance, though it is not large; but latterly the gates have been thrown down, and its limits thus rendered indefinite, and already large open squares and great buildings, out of all proportion to the rest of the city, are springing up on the outskirts.　It is, however, the great scientific and artistic institutions which inspire the greatest respect, and these mostly date from a period when the state was not so extensive by far as at present.　There also great dissatisfaction with the government prevails; but along with this there is great union and much hope in the constitution, which has already been granted and sworn to, and for the opening of which preparations are now being made.　People there showed me an amount of friendliness that I cannot sufficiently acknowledge, and old Jacobi was actually moved on seeing me. We endeavoured to come to an understanding relative to our views, but we got no further than to understand wherein the difference between us consists; and he always listened to me very good-naturedly when I told him that I thought his great mistake was that he confounded this difference with another, and sought its foundation in the disposition of mind.　I have learnt to like him very much, and have requested permission to write to him.　With his sisters, also, I soon found myself on a very friendly footing, and we playfully quarrelled and teazed each other a good deal.　We all three dined with

* A man who had been many years in his service.

Jacobi every day, and each time met some other guests: I always managed to be the first to arrive and the last to depart. Schelling was absent, which did not much distress me, more particularly as I have not read his last productions, and should have found it difficult to conceal this. Many interesting persons of secondary importance I also missed, but I had quite enough for the short time I was there, especially as there were picture and sculpture galleries to be seen. As it was, I could only give a very cursory glance at the library and the numismatic collection.

Yesterday morning we arrived in Augsburg, visited the town-house and the collection of pictures there, as also the cathedral; ran through the principal streets; and started again, after a hurried dinner, and travelled all through the night. How much we have to see in this place I do not know, but I hope we shall be able to leave to-morrow afternoon, and to spend Sunday afternoon and evening with Jean Paul.

Augsburg reminds one of Frankfort-on-the-Maine; Nürnberg has a much more antique character; and, in spite of their ugliness and want of fertility, the environs bear the traces of former wealth and of great commercial activity.

My thoughts are now constantly turning homewards, with great joy at the approaching meeting with you all, but also with some anxiety about the accumulation of work that awaits me, and which will hardly allow me to settle down at once to the quiet enjoyment of home-life. But you are already aware of all this, and many of the details of my journey, which I have saved for verbal communication, may, if you wish to have them, be imparted while we are taking our tea. In like manner, it seems, you have reserved for my return all the most interesting accounts about F——. Pray do not neglect to familiarize yourself gradually with the fact that, in the month of June, Napoleon was really quite safe in St. Helena, and modify your rules of interpretation accordingly. It would really be unworthy of your endeavours after truth, were you to insist upon not believing this.

Good-bye, dear heart, probably for the last time until we

meet. I have been once magnetized by Ringseis, and would have been glad to have repeated the experiment, but time would not admit of it. However, in spite of Jacobi's dinners and night travelling, my health is very satisfactory. Greetings to all in the house and out of the house. God grant that we may have a happy meeting.

As mentioned in the above letter, Schleiermacher had, during his interviews with Friedrich Heinrich Jacobi, reserved to himself the privilege of writing to the latter, to endeavour further to elucidate the differences existing between them. This agreement seems to have given rise to the subjoined letter, a copy of which was found among Schleiermacher's correspondence, but without date. A short correspondence between Reinhold and Jacobi, to which Schleiermacher refers, is also given.

[ccccx.]   *Reinhold to Jacobi.*

What a poor and miserable condition of things is not the present, even at the best, when men endowed with the purest love of truth and the greatest acumen, in spite of long years of inquiry, can attain to no result, concerning the questions most important to man, which really and truly satisfies them, or which, even supposing that it suffices to quiet their own doubts for a time, they are able to communicate to other equally upright investigators, so as to carry conviction to the minds of the latter also.

[ccccxi.]   *Jacobi to Reinhold.*

In your complaints, dear old friend, about the insufficiency of our philosophizing, I can, alas, join with all my heart; and yet I know no better remedy than to continue to philosophize or—to become Roman Catholic. There is no third alternative, as also there is no third alternative between Christianity and heathendom, that is, between the deification of nature and Socratic-Platonic anthropomorphism. Most willingly would I exchange my feeble, philosophical Christianity for positive, historical Christianity, and I cannot understand why, in spite of this wish, I have never been able to adopt the latter. You see, dear Reinhold, that I am ever the same. A thorough heathen as to the understanding, but in point of feeling entirely a Christian, I float between two waves, which, as far as I am concerned, will not commingle their waters, so that I might be upborne by both; on the contrary, when the one upheaves me, the other draws me down.

[ccccxii.]   *Schleiermacher to Jacobi.*

You refer me to your letter to Reinhold, and in this I find the same complaint that runs through all your writings, put forward in a couple of very simple formulas, which I am glad to lay hold of, in order to be able through their aid to place before you, for the present in an equally simple form, the difference that exists between us. You say you are a heathen in point of understanding, a Christian in point of feeling. To this my logic gives the following answer:—Heathen and Christian are, as such, opposed to each other within the same sphere, that of religion : have reason and feeling such equal claims within this sphere, as to allow of their dividing into these two contradictory forms? Religiosity belongs to feeling; that, which to distinguish it herefrom, we denominate religion, but which is in reality always more or less dogmatics, is only the interpretation of the feeling resulting from the reflective powers of the intellect. If your feeling be Christian, can your understanding put a heathen interpretation on it? This I cannot allow.

My proposition, on the contrary, stands thus : in point of understanding I am a philosopher; for to be such is to exer-

cise the original and independent activity of the understanding, and in point of feeling I am religious and a Christian,
and have entirely renounced all heathenism, or rather I have
never possessed any. You, however, as we all know, are
also a philosopher, as regards your understanding, and firmly
determined, in opposition to all those who think it necessary
to become Roman Catholic, to continue to philosophize. So
far we are entirely agreed; for I will not, either, in all eternity allow myself to be deprived of the right to philosophize.
When, therefore, you say that you are at the same time a
heathen, in as far as your understanding is concerned, this
can only mean, that your philosophizing understanding cannot adopt, along with its philosophy, that which your Christian
feeling gives it to construe. But, surely, supposing you had
a heathenish religious feeling, your understanding would not
either be able to adopt what this feeling would give it to
interpret, and you only call this negation heathenish, because
it is founded in the fact, that your understanding refuses to
overstep the bounds of nature; but as I will by no means
allow myself to be entangled in a contradiction, I have placed
myself on the footing to demand of others that they shall
prove to me where is the ultimate limit of nature. When,
therefore, my Christian feeling is conscious of a divine spirit
indwelling in me, which is distinct from my reason, I will
never give up seeking for this spirit in the deepest depths
of the soul's nature; and when my Christian feeling becomes
conscious of a Son of God, who differs from us in another
way than merely being better than the best of us, I will
never cease to search for the genesis of this Son of God in
the deepest depths of nature, and to say to myself, that I
shall most likely learn to understand the second Adam just
as soon as the first Adam, or Adams, whose coming into existence I must also admit without being able to understand.

This is my mode of establishing an equilibrium between
the two waves; it is in reality, likewise, an alternation of the
rising of the one and the sinking of the other. But, dear
friend, why should we not be content with this? Oscillation

is, after all, the universal form of all finite existence, and there exists in me at the same time an immediate consciousness that the undulation is, in fact, caused by the two foci of my own ellipse, and that through it I enjoy the fulness of earthly life. My philosophy and my dogmatics are thus firmly determined not to contradict each other, but for this very reason, neither pretends to be complete; and as long as I have been able to think they have always been more or less attuning themselves to each other and drawing nearer to each other.

After what I have said, I think it will hardly be necessary for me to lay before you my confession in regard to the present return to the letter of Christianity. One age bears the penalty of the misdeeds of another, but seldom knows how to redeem itself, except by the perpetration of a new misdemeanour. By the utter subversion of the letter of the Scriptures all historical continuity was dissolved, and it is as great madness to destroy such continuity in religious matters as in political matters. *That* had, therefore, to be re-established; but, as Tieck has admirably expressed it, in attempting to screw the thing back we shall only be destroying the historical continuity in the opposite direction.

The Bible is the original interpretation of the Christian feeling, and for this very reason so firmly established that we ought not to attempt more than further to understand and develop it. This right of development, however, I, as a Protestant theologian, will allow no one to defraud me of; but at the same time I am of opinion that doctrinal language, such as it has been formed since the time of Augustine, is so deep and full of meaning, that, if handled with good sense, it will be quite adequate to bring about such approximation between philosophy and dogmatics as is possible. But I will say no more of this, but, in reference to the difference in our philosophy, address myself to your second proposition : " There is no third alternative between deification of nature and anthropomorphism ;" for I have been told that you were of opinion that I could not think very highly of you, because the foundation of your philosophy was the idea of a personal God, which I denied. This fundamental principle you have expressed in your letter to Reinhold in the proposition I have quoted. At least so it seems to me. Because you can see no third alternative, and because you will not deify nature, you deify human consciousness. But, dear friend, in my eyes the one is as much a deification as the other, and this view, that both are deifications, is in my opinion the third alternative. We can in no way escape from the antithesis between the real and the ideal, or however you may choose to designate it.

Are you better able to conceive of God as a person than as *natura naturans?* If you form to yourself a living conception of a person, must not this person of necessity be finite? Can an infinite reason and an infinite will really be anything more than empty words, when reason and will, by differing from each other, also necessarily limit each other? And if you attempt to annul the distinction between reason and will, is not the conception of personality destroyed by the very attempt?

On the other side I see the same. Anthropomorphism, or let me rather say ideomorphism, is, however, unavoidable in regard to the interpretation of the religious feeling : whether hylomorphism is not equally indispensable in regard to natural science, I cannot undertake to determine, because I am not sufficiently acquainted with the subject. But I make use of the first with full right within the domain of religion because of the view that I take, while within the domain of philosophy I maintain that one expression is as good and as imperfect as another, that we cannot form any real conception of the highest Being ; but that philosophy properly consists in the perception that this inexpressible reality of the highest Being underlies all our thinking and all our feeling; and the development of this knowledge is, according to my conviction, what Plato understood by dialectics. But further than this, I believe, we cannot get. This is my view; allow me to entertain the hope that you will favour me with yours.

One word more in reference to your simile of the two waves, the waters of which will not unite in you. In me they also refuse to unite; but while you desire this union, and miss it painfully, I submit cheerfully to the separation. Understanding and feeling in me also remain distinct, but they touch each other and form a galvanic pile. To me it seems that the innermost life of the spirit consists in the galvanic action thus produced in the feeling of the understanding and the understanding of the feeling, during which, however, the two poles always remain deflected from each other.

Schleiermacher to Henrietta Herz.

[ccccxiii.]   *Berlin, 23rd April*, 1819.

Being doubtful as to whether this letter will find you still at Rome,* dear friend, I send it to our friend Rühs, who will take care to forward it to you. . . . . Here everything is wonderfully quiet, with the exception of the dead Kotzebue, whose ghost is playing the very devil with us,† so that when any two men fall out, you may be sure he is behind it all. This makes many people very uneasy, lest the university should be dissolved; but I remain tranquil, because I know that difficult matters are not so easily carried through. . . . I am celebrating to-day my silver-wedding with the Church, and have invited my theological friends on the occasion. I have much reason to thank God for his merciful guidance during these twenty-five years of my office, and I would fain live through a part of the next quarter of a century also; see the end of it I shall not; but in the meanwhile others will have come forward to take my place. . . . . God bless you, dear friend! How I wish you were back again among us. Hearty greetings to all friends.

* Henrietta Herz was then travelling in Italy, with the family of Wilhelm von Humboldt.

† Probably an allusion to De Wette's case, who was dismissed from his chair at the university, because of his having written a letter of condolence to the family of Sand, Kotzebue's murderer.—Trans.

Schleiermacher to Charlotte von Kathen.

[ccccxiv.]   *Berlin, 14th February,* 1820.

Dearest Lotte, it seems an age since I communicated with you, but therefore I will also now give you most joyous tidings! The day before yesterday my wife was happily delivered of a boy!*

This time I had not felt so strong a wish that it might be a boy, as on former occasions. I was too much penetrated by the feeling that we do not know what we wish for, more especially in the present times. But among the children there was such a constant talk about the little brother that was expected, that I felt quite anxious as to how we should reconcile them to the fact, should the child be a girl. But when it proved to be a boy, you may conceive with what joy and thankfulness I received him, and that my first prayer to God was, to be inspired with wisdom and power from above to educate the child to His glory. Join with me in this prayer, I beg you, all you dear ones! . . . . .

Schleiermacher to his Step-Son.

[ccccxv.]   1821.

My hearty greetings also, I send you, my dear son, hoping that after this pleasant excursion you will set to work again with renewed zeal and earnestness, and begin your new *cursus* with the earnest endeavour to avoid in future such blame as is this time contained in the report of your examiners. However, this is the least that you have to do; you have now attained the age when you must no longer be content to do what you have been given to do, well and ably, but when your own zeal must carry you further than the tasks imposed in school. We will rejoice to find you renouncing all trifling, striving steadfastly forward, and exercising a beneficent influence on your sisters by your example and by your love. May God assist you herein, dear son. Think often of us.

* His only son, Nathanael, whom he lost again at the age of nine years.

Schleiermacher to Charlotte von Kathen.

[ccccxvi.]   *Berlin, 9th April, 1824.*

Dear Lotte, so badly stand matters with me, that Ernst arrives, and brings me a letter from you, and not until now, when he is again leaving us, have I been able to pen you a few lines in return. Thus life passes on while man is doing what he is bound to do, and little time is left for doing what he wishes to do. Could I but feel easy as to my doing all that I am bound to do!

Your son, dear sister, will tell you how our life passes. We have had a sad time of sickness among the children latterly. . . . . About myself there is a great deal to be said that Ernst cannot tell you, and which, in fact, I cannot myself tell you. My outward position is very precarious, perhaps more so than ever. The suspicions of demagogical tendencies in regard to me have, I trust, been allayed; but the ecclesiastical questions must soon be brought to a head, and should the result be violent measures, I must infallibly be one of the vfirst ictims. I cannot say that I am alarmed, or that in itself the thought of this troubles me; for in regard to these matters I know that I have done nothing but what I was bound to do, and I almost think I may say, also, that I have done all that I ought to do. But when such decisions are impending, one cannot help feeling very keenly, what under ordinary circumstances is less remarked, viz.: that in regard to our offices and their functions, we are dreadfully exposed to personal arbitrariness, and to feel this is very disagreeable. But this also must be borne, and all things will come to pass as God wills it. . . . .

In the summer of 1824 the health of several of the children rendered sea-bathing desirable. In consequence the mother went with all the children (with the exception of the eldest son, who was attending the gymnasium) and their governess to the island of Rügen, where she selected the remote and most romantically situated fishing hamlet of Sassnitz, in the district of Stubnitz, for their place of residence—an undertaking fraught with no little difficulty, as no preparations for the reception of strangers existed there, and two cottages had to be given up by their rural inhabitants before the guests could find room. Nevertheless, his "wife's idyl," as Schleiermacher called it, was carried through cheerfully, and it seems that this first visit of strangers to Sassnitz led to others, in consequence of which the little village has now almost risen to the importance of a regular bathing place.

Schleiermacher joined his family towards the close of their visit to Rügen, and spent a few days with them at Sassnitz. During the interval the following letters were interchanged between husband and wife.

Schleiermacher to his Wife.

[ccccxvii.] *Berlin, July 16th, 1824.*

My dear heart, I shall say nothing about how my thoughts have accompanied you and the dear little tribe, and how they still accompany you. . . . . I fancied that when you were gone I should feel as in my former days of bachelorhood. But that was very foolish; for I know and feel it every moment, that you and all of them belong to me, and even my outward life becomes quite different through this consciousness. God be with you, and let you enjoy much that is good and beautiful. Give my best love to all the dear Götemitz people, and more especially to our sister Lotte. I hope I shall soon receive accounts from you. Greet and kiss all my little folks. On Sunday it will be the anniversary of

the day at the Brunnenau.   Will you remember it, I wonder?
No, I think not ; dates are not your strong point.

[ccccxviii.]   *Tuesday evening.*
          . . . . . This forenoon we buried the old B——.
Nicolovius was present, and shed a few tears when I pronounced the prayer at the grave, because it reminded him of
his wife.   He begins again to see everything in black, and is
very anxious as to what evil may be brewing at Johannis-
berg, where, as I suppose you have heard, all kinds of ministers have been in conference with Metternich.   Indeed, it
appears that he even fears that I may be persecuted from that
quarter. . . . . .   While taking my solitary tea, I have been
working a little, and also giving audience to various thoughts.
They ended with the wish, that becomes ever more earnest,
that I may be allowed to devote a greater part of the latter end
of my life to you all, and to working for posterity, than I have
been able to do hitherto.   This wish has taken very strong
hold of me just now, but for the present I will conclude with
one that lies nearer still, viz., that I may soon learn where you
are, in order that I may be able to form a more vivid picture
of your condition.   This evening, I think I may with pretty
much certainty send my " good night " to Götemitz. . . . . .

[ccccxix.]   *Wednesday evening.*
     To-day I have dined quite alone with Lotte.   In the
afternoon came your note announcing your safe passage across
the water.   Thank God for this ; but now that you have
arrived at the port of your destination, I begin to see more
clearly how long our separation is likely to last.
     This evening, immediately after tea, Bettina came to take
leave.   She was exceedingly civil, and said many clever
things. . . . . .   Old Hennefuss* has seen you at an inn

* A remarkable old man, whose child-like piety and deep wisdom
will ever be remembered by all who knew him.   He believed himself
to be in daily personal communion with various good persons who
had departed this life, and even with the Saviour himself, and had

with all the children. I suppose it was when you sought refuge from the storm. . . . .

[ccccxx.]   *Monday, 26th July.*

. . . . . M——'s letter, about which I could not write more fully the other day, has, in fact, made me quite melancholy. I do not see how you will be able to exist where you are with any degree of comfort. Supposing even that the discomfort of the clay floor can be mitigated by the aid of planks and bedsteads, how will you all be able to manage in the daytime in the miller's one little room? And how is any reading or writing to go on there? I am very much afraid that when you are not in the woods, or on the sea-shore, you will be wretchedly situated, and I am longing intensely for your first letter from Sassnitz. A little taste of camp-life I had no objection to your having, and I even rejoiced at the thought that many little anxieties would be overcome in that way, and that you would learn to see that less warm covering and greater freedom in running about in the open air was quite compatible with safety in regard to health; but these privations seem to me too great. However, I trust entirely to you, and feel sure that you will do all for the best. . . . . Here, everything is as usual. I have not yet seen Lotte to-day, and do not know whether she is to dine with me *tête-à-tête*. After dinner, I am to attend an academical conference, and after that, I think I shall go to see the French Hercules, of whom S—— spoke so very highly last Friday when I went from the Spanish Society to the Spanish equestrians. I still feel the necessity of some diversion during the tea-time. To sit upon the sofa and swallow down two or three cups of tea, and then go back to the writing-desk, makes me too melancholy.

Yesterday I witnessed a very touching scene. I arrived rather early at the Werder Church, where I was to preach for

besides other visions. He was a mechanician by trade, and an industrious workman, and in no way connected with magnetism. He and Schleiermacher were much attached to each other.

Küster, and thus heard the end of Palmier's French sermon, and afterwards saw him and the other pastors of the church and the elders fall upon each other's neck in the sacristy, and weep bitter tears. They were taking leave of the church, where they might have remained in peace and quiet for another century, had it not come within range of the destructive building mania, and an edifice that is far too small has been assigned to them in exchange. This arbitrary mode of proceeding—this absence of all consideration for the feelings of others, is very revolting; and I was obliged to exert myself very much to prevent the impression that this scene had made upon me from disturbing me in the delivery of my sermon. . . . .

God be with you, dear heart, and with all our loved ones, and do write the oftener, the more uncertain the delivery of the letters is, that is to say, as often as the circumstances amid which you live will allow; and keep in your heart your old faithful husband.

The Wife to the Husband.

[cccccxxi.]   *Sassnitz, 29th July.*

My dear, dear husband, yesterday was a day of joy and jubilation to me, for it brought me your letter. Thank God! that it contains nothing seriously distressing, though a melancholy tone runs through part of it. The more important events, the results of which may be so serious, are in the hands of God, and I will not allow my thoughts to dwell on them, and will foster no anxiety in regard to them. . . . . My dear heart, I knew beforehand that it would be a severe trial to us both to be so long separated! . . . . We arrived here on Friday last in pretty good time and in pretty good weather. Bedsteads and bedding I brought with me from Götemitz ; so that by writing more explicitly, I might have saved you the anxiety you suffered under on that account. But the confusion was great until the bedsteads were put up, and everything brought in order. The miller's room is smaller than I expected, but the people are very kind and willing to serve. The house in which we are to sleep has indeed been whitewashed, but, nevertheless, the inhabitants had left enough of their own atmosphere behind them to make it very disagreeable for us the first nights and mornings, until habit, which reconciles us to everything, had come to our assistance; and now that we have had the clay floors covered with clean straw, over which we have spread linen sheets, we are tolerably comfortable. I console myself with the reflection that the air in the sleeping-house is more disagreeable than unwholesome; and the whole day long we are in the delicious, invigorating, open air. The situation of the village is very favourable. Against the west winds, that prevail during this season, it is quite sheltered by the forest-clad hills; and we take the most delightful walks, in spite of the cold, windy weather. The first evening, as you may have perceived by my last letter, was a very trying one to me. I felt so very desolate; anxiety about the children weighed heavily upon me, and I spent the greater part of the night in prayer to God to keep his hand over us, and to lead everything to a happy issue. . . . Provisions have as yet never failed us; on the contrary, we have had good and wholesome food every day, though of course, no variety, and everything is very plain; but this is so much the better. . . . . We have been taking a very nice walk, and been sitting in the wood, where I read aloud a letter which you wrote to me to Silesia, when I was in like manner separated from you and alone with the children during the war. I look forward with great pleasure to reading the subsequent letters also. I have brought the whole packet with me. What love and tenderness breathes from that letter! It has given me new spirit. Thank God that you need have no such anxiety about us at present, and that we can now calculate exactly when we are to meet again. I hope to God that I shall be able to bring back all the children in good health. The little ones are full of life and joy. Farewell for to-day, they are just bringing in our supper, which consists of sour milk, and potatoes with their coats on.

Schleiermacher to his Wife.

[cccCxxii.] *Saturday, 31st July.*

. . . . My Saturday evening with the students has again been somewhat spoilt. The weather was so fine that I gave orders that tea should be brought to us in the garden; but instead of coming at eight it did not come until nine, and to make matters worse, they had not put anything round the flame of the lamp, so that it went out every minute; and at last, after many vain endeavours, we were obliged to adjourn to the house in order to obtain boiling water. One of the globes of the garden chandelier was also destroyed on the occasion. That I must light the candles myself every evening, has become quite a matter of course, and so likewise that I must rest content with lukewarm water, because I get tired of repeating that they must let me have fresh cool water. But do not take these matters seriously, dear heart, but laugh at them; for they do not in the least affect me, and even such things as vex me when you are present, I bear with the greatest equanimity now that I am alone. The fact is, it seems to me that as you are not here, it is no matter how wrong things go ; but when you are here everything must be excellent and perfect.

I have a burdensome duty to perform to-day, that is, to be present at the election of a rector, where I shall probably see H. Krause, whom I have hitherto so studiously avoided. However, when you find that no one will imitate your mode of proceeding in such matters, you are at last obliged to give up. I did not know how to excuse myself without either telling a falsehood or saying something very bitter, and while I hesitated I lost the opportune moment.

The Wife to the Husband.

[cccCxxiii.] *Sassnitz, Wednesday, 4th August.*

. . . . Since I wrote last, we have been very dissipated. Mrs. W——, H—— and some of his daughters came to see us one beautiful afternoon; they were very friendly, and we endeavoured to do the honours as well as possible. With them came Carl Kathen on horseback, and the appearance of this youth, who is equally beloved by old and young, called forth shouts of joy. He had promised to pay us a visit, and the children almost tore him to pieces with their demonstrations of delight. A bed was made for him in the room at the mill. On the Saturday he persuaded us to undertake an excursion to Stubbenkammer. The weather was most lovely when we started, and we were all in high glee. On the heights we met a good many people, but we did not allow ourselves to be disturbed, but sat down under the green trees and eat potatoes and chocolate, which I had brought with me, without heeding the world around us; but a storm with heavy showers, soon poured its attentions upon us. We were obliged to leave our verdant bower; the sickly ones sought shelter in a house, the stronger ones remained before the door; and there we remained chained to one spot from two o'clock until six, while the rain poured down incessantly. At this hour it began to clear, and we set ourselves in movement, homewards. But, alas, the sunshine was but short! In a little while it began again to pour so heavily that our cloaks were not proof against it. Fearing that we might catch cold, I ordered the coachman to go round by Sagard, whereby also we avoided the bad road through the forest, which was quite dangerous after the rain. When it stopped raining we enjoyed a wonderfully beautiful spectacle; the sun shone forth just before it set, and shed through the surrounding mist, light and hues such as I have never seen before. My heart was very heavy on account of Gertrude, not knowing how she would bear it; and the next day we were all indeed somewhat upset, physically, and Gertrude was paler than usual. Ah, my dear old man, you may conceive that such moments are more trying to me here, than when living in the midst of our daily comforts, in the neighbourhood of the doctor and with all necessary means within reach. However, God holds his hand wonderfully over us, and the second day already we were all right again, and Gertrude the same as before. This morning early we had the joy of receiving your letter, and at the same time a message from Lotte Kathen, to say that she and her daughters and Wilhelm were in Bobbin, and intended to come hither in the afternoon. You may imagine the delight this caused. They were here from three o'clock until seven. We took coffee in " Schleiershall," and then went to inspect our bathing-place, which was pronounced lovely by everybody, and afterwards we took a sail for about half an hour, which proved very interesting, as the wind suddenly shifted to the east, and caused the waves to rise very high, and our boat was thus kept constantly in a kind of dancing movement. To-morrow we are invited to take coffee at Stubbenkammer with Aunt B——, whom I have not yet seen. You see, that without our doing anything towards it ourselves, we cannot quite avoid dissipation even here. As for lessons, they are not to be thought of; even the days that we remain quietly at home, very little work of any kind is done, and neither time nor the locality will admit of it. I rise at seven and waken up the rest. The children are always very tired, and it is no easy matter to get them out of bed. After breakfast we read a chapter in the Bible and some hymns of Albertini's; and then remain quietly together until ten o'clock, occupied with our needles. Often, however, various household matters also have to be attended to during this time. At ten I go down to the bathing-place and perform the part of bath-woman, helping one after the other to get into the water and out again. When all have had their dip, I send them forth to run about and get warm, keep Lina Kathen alone with me, take a good rest, and then myself descend into the azure waves, which, I can assure you, is much finer in idea than in reality. By this time the dinner-hour has arrived. After dinner we take a *short* rest, then drink coffee, then work a little, while one of the party reads aloud, and then walk until sunset, take our supper, and put the little ones to bed. It is then about nine o'clock; but we grown-up people remain up until ten, and then either in total darkness or in beautiful moonshine we leave the mill and wander a pretty good bit of way along the footpath, through the village to our " Ruhheim" (home of rest). This evening I have sent M—— to bed before me; and that she may not be too miserable when she is disturbed, I must now leave off and wish you good night, my own dear husband, you, my best and most faithful friend, you, greatest of God's blessings bestowed upon me.

[ccccxxiv.]   *Thursday Forenoon.*

Our delightful plan has, alas! come to nothing. The east wind, which blew pretty high yesterday, rose in the night to a perfect hurricane, accompanied by floods of rain. It was a fearful night. We were all awake, and M—— struck a light. Our sleeping-house is quite close to the sea-shore, whereas the mill-house is the last house at the other end of the village, and contiguous to the forest. When in bed we hear the sea roaring. However, in spite of the weather, we are all in good spirits; and M—— has even to-day, for the first time, given a French lesson. Nathanael is particularly well off here. When we are not out walking, on which occasions he is always of the party, I never see him except from afar, for the miller, a gentle, friendly man, has taken such a fancy to the child, that he has him always at his side. The door of the room we inhabit opens into the spacious mill, and there he sits the whole day long gazing at the great water wheel; or he follows the miller about in his various avocations, fancying that he is of great assistance to him. He is more especially happy when he is in the workshop, in one corner of the mill, where the miller planes and chisels, and where the child works away most zealously with a little tool that has been given to him, at a big rake which is being got ready for the harvest. As the miller is a quiet and sensible man, and Nathanael is so obedient that I feel sure he will never go near any place he is forbidden to go to, I am quite easy about him, and think that the boy cannot be in better company, or be better amused. He seems never to feel tired for one moment. Hildis also is on very friendly terms with the people of the mill (the family consists of a good old dame of seventy, her man, who seems, however, to be in reality master, and a maid-servant), and likes to be with Hanne in the kitchen. . . . . I rejoice that I may now say with truth, that it would not be in the least difficult for me, nor cause me one moment's unhappiness, were I to be obliged to live with you and the children in a little hovel. . . . . I am longing very much for your next letter, and now conclude this with a hearty wish that I could breathe all the love of my soul into this letter for you, my dear, dear father. Ever your own   HENRIETTE.

Schleiermacher to his Wife.

[CCCCXXV.]   *Sunday, 8th August.*

I have just returned home from the early morning service. What life there used to be in my room at this hour! You, with all the little ones, and sometimes another dear face or two. Now all is silent round me ; and when I send my thoughts over to you I do not know whether to seek you on the way to church, or whether you may again be obliged to rest contented with reading a sermon. If the weather be not better with you than it is here, you will not have much Sunday enjoyment. When you were at Stubbenkammer, dear Jette, did you think of old times? Of our first meeting, twenty years ago ? And of how, in the midst of the wholesome suffering I was undergoing, I was seized by a strange presentiment in Rügen ? How the love of your whole circle embraced me; how your bridal happiness cheered my heart, and how I was drawn towards you by paternal affection ? And how, during my second stay in the island, love unconsciously took another character in my heart? Then also we spent a delightful day at Stubben-kammer. The bench near the Brunnenau, where you gave me your "Yes," is, I suppose, no longer there ; and, perhaps, the bathing houses are also gone. I still remember that I emerged from my bathing-room a little later than you came

out of yours, and that I found you engaged in fastening up
your hair, which then fell around your neck in richer tresses
than now. Afterwards, we took a walk together through
the meadow, and my feelings would no longer be restrained,
but spoke out when we had seated ourselves upon the
bench. . . . .

Schleiermacher to Charlotte von Kathen.

[ccccxxvi.]   *Berlin, 9th August,* 1824.

  I have long been wishing, dear sister, to write to you
from my solitude, to thank you and your dear Kathen for all
the sisterly and brotherly love you have evinced towards my
dear ones, and to show you that I am ever in spirit with you
and with them. And now, you have anticipated me, and
surprised me with your most valued enclosure. What can
be more delightful to a clergyman than to find that his prose
has called forth poetry in a soul harmoniously attuned to his!
How I have rejoiced in your calm and pious inward life
while reading your effusions! Your image presented itself
bright and pure before my mind's eye, and the old times,
when we first learned to know each other, returned, as it
were, once more. I think we are both just the same as we
were then. You have, as little as I, lost taste and interest
for anything that we valued then ; but the relation to the only
ONE, who is the centre of all, has, I believe, become more
prominent in both of us. This, I dare say, you have seen in
the third collection of my sermons, which I was not aware
that you did not possess. I do not know how I have happened
to neglect sending them to you. I hope that the same is not
the case with the fourth collection. In fact, I am still opposed
to the publication of the sermons in a printed form, because
all sermons, and mine more especially, are only intended to
be heard. But when I see them bring forth such fruits as
your lyrics, then I feel that I should like to have all those
printed, in delivering which I have felt myself most excited.

The Mother to the eldest Son (who was studying in Göttingen).

[CCCCXXVII.]   *Berlin, 23rd May, 1826.*

My darling Ehrenfried, do you often think of me? Do you sometimes long for your mother—do you hear in spirit the words of love, which my heart is ever addressing to you? . . . . Now, let me tell you what we have been doing. As on the Saturday before Easter father confirmed fifty children, and was greatly moved, as you know he always is on these occasions—and there were a great many communicants on Easter Monday as well as Sunday—he was so much exhausted, that he stood greatly in need of a little strengthening excursion. On the Monday afternoon, therefore, he and Forstner * walked out to Werneuchen, where they remained the night over, and thence proceeded the next morning to Freienwalde. *All* the rest of us took our seats in the carriage on the Tuesday morning, and drove direct to Freienwalde, where we arrived almost as soon as the pedestrians. The children were delighted, notwithstanding the weather was wretchedly cold. . . . . . Your dear father, too, was very cheerful, though for several hours he walked about bent double by the cramp in his stomach. On the Wednesday, we drove to Neustadt, and inspected the manufactories and the smelting works in the neighbourhood, and again the weather was stormy and inclement. In the great brass works, near Neustadt, a student, by name N——, recognised Schleiermacher, immediately came up to us, and caused the inspector himself, in whose house he was tutor, to conduct us round the works; and when we had seen everything, we were, in spite of all that we could say, obliged to go in to take coffee with the inspector's wife, with whom we found a pretty girl, the betrothed of Mr. N——. The kind people were delighted to have met so unexpectedly with such "interesting" guests, and we derived great benefit from this little

* Alexander von Forstner, married to a daughter of Charlotte von Kathen.

adventure; for we were very hungry, and quite tired out by the wind. On the Thursday, we returned to Berlin. On the road back we spoke of the letter from you, which we felt sure would be awaiting us that day, as it was the anniversary of our marriage; and my joy was great when I found that I was not mistaken. . . . .

And now I will tell you a secret. Only think, that we shall probably adopt another little child, which will, most likely, be entirely like our own. Nanni's sister, in Gallicia, has lost her husband, and is left with four little children, the youngest of whom is not a year old. On the last anniversary of our wedding-day, we determined to adopt one of these, if the mother will consent to part with it, which I have no doubt she will.

I had long had a presentiment that something of the kind would happen. Last new-year's eve I was seated with Louise* at Mrs. F——'s side. The latter was unusually kind; . . . . and, turning to me, said : " I see a little child kneeling close to you, who is looking up so touchingly in your face, and asking,—Will you be my mother?" And even before this, she had told me that I would be called upon to be mother to another child to whom I had not myself given birth. It was a very affecting moment when your father and myself first mentioned the subject to each other ; for he had also been thinking of it for several days, though he had not spoken. As yet, we have not received the mother's answer, and therefore the matter is still a secret here. . . . .

Schleiermacher to his Step-Son.

[ccccxxviii.]   *No date.*

My dear Son, W——, who has returned, has intimated to your dear mother that your appearance gave him an unfavourable impression of your health. I entreat you, do not neglect yourself in regard to this point, but

---

* Daughter of Mrs. F——, who had been adopted into Schleiermacher's family from the time she was a little child, and was educated with his own children.

remember that the care we used to bestow upon your health must now be bestowed by yourself. Inquire from Göschens who is their family doctor, and consult him. A sensible physician will be sure not to overdose a youth of your age with physic; but he will, no doubt, give you advice in regard to your diet, and to this pray attend regularly. That you bathe and swim so frequently I am very glad to hear, but I cannot deny that I feel a little alarmed at athletic exercises which seem to exceed the exploits of St. Christopher himself. The more anxious I feel about your health, the more desirous I am that you should seek some beneficent recreation during the impending vacation. I should be best pleased if you could find some young man, who is agreeable to you as a companion, and with whom you could undertake a pedestrian tour. This is the most thoroughly enjoyable way of travelling, and of becoming acquainted with the beauties of nature, and it is, likewise, the most beneficial to health, if one takes care not to over-fatigue oneself. . . . . With what you write about your studies I am very well pleased; only, as regards the special studies for your profession, you have not been sufficiently explicit. It is a very good thing to follow up more thoroughly some point or other suggested by the professorial lectures, and also to acquire such a general knowledge of the leading scientific works mentioned, as to feel somewhat at home in them.

The idea of becoming a member of the Borussia or any other association, I have no doubt you will give up, on maturer reflection. The ties which one subjects oneself to by joining such an association, become burdensome and impeding, even as regards social intercourse; and considering your tendency to exclusiveness, I cannot otherwise than dissuade you. On the other hand, it gives me much pleasure that your gymnastic exercises are leading to an extension of your circle of acquaintances.

I presume that your mother and sisters write you all our domestic news and everything that relates to our family circle. Of myself I have nothing to say but what you already know·

There is no lack of annoyances, nay, even of serious crises in Church affairs and university affairs, and you must always keep in mind the possibility that I may not remain in my present position long enough to see you well started in your career. I am sincerely desirous that it should be so, but circumstances may occur which will render it imperative to set aside all such considerations, and I wish, therefore, that you would reflect as to how you would manage in such a case. Arndt's affair has been laid before the king for decision, but as yet I do not know the result, and this is another reason why I do not exactly wish you to go to Bonn during the ensuing vacation. You might arrive there at a time when your presence would be troublesome, and the serious matters to be settled might exercise a disturbing influence upon you. . . . . .

The Mother to the eldest Son.

[ccccxxix.]   *Berlin, 24th Nov., 1826.*

My dear boy. It seems to me that you have got so much into the habit of complaining of my not writing, that you even do so when there is no reason for it. You must have had several letters from me since my return, and the present has only been a little retarded by father's birthday, for which we were getting ready a piece of work which we had undertaken in common, and for which there were besides a thousand other preparations to be made. It was a most happy day, and nothing was wanting but that my dear son should have been amongst us—a day rich in joy and manifold emotions; for I think, I may almost say, that never before did such a host of people crowd in to express their affectionate devotion to father. At half past eight o'clock in the morning we sang a choral hymn, and the children crowned him with a wreath of moss and ivy. After that he went to the college and lectured till ten. During his absence a bower of verdure was constructed in the large drawing room, in front of the looking-glass, and in this was placed a table on which was spread a number of pretty presents, interspersed with flowers. Above all, a

beautiful carpet, embroidered for him by Emilie Braunschweig and Anna Redtel, and which was spread on the floor,
deserves mention. . . . . By degrees so many young
girls, and so many friends and acquaintances assembled, that
both rooms were crowded, and up to two o'clock there was a
constant coming and going. . . . . At eight o'clock in
the evening a great surprise was prepared for father. We led
him to the window, and here he saw a long procession of
students with torches advancing up the avenue of the garden,
accompanied by a band of wind-instruments—it was a beautiful
sight ! They placed themselves in a half-circle in front of the
window and sang (Luther's hymn), " A strong bulwark is our
Lord." Then came a deputation consisting of S——, O——.
and K——. The latter was the spokesman ; but he was so
moved that he could say but little. S—— presented to father,
in the name of all, a large, magnificently bound bible. You
may conceive, my son, how affecting this scene was to us all.
The three youths remained with us the rest of the evening, and
pleased us very much ; and, upon the whole, the company was
very merry, without being boisterous. The second supper table
was the pleasantest sight in my eyes, for it was almost exclusively occupied by a wreath of young maidens. At our table
Reimer presided, with the large crystal punch-bowl before
him, filled with cardinal, and performed his task extremely
well. Several very nice toasts were proposed ; one by father
in honour of the students, to which S—— replied in a very
good speech. I was seated between Nicolovius and Eichhorn,
and was delightfully entertained. Your dear father was very
cheerful the whole day. That you were often mentioned and
remembered with the tenderest affection, I need hardly tell
you. And now if you will take the trouble to note all the
little circumstances, you may, with the help of your imagination, form to yourself a correct and animated picture of the
events of the day. Many welcome letters were also received,
and among the heartiest, one from Bernhard Jacobi and Cornelia, who call him father, and express the sincerest affection
for him. To-morrow, Sunday, there will be a second cele-

bration of father's birthday. . . . . You see that we are living at present in the midst of joy and dissipation, but I hope that a nice long period of quiet will follow.

Nathanael has begun to learn Latin, and is to have an hour's instruction from a student every day. It is a new epoch in the little fellow's life, and he is greatly excited. Sometimes he wants to get out of bed at six o'clock already, because " he has so much to do." . . . .

Farewell, my dearly beloved son, I press you to my heart with joyful hope. May the love of God, and the truth that is alone life-giving, ever take more complete possession of your heart, and expel from it all darkness and all apathy. Write soon to me and very explicitly, for I often long very much for you; and write also quite candidly, for I understand you thoroughly. Father sends his tenderest love.

Schleiermacher to his Step-Son.

[ccccxxx.] *Berlin, 6th February, 1827.*

My dear son, I have long been wishing to write to you, but what I had to say could not be despatched in a few words, and I could not find time to write explicitly. First of all I wish to tell you once more my opinion of your ever-recurring complaints about yourself, which follow quick upon the most pleasant subjects. You occupy yourself too much with yourself, and dwell too much upon yourself. Man as an individual is much too insignificant an object to satisfy any one, and you remind me in your way of a couple of senti-mental lovers, who begin by wishing to be all in all to each other, but who soon become extremely burdensome to each other in the midst of their very vapid and tiresome life. Your case is indeed in so far different, that whereas they begin with the most exalted opinion of each other, you, on the contrary, are ever trying to acquire such an opinion of yourself. You desire to possess the consciousness of being noble and excel-lent, and because you cannot attain to it, you put yourself to the torture. But who demands this perfection of you ? At your age people are not generally noble and excellent characters, but are preparing to become so. But this inward operation, when it does take place, cannot and must not be watched, for watching would only impede it, just as bread never rises if they go on opening the oven door while it is baking, or perhaps even taking it out of the oven to look at it, or cutting off a bit to try. How a man has developed himself can only be ascertained subsequently by his acts; and at present you have no means whatsoever for making any valid experiment in regard to this. But one experiment you may make, and that is, to ascertain whether you are capable of taking such a deep interest in any matter as is the source of all true capacity. It is your wish to work in and for the state, and I have no doubt you desire to accomplish something great; you live in the midst of times when the most important matters of this kind are going on, when new states are being constituted and old ones are falling to pieces, and when old forms are getting into the most striking contradiction with themselves. But I can discover no evidence of your having made it your business to understand the connection between the various events, and to penetrate deeply into their causes. Questions connected with the internal administration of the various states are also at present discussed so publicly, that the newspapers are full of them. Were you to take an interest in these, you would soon cease to give so much attention to yourself, and a new life would gradually be unfolded in you. Should you not be able to feel an interest in these matters, then, my dear son, you are certainly not destined to play an important part in either of these directions; for without a great interest no man can work in a large-minded way, nor can he attain to a high position except by despicable means, and such you will never have recourse to. You will therefore, in that case, remain in the subordinate sphere of the profession you have selected; but even under these circumstances you will require some other scientific or artistic pursuit, to enable you to practise some independent activity along with the mechanical activity of your position. I can therefore only wish for you that your studies or your life may soon suggest some such pursuit.

The Mother to the Son.

[ccccxxxi.]   *7th February*, 1827.

I cannot let father write, my own dear son, without adding a few lines. . . . . Your father has undoubtedly described your state most correctly; your complaints are very foolish. . . . . If you could tell me one day of yourself, as you have told me about L——, that he could actually become quite enthusiastically interested in a lawsuit, that would be a feast for father's ears. When I recall to mind the tendency which manifested itself in everything you undertook as a boy, while constantly under my eye, this gives me a clue to the reason why you derive so little nourishment for your soul from the business of your profession. . . . . Ah! this precociousness, this early awakening of the idea, is doubtless very detrimental, when not connected with some decided taste, which from the beginning imparts a soul, as it were, to what is otherwise quite mechanical, and thus prevents any disgust from being felt. I am sure you entirely agree with me on this subject, and I can only wish for you, that God may grant you that true inward power of will, which, when resting upon a higher will, cannot fail to become creative, and which may therefore enable you to correct and to supplement such defects and failings as nature or early education may have left in your character. . . . .

In the months of July and August, 1827, Schleiermacher's wife took her friend Mrs. F—— and the daughter of the latter to Karlsbad, for the benefit of their health, and was subsequently joined by Schleiermacher, when both proceeded to Biala, in Galicia, to fetch their little adoptive daughter. The following letters date from this period:—

Schleiermacher to Charlotte von Kathen.

[CCCCXXXII.]   *Berlin, 26th July,* 1827.

. . . . Our dear Forstner will no doubt tell you all about me and my little people; and when you hear from him how constantly I am engaged in conflicts which I cannot avoid without doing violence to my conscience, you will, I am sure, feel sorry that the last part of my life should be spent amid so much turmoil, and that I should be obliged to waste so much time on these matters, which, according to all appearances, might be used to much better purpose. However, I do not repine, but think, on the contrary, that it is all for the best; and when my book of life is made up, I shall have greater reason for thankfulness than most people. From what I have heard from several quarters, things seem this time to have been very nigh coming to a crisis. As for myself, I rarely know how these matters stand, and generally do not hear the worst until it has blown over. May it ever remain so; for it is my endeavour to do nothing that I may have to repent of afterwards, and for the rest I leave the result to God. . . . .

Schleiermacher to his Wife.

[CCCCXXXIII.]   *Saturday, 4th August,* 1827.

My dear heart, your letter has been a great consolation to us all; for we have been sixteen days without news of you. . . . . Hildchen is as lively as a fish in the water, and went with me last night to see *Iphigenia*, and to hear Madame Schechner once more. Your old "house-cross" also is well again; and if I can only get a good sleep once in a way, I am all right.

The day that the B——'s left with my second letter for you, old Jänicke was buried. I followed him to the grave, but I cannot say that I was much edified, for a certain pastor H——, who was called from Potsdam to deliver the funeral discourse, as if there was no one here worthy of the

office, was affected, prolix, and dreadfully one-sided. From
what he said, you would suppose that the deceased had been
the only Christian preacher in Berlin, until eventually some
others, who had learnt their lesson from him, had come to
his assistance. What unnecessary trouble these good people
give themselves to contract their hearts! On the other side,
there is the philosophical Marheineke, who is proving himself
still more narrow-hearted, and the affairs, which, I believe,
I mentioned in my last, are still going on. Hitherto I have
escaped pretty well from being personally mixed up in them,
but this can hardly last. However, the result cannot in any
case be such as to cause uneasiness.

My dear heart, though I was not exactly alarmed at your
long silence, I am, nevertheless, quite another being since we
received your letter. . . . . Last Thursday week the
girls went with Nicolovius to Rust's. I was very busy, and
felt myself as forlorn as if my former days of bachelorhood
had come back. However, I was forced to rouse myself and
go to work, and soon the consciousness of my real condition
returned, and with it a feeling of sincere thankfulness. . . . . .
I was obliged to break off suddenly, as is often the case now,
so that I can only send you a short farewell. You very often
send me no parting words at all, and thus it will be with my
present letter also. I must keep all my tenderness in my
heart, and see what I can make of it there.

[ccccxxxiv.] *7th August.*

  Our letters are so constantly being conveyed without
the mediation of the post, that I cannot help wishing that I
had a great deal to tell you which the post ought not to know.
But everything is going on so quietly, in the house and out of
the house—the old well-being and the old woes—that I have
nothing but what is consolatory to write. In regard to official
matters, also, everything is as it was, only that I have learnt
through a third party that the crown prince is said to have
expressed himself very much pleased with my memorandum
to the ministry. In the theological faculty a disagreeable

affair has taken place between Marheincke and Neander, but it is too complicated for me to explain to you now. What will be the consequences, and how far I shall myself be drawn into it, I cannot as yet say. However, the general desire to patch up all evils as speedily as possible, will, I suppose, in this case also, be followed by the usual result.

Good-bye, dear heart. I am expecting the boys whom I am preparing for confirmation; after that, I am to accompany Twesten to the Solly collection; and later, I am to have a small gentleman's party in honour of Twesten, who is to leave to-morrow or the day after.

[ccccxxxv.]   *12th August.*

. . . . . Just as I was writing the above, Eichhorn sent me the sad news of Canning's death. No individual man in Europe is of equal importance at this moment, and for the present I can hardly think of anything else. A moment ago my thoughts were so entirely with you, and now sorrowful sympathy with the state of the world spreads them abroad. Well, God will provide! But what may be His will in this matter, it is very, very difficult to discern. How every old evil will again raise its head! How many backslidings, how many new struggles may be in preparation! . . . . .

Strangers, who take up much of my time, are pouring in at present. The Twestens had not yet left, when the Swedish Count Schwerin arrived, and he is still here, and in consequence of his presence, the Schwerin from Putzar has been here a couple of days, so also a Swiss professor, who is to dine with me to-day in company with Pischon. Then there is a new American, who has brought a letter from Bancroft, and a young Scottish divine. But as the vacations are so near at hand, I suppose there will be no new work to do, at least not in connection with the university.

The Father to the Son in Göttingen.

[cccoxxxvi.]   *Berlin, 8th August,* 1827.

My dear son, I have long been wishing to write to you, but I have been overwhelmed with business, partly of a very disagreeable kind, and also with visitors, some very dear to me, others indifferent, and thus I have been prevented. . . . . The enigmatical expressions of Nicolovius I do not know how to solve; for even though he ascribe to me a hundred times the paper which I suppose you allude to, I do not see how this affords any explanation in regard to his official relations, except in as far as it shows generally that the contest is still raging with a certain fierceness, and that it is not likely soon to come to a conclusion. Should you, in the meanwhile, have seen in the papers that " the twelve "— for thus we are generally called here—have received a reprimand, do not picture this to yourself as something very dreadful. The person I pitied the most was President von Bassewitz, who had received the disagreeable mission to read the reprimand to us. Very severe things were indeed said in it; but I have already sent in a written defence, and the whole affair has not caused me a moment's uneasiness, and the less so, as it was announced so long beforehand, that no one was taken by surprise. . . . . I shall also be glad when the Semester draws to a close, for I feel more overworked than usual. And now farewell, dear son, and let me soon have pleasant news from you.

[ccccxxxvii.]   *Berlin, Wednesday, 29th August,* 1827.

. . . . I also have been greatly affected by Canning's death. Such a man, in such a place, is a rare phenomenon; and, holding in view the present state of Europe, we must confess that it is long since so much has depended on a single individual. However, the fact that his system is maintained even after his death, and that there seems not to have been any serious attempt to overthrow it, denotes considerable progress.

Respecting my own affairs, everything is still in the old state, and probably will remain so. What I most regret is the time that seems to have been spent in vain. However, there is no knowing what may be prevented and what may be prepared by such opposition. All send their love, and are looking forward with pleasure to your coming. Therefore, keep yourself bright and cheerful, and come to us thus. Some improvement I do discern in you in this respect; but it is not yet the right thing. As long as you continue to account for your inward state by reference to your outward position and circumstances, and, consequently, to look to the latter for assistance, you have not reached the proper point; because as long as this is the case, you are wishing, and not willing. Willing is to wishing, what the proverb, " Hope puts no man to shame," is to the proverb, " Hoping and waiting makes many a fool."

Schleiermacher to Henrietta Herz.

[CCCCXXXVIII.]   *Berlin,* 1827.

Dearest Herz, you may conceive in what a state of bustle I must be living, since I have not written to you before this. It is with my writing to you as with my working at Plato: over and over again I determine to do so, and yet I leave it undone; so that the *Republic* gets on even slower than my grandfather's wood, which was carried into the house by an old invalid, who lugged in one log every half-hour.

It is true, if you could be invisibly in my room, you would probably often inquire, " But, Schleier, what are you doing now, in reality?" There is a kind of leisurely inward putting things to rights, which I cannot do without, though I envy all those, and I believe you are of the number, who can get on without anything of the kind. Towards our dear L——, I am as great a sinner as towards you, and yet she stands even in greater need of a cheering word than you do. You must console yourselves with the assurance that I am much with you in spirit, and that I sincerely sympathize with you in your various cares and troubles. I feel quite vexed that you should have spent my birthday—on which you must know, we missed you much—in the midst of the worst confusion, when it is so difficult to have one settled thought, and still more so, to be conscious of any strong feeling.

The most urgent matters on which I am at present engaged are the lectures on Church history, which I have only delivered once before, and which lead to numerous researches which I cannot resist, though by far the smallest number is turned to present account; and in addition to this, the labour connected with the commission for the reform of the hymn-book, to which I devote myself very assiduously—the secret of my industry being that I wish as soon as possible to get out of this commission, as I can feel no pleasure in the relations it forces me to keep up, since we have all fallen out about the question of the ritual. This matter becomes daily more complicated; E—— and his party are growing more and more violent, and affairs may still take a tragic turn. What distresses me the most is, that if anything should happen to me, Jette and the children will be the greatest sufferers after my death. For, after all, I am no General Foy. However, I cannot alter my conduct on account of these considerations, and with this assurance I must conclude, as I must not write on the fourth page. God bless you, my dear Herz. Everything between us remains as it ever was.

Schleiermacher to Charlotte von Kathen.

[ccccxxxix.]   *Berlin, 18th December, 1827.*
        Dearest sister, I wish I could describe to you how, in spite of all the inexpressible blessings that God showers upon me, I am still a troubled individual, and how the pressure of business often prevents me from enjoying with all my heart, as I ought to do, even the sweetest gifts that God has bestowed upon me. What place you hold among my treasures I trust you know. However, you are not included in the complaint to which I have just given utterance, inasmuch as I often think of you with heartfelt joy, and thank God

with all my soul for having given you to me as a sister. In like manner I thank you for the token of affection that you sent for my birth-day, which was again so rich in remembrances of this kind coming from all sides, that I ask myself how it is that I am so favoured. When the year is drawing to a close, as at present, I look back with a sense of humility to the manifold ways in which the grace and mercy of the Lord have been manifested in our family; and my gratitude gathers strength from comparison with the many sorrows that we see around as. Thus lately two young men have been called away in quick succession, who I hoped would in the future have worked much good in the profession which they shared with me, and one of whom was intimately connected with our family. They have been taken away, and I—who can do so little in the future, most of whose work has been done, for my present activity is but an echo of the past—I am left.

Another complaint that recurs often, with no little bitterness, is, that the general stupidity of mankind obliges me to waste so much time and strength unnecessarily; for it is this stupidity which, on the one hand, causes everything connected with public affairs to be overlaid with formalities, and on the other hand, leads to numerous foolish acts, frequently originating in high quarters, which I am obliged to combat with all my might, within my own circle at least. It seems hard that so much of this should fall to my lot; and this year more especially has abounded in such annoyances. Few would believe how little excitement there is to me in such controversies, and how deeply I deplore that so large a portion of life, which might be spent much more agreeably, should be consumed in this way. It is with my intercourse with absent friends especially that this state of things interferes; but this makes the hope of meeting them once more face to face all the more delightful; and when I think of your coming to see us, it is as if a bright star arose towards which I look with longing heart. Ah! do try to realize your project! . . . .

In the autumn of 1828 Schleiermacher paid a flying visit to England, by way of the Rhine and Rotterdam, accompanied by Alexander von Forstner, and stayed a few days with his sister and Arndt at Bonn. The following letters were written during his absence on this occasion :—

[CCCCXL.]   *Bonn, Saturday morning.*
        Yesterday we dined alone (with the Arndts), and Siegerich * said a little prayer in the true Arndt style. After dinner we took a nice walk to Blittersdorff, likewise without any addition to our party. Nitzsch was, indeed, to have joined us, but he did not arrive until tea-time. The little flock looked very sweet. Harthmuth (surnamed Sparrow-hawk), and Wilibald, clad in little pink striped frocks, were drawn in a little waggon. The other three, in blue blouses, ran gambolling before us. We revelled for some time in the glorious view across the Rhine, while indulging in pleasant conversation and in a glass of wine and a cup of coffee, and then we strolled slowly back, so as to be home by tea-time, after which we " theologized " for some hours with Nitzsch, who is an excellent and very pleasant man. The next morning we paid our visits, and dined at Sack's. The people from Siegburg had come over, father,† mother, and Dora, who had just returned from Kling's. They brought with them the Niethammers from Munich, who are staying with them; and Nitzsch and Nasse were also among the guests. The mother Jacobi ‡ won my heart at once with her sweet and hearty manner. We had a good deal of discussion at table. After dinner came the little president § and Schlegel to return our visit.

---

* One of Arndt's children.
† *Geheime Medizinalrath* Jacobi, the director of the lunatic asylum in Siegburg, and a son of the philosopher Jacobi.
‡ A daughter of Claudius, the *Wandsbecher Bote.*
§ Another son of Jacobi's.

In fact, dear mother, the only evil that I have to complain of is, that I shall be so long without accounts from home. May you all be well and happy under the merciful protection of God. Remember me most heartily to all the dear children, and tell them that they are daily before my eyes. From the bottom of my heart I commend you to God. May He be with you and the whole house.

[CCCCXLI.]   *London, 4th September, Evening.*

I must write you a few lines on the first evening of our arrival, my heart's own wife, and, through you, to all our dear ones, to let you know how very fortunate we have been. When we got into the diligence on Tuesday morning, to proceed to the Hague, we met there an honest paper-merchant from Wesel, with a daughter of fifteen, who had been on board the steamer with us during the latter part of the trip, and who were, like ourselves, *economical* sight-seers. We made up a party with them at the Hague, and thus escaped with very little expense; and if our sight-seeing was limited, it was by time, and not because of the want of funds. The most interesting sights of all were the town itself, which presents a striking picture of Dutch neatness, and the picture gallery, which, however, we had only time to rush through. Nevertheless, I had leisure to mark many a Rubens, Ruysdael, Van Dyk, Potter, De Steen, Sachtlevens, &c. Of the Italian school there is little or nothing, and of the old Netherland school also very little, and that little not good. Next to these in interest was the *Bosch*, the *Thiergarten* of the Hague; but we did not get so far as *Huys tot dem Bosch*, which one might term its Charlottenburg, but turned off just as it was coming into sight, because we preferred renouncing the inspection of the palace, however beautiful it might be, to giving up the walk to Scheveningen—a Stralau on the Northsea— whither we went to pay our respects to the latter, and to recommend ourselves to its good graces for the morrow. The young maiden, to whom I was obliged to pay court, because Forstner neglected doing so, had never before seen the sea, and I therefore led her far enough out to allow it to moisten the soles of her feet, and presented her with pretty little shells, some of which I bought for a stiiver, and others of which I picked up myself. Notwithstanding the cheapness of this excursion, our fears as to the sufficiency of our funds were again roused, on the Wednesday morning, when we heard a Prince Gallizin making a tremendous uproar in the hotel about the shamefully exorbitant charges, and I made up my mind that Forstner would be obliged to pay a second visit to our friend the merchant, to negotiate another loan. However, when the bill came in, we were delivered from this fear, and when we went on board the steamboat, *The King of the Netherlands*, just in front of the house, we had still half a Wilhelmsd'or in pocket, which we exchanged on board for English money, but which, in this shape, vanished from our possession the moment we landed.

Our course up the Thames was greatly favoured by wind and weather. Everything was beautifully lighted up by the sun, so that we could recognize from afar every important edifice on the banks, and up and down the river went ships in great numbers, some with full sail, and yet the Englishmen on board told us that, comparatively, there were not many that day. From Gravesend to the Custom House, a whole world is disclosed to you ; but a great view of the entire city cannot, of course, be had from the Thames, and to obtain this, I suppose, we shall have to mount up to the top of the Monument or of St. Paul's. As yet I do not know what we are going to do this morning. . . . . .

[CCCCXLII.]   *Afternoon.*

Everything, with the exception of the visit to the Prussian consul, came otherwise than we had planned, and time has run on so, that I have barely a moment to say that we have been in St. Paul's—only in the lower part—and that neither in point of devotion nor of artistic taste have we been rewarded for the trouble.

[CCCCXLIII.] *Sunday, 7th.*

I do not mean to say that St. Paul's is not beautiful, but the funeral service at which we were present was anything but beautiful; it was excessively dry, and the female mourners, who stood around the grave, were wrapped in black draperies, which are probably kept in the church for the purpose, for afterwards, when I saw them within the edifice, they were no longer clad in this manner. The clergyman read the service with great indifference, and the whole was very unimpressive. The church itself is, however, very imposing, and nothing can be more glorious and elevating than the monuments that indicate the gratitude felt by a whole nation towards single individuals; and there are here not only monuments to great heroes, such as Rodney, Nelson, St. Vincent (if these names should be unknown to any of you, look for them in the *Encyclopædia*), but also to more subordinate characters, more especially young naval officers, who distinguished themselves by bravery and fidelity. The deeds of all are mentioned shortly in simple inscriptions, but their memory will be kept alive as long as this edifice, destined to withstand the power of ages, shall rear its head aloft. . . . .

[CCCCXLIV.] *Saturday, 13th.*

. . . . . What will you say when I tell you that, after all, I have been unfaithful to my determination, and that I have engaged to preach here to-morrow week? The first proposal of pastor Schwabe I triumphantly resisted, but Steinkopf conquered me yesterday, having surprised me by the sincere and earnest manner in which he entreated me to do so, when we were alone. He begged me not to give him a decisive answer until this morning; and before writing to communicate my assent, I have examined myself well, to ascertain whether vanity had any share in my motives. I believe, however, that I may feel quite easy in this respect, and more particularly because, as far as I have understood, his congregation mostly consists of persons who do not belong to the

upper and highly-educated classes.   In my plans, however, it
makes an entire upset.

[ccccxlv.]   *Wednesday Evening, 17th.*

   I dined to-day in the country with a thoroughly
English family, but, unfortunately, one without children.
We were only four, and I was obliged to help myself through
with the very little English that I know.   Even here, this
Mr. G—— is a phenomenon, he being a banker, who not
only possesses, but also reads Greek authors, and who is
engaged in writing a history of Greece. . . . . You
must rest contented with these few dry outlines, for I have
here neither the time, the quiet, nor the conveniences necessary for writing.   But the short notices in my memorandum-
book will afford subjects for many a narrative when I shall
be with you again.   Once more, good-bye!   I embrace you
in spirit, dear mother, and all our loved ones.   How delighted
I shall be when I find myself journeying homewards !   May
you all, likewise, rejoice at the thought of getting back.

                              Your old father, Schl.

In January, 1831, Schleiermacher, who had until
then never received any decoration, was honoured with
the Order of the Red Eagle (third class), and he interpreted this as a sign that the favour of the King, of
which he had long been deprived, had been restored to
him.   The great value which he placed upon this, and
the importance with which, in consequence, he invested
an event that would otherwise have had no significance
in his eyes, is shown in the subjoined letter.

                Schleiermacher to the King of Prussia.
[ccccxlvi..]
   In graciously bestowing upon me the Order of the Red
Eagle, your Majesty has given me a proof of your favour that

has caused me a degree of emotion such as few things could call forth, and that has arisen like a bright star over my old age, and will shed a lustre over the future, the reflection of which will serve to dispel much of the gloom of the past. Although I am deeply conscious that nothing that happens to me personally, however much I may feel honoured and gratified by it, can increase the sentiments of reverential fidelity and devotion which I entertain for your Majesty, nor the pure love which I bear to my beloved country, the well-being of which has been so greatly promoted by your Majesty's Government, whose efforts in this direction have been signally blessed by God, I can, nevertheless, not refrain from laying at your Majesty's feet the expressions of a grateful heart. Henceforth may everything that I conscientiously endeavour to effect, for the good of the Evangelical Church, in my capacity as clergyman and as teacher in the university, be so fortunate as to secure the gracious approbation of your Majesty.

Somewhat later in the same year, a circumstance occurred which afforded Schleiermacher a welcome opportunity for expressing publicly the relation in which he stood to the political parties of the day, that is, of the period of fermentation immediately succeeding the July Revolution in France. In the Parisian journal *Le Messager des Chambres*, there appeared in February, 1831, a series of fictitious letters from Berlin, which caused great sensation in that city, and in which, among other things, Schleiermacher's political position was represented in a manner which he felt himself bound emphatically to disavow. This he did in a letter to the *Messager*, which was not, however, inserted, but which, at his own request, appeared subsequently in the *Allgemeine Preussische Staatszeitung*, accompanied by a complaint of the unfairness of the *Messager*, in refusing to insert this refutation of matters of a personal character. The letter to the *Messager*, written in French, was as follows :—

To the Editor of the "Messager des Chambres."

[CCCCXLVII.]   *Berlin, 8th March.*

SIR,—As it has pleased one of your correspondents in this city to allude to me repeatedly, I trust that you will allow space in your columns for the subjoined answer to his remarks, if for no other reason, at least for the sake of your German readers.

First of all, I must disclaim the surname of *great*, as we Germans use this word so very sparingly that it can hardly be applied to a man like myself, except for the purpose of throwing ridicule upon him, which I am not aware that I have deserved.

Secondly. I am equally far from being " the most eminent Christian preacher in Germany "—I believe that was the expression used—and my sermons and discourses cannot possibly be models of eloquence, as I never write them before delivering them. To attempt to be " sublime," as a preacher, would even be contrary to my principles; for the more sublime the Gospel, the more simple may the sermon be.

Thirdly. We pray every Sunday that God will grant the king such wisdom as he needs for the fulfilment of the duties imposed upon him by God : but when doing this we are not aware that we express any other " wish of the people," than that it may lead a tranquil life under the rule and protection of the king, and ever draw nearer to the goal of Christian perfection. Such, sir, is the language of our Protestant church, and from this I have never diverged.

Fourthly, it is very true that I was "for a time forbidden to preach;" but it was from my doctor that the order emanated.

Fifthly. I belong to no party of the Left. Your expressions, right and left, right and left centre, are quite foreign to our relations ; and were your correspondent in truth a Prussian, he would not have made use of party appellations which, among us, no one would apply to himself. More especially, he would not have spoken of a party of the Left, secretly intent on revolutionary thoughts. We have made enormous progress since the peace of Tilsit, and that without revolution, without chambers, nay, even without liberty of the press ; but the people have ever been with the king and the king with the people. Under these circumstances, must not a man be out of his senses who would pretend that henceforward we should progress more rapidly by means of a revolution ? I, for my part, am always sure to be on the king's side, when I am on the side of the most enlightened men of the nation.

Finally, in order not to be utterly opposed to your correspondent on all points, I am willing to express to him my thanks for the honourable place which he assigns to me among the teachers of the university, though I am bound to confess at the same time, that I would rather be confounded in the comprehensive *etcetera*, under which he conceals the names of a number of highly distinguished men. Accept, &c.

SCHLEIERMACHER.

*Schleiermacher to his Step-Son.**

[CCCCXLVIII.]   *Berlin, March,* 1832.

Accept also my hearty greetings, beloved son, on occasion of your birthday, and my best wishes that you may advance in your career through healthy, cheerful activity, remaining united with us in spirit, though distant in body. Remember that your old father is daily drawing nearer to the last goal, and that it would be a great consolation to him could he live to see you in an independent position, so that your mother might be left with fewer anxieties weighing upon

* The son had a few months previously received an appointment as Referendary to the Government in Aix-la-Chapelle.

her. . . . . You did quite right to participate in the merriment of the late carnival ; but I am not so pleased to find that you write letters while the board is sitting. You must endeavour to acquire the power, not only of listening attentively to an uninteresting discussion, but also of learning something from it. It is this that leads to the position of *Ober-Regierung-Rath* and of *Präsident.* During the vacations I will write more fully. I commend you to God, dear son of my heart.

*Schleiermacher to Christlieb Reichel, Bishop of the Con-
gregation of the United Brethren in Berthelsdorf.*

[CCCCXLIX.] *Berlin, 3rd April,* 1832.

Beloved and honoured friend, I have long owed you an answer to your kind and lengthy communication relative to the departure of our dear Albertini. The news came very unexpectedly upon me, for it so happened that I had not for some time seen the good Stobwasser,* who has now also been called away, and who was then already very ailing ; and the last news which he had communicated to me regarding our friend, and which was most gratifying to me, was that he had specially requested to have the narrative of the life of my late sister† sent to him without any curtailment.

That he also remembered me so kindly in his last days has been like a soothing balsam to the wound inflicted by his death. What can we say to it ? It is a sad loss to the congregation, and to many kind, pious souls beyond its limits. But new seeds are ever sprouting forth with gladdening promise; and though the work of the Lord may not seem to prosper equally at all times, it will not suffer because individual labourers have been called away, even in the midst of the most energetic activity. It has, more especially, long been evident to me, that in the congregation, as in the church, the presence of pre-eminent individualities is far less important

---

* Preacher to the congregation of the United Brethren in Berlin.
† Schleiermacher's sister Charlotte died in the year 1831.

than the faithfulness of the great mass, and a right understanding of the Gospel by them, and that the necessity for remarkable individual combatants will grow ever less urgent. This is more particularly applicable to the community of the United Brethren, among whom certain maxims are once for all established, and the internal conflicts cannot, thank God, be so violent. Nevertheless, even this faith does not suffice to soothe the wounded heart at first ; the feelings will vindicate their rights, and I have, therefore, wafted many a sigh after our beloved friend, and rejoice at every word from his lips in each new number of the *Gemeinenachrichten* (the Journal of the Congregation), and am always fearing that it may be the last. For this reason, also, I have been much pleased to learn that we may expect the publication of a collection of his discourses. Not long after your valued letter came to hand, I received the account of his life and the discourse by dear brother Kölbing. . . . .

I always thought it probable that he would leave no record from his own hand of the providential guidance of his life, and I cannot attach any blame to him on this account, though I hope his example herein may not be too extensively followed, and that the custom of recording the events of their life may not fall into total desuetude among the brethren. What he says about his want of diligence while in the Pædagogium, must refer to the time previous to my arrival, and I know that it was from me that he received an impulsion towards the study of botany, and also of mathematics, which latter he had, strangely enough, entirely neglected. But as regards our other studies, the impulsion came more from him than from me.

I would fain have learnt something more explicit about the various changes that had taken place in his mind since the period of our separation; but even had I questioned him on the subject, I should hardly have learnt much. I can only say that in spite of all the sceptical tendencies that had been developed in us, he was even at the time of our separation, firmly determined to remain in the Congregation. And thus in reference to him also the appositeness of the observation has been proved, which the reverend old Zembsch addressed to me when I paid him a visit, during my professorship at Halle: "Brother Baumeister," said the reverend old man, "seems at that time not to have taken into consideration that it is only through scepticism that theologians are formed." For myself I may say in reference to this, that amid the various conflicts which I am necessarily exposed to in my career, and amid the numerous misunderstandings of the extreme parties on both sides, through which I am obliged to wind my way, it is ever a great encouragement to me when I discover even a faint glimmer that leads me to think that we hold the same goal in view and are labouring for the same end. Therefore, your expressions on this head have been highly gratifying to me; they concur with my clearest consciousness, yet I do not marvel when many minds, though resting on the same basis, nevertheless fail to understand me. However much this pains me on the one hand, on the other I must confess, that the more I reflect, the more confirmed I am in the conviction, that I am walking in the path assigned to me, that in so doing I am effecting that which I am destined to effect, and that I ought not for any consideration to diverge from that which is natural to me, if I would not by my own act destroy the blessing that attends my vocation. Thus at least I learn to unite, quietly within myself, with many who believe themselves far distant from me, and herein dwells a peculiar life-giving energy. . . . .

My dear Albertini is one more added to the number of those who have stood nearest to me during some period of my pilgrimage, and who have gone before me. As for my dear sister Lotte, I rejoiced when she was relieved from the yoke, as she herself so much desired it; yet it is a heavy trial to have lost so faithful a heart, one who had lived through my whole life with me, and who had ever clung to me with faith and love. But she was called away in the right time, for had she lived to see the departure of our dear Stobwasser, to whom and also to whose wife she was most tenderly attached, it would almost have been too much for her.

Should I be able to carry out a little plan which I have sketched out for the Easter holidays, it is possible that I may pay a flying visit to Herrnhut. My hearty greetings to . . . . I commend you all most heartily to the Lord.

Your faithfully attached
SCHLEIERMACHER.

The Mother to the Son (at Aix-la-Chapelle).

[CCCCL.]   *Berlin, 6th May,* 1832.

. . . . I am sure that you will be pleased to hear that your dear father is taking a little tour for his recreation. He left on the second holiday, immediately after church. I shall never forget the impression it made upon me, to see dear father in his blue blouse, with his silvery white hair, as lively and youthful as a young lad about to wander forth into the world for the first time, giving a parting word to all, who pressed round him with joyful emotion. . . . . On the 10th they will be back, and father will then no doubt at once answer your letter about your travelling project. . . . .

Schleiermacher to his Step-Son.

[CCCCLI.]   *Berlin, 19th May,* 1832.

My dear son, immediately before my departure, as well as since my return, up to the present moment, I have been so pressed with business, that I have not been able to write you even a few lines. Even to-day the time for so doing is very sparingly measured out to me; but I dare say you would rather put up with a few words only than remain longer in suspense. It has long been my intention that you should travel, but the present period does not seem to me suitable for the purpose. Once only you can enjoy this privilege, and therefore you ought not to rest satisfied with revelling in the beauties of nature, but ought also to endeavour to make yourself acquainted with the social conditions of the various countries, and to acquire knowledge that may be useful to you in your vocation. But at this moment you would not even be able to enjoy the former in peace. In Switzerland you would find the populations in a state of such intense excitement, that no one would be ready to impart the information you might desire; besides which the various constitutions are in a state of perfect dissolution, and there is great reason to anticipate the outbreak of a civil war. In Italy things are pretty much in the same condition, and under such circumstances, every traveller in the Austrian territories may be sure to be beset by difficulties and annoyances that may occasion a waste of time and money which he ought not in reason to incur. Upon the whole it seems to me better that we should defer this undertaking until after your final examination. Should even the travelling then cost a little more, it will not at all events upset you in regard to your studies, as would be the case at the present moment, and you would also derive more solid advantages from it. Try to follow my advice for this once with a willing heart, but nevertheless keep the project in your thoughts, and in your choice of reading hold your travels in some measure in view. . . . . .

[CCCCLII.]   *6th August*, 1832.

. . . . . The resolutions of the Diet which, according to what people say, have been passed in consequence of the urgent representations of the constitutional German governments, and which therefore spring, not from any misunderstandings that may prevail at a distance, but from a home source, have also produced a very painful impression here. It is rumoured that the king has expressed himself to the effect, that he would be very willing to support the gentlemen, if he could but be sure that they would really govern well. Everybody must at present be looking forward with great anxiety to the new press law, which it is thought will remedy many evils. I do not think, however, that it will succeed in so doing. . . . . Otherwise our social circle is again extending a little in consequence of the arrival of the

Steffenses and the Winterfelds. My dear Steffens I find, as far as I am concerned, quite unchanged. . . . .

*Schleiermacher to his Wife.**

[CCCCLIII.]

My dearly beloved wife, it is very long since I wrote to you, and yet I have been wishing very much to do so. I had to write an essay (not merely a flourish of the pen) for the academy, which I read to it the day before yesterday, and besides that there was an accumulation of smaller matters to be attended to. In the meanwhile you must have had the children's letters, and cannot therefore have been uneasy. . . . .

In reference to your letter to Hildchen, darling mother, I have something on my mind. You have adopted the way of speaking constantly of the Saviour and placing God quite in the background. If it be the Saviour also who speaks to us from nature, then there can hardly be any direct relation more between us and God. And yet Christ himself seeks above all to impress upon us that through him we come to the Father, and that the Father abides in us. In your way the true simplicity of Christianity is absorbed in some self-made system that Christ would not have approved. I am so afraid that the poor girl may get confused between your ways and mine; for she is no longer so wanting in reflection as not to be struck by the discrepancy. Dearest heart, do try to hold fast the belief that *with* Christ and *through* Christ, we are to rejoice in his and our Father.

The Wife to Schleiermacher.

[CCCCLIV.] *Salzbrunn, 15th August.*

. . . . . The rebuke contained in your last letter but one, darling father, I accept with childlike submission, and I will not fail to watch over myself, that I may not give

---

* She was absent at a bath with one of her adopted daughters, who was suffering from ill health.

cause for misapprehension. As regards myself, I must confess to you, that I never feel any desire or necessity to keep God our heavenly Father, and God our Saviour, distinct. I know not to whom it is I raise my heart in prayer or thanksgiving—to my feelings they are one—and I only become conscious of the distinction when I think of the human life and activity of the Saviour. If there be in this a confusion of ideas against which I ought to struggle, do tell me so. Farewell, my own dear life.

Schleiermacher to his Wife.

[CCCCLV.]   *Berlin, 5th September, 1832.*

My dear mother, on my return from church last Sunday, I found Hückel in my room, and was gladdened by the receipt of your dear letters, and of all the accounts he gave me of you, which, thank God, contained nothing but what was good. . . . . Our Jonas left yesterday. He seems to have made a very favourable impression on Bishop Neander, which gives me much pleasure. To-day, I had a long conversation in the street with A. von H——, who, as an ultra-liberal, is furious at the present state of German affairs. I do not quite participate in his feelings, but I am not either so easy in regard to these matters as our dear Eichhorn. It often makes me sad to think, that after all our bright hopes and good beginnings, I shall, when I depart this life, leave our German world in such a very precarious state—for this will most probably be my lot. But I will not now give way to these reflections, or my letter will be too late for the post. May I only be allowed to continue my life of domestic contentment with you and the children. God be with you, my dear, dear heart.

The Mother to her Son.

[CCCCLVI.]   *Berlin, 26th November, 1832.*

. . . . . How merciful is God to allow us to be all gathered again in renewed health and spirits around your dear father, who is always the most precious figure in the picture! On his birthday, he was so cheerful, so indescribably amiable. The detailed account of the festivities I leave to the girls to give you. You will receive an abundance of letters, and, taken all together, I have no doubt they will afford you a very lively picture of our present state. Our home life is just now very cheerful and animated, and I am greatly pleased with all the children. . . . . How uncertain, however, is the future, and you also, my dear son, may be thrown out of your present career by the war—in what an unsettled state are all the great common interests of mankind! I thank God that He has given me faith to trust so entirely in His fatherly love that no cares or anxieties can trouble me, but that I feel ready to submit cheerfully to all his ways, and that I can rest in Him. My prayer is that you also will allow yourself to be guided by Him; for He will guide you better than any thoughts or wishes of mine. . . . . .

[ccccLVII.] *Berlin, 11th May, 1833.*

These lines will be delivered to you by Mr. von St——, of whom we have unfortunately seen but very little. . . . . But now, let me turn to you, my dear son, with whom I have not exchanged a word for so long a time. I often yearn for a voice from your heart addressed to mine, and cannot conceal from you that I miss it sadly. For I cannot allow myself to believe that my Ehrenfried is entirely devoid of all inward life and emotions, and I therefore think that in his letters he only shows us the one side of his life—that which is turned towards the outward world. How could I doubt that in his soul also there are quiet depths which reflect the images and re-echo the tones of the Eternal and the Holy! I will not warn you not to allow too great a preponderance to that half of your being that is turned towards the outward world, for you will find this warning in every line of the Book of books, which I trust you do not fail to open every day; but I would fain beg you to bestow from time to time upon your mother, who feels little interest in the things that belong to the noisy mart of life, some word from the quiet depths of your heart, or some earnest thought, gained as a solid acquisition amid the noisy bustle.

Do not suppose, my dear Ehrenfried, that I do not from my heart rejoice that you should learn to know life from its outwardly attractive sides likewise, and draw lessons from it in this way also; I do not object to this, I only say, Beware that you do not habituate yourself too much to leave the deeper wants unsatisfied. If these cravings have once been entirely suppressed, it may at another time be too late to try to call them forth again. . . . .

As concerns our social life, I suppose your sisters have told you that our Wednesday receptions are very much frequented, so that we cannot be said to live in great retirement. Mr. von Haxthausen in particular, has requested me to remember him very kindly to you. He is again here, and a very welcome Wednesday guest; for he never talks for the sake of talking; but the things that he has seen he has judged with understanding, and his culture has penetrated deeply —that is to say, it has assumed an original character—and how few people are there of whom this can be said! . . . . The Wednesday evenings are often rendered doubly cheerful by a great number of young people. The circle of young maidens in our house, is a spectacle which gladdens many hearts; and how this fresh and youthful circle gathered round your father embellishes and sweetens his old age, you will readily conceive.

Schleiermacher to his Step-Son.

[CCCCLVIII.]   *Berlin, 19th May, 1833.*
. . . . . For the rest, my dear son, I almost upbraid myself for having yielded to your wish to go to Aix-la-Chapelle, because your life there, independently of your official occupations, seems to me to be very empty. I can hardly conceive that there should not be among the officials

in the place, some men from the other provinces, in whose homes there is some kind of family life, to which you might gain admission. . . . . I am willing to believe that this exclusion has not caused you to lose all taste for a better mode of life, but at all events this taste has found no nourishment. . . . Your sisters have told you, I presume, how many melancholy losses we have sustained latterly in our most intimate circle. Poor Jacobi!* I do not know how he will ever get over it. The unexpected and sudden death of Prince Radzivill and the almost hopeless illness of the Princess Elizabeth have also affected me very much. Indeed for some time one painful call on our sympathies has followed close upon another. . . . .

. . . . However, these considerations have no part in my proposal to you to get yourself removed this last year to some other centre of administration; for herein I have only been guided by what you say about the different arrangements that prevail. For on the one hand I am not quite sure that total unacquaintance with certain branches may not injure you at your final examination; and, on the other hand, I also fear that, by remaining where you are, you may in future be considered as being exclusively destined for that locality, which would, I confess, be far from what I wish for you, as the higher elements of life are thrown too much into the background there. However, I may and will leave this entirely to your own judgment and decision. If, therefore, you feel sure that your stay at Aix will not entail either of these disadvantages upon you, I am content that you should remain. . . . .

In July 1833, Schleiermacher's wife went with her invalid friend Mrs. F——, and the daughter of the latter, to Putbus in Rügen for sea-bathing. Subsequently Schleiermacher took the rest of the family to

* He had lost his wife, a daughter of Nicolovius.

Putzar in Pomerania, the estate of Count Schwerin, whence they afterwards joined their mother in Rügen, while Schleiermacher undertook a journey through Sweden, Norway, and Denmark, with his friend Count Schwerin.

[In a letter to his wife, previous to his departure, Schleiermacher speaks of this tour as probably the last he will undertake, "with the exception of the long one" from life to death, and thus in truth it proved; and as if this feeling made him cling more tenderly than ever to those who had constituted his greatest happiness through life, his letters during his passage through the Scandinavian countries contain little more than the expressions of his intense uneasiness at not receiving news from his dear ones, whose letters had been unaccountably retarded, in consequence of which he even at one moment contemplated returning home directly. In addition to this there is a bare mention of the places he has visited, and the distinguished personages to whom he has been introduced, among whom, to his great delight, was *not* the king. Whether he was in any way specially prejudiced against Bernadotte, or the fact of the latter being a Frenchman, and originally one of Napoleon's marshals, was at the bottom of it, does not appear in the letters; but in writing to his wife of the urgency with which his friends press him to allow himself to be presented to the king, who was in the habit of receiving all foreign *savants* who visited his capital, Schleiermacher says: " I have not the slightest desire to make myself ridiculous with my bad French before that Gascon, and if it be at all possible to avoid it, I will not go to him." But more than all, these letters (which are included in the German edition, but have been omitted by the translator because of their trivialness) are remarkable for the absence of every indication of the fact, that his progress through the three northern kingdoms was a continual ovation. In Copenhagen more particularly, his arrival was hailed with the greatest enthusiasm, and the professors and students of the university, as well as a number of distinguished men of all classes there, joined in a public banquet in his honour, which ended with a torch procession, the never-failing feature in German and Scandinavian ovations.]

Schleiermacher to his Step-Son.

[CCCCLIX.]   *6th November,* 1833.
     My poor son, you have indeed had to wait long for accounts from me! When I think that the day after-to-morrow it will be four weeks since I returned, it seems too bad not to have written to you before this, and one of your sisters, at least, ought to have put pen to paper for you. I, for my poor part, have been thrown at once into such a turmoil of business, that 1 may be absolved from all blame. That I should respond to your pleasant and circumstantial account of your excursion by a similar narrative of my travels through Scandinavia, is, alas, out of the question. Such narratives must be written on the spot, as my dear travelling companion did, while I did nothing more than jot down short notices in my memorandum book to aid me in the circumstantial account of my wanderings which I knew I should have to give, when we should all be assembled round the tea-table ; but in which I have not, during the four weeks I have been back, got further than to the northernmost points of our journey.

     . . .   Of the kindness with which I was received everywhere, I cannot say enough. I was only sorry to find, when I returned home, that so much ado had been made about it in the newspapers. It was amusing to see how at one moment the Count took me under his protection and at another I took him under mine ; he me when among the great in rank, I him when among the learned; and how we got on without a knowledge of the language of the country (which indeed I understand pretty well when I read it, but which I can as little understand when spoken as I can speak it myself) by the help of an interpreting coachman, when we had to communicate with the *plebs*, and in society with the aid of a mouthful of French. . . . . For the rest, I am delighted that you were able to make that tour. Your letters, written at the period, have given us all, and I think me more especially, very great pleasure. You were intent upon improving yourself rationally, and I believe you have succeeded, and that you sympathized so warmly with the life at Ehringhaus, has given me greater confidence even than before in regard to your future. . . . . I see that mother has already made out a clean bill of health for me; and, thank God, I can fully confirm it. During the four weeks that I have been at home I have tried myself in various ways, and have borne all very well. Could I but get rid of some of my business occupations, so as to be able to devote myself more to literary labours; but I am afraid that will not be possible. . . . . I hope you will let us know in your next how the crown-prince* has been received at Aix. I am very much pleased to find that his journey has been a kind of triumphal procession. I believe the best of him, and hope for the best from him, and neither fear the aristocratic nor the pietistic tendencies which people attribute to him. And now, farewell, for the present, dear son ! May God continue to be with you as we desire.

---

* The present King of Prussia.

Schleiermacher to his Son.

[CCCCLX.]

I see that neither mother nor daughter has dated her letter, and I will, therefore, tell you that this sheet has been put into my hands to-day, *the 30th of January,* but too late for the post.* . . . .   I look upon it as an over-sanguine expectation, even should you intend to finish your studies here, that you will be able to be here by Easter; and I intreat you not to neglect anything to effect this, however pleasant it would be, but to follow up your course of studies to the last. But that you may be here for our silver-wedding on the 18th of May, that I consider more feasible, and if we could then have you all together, as many as you are, that would indeed be delightful. Immediately after we had sent off our last letters, the Count† came here for a few days, and seemed no less impatient than his son to see Hildegard bear his name; but, before the vacations, it will not be possible; and, for my part, I would rather it should be at the end of the vacations than at the beginning; but whether I shall be able to carry the question is very dubious. That mother has all hands full of work, you may suppose. . . . . .   Hildis is already strutting about with a beautiful little gold watch, *à quatre couleurs,* presented to her by her future father-in-law, during his stay here, and accompanied by some pretty verses. Our Elsbeth has long been suffering, and has to-day ventured out, for the first time, to her sister, whose little Siegfried is at present the general attraction and delight of the whole family. By the time you arrive, he will probably have developed his linguistic talent a little more, and also be able to move with greater ease. At present, he begins to be able to stand when he is held, and his speaking powers are limited to a very doubtful " papa " and " mamma," and a few monosyllabic articulations. I have been forced to keep the house these last three days, on account of a cough and hoarse-

* Probably the last letter that Schleiermacher ever wrote.
† Count Schwerin, of Putzar.

ness, which made it impossible for me to lecture. To-day I was obliged to go out to christen a child, and I also attempted to lecture for an hour, but it went off very badly. From to-morrow, however, I will commence again, as usual. And now, my dear, God be with you. This letter will be sent to the post to-morrow.

Thirteen days after the date of this letter, the 12th February, 1834, Schleiermacher breathed his last. He died of inflammation of the lungs. The subjoined account of his last days and hours was drawn up for their most intimate circle by his widow, who survived him only six years :—

" For twelve days our beloved father had been suffering from a cough and great hoarseness, and though bright and cheerful, he looked very pale. To our anxious entreaties that he would be more careful of his health, he always replied with the assurance that he felt perfectly well, that what he was then suffering under was a mere outward ailment, and that it did not in the least interfere with his inward health.

" The evening of Thursday, 5th February, was the last that was spent in cheerful tranquillity in the home circle. In the night, the disease began with the most fearful pains in every part of the body (he had had similar symptoms the previous night, but they had passed off, and he had not mentioned the fact), so that our dear father said that he could not describe where the pain was, but that every fibre of his body ached. His looks were those of a dying person, and he expressed his firm belief that he would not survive. I had sent immediately for the doctor, who declared the case to be very serious; but the remedies applied by him relieved the pains after a few hours, and the patient lay calm and without suffering in his bed.

" On the Sunday there was a consultation of four physicians. The inflammation increased rapidly on this day, and in a few hours attained its highest degree. The patient was twice bled in one day, and though the doctors still gave hope, it was evident to those around that they did not entertain any themselves. I did not move from his bedside. The children and friends, who waited on my bidding in the next room, brought me everything I asked for. I required no other aid in nursing him, and the utmost quiet had been recommended. I obeyed the order so conscientiously, that I did not cause him to speak even one dear word to me.

" He often assured me that he did not suffer so much as, perhaps, it appeared. During the whole of his illness, his mind was calm, collected, and gentle; he obeyed punctually every order of the doctor, never uttered a complaint or a murmur, and was throughout friendly and patient, though serious, and as if his thoughts were turned inwardly.

" On the Monday morning, the physician, after examining his pulse and his features, announced the approach of death.

" The following are a few of his last, precious words that I have been able to retain. Once he called me to his bedside, and said, ' I am, in fact, in a state between consciousness and unconsciousness (he had been taking opium, which caused him to doze frequently), but inwardly I enjoy heavenly moments. I feel constrained to think the profoundest speculative thoughts, and they are to me identical with the deepest religious feelings.' Another time he raised his hand, and said, in a very solemn tone, 'Here light a sacrificial flame.' Another time, again, 'To the children I bequeath the saying from St. John: "Love one another."' Again: 'The dear children, what a blessing they are to us!' Again: 'I charge you to greet all my friends, and to tell them how sincerely I have loved them.' 'How I rejoice at the thought of our silver-wedding, and of Hildchen's wedding; I seem already to be enjoying the precious days. I would willingly have remained longer with you and the children;' and when I expressed a hope that it might still be so, he said, 'Do not deceive yourself, dear heart,' and then, with the deepest tenderness, added, 'There is still much for you to endure.' He asked to see the children; but when I begged him to avoid everything that could cause him emotion, he at once submitted, and was content that one of them at a time should come into the room to bring something. He asked several times who was in the next room, and when I named the dear friends, and told him that they were engaged in silent prayer with the children, he seemed pleased.

"The last morning his sufferings greatly increased. He complained of excessive internal heat, and the first and the last murmur escaped his lips in the words: 'Lord, I suffer much!' His features assumed entirely the character of death, the death film spread over his eyes, the death struggle had been fought.   He then placed his two fingers on his eye, as was his habit when reflecting deeply, and began to speak.

" 'I have never clung to the dead letter, and we have the atoning death of Jesus Christ, his body and his blood.   I have ever believed, and still believe, that the Lord Jesus gave the communion in water and in wine.'*

" While saying this he raised himself up, his countenance lighted up, his voice became clear and strong. He then asked with priestly solemnity : ' Do you agree with me in this belief, that the Lord Jesus consecrated the water also that was in the wine ? ' to which we replied with a loud yes !   ' Then let us take the Communion : the wine for you, the water for me,' he added solemnly ; ' but there is no time to fetch G——,† quick ! quick ! Let no one take offence at the form.'   The necessary things having been brought in while we waited in solemn silence, an expression of heavenly rapture spread over his features, a strange lustre shone in his eyes, a look of beaming love fell upon us all, and after a few devout words of prayer, he commenced the holy ceremony.   He first gave me the bread, then each of the other persons present, and lastly himself, pronouncing each time in a distinct voice, the words, 'Take eat,' &c. So loud, indeed, was his voice, that the children, who were kneeling at the door of the adjoining room, heard him quite plainly.

* He had been expressly forbidden to take wine, and it is a well-known fact, that throughout antiquity the Jews never drank wine except mixed with water.

† The clerk.

"In like manner he gave to each the wine with the usual words; then addressing himself likewise, he took the water, and then said: 'On these words of the scripture I rely, they are the foundation of my faith.' After he had pronounced the blessing, his eyes turned once more to me with a look full of love, and he said, 'In this love and communion we are, and ever will remain united.' He sank back on his pillow. The expression of heavenly rapture still dwelt on his countenance. After some minutes he said—'Now I can no longer remain here;' and in a little while he added—'Place me in another position.' We placed him on his side. He breathed heavily several times, and life was gone. In the meanwhile the children had come in and were kneeling round his bed. His eyes closed gradually."

THE END.

Printed by SMITH, ELDER & Co., Little Green Arbour Court, Old Bailey, E. C.